Praise for The Dandelion Insurrection

"This novel will not only make you want to change the world, it will remind you that you can." - Gayle Brandeis, author of *The Book of Dead Birds*, winner of the Bellwether Prize for Socially Engaged Fiction

"Close your eyes and imagine the force of the people and the power of love overcoming the force of greed and the love of power. Then read *The Dandelion Insurrection*. In a world where despair has deep roots, *The Dandelion Insurrection* bursts forth with joyful abandon." - Medea Benjamin, Co-founder of CodePink

"THE handbook for the coming revolution!" - Lo Daniels, Editor of Dandelion Salad

"*The Dandelion Insurrection* is an updated, more accurate, less fantastical *Brave New World* or *1984*." - David Swanson, author, peace and democracy activist

". . . a beautifully written book just like the dandelion plant itself, punching holes through the concept of corporate terror and inviting all to join in the insurrection." - Keith McHenry, Co-founder of the Food Not Bombs Movement

"*The Dandelion Insurrection* is a prayer seven billion hearts strong and counting." - Megan Hollingsworth, Founder of Extinction Witness

"Rivera Sun is an author in a league of her own." - Marirose NightSong, Transformational Holistic Care, Healing Wise Center

"This is a very inspiring read . . . the words are contagious!" - Sheila Ramsey, author, Founder of Personal Leadership

"Rivera Sun's *The Dandelion Insurrection* takes place in a dystopia just a hop, skip and jump away from today's society. A fundamentally political book with vivid characters and heart stopping action. It's a must and a great read." - Judy Rebick, activist and author of *Occupy This!*

"This is the book that our generation has been awaiting. I predict it will be a major contributor to change." - Malathy Drew, Founder of Whispering Energy

"I give the book 7 gold stars . . . and a huge Right On Sister!" - Joe Hock, OWS, March Against Monsanto

"It's a rare phenomenon when a writer can move a reader to tears in the beginning chapters of a fictional novel." - Kevin 'StarFire' Spitzer, radio host, writer, mentor, visionary thinker

"Rivera Sun is a fabulous, creative author who weaves the kinds of stories that inspire me to create life differently." - Cindy Reinhardt, Founder of The Success Zone

". . . Rivera Sun beckons us to address the crises of our day with kindness, in community and from courage. With these tools, we can change the world one heart, one home, one block at a time." - Anne Symens-Bucher, Canticle Farm

"If you are seeking to understand our evolved world and how to unite and prosper, I urge you to read this book." - Lauren Taite Vines, author of *The New Dawn on Planet Earth*

"Written on the winds of hope, this book presents a political prophesy showing how a people united can defeat corporate tyranny through the force of their will." - Steven Jonas, MD, MPH, author of *The 15% Solution*

"This opus is a well-written allegory of what could happen in the future and how only through the power of love we can make real change in the world." - Ted Zeff, Ph.D. author of *The Highly Sensitive Person's Survival Guide*

"Rivera Sun nourishes us with her warm rays of kinship and waters our hearts with the storytelling of courage . . ." - Pancho Ramos Stierle, Occupy Oakland, peace activist

# The Dandelion Insurrection

## - love and revolution -

The Dandelion Insurrection

Copyright © 2013 by Rivera Sun

Rising Sun Press Works
P.O. Box 1751, El Prado, NM 87529
www.riverasun.com

*Library of Congress Control Number:*
2013947460
ISBN 9780984813254
Sun, Rivera 1982-
The Dandelion Insurrection

Photos by Steve DiBartolomeo
*198 Methods of Nonviolent Action* is reprinted with permission from The Albert Einstein Institution www.aeinstein.org

# A Community Published Book Supported By:

Anonymous
Jennifer & Peter Simonson
Farrokh Namazi
Ellen Cook
John Jordan-Cascade
Libby Dickerson
Marada Cook
Crown O' Maine Organic Cooperative
GODeepWITHIN Consulting
Aunt Lynne and Uncle Ted
DrSuRu
Land Cook
Annie Kelley
Atlantis Thyme
Karen Lane
Garimo
Patti & Bob Oldmixon
Madeleine Le Fevre
Angel Imaz
Sarah Roche-Madhi
Deb Colbert

And with the support of many more!
Thank you.

**Dedicated to Dariel Garner**
. . . and dandelions, everywhere!

Other Works

by

Rivera Sun

**Novels, Books & Poetry**

The Way Between

Billionaire Buddha

Steam Drills, Treadmills, and Shooting Stars

The Dandelion Insurrection Study Guide

Skylandia: Farm Poetry From Maine

Freedom Stories: volume one

The Imagine-a-nation of Lala Child

**Theatrical Plays & Presentations**

The Imagine-a-nation of Lala Child

The Education of Lala Girl

The Emancipation of Lala

RISING SUN

PRESS WORKS

# The Dandelion Insurrection
## - love and revolution -

by
Rivera Sun

# Table of Contents

# The Dandelion Insurrection

In a time that looms around the corner of today, in a place on the edge of our nation, it is a crime to dissent, a crime to assemble, a crime to stand up for one's life. Despite all this - or perhaps because of it - the Dandelion Insurrection began . . .

# CHAPTER ONE

. . . . .

## *Little Bird*

The seasons wrestled in the sky. Battalions of black clouds collided. Cold and warm gusts of air slammed against each other. Sleet rained like gunshot.

A little bird flew north.

She was the lone hatchling in a nest of deformed eggs, the last survivor of the fledglings that perished in a shocking bite of cold; the sole remainder of a once mighty flock . . . but she would not think of those stiffened feathered bodies now.

She winged hard and fast in the great battering of winds. All across the continent, the earth railed against the destruction wrought by humans. The eastern skies whipped furiously. Western clouds refused to rain. Soil cracked. Wind swept up walls of dust. Along the coasts, the rivers spilled their banks and the oceans attacked the shores.

Humanity marched onward despite these warnings. The earth was ravaged without distinction. Mountains crumbled. Lakes vanished. Forests fell. Prairies burned. Black plumes filled the sky.

The bodies of the birds lined the highways of migration.

The little bird struggled over fallow fields where the poisoned farmlands held no food. Failed crops mocked her hungry eyes. Urban scavengers congregated over dumpsters. Human children fought rats for rotten produce. Pigeons drew blood for crumbs. The cities heaved with hunger. The stench of fear choked everything. The little bird fled quickly.

She winged northward too soon in the turning of the

1

seasons, but spring called to her with hints of hope. The ground rebelled against the grasp of winter. A spark of life emerged that could catalyze the courage of the world.

*Don't wait! Don't wait!* the little bird sang. Death litters the animal highways. *You are next. You are next. In the war that humans wage upon the earth, the young ones will be next.* The bird flew north against the wind, warbling *don't wait!* Death creeps ever closer; not one of us can wait.

# CHAPTER TWO

· · · · ·

## *The Man From the North*

At the edge of the nation, a fist cracked down on a weathered table.

"That's it! They've gone too far!" leathery old Valier Beaulier declared.

A riot of voices shot out loud enough to disturb the guards on both sides of the Canadian-American border. The women immediately hissed at them to shut up. Police patrolled the small town's streets in droves. The squabble of questions puttered out nervously. The curtains were drawn tight across the windows. Pierrette's Cafe bulged at the seams, grossly defying the new laws that restricted gatherings to fewer than twenty people. Every rickety chair held an equally creaky collection of arthritic bones. Younger men were relegated to leaning postures against the walls, perched on the narrow sills of the storefront windows, or shoved up against the cream and sugar shelf. Charlie Rider squeezed into the corner as his grandfather called for the family's attention.

"Rick Dumais, tell them what you told me!" the old man insisted. He nudged his agitated companion, who burst out talking so fast that his French and English tripped over each other in stumbling consternation.

"*C'est vrai,* I swear, it's true. I went to the bridge, there-*la,* to go across to Canada - my *ma tante,* she wanted me to take her to church today - but *l'agents des douanes* - the guards - they said I couldn't cross. The bridge is closed!"

"For what?" Jean Pierre demanded to know. "Repairs?"

"*Non*," Rick answered. "It's the border . . . they've closed the whole border!"

"*Ah voyons, there-la,*" Bette burst out, skeptical of the news. "They'll let me across. I got that new identification."

"I tried that. They say it makes no difference," Rick told her.

"*Mais, je suis un citizen du Canada et des États-Unis!*" Jean Pierre declared in French, pulling dual citizenship papers from his wallet.

"They don't care. Only official business, they say."

"Is my daughter's wedding official enough?" Pierrette snapped from behind the cafe counter. "Are they going to reopen the border before she gets married next week?"

A collective gasp sucked the air from the room. Jean Pierre's white eyebrows shot up. Round eyes swung to Pierrette's daughter. The girl's face turned ashen. She protested quietly that certainly something would be worked out, after all, she was almost married to her fiancé: the wedding was next week, the papers were all in order, and they had a house together in Canada. Couldn't the border guards make an exception?

Valier's deep voice cut sharply through the rumble of the others, demanding to know the reason for the closure.

"*Pourquoi les douanes sont fermées?*"

"Terrorism, they say," Rick answered the old man respectfully.

Terrorism. The family groaned in collective exasperation. Everything was because of terrorism these days; the unending wars overseas, the soldiers on the streets at home, the restrictions on gatherings, the censoring of newspapers, the police checkpoints, the ballooning military budget, searches without warrants, and now, the closure of a peaceful border after hundreds of years of open travel.

"But we aren't terrorists!" Jean Pierre exploded. "*Nous sommes les Acadians!*"

*We are Acadians!* They had lived in this valley for four hundred years, marrying back and forth over the international border that crowned the northern tip of Maine. The sharper tones of the sisters and aunts blended into the gravel pit of men's voices. The rumble of the old backhoe, Jean Pierre, kept pushing and shoving everyone else around. The reverberating engine of Valier leapt from idling mutters into roars. The sighs of his ancient, oldest brother, Mathieu, slipped between the voices like wind through the trees. This was a family that knew the pinch of hunger, the births and deaths of babies, the callousing of hands, chapped lips and rugged cheeks, the etching of dirt in skin, the crash of timber falling, the roar of tractors, the scent of opened earth, the cool roundness of potatoes, the drip of sweat from the brow . . . and the feel of French upon their tongue.

*Nous sommes les Acadians.* We are Acadians.

Valier Beaulier sat in the center. *Valier*, they had named him, from the old *Valere*, dweller of the valley. The family that ringed him had endured in *La Vallée Saint-Jean* through the turning of four centuries. Southward, the land stretched out in rolling farms. Due north, the blue-gray corrugated steel of the paper mill sat in the middle of the town like an intractable giant, smoking a pipe that reeked of damp pulp. Beyond that, the country stopped. Politics drew a line at the river, claiming a division that the families of the valley all ignored . . . until now. Carefully keeping their voices low, they demanded to know what idiot had ordered the closure.

"The guard said that it's closed on the orders of the President himself!" Rick Dumais told them.

"*Le président-illégitime!*" Jean Pierre howled. His palm

slapped the table so hard the salt-and-pepper shakers jumped in alarm. "Who voted for the scoundrel? Rick? *Non.* Valier? *Non.* Henri? Marc? Mathieu? *Non.* No one voted for him. He stole the election!"

The thin voice of Mathieu rose through the rest.

"It's so easy with those computers! One click and all the votes are gone! *Mon Dieu!* In my day, we had paper ballots."

"In your day, *grand-père*," young Matt teased, "they stole the elections on horseback!"

Laughter shot out in bellows and chortles, hefty snorts and quiet chuckles. Old Mathieu swiped a lazy hand at the youth, his lips curling in an indulgent smile. In the center of the cafe, Valier rapped the wooden floorboards with his cane.

"Shhhh! Keep your voices down and listen to me. *Écouter!* We will get through this! Mathieu, Jean Pierre, and I have voted in every election since Truman beat Dewey, and I say, politics come and go. People endure. The Acadians have been citizens of France, England, and the United States. We have survived Federalists, Populists, Whigs, Tories, Know-Nothings, Democrats, and Republicans, alike. The English rounded us up and drove us away, but we returned. They tried to suppress our religion, but by the grace of God, it remains. The Americans whipped us for speaking French, but - "

He paused, looking around proudly.

"*On parle français ici!*"

French is spoken here. It was their motto, their creed. Wrinkled hands leapt into applause. Lined palms slapped the tables' edges. Old shoes pounded the floor. Fists curled approvingly on knees. English, on the tongues of both the British and Americans, had dominated the region for hundreds of years, yet French was still spoken here . . . and the Acadians had endured. *On parle français ici!*

"*Mais oui, c'est vrai,*" Jean Pierre conceded, "but remember when the border was easy to cross? Back then no one needed papers. You knew the guards on duty! That was before they transferred our men to New York and brought those cold-hearted bastards up here!"

"In my day," old Mathieu began with a weary shake of his head.

"In your day," young Matt interrupted cheekily, "you were sneaking whiskey across the border in your grandmother's coffin during the Prohibition!"

Again, that beautiful symphony of laughter rang out. The sound flared in the heart like a lamp during a bitter-cold night, clearing the shuddering fear, keeping the darkness at bay if only for a moment. Eyes jumped nervously to the door. The wick of humor fluttered and died out. Old Mathieu waved a feeble hand and insisted that he hadn't been born then; it was his father, and, anyway, those days were gone. The border was closed and how was their sister, on her deathbed and all, how was she going to be brought across to be buried in the family plot now?

"*Ah, voyons,*" he sighed, "what is the world coming to?"

Shoved up in the corner, Charlie gritted his teeth. How could they ever know what the world was coming to? He was a journalist for the local paper, but if it weren't for his relatives, even he would know nothing about global news. The only uncensored information that passed back and forth across the Canadian-American border came via his cousins, aunts, and the little old *mémères*. For this, Charlie Rider often escorted his grand-père to bingo night, accompanied his uncles to the bowling alley, volunteered with his aunts at church socials, and wedged himself into the corner of this cafe, shoulder-to-shoulder with the comingled musk of men and bitter coffee, eavesdropping on a vital flow of information which invariably began with *my brother heard* or *my sister-in-law's cousin said.*

Not the most reliable of news reports, but it was better than nothing; better than the syndicated fairytales the local paper expected him to write; better than the insulting stream of government propaganda he was expected to believe; better than the lies that had the gall to parade around as journalism. A pit of frustration fumed in Charlie; a frustration stoked by the restrictions of his editor, who threatened to fire him for his inflammatory articles and reminded him that his employment contract stated:

- No anti-American sentiments.
- Stay on predetermined subjects.
- Any potential aids to terrorists will be edited out.

Journalists vanished like flies swatted by government agents. Entire newspapers choked and died overnight. The slightest hint of dissent triggered raids by the long arm of the censors. Charlie's work was riddled like Swiss cheese by the time the paper reached the public. His description of the proliferation of soldiers and tanks on the streets was removed because it aided terrorism by revealing military maneuvers. His report on the erosion of civil liberties was cut for criticizing the new security measures and was, therefore, anti-American. When drought destroyed forty percent of last year's grain crop, his editor shredded Charlie's report and, instead, told people that global warming was *Nothing To Get Hot and Bothered About.* Once again, indefinite detention without trial passed through Congress, but the newspaper merely said, *Security is Important.* Corporate taxes decreased while the already cash-strapped and debt-ridden average Americans paid more, but the local paper stuck to the official line of *Business Fuels the Economy.* Charlie asked to have his name removed from the articles.

"This country has gone to hell," Charlie muttered under his

breath.

"Watch your language," Jean Pierre barked.

"*Pourquoi?* Why?" young Matt retorted, springing to Charlie's defense. "It's true. Democracy is dead. We live in a police state. Haven't you seen the soldiers crawling up and down the valley?"

"Mmph," the family assented. A week ago, the latest hybrid of militarized police had shown up in the valley carrying automatic assault rifles and carte blanche to stop and question citizens. Young Matt's impertinence had earned him a black eye and a harsh warning.

"Fear of terrorism has destroyed our country," young Matt complained. "The terrorist attacks started and the military took over everything!"

"*Non,* it didn't happen overnight," Jean Pierre argued. "It was like the weather in the spring, blowing hot, then cold. Congress passed laws. The courts struck them down. They passed them again. The old president vetoed a few."

"He passed others," Matt interjected. "Even that liberal president was a nightmare for the Bill of Rights!"

"Bah," Jean Pierre said, waving his hand in disgust, "all politicians are nightmares. You're too young to remember anything."

"Maybe you're too old to - "

Stiff looks from the family silenced the brash young man. He backed down and leaned up against the wall next to Charlie. The cousins exchanged a long look and let their elders take a turn.

"Sure," Rick Dumais began, "terrorism changed things, but this goes back to when the corporations stopped paying taxes and became more powerful than God!"

"*Mon Dieu!* It is like false idols, eh?" Jean Pierre burst out.

"We worship money and it corrupts the soul!"

"Well, we're so broke now that we ought to be saints," Pierrette snapped sharply.

"That's what I told my wife," Rick agreed. "Money is the only vote that matters . . . and we haven't got it!"

The grandfathers nodded at his sensible comment.

"*Mais oui*," Jean Pierre agreed, "if only millionaires can run for Congress, isn't that taxation without representation? Have we got King George running the show again?"

"*Non, non, c'est les trois hommes dans le bain!*" young Matt called out.

The three men in the tub! The old men wheezed and howled, slapped their knees and roared back with laughter. Heads shook at the flippant reference to the nation's powerful: *the Butcher* at the head of the military, *the Banker* who controlled the major banks, and *the Candlestick Maker* who ran the fossil fuel industry. *Le président-illégitime* was nothing more than a rubber ducky floating in their bubble bath. The women laughed into their fists. Shoulders bobbed in amusement.

And yet, it was nothing to joke about. Just last week, a high school student had been arrested for making anti-American jokes. *Humor lights the wick of dissent*, it was said, *and dissension ignites into terrorism*. Censorship grasped the nation in a tight fist of control. The media stayed in line or disappeared overnight. Mail arrived opened at the postbox. Phone conversations were recorded and analyzed in a huge surveillance center out west. The Internet Censors pounced on anything criticizing the government or the corporations, and showed up at your door to arrest you. Nothing was secret. The common expression ran *just between you, me, and the government's spies . . .* Even in this family gathering, it could be risky to voice opinions too loud. Rick Dumais surreptitiously parted the curtains covering the cafe door and squinted up and down the street. An uneasy lull fell over the family as they waited for his shrug.

"Nothing," Rick assured them.

"We're headed toward trouble," Jean Pierre blustered. "They've closed the border and there's no escaping now. Those three men in the tub own everything and control the rest. Half the country works for them and the other half is starving!"

"I read somewhere that it's called plutocracy or oligarchy or something like that," Rick interjected.

"It's corporatocracy, that's what it is," shot out young Matt, his Adam's apple bobbing.

"*Non,* you don't know what you're talking about, any of you," Old Valier said dismissively. He frowned until his wrinkles reached the bottom of his chin. "It's worse than that: *une dictature.*"

A dictatorship? The older men drew in sharp breaths and began protesting. The younger generation argued against the notion. The women crossed their arms over their chests and pursed their lips. Old Valier shrugged. He preferred to call a horse a horse.

"Well, I am not the only fool who thinks this way. Listen to this," he sniffed dramatically. He pulled a folded paper from his breast pocket and slid his reading glasses up his nose. After peering around to be sure they were listening, he began to read.

"*You can call it by a thousand names, but it's all the same. When an elite group of people function in sneaky, undeclared tyranny, they have become, in essence, a closet dictatorship.*"

Charlie swallowed. Where had his grand-père grabbed hold of that article?

"*. . . due to rampant militarization, unchecked corporate influence on politics, restrictions on civil liberties, and a severe narrowing of the power elite, the United States is no longer a* *functional democracy . . .* "

Charlie's eyes flicked nervously to the door.

" *. . . unless the people rise up to restore it.*"

He slouched low in the corner. Every last one of them could be thrown in jail for anti-American activities. Charlie silently quoted along as Valier read the banned article. Every word was utterly familiar to Charlie. After all -

"*L'homme du Nord* wrote that!" Matt called out in sudden realization.

*The Man from the North.* The room flinched at the sound of the name. Eyes flicked northward. The blood stirred. One man crossed himself automatically. *L'homme du Nord.* Even the mention of the writer evoked a sweat of admiration, envy, and fear. Because of the Internet Censors, his articles were slipped hand-to-hand, smuggled across the border from Canada, taped in the back of pocket Bibles, Uncle Henry's Swap 'n' Sells, and Old Farmer's Almanacs. All through the winter, their woodstoves had been kindled by the man's incendiary remarks. He tore apart the corporate-controlled government, decried the rising tide of militarism, and lambasted the grind of economic injustice that held millions in a death grip. *The Man From the North* also regaled his readers with real life stories of courage in the face of oppression. He touched their hearts with passionate tales of kindness in a time of darkness. People looked out their windows at night and thought: *we are not alone in wanting a better world than this.* Prayers had been uttered for the continued protection of this man's life. They gave thanks for his fearlessness in speaking out when no one else dared. Up and down the valley, they had been stopped and questioned by the authorities about the possible identity of *the Man From the North.* The federal government hunted him on both sides of the border, trekking far up into Canada in search of the elusive man.

"*Pardon?*" Valier blinked at young Matt. "This could not possibly have been written by *L'homme du Nord.*"

"Sure it was," the youth replied. "*Mon oncle* sent that article from *Québec.*"

Valier's voice cracked across the room.

"Charlie!"

Charlie bolted upright. Valier's rheumy, wrinkled old eyes pinned him to the corner. His grandfather shook the article at him. The handwritten scrawl of the pen was clear to all.

"Tell me why - "

The door jingled open. A figure stepped inside. Valier barreled onward.

" - this is written in your handwriting!"

"Because," a soft voice replied from the doorway, "Charlie is *the Man from the North* . . . the voice of the Dandelion Insurrection."

# CHAPTER THREE

· · · · ·

## *Zadie Byrd Gray*

Zadie Byrd Gray. She stood on the cafe's threshold like a breath of fresh air. A white scarf covered her black curls. Her boots climbed her calves. Red leggings scaled her thighs. Her jean jacket hugged her like a sailor on shore leave. And that short, tight skirt, Charlie laughed to himself, was nothing but honest. She released the door. The bell tinkled. The cafe was silent. Her lips curled in a slow smile.

The past and present collided in a sudden short-circuiting of time. No one spoke. The family breathed in unison. Eyes leaped back and forth from the young man to the woman. Years of memories were stacked inside them like a set of nesting Russian Zadie-dolls, from the twelve-year old hellion dragged north by her hippie parents to the precocious adolescent strutting the halls of middle-high school like the Queen of America, to the daredevil teenager boasting about her victories in the wild west of adolescent love while young Charlie died in the agonies of unsuspected adoration, to the gorgeous sixteen-year old who broke his heart by running away in a fit of spontaneity, stringing him on with long distance phone calls and whirlwind visits right up until today. She stood in the doorway with that sphinx's smile while Charlie's breath slipped out in a sigh. Zadie Byrd Gray. She'd rescued him and ruined him, run wild with him, revived him, released him and returned to him. He couldn't love her one iota more . . . and everyone but Zadie knew it.

Smirks grew. Valier folded his gnarled hands over his cane

15

and fixed his eyes steadily on his grandson. *Be patient*, he had once told the teenage boy, *be patient with that girl*. All these years later, Valier could see that Charlie's patience would not last another month. A lit fuse crackled in the young man; explosion was inevitable. Charlie ran a hand through his sandy hair and swallowed hard.

"Welcome back, Zadie," he managed.

"Thanks, Charlie."

She flashed her lightning strike of a grin. Charlie's heart burst into flames. A rumble of snorts and titters broke the silence. Valier rapped the floor with his cane.

"Come, *belle*, give an old man a proper French greeting," he demanded imperiously.

Zadie swept through the assembly to kiss the old man on each cheek. Charlie died a thousand deaths of envy, stuck in his corner, hemmed in by shoulders and chairs. His mother, Natalie, arched an eyebrow at Zadie's short skirt. Charlie sighed. There was no lost love between those two.

"Now," Valier demanded, holding Zadie's hand and shaking it a little, "tell me why my grandson is making trouble."

"I am not making trouble," Charlie retorted.

Valier rattled the article at him. *This* was making trouble. *This* would bring the authorities down on their heads. *This* was kicking a hornet's nest, smart-mouthing your elders, setting off fireworks in church . . . in short, Valier scowled, *this* was exactly Charlie's brand of trouble.

Zadie pointed to the article in Valier's hand.

"*This* is flying like a little bird across the country, delivering messages of courage and waking people up. Charlie's writing is the rallying cry of the Dandelion Insurrection."

Mouths dropped open. Half legend, half real, the stories of the Dandelion Insurrection's spirited resistance rode the rumor-

16

winds that swept across the country. The tales were murmured in barbershops and whispered in kitchens, passed between the church pews, and told in hushed tones late at night when husbands and wives climbed into bed. From all directions and corners of the country, the stories came, sharing a common message of hope: *the golden soul of humanity was rising up.*

*When?* the hushed voices asked.

*In the spring,* the rumors replied, *when the dandelions bloom.*

The wind swept down the prairies with the question.

*Where?*

The echoing answer leapt from mountaintop to rolling hill to valley floor.

*Everywhere.*

The Dandelion Insurrection was as small as baking bread in the oven and as large as bringing down dictators. It was practical and metaphorical, symbolic and literal. It was real. It was legend. It spread hope. It grew kindness. It sowed the seeds of resistance in the ground of adversity. Everywhere the concrete of control paved over the goodness of the heart, the Dandelion Insurrection sprang up through the cracks.

In the cafe, an explosion of questions erupted. A barrage of sound roared out as they shouted above each other, thundering, rasping, thumping the floor with their boots, pounding the tables with their fists until Zadie threw her hands over her ears.

"QUIET!" Charlie bellowed.

A score of mouths snapped shut.

"The Dandelion Insurrection," Charlie told them, "is the last hope that people have as our democracy is strangled in the grip of this hidden dictatorship. It is the refusal to be squeezed to death by the hand of fear and greed, but instead, to spring into action to *live!*"

For a moment, the family stared at him in disbelief. Then

every throat broke out once more in a tangle of French and English. A few voices hastily shushed and silenced the others, muting the noise into a dense thicket of whispers. Curiosity strained against the stranglehold of safety. The questions broke free, rising and falling in a tumbling cacophony of sound. Charlie and Zadie stood quietly as the storm raged around them.

*Hello*, he mouthed silently. She smiled. Charlie's pulse hammered until he couldn't breathe. *Forget my earlier words*, he thought. *The Dandelion Insurrection is what happens when the heart breaks open with love!* The breaking open itself *is* the insurrection. It is what happens when our love for life and for each other rises up so powerfully within us that we can no longer keep silent, but must leap into passionate action!

This sudden understanding beat ferociously through his veins as the family argued about the hidden dictatorship and democracy's demise. Charlie waited them out. They could bicker until they were blue in the face, but the facts were clear; the police were armed like soldiers, the army swarmed like mosquitoes, the military marched up and down the streets, and what could you do? Nothing. You could not sign petitions. You could not speak out against the government. You could not rally together in the square. Grunts and growls shot around the room. Heads shook. Beards waggled. Sighs and appeals to God slipped out. Elbows leaned on tables. Mouths spat out complaints.

"Charlie?" young Matt asked, nudging his elbow. "Is it true? *The Man from the North* . . . is that you?"

The cafe silenced abruptly. Natalie's eyes bored sharply into her son. The members of her family were salt of the earth farmers and foresters, not radicals, certainly not revolutionaries! The family stared at the young man as if he had suddenly sprouted horns. Charlie shifted awkwardly.

"Well, yes," he replied.

"*Holy boys!*" Matt burst out in awe. "I never figured!"

"Well," Charlie answered, "I didn't figure anyone around here was taking those articles seriously."

"I do," Bette confessed.

"*Et moi,*" Jean Pierre admitted.

"Ah, well," Rick put in shyly, "my wife has them all hidden in her underwear drawer." He blushed beet red as the others burst into laughter. Charlie's mother pushed furiously off the cafe counter and threaded through the chairs. When she reached her father's side, she snatched the handwritten article from the old man's hand. Her eyes scanned it in disbelief.

"Charles-Valier Rider," she snapped, calling her son by his full name, "have you lost your mind?" Natalie's face was pinched with distress. There were soldiers on the street, hunting *the Man From the North!* "Who put you up to this?" she demanded.

Charlie froze as Natalie glared at Zadie and memory cut him as keenly as a sharpened blade.

"We need a voice, Charlie," Zadie had told him. "The stories of the Dandelion Insurrection must be told. People are rising up against this oppression, but they are few in number and we need more. We need you to plant the seeds of love, creativity, and courage. We need your poetry."

"But I'm a reporter, not a poet," he protested.

"Wrong," Zadie had contradicted, "you're a poet, not a reporter. Your writing has a revolution of metaphor and beauty beating against the jail of your practicality."

Charlie stared at her.

"How did you know that?" he asked.

Zadie smiled.

"It keeps escaping. Besides," she went on, "it's not enough

to report the *facts* of the Dandelion Insurrection. You'll need poetry to capture its essence. The Dandelion Insurrection slips out of its own parameters. It's as big as restoring democracy and as small as saying hello to your neighbors. Sometimes, it looks so ordinary that you don't even know it's there."

A blaze of writing had hurtled from him like a firebrand of resistance. *Be like the dandelions,* he had written, *spring up in intolerable soils, dare to stand up against violence and hatred, blossom into love.* Charlie translated the articles into French so the authorities would suspect he was Canadian. The underground presses across the border switched them back to English before sending them anywhere the seeds of resistance would take them. All winter, he had used the stories Zadie told him to ignite the dormant courage of the nation. The words couldn't fly fast enough from his fingertips. He raked the coals of frustration, stirred up the smoldering piles of despair, and tore off the smothering effects of fear. *Be like the dandelions,* he wrote, *courageous, bold defenders of the golden soul of humanity, fearless in the face of adversity.*

Zadie sent word back to him: people were listening. Charlie watched in awe as rumors of his infamy circulated. In America, they began to call him *the Man From the North.* Following the French clues, the authorities searched in Quebec, Montreal, even as far as France. The dark fist of oppression tightened. Charlie wrote despite its shadow. The fingers of the government crawled across the land. Charlie kept churning out his articles. The hot stench of infuriated tyranny fumed. Charlie held his breath . . . and kept on writing.

Two weeks ago, Zadie had left a cryptic message on his landline.

"Get ready to go."

She didn't say where. She didn't hint when. She left

Charlie, as always, hanging in breathless uncertainty. He eyed the border nervously. He waited for her call. He crossed his fingers, prayed in church, packed his bags, and hoped-against-hope that Zadie would reach him before the federal agents. For days, he had tiptoed nervously around his Ma, hating to lie to her, knowing that he would vanish and she would not know the reason why.

*Now she knows,* Charlie sighed, *but that doesn't make it any easier.*

Natalie drew all five feet and two inches of herself up in a storm of outrage. The entire cafe hunkered down. Valier murmured in a conciliatory tone. She sliced him with the steel in her eyes.

"Charlie, you must stop writing these at once!"

Charlie clenched his jaw.

"Ma, I'm not a little boy anymore."

"*Non.* By now, you should have better sense," Natalie snapped.

"How many times have you said that God took away all my common sense and gave me curiosity instead?" Charlie shot back.

Old Valier sighed. That boy got his fire from his father, Scott Rider, may the man rest in peace. Even now, he could see that rebellious, motorcycle-riding atheist in the determined lines of Charlie's face. Stubborn. Headstrong. Insistent. Valier's eyes flicked up to his daughter. *Ah voyons!* Who was he fooling? Look at the woman, hands on her hips, one toe tapping; still wearing tight blue jeans just like the day she had ridden off on the back of Scott Rider's motorcycle; still poking her stubborn chin up as defiantly as when she had returned to the valley pregnant with Charlie, not yet married to Scott, unashamed and unrepentant. Valier sighed. The boy got his stubbornness from both ends.

"Charlie," he said gently, "you are in danger, maybe we can hide you. We can make sure the police don't know you are *the Man From the North*."

The family nodded solemnly, but Charlie shook his head.

"No, grand-père. The time of winter and hiding is over. Haven't you heard the river? The ice is on the move, cracking and booming, yearning to break free. It is spring. The dandelions are erupting from the soil. It's not time for hiding. . . it's time for action."

He had their attention now. No one stirred.

"How long will you sit around, talking, talking, talking, but doing nothing? Already, the border is closed. Already, we risk arrest just for speaking in this way. What will it take for you to say, *enough?* We tuck our heads between our legs, trying to spare our loved ones suffering . . . but the road of complacency never leads to the end of suffering. It leads to death!"

The younger men along the walls were throwing glances at each other, agreeing with Charlie's words. The ring of older men who had lived through hardship and bitterness wore their weary cynicism on their scowling faces. To them, Charlie made another appeal.

"What is life without freedom?" Charlie asked. "Real freedom, not just from terrorists, but from oppressive control? *Nous sommes les Acadians.* We are Acadians. We have pride in ourselves, our families, our land, and hard work . . . but one day, we will hide our heads in shame, looking back at these times and knowing that *we did nothing.*"

"Bah," Jean Pierre dismissed him, "you are a boy. You have never fought for anything. I have spilled blood for this country. I have lost brothers for this country. I will not take up arms against my country!"

Charlie regarded him steadily for a moment.

"Nor I," he agreed softly. "I will not take up arms against any man. But I will stand up for the principles this nation was founded upon; the freedom of speech and assembly, the right to a fair and speedy trial, and the equality of all human beings."

"Huh," Natalie snorted, folding her arms across her chest, "and you plan to do all this with your bare hands, eh?"

"Yes, if I must," Charlie answered. "But my bare hands wield the tools of nonviolent struggle; the tools of Dr. Martin Luther King, Jr., Jesus, Gandhi, and countless more through history. Matt knows about them. He has read my articles."

Matt looked up red-faced.

"Yuh, and I can tell anybody what they want to know." The young clown of the family was not laughing now. He appealed to them in earnest. "We've got to take a stand. *The Man From the North* - Charlie, that is - he made good points in those articles." Matt looked from one face to another, expecting to be rebuked by the elders, but they were grave and silent, weighing his words. "I joked about the three men in the tub, but, by god, when just three men control us all, it is not funny! *The Banker* has been foreclosing on families all over the country. How long will it be before it starts to happen here?"

Old Mathieu spoke up.

"They're not going to get my land. We've worked that land for four hundred years."

"If they can't get you off by economics, they'll do it by military force," Charlie warned them. "Remember *le Grand Dérangement?*"

The faces grew stony around him. He had tapped the root of centuries old bitterness from when the British had expelled the French families from the valley.

"It didn't work," Jean Pierre said stiffly. "We returned."

"It can happen again," Charlie replied. "It is happening now. In other regions of the country, where the land rests above minerals or gas, they are pushing out the families by economics, by laws, and by force."

Zadie spoke up softly.

"If we don't do something now, our kids won't even remember the freedoms or rights that our forefathers fought for. We must resist this slide into authoritarian control! My parents will help you. You joke about them being hippies, but they have a wealth of knowledge to lend. They have trained in nonviolent struggle and they are connected to Dandelion Insurrectionists all across the country."

"And," Matt added proudly, "we've got Charlie; *the Man from the North!*"

Zadie shook her head.

"The authorities are raking their talons through this valley looking for *the Man from the North*," Zadie told them solemnly. "That's why they closed the border. I came to take Charlie out of the country, but I got here too late."

"It doesn't matter, anyway," Charlie said. "We can't run away from what's happening in this country. We've got to meet it, head on."

Natalie stiffened as if the air had just left the room. Her heart clutched her chest. Her boy was gone, swept like a ghost from the stark reality of the present. Her son was a stranger, a man with burning determination in his eyes, sandy hair left uncut, a leanness to his angular cheeks, the heat of his youth tempered by a fierce winter of thought, now standing there, a man, yearning to give himself, his words, his breath, and his life to this troubled world.

"Charlie."

He flinched. The way she *shhhed* the 'Ch' and bit down on

the 'r' and raised the pitch of her voice right at the end . . . that was her warning tone of trouble, often followed by a tirade. Natalie was the youngest of Valier's children, spoiled and cossetted by her seven older siblings, but she had grown into a woman made of iron sinew . . . short, petite, and tough. She pinned her son with a fierce look.

"I will never forgive you for being an idiot," she said shortly.

Charlie groaned.

"Ma - "

"But," she cut him off, "I have read the articles of *L'homme du Nord*, in English and *en français!* And I agree, we must do something." He blinked at her unexpected and sudden support. She straightened up and looked at the family.

"They closed the border a week before my niece's wedding. Are we going to do nothing about it?" she demanded.

They shifted uncomfortably.

"Eh, but what can we do?" Rick Dumais answered.

"Resist," Charlie urged them. "Push back. March across the border dressed in your wedding finery, if you must."

Zadie supported him.

"All across the country, people like you are in this position," she said. "They can't hold a baseball game without a permit. They can't recite the Declaration of Independence without being hauled down to the police station for an interrogation. People are rising up because they *must*."

"*Mais oui*," Natalie agreed, "and so must we! If the whole valley goes across the border together, they will have a hard time stopping everyone, won't they?"

The young fiancée blanched.

"I don't know, Aunt Natalie . . . that is . . . what if we are all arrested?"

"Lynnette," Natalie shot back, "do you want to get married

next week?"

"*Mais oui!*"

"Then we're going to have to stand up for your right to do so!"

Charlie smiled. Grand-père always said that Natalie had inherited her mother's spirit. She stamped her heel on the floor and glared at the rest of the family.

"It's time we made a fuss about these restrictions on assemblies over twenty," she declared. "I can't even have you all over for Sunday dinner without a permit. *C'est absurde!* We need to make a stink about how the government is destroying *l'héritage culturel Acadians* with their senseless laws. We aren't terrorists - "

"*Nous sommes les Acadians!*" Valier roared out, completing her sentence with a bark of laughter. Hands clapped in approval. The family broke into conversation, gnawing on strategy and worry, bursting out in small explosions of epithets for the stupidity of the boy, of the government, and of them all! In the ruckus, Natalie reached over and grabbed her son.

"When are you leaving?" she demanded.

"Now, I think," he answered, glancing at Zadie for confirmation.

"It would be best," Zadie told Natalie softly.

"Oh!" She pulled her son into an awkward hug, telling herself it would not be the last time. "Well," she said, lost for words. "Charlie, I - " Natalie bit her lip. Tears pushed to come out, but she was determined not to make a scene. Behind them, they heard Valier bark out a command. Charlie swore under his breath and bolted for the door. How many times had the old man played this trick on him, ordering his cousins to -

"Catch him!" the old man's command burst through the room. Matt and Rick pushed off the walls and leapt for Charlie, shaking the cafe with their commotion. Chairs crashed to the floor as Valier yelled to them.

"My own grandson is *the Man from the North*? Catch that wicked boy! I will smack him for his stupidity . . . and bless him for his courage!"

Smiles broke out in the melee of tumbling bodies. Rick Dumais seized his torso. He shot a quick nod to Matt and they swept Charlie off his feet, hoisting him up onto his back in the air.

"*L'homme du Nord! L'homme du Nord!*" they chanted.

"Put me down!" Charlie cried.

Zadie started laughing.

"You're not helping!" he told Zadie.

Natalie began to chuckle, too. Bette's wheeze broke loose from her chest. Jean Pierre's snorting guffaws shot out. Matt and Guy's hands shook. Charlie bobbed midair.

"You're all crazy!" he hollered at them.

The bell above the door jingled.

Heads swung toward it.

A policeman entered.

Everyone froze.

"*Bonjour*, Officer," Valier said politely as the uniformed man scanned the scene with a fierce scowl. Startled eyes and shocked faces instantly alerted the policeman's suspicion.

"What is going on here?" he growled.

"Oh, eh? Nothing. A little family gathering," Valier replied.

The officer's teeth clicked as he began to count the occupants of the room.

"Assemblies of more than twenty must have a permit."

"This is a restaurant," Pierrette called out, trying to keep her voice from shaking.

"You are not eating. This is a meeting of more than . . . "

He tried to tally their numbers, but Jean Pierre blocked his view.

"Eh? There cannot be twenty of us here!" Jean Pierre protested. A sudden flurry of relatives ducked behind the counter and into the kitchen. The rest stayed frozen in place, hearts thumping in their throats.

"What are you doing with that man?" the officer asked, pointing at Charlie.

"Huh? Oh. Uh . . . we are just - " Jean Pierre stammered as they searched rapidly for an explanation. They certainly could not say that they had, at this very moment, taken hold of *the Man from the North*. Rick Dumais coughed. Old Mathieu creaked in his chair. Natalie scuffed the floorboards with her shoe. Valier shoved Charlie's article out of sight. The officer waited for an answer.

"Eloping!" Zadie exclaimed breathlessly. "We are eloping. Me and him." She pointed at Charlie.

"*Oui, monsieur,*" Valier agreed quickly. "It is an old French tradition to carry the groom out on his back . . . eh . . . as if he is on his way to his funeral!"

There was an old tradition of bullshit, too, Charlie thought, but now was not the time to point that out. The relatives quickly supported Valier, explaining in convoluted French-English sentences *l'héritage culturel Acadians* in a contradictory tumble of invented traditions. The policeman's frown bent in confusion, but before the officer could piece together the glaring inconsistencies, Valier leaned on his cane and stood.

"I am the boy's oldest blood relative," he announced, frowning severely as if preparing to give or withhold his benediction upon his grandson's proposed marriage. Valier pondered Zadie solemnly, shaking his head. Matt and Rick muttered something about hurrying it up . . . the *boy* weighed

28

more than a barrel of potatoes.

"Yes," Valier continued, "the boy has pleaded his case. He is headstrong. He wants to go forward with this. It is foolish. It is crazy."

Charlie held his breath, realizing that Valier was talking not about the imagined elopement, but about the Dandelion Insurrection. Valier cleared his throat and took Zadie by the hand.

"What this girl is asking our boy to do, is to . . . eh," he paused, looking askance at the policeman. "Well, she wants him to stand up for the rights of all men to determine their own lives."

The old man switched to French, declaring that the essence of freedom granted everyone the right to live and love. It was a holy trust from God, and must be protected by all.

"Life? Liberty? Love? Who are we to stand against such things?!" he asked them. He stood up straight and rapped the floor with his cane. It was the moment of truth, were they for or against Charlie?

"*La vie. La liberté. L'amour.* Who will stand up for it?" Valier demanded.

"*Moi!*" cried out Matt.

"*Moi aussi!*" seconded Rick.

"*Pour la vie!*" hollered out Mathieu.

"*Pour la liberté!*" yelled Jean Pierre.

"*Pour l'amour!*" roared petite Natalie.

Zadie let out a whoop of delight. Valier thumped his cane, gesturing, *carry him out!* He hobbled quickly through the door as the policeman held it open. Matt and Rick paraded Charlie out. He lay stiff as a board, his heart pounding, turning his head away as the officer looked curiously at him.

"Wish us luck, Officer," Zadie requested, pulling on the

man's arm to distract him. Charlie choked. Leave it to Zadie to have the gall to ask the police to wish good luck upon an insurrection. The officer glanced up at Charlie, unimpressed.

"Seems like you might need it," he said.

Charlie rolled his eyes. *Officer*, he longed to say, *you have no idea.*

# CHAPTER FOUR

. . . . .

*A Radical By Spring*

The ice was on the move! Along the valley floor, the roar of spring released the cracking ice in the river. Stretches of potato fields turned piebald as sunlight stung the snow away. The trees teased the eyes with signs of yellow-green buds. The sun and wind flirted with the air, seducing the temperature to swing from cool to warm and back again.

"Do you have any idea what's going on out there?" Zadie exclaimed as they raced down the back roads. She reached across the narrow cab of Charlie's station wagon and began punctuating her words with a little shake of his shoulder. "Do - you - know - what - you - have - done?"

"I would," Charlie retorted, "but *somebody* hasn't called me for two weeks! Where on earth have you been, Zadie?"

"Everywhere!" she answered, flinging her arms out in a sweeping gesture. "I've been across the continent twice this winter, setting up underground networks, spreading your articles, seeing what's going on."

He glanced at her.

"And?"

"Well, thanks to the government, *the Man from the North* and *the Dandelion Insurrection* have grown into household names," Zadie said with a wry expression.

"So, the ban on my articles last February did some good?" he groaned.

"Sure," she laughed. "As soon as you were blacklisted as a *seditious polluter of minds*, everybody started reading you!"

He sighed in exasperation.

"You're a legend out there," Zadie told him. "Everybody's got copies of your articles hidden under the kitchen sink."

"All I did was write their stories down," Charlie said, humbly.

"All you did was put the name of the Dandelion Insurrection onto every spark of resistance in America, codify chaos into an umbrella strategy, outline the philosophy of *what, why,* and *how* they need to resist, and describe their own strength to them. That's not a minor accomplishment, Charlie."

"But it has hardly even begun," he sighed. "This is just the start of the struggle."

"Yeah, but Charlie," she pointed out, "because of you . . . people are ready."

"How many?" he questioned sharply.

"Not many," she admitted, "but enough."

He nodded, his suspicions confirmed. The real insurrectionists still belonged to a fringe minority, but their numbers would grow. Every outrage and injustice could be used to swell the support for the Dandelion Insurrection. Every story of hope and human kindness could act as fertilizer to the seeds that had been planted in people's minds. The words of *the Man From the North* were whispered in every household. Even if people only heard the government's lies about him, they at least knew that one person dared to stand in opposition to oppression. That was enough. *Be like the dandelions,* he had written, *take root in the most inhospitable of soils.*

"Zadie?" Charlie said as he swung around a bumpy curve.

"Mmm?"

"It's good to see you."

She turned to him, noticing the tiny differences in his face, the lines that crept into places they had never been before, the tired eyes from too many late nights spent writing, and the way he now bit the corner of his lip in a vague unease that never left.

"Have you been alright, Charlie?"

He nodded.

"It has been a long six months," he admitted. "Your dad decided my education in American history and politics was severely lacking."

Zadie rolled her eyes. Her radical father, Bill Gray, ran an organic farm and had been involved in every social justice movement she could remember. The rise of militarism and suppression of dissent had boiled the temperamental man into a pot of simmering frustration as the longtime activist was forced to lay low. He kept a lid on his opinions, a tight rein on his temper, and a provisioned boat hidden on the banks of the St. John River, ready to split at a moment's notice.

Between tractor repairs and potato picking, Bill had subjected Charlie to a crash course in what he dubbed, *the real history of America*. As the last cold days of potato harvest came to a close, the tree of Charlie's education shed its leaves. Glaring lies and half-truths fluttered to the ground. In a startling fury of speed, he found himself stripped bare-branched and starkly disillusioned about his own country, appalled by the history of violence and conquest that brought Europeans to these lands and continued to bleed deep red through the strands of the American Dream. Betrayals and broken promises lay like shattered glass on every hilltop, valley floor, and open plain. His old map of America became a marker of graves. Here, the Black Foot Indians were butchered. There was the Trail of Tears. On this mountain, a hundred coal miners had been murdered. At this site, the suffragettes were beaten, imprisoned, and starved. These were the places in Texas where the immigrants blistered in the heat before they were deported.

He learned that abject lies, misinformation, and propaganda had been perfectly legal in the mainstream news of his country for decades. The newscasters spoke of the upturn in the economy, but Charlie discovered the dark underbelly of the beast: the so-called economic upturn dove into the pockets of the wealthy, and the gap between rich and poor kept widening. He gritted his teeth in frustration as Congress played to the profit-piper's tune and passed rich men's legislation while the unemployment lines grew. The soup kitchens scraped the bottom of the pots long before the hunger of the people stopped. He wrote madly as concerns over food shortages and riots rose.

*I hear your despairing rain of cries. I sense the burning fury in you, that lustful ache for retaliating lightning strikes. In the distance, I hear the thunder rolls of violence. Remember: weapons never built a house, fed a child, or planted fields. We must turn to tools of nonviolence to build a chance for life.*

The prairies, the mountains, the farmlands, and the river basins were stripped of protections, reverting to environmental lawlessness under the legislation of the *American Freedom of Open Lands Act.* Charlie's gut clenched as he watched politics prepare to wreak environmental havoc under the false flag of liberty and freedom.

"Times are changing," the old men of the valley muttered as they watched rural people in other parts of the country get forced off their land by tax increases, mortgage failures, and denials of farm loans for seed and tractor repairs. Agribusiness took up residence, owned by *the Banker,* dependent on *the Butcher's* surplus chemicals from the war industry, and fueled by *the Candlestick Maker's* cheap oil. Out moneyed, out subsidized, out gunned in the courts and Congress, the local farmers despaired.

On top of it all, the weather defied everyone's predictions. Early frosts threatened the late summer crops. A heat snap surged for a week before giving way to pouring rain. Fall floods turned fields to mud. Rot and blight proliferated. Charlie's grandfather and granduncles slid deeper in their chairs, depressed as only old farmers can be as the earth turned wild against their claims of wisdom. As the winter whipped from blizzards to heat waves, they burned their old almanacs, solemnly feeding the pages into their woodstoves, conceding to a changing climate that the National Weather Service refused to report on.

*Times are changing,* Charlie wrote for the Dandelion Insurrection, *and we must change faster, growing in our hearts and souls, embracing our diversity as our saving grace as we work to stop our corporate politicians from waging this destructive war upon humanity and the earth.*

Midwinter, when the high school band kicked off the basketball season, Charlie discovered the national anthem now made him queasy. He could no longer believe his country was the greatest nation in the world. He could not wave the flag or sing along with its slogans. Yet, as he watched the students trumpeting out the anthem with heartfelt effort, he loved them all. They were lambs on the way to the slaughterhouse, playing homage to a government that cared nothing about them.

His heart broke a thousand times a day.

He took long walks over the hard cold earth as the clouds spit out flakes of snow. Charlie felt stretched across two realities; the beautiful curves of his valley and the starkly brutal landscape of his nation. He paused on the crests of rolling hills, patched with fields both fertile and fallow, and let sorrow and love sit quietly together as he watched the snow tremble earthward.

*It is our love that calls us into action now*, he wrote. *Our respect for life and our compassion for creation require us to stand up to the forces that cause oppression, suffering, and destruction.*

Everything mattered, not just this valley, but every nook and cranny of the earth; every stand of trees; every cluster of children in the school yard; each block of the teeming cities; every language that cried out on the tongues of immigrants; every joy; every sorrow; everything mattered. Charlie knew the heartbreak of his grandfather's God, watching over the preciousness of all creation and weeping at its suffering. He felt the apathy his own pain sometimes drove him to, and the coldness with which he silenced his compassion when it became too much to bear. But, he also sensed, before long, the tenderness of love reaching out to him again.

Each day, this love penetrated further into his bloodstream, pulsed in his veins, rewrote his cells, his muscles, even his genetic coding. In the heat of writing, he would look up in wonderment, feeling tears prickling the corners of his eyes. It was all precious: the snowflakes, the deep night, his grand-père's snoring in the room next door, Zadie's voice long distant on the telephone, the scrawl of ink running across the page, the people waiting for his articles . . . everything. It had been a lonely winter full of the heartache that comes from loving the world too much.

But now, spring pushed against the weight of winter. The air pulsed with fresh starts and new beginnings. The ice was on the move . . . and so was he!

The station wagon swung around a curve in the back road and Zadie rolled down the window. The scent of snowmelt dampened earth whipped into the car. She scanned Charlie's face with her blue-grey eyes, noticing the carved slope of his cheekbones, the angle of his nose, the rebellious temper of his spirit. He had always chafed at the confines of this valley, and now his whole body leaned into the winds of change, ready to take flight.

"Zadie," Charlie said, his eyes glowing with readiness for this journey, "there's a world of trouble right beyond the doorstep of this valley. We've got to find a way to stop it, or that trouble is going to march right into our homes and destroy everything."

Zadie reached over to tug the front of his jacket with one hand.

"You sound like a soldier in the old days going off to war."

"This isn't the old days," he answered, shaking his head. "There is no war. No enemy. Soldiers and guns are part of the problem, not the solution. Zadie, I've got to spread the seeds of this Dandelion Insurrection as fast as I can."

"Can I come with you?" she asked.

"What do you mean, *can you come with me*?" he exclaimed. "You're practically kidnapping me!"

"Well, technically, we're eloping," she grinned.

"Don't tease me, heartbreaker," he shot back. "What exactly does that mean, *we're eloping*?"

"You drive and I tell you where to go."

"Well," he sighed, "that's a relief."

"Why's that?" she asked.

"Because I don't have any idea where we're headed."

\*      \*      \*

The itch of the road burned in them, but they detoured toward Zadie's parents' farm. The house hunkered down at the top of a long driveway, sagging and comfortable. As Charlie shut off the engine, the last adrenaline sputtered from his veins.

Zadie shot out of the car and took the porch steps three at a time. Charlie got out slowly, absorbing the tumble of Bill and Ellen's cluttered yard one last time. His eyes stretched westward toward his town, then swept along the familiar horizon. *Goodbye,* he said silently to it all.

"Mom? Dad? Charlie and I are headed south!" Zadie yelled as she raced into the farmhouse.

He climbed the steps and threaded through the narrow hallway into the kitchen where Zadie was animatedly recounting the morning's events to her mother. Ellen Byrd rose from the table and reached out to pull Charlie into her embrace. It was like greeting a tree. Ellen's branch-like limbs wrapped around him. Her black curls canopied out from her head, lined with a few tendrils of silver; a birch tree in reverse. She towered over Charlie in her loose white clothes, splattered with paint. The telltale signs of her profession were etched in the cuticles of her fingernails.

"Hold on a moment!" she told Zadie, halting the story with a wave of her hand. She leaned out the front door and called down the driveway to her husband. Bill jogged up from the barn and clomped inside, shedding his coat, kicking off his boots, and breathing hard. His wide feet flamed red in their thick wool socks. Above his ruddy cheeks and bushy beard, a grave look deepened the wrinkles around his dark eyes.

"Just in time," he wheezed. "I've got some disturbing news."

"What do you mean?" Charlie asked him.

Bill gestured to the kitchen table. Ellen bent her head for a kiss as he stomped past. She was nearly a foot taller than her solid-as-the-earth husband; quiet where he was explosive; mild where he was dramatic. She settled back into her chair while Bill paced back and forth on the narrow track worn in the linoleum by years of his tirades.

38

"I just got a call from Aubrey Renault down in New York City. The latest budgetary cuts have gone into effect. The Food Assistance Program shut its doors today."

A chill ran down Charlie's spine. Ellen's mouth tightened into a thin white line. Zadie's eyes stung. It had been inevitable. Everyone knew it. With the military receiving seventy percent of the entire United States budget, the last crumbs of social services had slid down the endangered species list into extinction. For weeks, the television had been relentlessly screening World War II style advertisements to convince people to accept the food shortages as a patriotic contribution to the war on terror. Public service announcements on the radio urged people to *sacrifice for our soldiers . . . they risk the highest sacrifice for you.* The latest billboard ads brazenly told people to *pull in your belts and suck up your guts . . . the boys at the front need to eat!* One of Charlie's aunts was participating in the nationally sponsored weight loss program that featured a boot camp instructor who barked out, *drop down and give me ten! What's good for the soldiers is good for us all!*

The poor didn't have ten pounds, ten dollars, or ten *anything* to give. They had borne the brunt of the recent food shortages, the economic downturn, and the budgetary cuts. The impending closure of the Food Assistance Program had shot panic through the poverty-stricken neighborhoods that had come to rely on it for survival. Political leaders said the churches and charities should cover the gap as a service to God.

*The Man From the North* wrote that if the allegedly Christian politicians were so keen on *services to God*, they might stop spending the food assistance money on bombs that destroyed God's creations. A great service to God would be to tax the rich to feed the poor. *The hunger of the poor grows as fast as the pocketbooks of the wealthy,* he wrote.

Last fall's crop failures exacerbated the volatile situation. Grain prices spiked. The international market scrambled to buy up the grain reserve. *The Banker* raked in a fortune. The poor stood dumbfounded in the supermarkets, unable to afford a loaf of bread or a box of cereal. Soup lines grew. Food assistance applications flooded in. A high profile bureaucrat committed suicide, leaving a note about the impending genocide from starvation caused by the closure of the Food Assistance Program. The matter was quickly hushed up with rumors of the man's mental imbalances.

"The authorities are anticipating riots," Bill told Charlie and Zadie. "They've established police barricades and patrols throughout the cities. Aubrey said they've got the neighborhoods completely blocked off after dark, no in's or out's."

"Curfews," Charlie muttered. "Ghettos."

The four faces around the farmhouse table grew grim and somber. Bill's sigh rumbled with a groan. The lines in his face had deepened.

"This is the worst possible moment for you two to head toward the cities," Bill said slowly, "but I'm afraid you've got to go."

Charlie and Zadie looked at him in surprise. Bill's face was scrubbed with inner conflict. Ellen crossed her arms tightly over her chest. The echoes of a heated discussion were raw and palpable between them. Ellen raised her eyes up to Zadie and spoke.

"The threat of riots is very high right now," Ellen pointed out. "We're worried that if no one speaks out, people will fall back on the violence they've been indoctrinated into by the media."

Charlie shuddered. Every other television program featured

people murdering and beating each other up. A violence-lusting populace provided fuel for the war machine that required more and more bodies as the war on terrorism stretched around the globe.

"We think you should go down to the city," Bill said, "connect with the insurrectionists, and help Zadie's activist friends organize a productive response to the closure of the Food Assistance Program."

"If people are really panicked about food shortages, I doubt they'll listen to me," Zadie admitted.

"I bet they'll listen to Charlie," Bill replied.

"Me?" Charlie exclaimed.

"Yes, you. *The Man From the North*. Your articles have been circulating all winter. People think of you as a leader."

Charlie shuddered.

"That's a frightening thought."

Bill shook his head.

"It's time to step up, Charlie."

Charlie looked from one intense face to the next. Bill's was lined with grim predictions. Ellen's carried a powerful conviction in the strength of love and life, a mother's ferocity to feed and shelter people. Zadie's blazed like a young hero on a ship's bow, leaning into the winds of a great adventure. Perhaps, Charlie thought, there was a chance he could take the outrage of the people and channel it toward change.

"Alright," he said. "There are three hundred million hearts beating out there. Let's go rally the dandelions of the soul and stop this madness before it begins!"

*Rivera Sun*

# CHAPTER FIVE

· · · · ·

*Strategy For Life*


Just past the Portsmouth Bridge, the river of humanity began to swell, growling and growing with every mile. The scattered houses of Maine gave way to a mountain range of urban buildings; rising slopes of suburbs, foothills of concrete industrial buildings, peaks of coastal districts, and finally, the summit of New York City.

Zadie tucked the car away and pulled Charlie down the city blocks. He tried not to gawk as he hustled after her, half-running to keep up with her longer strides. The buildings towered over them more densely shadowed than the pine forests up north. The roar of traffic flooded his ears. Zadie grabbed him by the elbow and hauled him behind her like a trout on a fisherman's hook. He hesitated on the street corner. She plunged into traffic. The lifeline of her grip snapped loose. Charlie floundered in the stream of people, bumped and pummeled without a word of apology. The current of the city throbbed and ached like a churning snowmelt flood, dark with dissatisfaction, ripping at the shores, pulling the muck of the river's underbelly to the surface. Swift-flowing bodies rushed past Charlie. Their unspoken roar deafened him. Desperation stung the whites of their eyes. Hunger gnawed gaunt hollows into their cheeks. Anger tightened lips and tensed shoulders. Hands begged like barren tree branches, uprooted and clawing for a foothold.

Charlie drowned in the river of humanity.

The city heaved ceaselessly, throbbing and clattering. The

air tasted like bitter anxiety. A sharp yearning burned, the scent of souls longing for escape as the city tore itself apart in its frantic self-devouring. The urban behemoth ripped itself to shreds, pounded itself into pulp, smashed itself into paper, wrote down its story, incinerated every word, swept up the ashes, tossed them into the howling winds, and lodged the seed of its own fertility back into concrete cracks.

Somewhere in this madness, dandelions grew.

Charlie gasped for breath, shoved off the bottom of the river, and lunged for life again. He kicked and twisted, pushed his way through jam-packed shoulders, and swam upstream against the tide. He caught sight of Zadie's bobbing head and hollered out. She spun around and dragged him from the torrent.

"We're here," she told him. "Catch your breath."

He nodded. The sweeping current raced up and down the streets. The frantic pulse of the city throbbed mercilessly. Down the blocks as far as he could see, the city screamed for change. Charlie took a breath. There was no turning back. The rhythm of this place pounded in his heart. He nodded to Zadie and they entered the slower-turning eddy of the alleyway. Tall buildings cast them into shadows as she led them toward the hangout of her radical friends. They passed a row of dumpsters, rounded the corner, and stepped through an unmarked backdoor that opened onto a dim, tight hallway. Two figures swiveled toward them. Charlie gulped as his first impression hit him.

Sharks! Black clothed, safety-pinned, patched up sharks; pierced in nose, ear, lips, and necks, tattoos spreading underneath. Even the way their hair curled looked sharp. Bicycles hung from the ceiling above them. His nostrils flared on the smells of grease and rusted steel. Spray painted prints plastered the walls; revolutionary fists thrust upward, gas masks, olive green grenades.

"Is that Zadie Byrd Gray?" a voice asked.

"The one and only," Zadie replied. "Is that you, Hawlings? Who's behind you? Spark Plug?"

They stepped forward through the gloom, staring coldly at Charlie's blue jeans and plaid shirt. Unimpressed looks flitted from face to face. *Well, thanks, I'll just go crawl back into my backwoods hole now,* Charlie thought sourly. He made no comment about their odd names, but uncharitably observed to himself that Spark Plug's half-shorn haircut looked like a kid sister's midnight prank. His tentative hello was met with stony silence.

"Nice to meet you, too," he muttered. "Is this your bike shop?"

"It's a tool co-op and recycled parts store," Hawlings answered.

Spark Plug hissed at him to shut up.

"And what're you? A lumberjack?" he asked, pointing to Charlie's plaid shirt.

Zadie pinned him with a ferocious glare.

"Didn't your mother teach you any manners?"

"Nah, she taught me how to smoke dope," Spark Plug snorted.

"Your mom?" Hawlings exclaimed. "No way. She's so straight, she'd mistake weed for tea leaves and try to steep it."

"Haha," Spark Plug snickered back. "She's so straight, she thinks Guantanamo is that foreign word for bat shit."

"No, no, I got it . . . your ma's so straight, she thinks 9/11 was done by terrorists."

Charlie blinked. Wasn't it?

The door shot open behind them, kicking Charlie in the

back.

"Oops, sorry," said a man's voice.

Zadie spun around.

"Zipper?!"

"Zadie?" he cried out. The lanky guy threw his arms around Zadie, squeezing her enthusiastically.

"What're you doing here?" the man exclaimed. "You didn't call or anything!"

"I was hoping there was going to be a meeting tonight," Zadie answered. "I brought someone special along."

"It's a private meeting, Zadie," Spark Plug growled. "No outsiders."

Zadie put her hands on her hips.

"What do we look like, Sparky? The FBI?"

"No one's doubting *you*, princess," Spark Plug spat out. "This guy, though . . . "

"Spark Plug," Zadie snapped as she lost her temper, "this is *the Man From the North*."

Spark Plug blinked. His eyes raked over Charlie. Zadie saw a strange expression dart over his face. She frowned. Then Zipper let out a thrilled whoop that broke the moment.

"No way!" Zipper crowed in delight. "*The Man from the North* is here?!"

Hawlings laughed in amazement and elbowed Spark Plug.

"Dude, look at him. It's brilliant. I mean he's so damn straight we could elect him for President!"

Spark Plug's stony expression didn't crack.

"Hey, no hard feelings?" Hawlings asked Charlie. "We didn't know who you were . . . it's our job to give newbies a little shakedown."

"You might want to reconsider your welcoming committee's approach," Charlie suggested. "If I wasn't *the Man From the*

*North*, I'd be halfway down the block by now."

"If you weren't *the Man From the North*, I'd be running you out of town," Spark Plug muttered.

"Why?" Charlie shot back.

"'Cause I don't like your face."

Zadie shoved her way between them, pulling Charlie by the arm.

"Come on," she muttered. "Just ignore him."

"Hey," Hawlings called after him, "no offense about dissing your shirt."

"Plaid's the new black," Zipper joked quietly to Charlie. "All the anarchists are gonna be wearing it soon."

Charlie laughed a little, catching the friendly gleam in Zipper's eye.

"Zipper, no filming tonight, alright?" Zadie said, pausing to point at his camera bag. He started to protest. "Look, the Feds don't have a face on Ch - *the Man From the North* and it's important to delay the inevitable as long as we can."

"But, Zadie, this is historic! I'll protect the footage, I promise - "

"Don't make promises you can't keep," she said.

Zipper sighed, but agreed.

"You make films?" Charlie asked.

"He makes *amazing* films," Zadie answered. "He has been on the front line of every protest, inside people's homes, down to the police station, in prison, up at City Hall. If you want the image of what's going on, Zipper has it."

"How come I've never seen them?" Charlie exclaimed. "We could send some short films through the same networks as my articles."

"Can I use some of your words in my next film?" Zipper asked.

"Yeah, yeah, of course," Charlie answered. "They say the pen is mightier than the sword, an image is worth a thousand words, and if film rolls thirty-two frames per second . . . you do the math!"

Zadie cleared her throat.

"Just one thing, Zipper . . . don't use his writing to advocate violence. No destruction of property. No *strategic* violence. No posters with Molotov cocktails or short films of intentional clashes with the police. No chants of 'death to so-and-so.' No cyber hacking that results in harm or injury to any person - "

"Hey, hey, you're preaching to the choir," Zipper protested.

Their eyes flicked toward Spark Plug, but neither said another word. They walked down the crowded hallway. Square metal lockers were bolted at head height. Jackets hung from hooks underneath. Packs were stashed on top. Voices argued down the hall.

"Look, they've set down city-wide curfews - " the speaker broke off, truncated by a second voice.

Charlie followed Zadie around the corner into a room crowded with bike stands and a couch that looked like it had survived the Armageddon. The front door was solid steel and behind the curtains a chain-link fence had been bolted to the window frames as a security measure. A rough dozen people sat in a haphazard circle of beat up chairs, talking at once, tromping over each other's sentences.

"They've closed off the neighborhoods - "

"I say we have to organize and fast - "

"Organize?" Zadie laughed. "Did someone in an anarchist collective just say organize?"

The group swiveled in their seats at Zadie's voice and a few people burst into smiles as they recognized her.

"We're having a philosophy and strategy session," someone

48

explained.

"Uh-huh, that's what it sounded like," Zadie chuckled.

"We're working on particulars," a young man clarified. "We know the grand strategy."

*Damn straight, they better know it,* Charlie thought to himself. He had spent months researching the article that outlined the overarching strategy of the Dandelion Insurrection, critiquing it rigorously before distributing it. The final article laid out a succinct plan of action to restore democracy. It wasn't rocket science, Charlie shrugged to himself, but it wasn't a cakewalk either. The people must be taught that they had the right to resist tyranny *and* the capacity to do so nonviolently; they had to dissolve the barriers of class prejudice that the power elite used to effectively segregate the populace; they had to undermine the pillars of support for the corporate-controlled government through boycotts, noncooperation, and refusal to obey orders; the police and the military had to be convinced to serve the people rather than the powerful; the Dandelion Insurrection had to be strong enough to push the current regime over when it began to topple; and, finally, the movement had to develop a clear strategy for moving forward, a list of reforms, a plan for holding elections, and candidates that reflected the values of the people. Each phase required tremendous effort and courage. Many obstacles needed to be overcome; culturally ingrained apathy, fear of retaliation, the general ill health and drug addiction issues of the populace, the tremendous misinformation spread by the corporate propaganda machine, and the current set of repressive laws. Education had been the focus of Charlie's articles over the winter . . . and instilling courage for action.

"So," Charlie asked, "what are you working on?"

"Well," the young man answered, "it's about the closure of

the Food Assistance Program and how to address it. We've been waiting to see if *the Man From the North* would put out an article on the subject - "

Zadie bit back a smile. Charlie's eyes flicked to meet hers.

*Don't tell them, yet,* her expression hinted.

"Why wait?" Charlie asked the guy. "You're probably as smart as him. He would be the first to tell you that he doesn't have all the answers."

"Yeah, but see, he knows what's going on. We don't. We're not connected to the whole Dandelion Insurrection or to the leaders. It may be that riots are needed to wake people up!"

The woman next to him blew a hot sigh of frustration.

"I keep telling you, that's crazy. If riots start, soldiers will be brought in and the police will start arresting people left and right. Violent unrest is exactly what the power elite wants. They're prepared to deal with it. They expect it. It gives them an excuse to tighten the reins and use military force."

The young man argued with her.

"The unrest will backfire on the government. They'll be blamed - "

"No, they won't. The poor will be called the culprits, like always."

"Well, at least people will know something is terribly wrong."

"I wouldn't count on it," the woman argued. "People in suburbia don't have a clue what goes on in the cities. They don't even know about the prison camps or the debt-labor laws - "

"See, this is why we should wait for *the Man From the North* to say something."

Spark Plug slunk in from the hallway and leaned against the doorframe.

"Why don't you ask him? He's standing right there."

Spark Plug gestured to Charlie. Eyes flew open. A sudden silence fell. Every gaze in the room fixed on Charlie. He gulped. Spark Plug snickered.

"So, Mr. Expert-on-the-Dandelion-Insurrection, tell us what to do."

"Well, it's not all up to me - "

"Haven't you tracked down the organizers? Who are they?" Spark Plug demanded.

Charlie blinked at the fierceness of the question.

"There aren't any organizers to the Dandelion Insurrection," Charlie stammered. "As far as I can tell, it's simply bursting out of nowhere."

"I knew it!" Hawlings exclaimed in excitement, rattling off a stream of activists' verbiage. "It's a multi-nodal, non-hierarchical, horizontally-structured, self-organizing emergent movement."

Spark Plug crossed his tattooed arms and glowered at Hawlings.

"If you're talking about the disorganized inefficiency of leaderless movements, forget it. They don't work."

"Hey!" Hawlings bristled. "They're still new. They've only been in development in the last decade or so."

"Actually," Zadie chimed in, "self-organizing structures are as old as the planet. They're the foundation for this basic thing called Life."

"How come they don't work, then?" Spark Plug pushed.

"They do work," Zadie answered defensively. "You're alive because they work."

"Well, they don't work for social change," he shot back.

"It's not that *they* don't work," Zadie told Spark Plug in a challenging tone. "It's that *you* don't know *how* they work. If you understood anything about life, you'd see how the theory of natural systems could be used to create truly effective social movements."

"Well, wonders be," Spark Plug said nastily, "our ole pin-up girl has got a brain behind those curls. Gonna get a Ph.D.? Oh wait, you're still working on your G.E.D., aren't you?"

Charlie bristled in defense of Zadie, but she snapped back first.

"You don't need a degree to notice the way life works."

They locked eyes in a fierce battle of glares. Spark Plug dropped his gaze. Zadie sniffed.

"What I was trying to say is that life has mechanisms for success," she explained, ticking the concepts off on her fingers as she outlined them. "The first one is the capacity to create an idea, the second is an ability to copy a preexisting idea, the third is being able to improve on an idea, and the last one is the capability of sharing the idea. Do you get it?"

"Create, copy, improve, share," Charlie repeated back.

Hawlings objected with a wave of his hand.

"We're already doing this. Every time we hear a slogan, make a bumper sticker, print copies, and send them to our friends, we're doing those four things."

"I didn't say it was an original concept," Zadie replied calmly. "I'm just saying that when people recognize that those four abilities are the tools of self-organizing structures, then they can use them powerfully."

She looked around the group.

"For instance, take those bumper stickers. Most people see a bumper sticker and think; *where can I get one?* I want every person involved with this movement to see a brilliant bumper sticker and think; *cool! I'm going to make a thousand of those and put them in every auto shop in town.* People tend to wait for leadership, but with the power elite poised to destroy any leader they can spot, we have to work differently."

"That's for sure," Hawlings sighed.

"This system has been called *leaderless*," Zadie said, "but I see it more as *leader-full*. If every person thoroughly understands the overarching strategy and is empowered to lead, then you've got innovation and organization working together effectively, creating a tremendous explosion of activity without a chain of command."

"Beautiful," Zipper laughed, pounding his knee with his fist. "It's the opposite of the power elite's top-down, corporate dictatorship. They can't control it. They can't stop it. They never know where it's going to be or what it's going to do. They can't break the power chain because there are too many links. It's the best organized anarchy in the universe, second only to life itself!"

Charlie smiled at the accuracy of that oxymoron. *Organized anarchy*. It might not make logical sense, but then again, life didn't either. Next to him, Zadie bolted upright, thunderstruck by a thought. She gasped. She started laughing. The others stared at her, perplexed. Her face turned red. Tears came out her eyes. She lay back against the couch and kicked her heels. She sat up to speak, collapsed back into giggles, held up her hand for their patience, and whooped so hard she started choking. Charlie pounded her on the back. Finally, she gulped back her chuckles.

"Oh my god! What if - hahaha - what if - oh ho!" she collapsed again.

"*Zadie*," Charlie groaned. She was killing him with curiosity. "Let us in on the joke, huh?"

"The joke . . . is . . . on . . . them," she managed to say. She wiped her tears away. "Don't you see? *We're not resisting them! They're resisting us!*"

Everyone stared at Zadie, bewildered.

"Look, they may be an absurdly powerful group," Zadie said, cutting back her laughter, "but they're teeny-tiny compared to the forces of the Dandelion Insurrection. We're seven billion strong. We're as vast as the planet and as microscopic as infectious disease. The Dandelion Insurrection isn't a handful of radicals. It's all of Life itself!"

Charlie chuckled as he suddenly saw it. "You've got to admire the audacity of those poor little men and women trying to destroy the world. They're doing a tremendous job in the face of overwhelming opposition."

Spark Plug frowned.

"I can't feel too bad for the bastards. Even if they win, they're going to die."

Zadie whirled on him.

"Sure, but if we win, everybody lives."

She turned to look at each of them in turn.

"The most terrifying powers known to man may be lined up to protect the few in their greedy desire to destroy everything, but life has triumphed every single day and it's triumphing still. In a way," Zadie pointed out, "pesticides, weapons, and bombs are just mechanisms of resistance to the absurdly powerful force called Life."

"Very impressive," Spark Plug scoffed sarcastically. "I'll try to remember that when a soldier fires a bullet into my chest."

"What's your other option?" Zadie shot back. "Fighting destruction with destruction leaves the whole world destroyed. Resisting destruction with vitality is the most powerful and natural process on Earth."

"Whoa," Zipper said, a look of dawning understanding growing on his face, "that's why multi-nodal, horizontal structures work. They mimic Life! They're the ivy crawling up the buildings, the moss breaking down the bricks, and the dandelions shooting up in the sidewalks."

Charlie leaned his head back against the couch. That's what had been happening with the articles. Every time he wrote one story about the Dandelion Insurrection, a dozen more popped out of the woodwork. The writing both revealed and inspired the events.

"Did you all ever see that video of starlings in biology class in high school?" Charlie asked. "You know, where they're doing the flocking thing . . . what's it called when they dive and cluster in those crazy shapes?"

"Murmuration," Zadie answered.

"Yeah, exactly! The starlings only have a few rules; fly forward, the leader changes at every shift in direction, keep equidistant, and don't leave your wing-mate out on a limb. Those are fairly simple parameters that everyone can grasp, but they give rise to an incredible patterning of thousands of birds, never crashing, never falling, unpredictable, and absolutely beautiful."

Charlie leaned forward in excitement.

"If each person in the movement can articulate the parameters of the Dandelion Insurrection as clearly as that, then Zadie's theory *will* work. If we move from a common set of principles, anyone can become an effective leader."

"Let's define the principles," Hawlings said eagerly.

"*The Man From the North* has been writing about them all winter," Zadie pointed out. "The Dandelion Insurrection is what happens when the heart breaks open with love . . . do you remember the guidelines for when it springs into action?"

"Don't hurt anyone or anything," someone said immediately.

"Create human connections everywhere," Zipper added.

"Stand up for our democracy by *using* our constitutionally granted civil liberties even if the government has outlawed them," Hawlings answered.

"And work to keep human suffering and environmental destruction from occurring," Zadie mentioned.

"That's it," Charlie said with a smile. "Nonviolence, create connections, use our civil liberties, and keep humanity and the planet alive . . . that's the Dandelion Insurrection in a nutshell."

"Give me a break," Spark Plug scoffed. "There are soldiers on the streets with guns! This is not going to topple a psychopathic power-mad elite."

Charlie looked at him. Spark Plug's arms crossed tightly over his chest, and his jaw clenched his lips so tight that the blood drained out of them, leaving a white, deathly line across his mouth. Charlie answered quietly.

"When fear is used to control people, love is how we rebel."

"Throw me a potluck and bring me a beer," Spark Plug sneered. "That's hardly going to fix anything."

"What did you have in mind, then?"

Spark Plug clamped his lips shut.

Charlie got a bad feeling.

"Maybe you should spit it out," Charlie said tersely.

"All I'm gonna say is that people respond to violence," Spark Plug shrugged.

"Only an idiot would use violence against the biggest military force in the world," Charlie argued.

Spark Plug shot Charlie a challenge of a look.

"Somebody needs to be the hardcore edge of the Dandelion Insurrection - "

Charlie jumped to his feet and cut him off.

"Don't do this under our name. The Dandelion Insurrection is what happens when the heart bursts open with love," he said.

"*Violence* is the strategy of shit-ass cowards without the balls to do the real work."

Spark Plug leapt up and crossed the room in a flash.

"Say that to my face, hick."

He put his tough scowl in Charlie's face.

"Violence is the weapon of cowards," Charlie told him.

"Yeah, well, violence is what we got left, 'cuz you know what?" he grabbed Charlie's shirt and started shaking him with every word he spoke. "The god-damn-government-has-got-our-backs-against-the-wall!"

Charlie winced as he was slammed up against the side of the bike shop. The gears above his head clattered. One fell off its hook and rolled, spiraling to the ground.

"Well, they've won, then," Charlie gritted out, "because as sure as my back is against this wall, you've become a tyrant just like them."

"Don't you see?" Spark Plug hissed. "They've got the guns, the money, the law, the police. They took away our right to protest, to assemble, to petition, and to speak out. They took our tools! They took 'em all!"

Charlie felt his shoulder blades pressing painfully against the uneven surface behind him.

"You got my back against the wall," Charlie said, "but I've still got tools you aren't ever going to pry from my grip."

Spark Plug's nose was inches from his own. He could see his reflection in the other man's eyes.

"You can't make me hate you," Charlie said, so quietly that only Spark Plug could hear. "You can't make me angry. And you can't stop me from feeling only love toward you."

"Fucking bullshit!" Spark Plug snapped. He flung himself away from Charlie.

"Sure it is," Charlie called after him. "Love is just hippie bullshit . . . until the day the cops lay down their guns because they're tired of hurting people who love them. It's bullshit until you see thousands of lives saved because one little old lady couldn't step quietly aside without trying to help people. It's bullshit until you realize that the neighbors won't spy on each other because they *know* each other too well. It's all bullshit, but you know what?"

Spark Plug's back was to him, but he continued anyway.

"It works. And it's the only thing that's going to work. Our fear and hatred isn't going to create a better world than the one their greed is working on right now. *In a time of hate*," Charlie quoted, "*love is a revolutionary act.*"

Spark Plug kicked the back of the couch.

"You're all a bunch of crazy idealists," he muttered, "and when they march you away to your collective grave, I won't say I told you so!"

"Spark Plug," Charlie retorted in a tone so sharp it chilled the room, "do you want to do something truly radical?"

Spark Plug froze.

"Be kind. Be connected. Be unafraid."

Spark Plug slammed out into the night. They sat silently for a moment, a little breathless at his abrupt departure.

"I'll watch him," Hawlings muttered, grabbing his coat. "I suggest we break this meeting up. Ole Sparky used to be one hundred percent trustworthy, but recently . . . " Hawlings let the sentence dangle as he gathered up his pack.

Zipper shrugged.

"I doubt he'll do anything without a group at his back. For all that he professes the tenets of anarchy, he's always looking to be a leader, not a lone wolf."

"*Le loup garou*," Charlie said. He looked up at their curious expressions. "It's an old French Acadian creature. A *loup garou* is a human who has turned into a werewolf, but as soon as someone draws its blood, it returns to its original human nature."

Zipper looked appraisingly at Charlie.

"I think he's just jealous."

"Of me?" Charlie laughed. "The backwoods hick in a plaid shirt?"

"Sure," Zipper exclaimed. "You pointed out something important."

"What's that?"

"The greatest radicals are all revolutionaries of the heart."

*Rivera Sun*

# CHAPTER SIX

· · · · ·

*Greenback Street*

At night, the city bared its teeth and hissed. Doors shut tight. Curtains drew over windows. The subway closed down. Police patrolled the streets between neighborhoods. The few late pedestrians scurried quickly toward their destinations. Zadie no longer pulled Charlie pell-mell along the sidewalk, but matched his somber stride, alert and watchful.

"The first thing we need to do is break through this fear," Charlie muttered.

"Can't blame people for being scared," Zadie murmured. The streets were crawling with cops that looked like a cross between a tank and the terminator.

"Fear won't help anything," Charlie replied. "The government's whole game is based on fear and intimidation. They're fully prepared to deal with terrified mobs. What they can't handle is fearless, organized resistance. We have to stop seeing guns and start seeing people. We've got to connect with each other, human to human. Not just in the movement, but everywhere. The police officers need to see that we're not statistics; we are as alive and worthy of life as they are," Charlie said. The mind was the first defense against tyranny. As long as the people kept playing the role of the faceless masses, they were never going to succeed. He nodded to the officer on the corner. The uniformed man gave him a startled look before quickly hiding it under a scowl.

They walked in silence for a few blocks. The streets were nearly deserted, but images of humanity still rushed through

Charlie; soldiers, anarchists, housewives, executives, bureaucrats, all genders, races and religions. Words and thoughts pummeled him.

"Zadie, I need to write - "

"What you need is to eat dinner and sleep soundly," she countered.

Her words crash-landed his racing mind back into his exhausted body.

"You're right," he admitted. "Where are we going?"

"Uptown . . . if we can," she muttered as a group of police appeared on the next corner, enforcing a blockade between this neighborhood and the more upscale section down the street.

"Let me talk," Zadie whispered as they came up to the intersection. "You there!" she called imperiously. "Which street is the safest way to get to Greenback Street?"

One of the police officers turned.

"Greenback Street?" he repeated, scrutinizing Zadie's face in the streetlight.

"Yes, I'm meeting my father at Café Renault, but we're running late and the taxis . . . what on earth happened to all the taxis?"

"Curfew, ma'am."

"Oh!" Zadie stamped her foot. She shot an exasperated look at the astonished, poker-faced Charlie, and then leaned toward the policeman. "We simply can't keep my father waiting . . . it's bad enough already. I know he won't like him." She tilted her head to indicate Charlie, who shifted awkwardly.

"First time meeting each other?" the officer replied sympathetically.

"Yes," Zadie answered. "And you know my Dad! He's a holy terror!"

"It's just a few blocks that way and two over," the officer

pointed out helpfully.

"Thank you, sir!"

As they moved past the officer, he gave Charlie a wry grin.

"Good luck," the officer said, jerking his head toward the cafe and the imagined terror of the old man.

"Uh, thanks," Charlie answered back.

Zadie grabbed his waist like a tipsy love-smitten girl and hauled him down the street urging him to hurry.

"Well," she confessed when they were out of earshot, "after a lifetime of getting in trouble, I've learned some good tricks along the way. Number one, never lie if you can help it."

"You just told that officer that we're going to meet your father," Charlie pointed out. "Last time I checked, he's up on a farm by the Canadian border."

"Yeah, but my *surrogate* father runs a restaurant so exclusive, no one but the very rich even knows it exists."

"That officer did," Charlie mentioned.

"He used to work that neighborhood as part of an elite corps. He recognized me, but didn't remember that I was a waitress, not a customer."

"Zadie, you're amazing," he said.

"Me? High school dropout, Zadie Byrd Gray? Juvenile delinquent, runaway, troublemaker, slut, no-good - "

Charlie touched her lips.

"Don't say that."

"It's all true, Charlie," she said quietly. "Don't get any romantic ideas about me."

*Too late for that*, he thought. *Twelve years too late.*

They turned a corner. Charlie reeled. Greenback Street spread before them in its legendary splendor. About a decade ago, the wealthy had created a cultural oasis, or so they said, renaming one of New York City's streets and claiming it as their own. Television shows frequently aired specials on Greenback Street fanning the flames of envy in the lower classes for the lifestyles of the rich and famous. The Mayor of New York had even allocated a special police force for the area. Unpleasant elements were bounced out of the street at the drop of a hat. In contrast to the other sections of town, Greenback Street glowed in its own self-absorbed glamour.

"Curfew doesn't apply here," Zadie said. "For the rich, the party goes on."

A bustling scene of nightlife lay before them; brilliant window displays, glossy boutiques, expensive shops, a hum of chatter. The trees were illuminated with little lights. Open air cafes took advantage of the lusty warmth of the spring night. They walked by fountains, expensive cars, red carpets, and chandeliered lobbies with white-gloved bellhops and doormen.

"That's the Chief of Police," Zadie whispered, nodding her head toward a well-dressed man waiting for his wife to step out of their chauffeured armored car. They entered the club followed by their burly security officers.

"Private guards?" Charlie gasped. "An entire police force isn't enough?"

"Not for these folks. These are the wealthy class, Charlie. You're looking at the power-elite that you've been writing about all winter. That fellow is a Senator. Those two with him are military men, probably generals. That guy is a weapons contractor. I think those folks are oil executives. I'd have to guess on the rest of them. Oh, that woman? She's the Secretary of Defense." Zadie frowned in thought. "I wonder what she's doing in New York instead of Washington?" She shook her head and shrugged. "Doesn't really matter. It's only a short flight by private jet."

"I'm starting to understand why Spark Plug felt powerless,"

Charlie muttered. "These people don't care about the masses of people in poverty. They don't even know they exist."

"Spark Plug doesn't know the half of it. He only suspects." Zadie bit her lower lip pensively. "The thing is, Charlie, the wealthy are just people. Most of them don't think what they're doing is evil . . . and I can't say that they're all monsters. Some may be callous, power-mad, and inured to violence, but good ole Sparky is, too, in his own way. If pushed, he'd do a lot of the same things as these people. He'd close off his heart, his ears, and his mind if he thought he could live in this delusional fantasy . . . most people would."

She gestured to the street. It was a tantalizing scene for a world-weary soul. The manicured greenery and flower displays gave an illusion of safety. The carefully designed lighting established a buffer zone between this street and the rest of the darkened city. Private security officers discreetly and calmly patrolled the area. Chauffeurs, maître d's, and white-gloved bellhops reassured the wealthy that they were respected, protected, pampered, and adored.

Charlie thought of the flea-ridden couch, the bare bulb of the bike shop, and the gaunt lines in Spark Plug's face. He thought of his own dark nights when he felt the creeping hand of the government tracking him. Better men than he had cast morality aside to live in the mouth-watering world of wealth. Smarter men had seduced themselves into positions of power with half-truths and shoddy rationales. He had never been offered a chance to live in this Garden of Eden, but if he was, he suspected that the shiny red fruit of knowledge would send him tumbling away from the paradise of the wealthy. Charlie knew worried fathers who could not feed their families. He knew mothers who worked two jobs only to send their children to bed hungry. He had peeled apart the intricate layers of a socio-economic system that was riddled with rotten deals that screwed people over. He had tasted the bittersweet fruit of truth and his understanding of right and wrong barred the gate to a blissful existence in this garden.

Zadie took him by the elbow.

"Listen, watch, and learn, Charlie. You're going to see things tonight that only a small handful of people in this country truly understand. Most of the people can only imagine the extravagances of the wealthy class. You're going to experience them firsthand."

She gestured to the discreet entrance before them. He gallantly offered her his plaid-shirted arm. The maître d' opened the glass door. His eyes glowed as he recognized the young woman.

"Zadie! A pleasure to see you!" he said with genuine warmth.

"Louis," Zadie began, "we're bone-weary and starving. Will you tell - "

"Not another word! It is done already. Aubrey will be overjoyed to know you are here! *Bonsoir monsieur. Bienvenue a la Café Renault!*"

The maître d' escorted them to a quiet table and swept off to speak with Aubrey. Charlie slid into his chair, making an effort to keep his mouth from dropping open. They were hidden behind a canopy of plants that were better groomed than he was. Through them, he could see the coiffed women in evening gowns. Gold and gems glinted as manicured hands reached for crystal glasses. A live string quartet strummed softly in the corner. Somewhere, a fountain trickled just loud enough to blur the individual voices into privacy. The men, without exception, wore dinner jackets and gold watches.

"I feel underdressed," Charlie commented.

"Me too," Zadie laughed. "I should be wearing a diamond that could feed an African nation for a year."

"Will they throw me out if I eat my dinner with the dessert fork?" he asked, picking it up.

"That's your salad fork," she told him, "and no, they won't. The Mayor of New York confuses his silverware all the time."

"Get out," he said.

"It's true," she replied, smiling. "Quite a show, hmm?" She leaned her chin on her hand and peered through the leaves. "Those women are wearing more money on their backs than most people make in a year. Disgusting, isn't it?"

"I dunno," he confessed, pointing to one lady. "I think you'd look great in that red evening gown."

"Looks can be deceiving," Zadie retorted, leaning close to Charlie. "That gown is bought and paid for by selling drones that dump depleted uranium on Middle Eastern children. See the guy she's with? That's *the Butcher.*"

Charlie gaped at the stiff, irritable-looking man. Zadie hissed at him not to stare. He turned his head away, but continued to sneak looks at the man's sharp nose and short crew cut. He fidgeted, nervous to be so close.

"Relax," Zadie told him. "This is the last place they would look for you."

"Zadie, what else do you know about all this?" Charlie asked, suddenly burning with curiosity. "You worked here, right?"

"Two years, and then some more, on and off," Zadie said with a shrug. "I know that every glistening bit of gold that they're wearing was hauled out of the mines by modern day slaves. I know that the women over there are enjoying a three thousand dollar bottle of wine while their nationwide chain of stores refuses to pay a living wage to the employees. That guy is consuming his next triple bypass surgery that he'll pay for by the profits he makes on everybody else's extortionist healthcare programs. I know a lot of things, Charlie."

She looked around the room, her gaze shadowed and sorrowful. The glitz and polished marble surfaces didn't bedazzle her eyes anymore. The beautiful evening gowns didn't quite cover the sordid cruelties that paid for them. The plates of stunningly arranged dishes screamed at her, echoing the hungry bellies that had been sucked empty by the greed of others. The scene around them wasn't beautiful to her. It was heartbreaking.

"When you know the real price of wealth, Charlie," she said softly, "everything looks different. The gleam of riches hurts your eyes. The taste of extravagance is bitter in your mouth. The gentle strains of those string instruments carry an echo of the cries of everyone who suffers to pay for this night. And we're all part of it. Every time we idolize the wealthy and try to become rich like them, we're perpetuating the suffering of billions. I wish people would see excessive wealth as shameful, not glamorous. *This,*" she said, gesturing to the opulent room, "ought to be considered disgraceful when the children in the next block are scrounging in the dumpster for food."

Charlie sat back in his chair.

"We've got to work on that, then," he said. "The Dandelion Insurrection needs to address that mentality. Because, you're right, if people keep lusting after money and power, no amount of revolution is going to help us."

"Well, it's the same as worshipping our soldiers and glorifying the profession of murder," Zadie said passionately.

Charlie choked on his reply. That wasn't a very popular sentiment, but she had a point. Peace would never be found through celebrating militarism and idolizing the wealth of the war industry. They fell into a somber silence, each lost in thought, until a voice behind them chuckled.

"Well, well, little bird, you decided to fly back to me, eh?"

"Aubrey!"

Zadie shot up so fast that the silverware rattled and the votive candle gyrated. She threw her arms around a thin, dark Frenchman in a tight and intimate embrace. Charlie toyed with his fork and tried not to blush, wondering with discomfort if they had ever been lovers. When they stepped apart, the man kept a proud - and to Charlie's mind possessive - arm around Zadie's waist. Aubrey Renault was an intense man with carved features. Obsidian glinted in his eyes and a few wrinkles graciously lined his face with signs of good humor.

"*Bonjour, je m'appelle Aubrey Renault,*" he introduced himself, extending a hand to Charlie.

"*Je suis Charlie Rider,*" he replied in French, shaking the man's hand.

"*Ah! Un Français?*"

"*Un Acadian,*" he clarified.

"*Bienvenue,*" Aubrey welcomed him. He motioned for them to sit. "I have only a few minutes," he said, gesturing to the rest of the clientele, "but I must say hello to my bird, no?"

A waiter brought soup to the table. Aubrey pulled up an empty chair and waved at them to eat, ignoring their sighs of appreciation and thanks.

"*Sans les oeufs, le fromage, le lait, et le crème,*" Aubrey told them, throwing his hands up in despair and turning to Charlie for sympathy. "Can you imagine a French chef cooking without cream? The things I do for Zadie Byrd Gray!" He looked ruefully at her as she delighted in the soup.

"Zadie-*cherie,*" he sighed, "you could have been the love of my life, if only you were not a vegan. *Mon Dieu!* I could never live without cheese!"

Zadie rolled her eyes at the joke she had heard a thousand times before.

"And all these years, I thought it was your love for men that kept us apart!"

"Well," Aubrey winked, "there was that, too."

Charlie started to smile.

"Phew," Zadie laughed. "I'd have hated to have been upstaged in your affections by rotten cow's milk."

"Aach!" Aubrey exclaimed. He turned to Charlie. "This girl! She has no class. None. She comes into the Café Renault and *dares* to talk of rotten cow's milk?!"

"I could talk about the bacteria-ridden grape compost," she offered, pointing to the wine bottles on the other tables. Aubrey shook his head in mock horror and waggled his finger at her nose.

"Only you. Only because of my undying devotion and love do I allow you to say such things here! My restaurant is the best in the world and you call it all poison!"

"Look at him, Charlie," Zadie said, pointing at Aubrey with her spoon. "He looks so charming, doesn't he? But inside, he's a putrefying mass of dead animal souls."

Aubrey held his hands to his heart and leaned over to Charlie. "This girl? Watch out for her. She is a heartbreaker."

*Tell me something I don't know,* Charlie thought, but he was saved from responding by Louis, who swept over to whisper something in Aubrey's ear. The chef frowned in displeasure and rose to return to his duties. He told Zadie that they were welcome to stay at his apartment tonight, but he would be working late.

"You still have the key, yes?" he asked.

"Of course," Zadie answered.

"My home is yours. Charlie? A pleasure to meet you. I hope

we will speak more."

Charlie thanked him for his hospitality and especially for the dinner. Aubrey waved his extravagance off as nothing.

"I always take care of my bird!" he called as he returned to the kitchen.

"Wow," Charlie managed to say.

"That's Aubrey," Zadie grinned. "He took me in when I ran away from home, saved my life a million times over, and still won't let me thank him. Now, eat up! He'll be heartbroken if you send anything back."

A dinner unfolded, course after course. Charlie's tongue exploded with flavors. His nose went wild with aroma. Zadie laughed at every one of his heartfelt expressions, challenging him to make up poetry to describe the sensational cuisine. Zadie savored his reaction. Charlie had lived in a small town all his life; a new car the most fancy thing he had ever considered buying. *Charlie, my friend,* Zadie thought, *some of us are born adventurers, others have adventure thrust upon them. You, however, are an interesting blend of both.*

"Zadie," he asked at one point. "Am I dreaming? I mean, an hour ago we were in an anarchist tool co-op lit with a single bare bulb, right?"

"Welcome to my surreal life, Charlie," she answered with a sigh. "Friends in high and low places." She put her spoon down. "Very few people really understand the size of the gap between the rich and the poor, and fewer still experience it like this. That man over there," she pointed, "makes more in an hour and fifteen minutes than Zipper makes in an entire year. And chances are pretty good that in a hundred lifetimes, I couldn't make as much money as his wife was born with."

Zadie pressed her lips tightly together before continuing.

"When I hear the wealthy politicians blathering on about

*pull yourself up by your bootstraps*, I just get shaking mad! What world are they living in? *Nobody* has bootstraps anymore! Our shoes are all made in sweatshops in China. The wealthy claim to be self-made success stories, but that's like saying Wilt Chamberlain's height had nothing to do with his basketball prowess. They've got inheritances, tax loopholes, private school educations, job opportunities, trust funds, insider information, investments, start-up money, financial backers; not all born equal in these things, Charlie, not in America. The rich get richer, and the poor get poorer. That's how it goes in America."

She stopped and sighed.

"I'm ranting. Sorry."

"They're all good points," Charlie said.

"Yes, but I should just shut up and let you enjoy the most exclusive food on the planet."

"It is really good," Charlie admitted.

"The best meal I ever had," Zadie reminisced, "some French guy made for me. He didn't know how to cook vegan, but he made the most amazing butternut squash soup and - "

"Hey, that was me!" Charlie exclaimed, flushing. "You remember that?"

"Yes," she answered. "It was like you poured your whole heart into it."

*I did*, Charlie silently agreed. *I poured every drop of love I had for you into that meal.* He had been hoping it would exhaust his love for Zadie, but no, the feelings had returned, stronger than ever before. *Maybe I should tell her*, he thought, but he hesitated to unpack his heart with *the Butcher* sitting at the next table and Zadie seeing blood money laced into evening gowns. He would rather just enjoy her ranting, watch the color flush into her cheeks, and admire the way her eyes turned hot with passion. *Someday, I'll tell her*, he promised himself, *someday soon.*

As dinner wound down, Charlie began to study the expressions of the men and women at the other tables. He watched lips curl and frown, purse and smile, or twitch with words. He looked for joy or sorrow, irritation or anxiety, and found boredom and dissatisfaction often flitting across the faces. Zadie was right; they were just people. Strip away the luxury, the spa treatments, the make-up, the facials, the jewelry . . . throw them in a pair of blue jeans and an old tee shirt, dump them in a rundown diner . . . and they'd be just like any other human heap of heartache, misery, and hope.

"I thought they'd be different," he said quietly to Zadie.

"Monsters with red eyes and bloodthirsty mouths?" she teased.

"Something like that," he admitted. "I thought they'd look powerful, not dyspeptic."

Zadie snorted with laughter as he flicked his eyes to a particularly red-faced man whose mouth pulled down in discomfort as his double chin folded up with a belch.

"That's one of *the Butcher's* government contractors for the military."

"Frightening," Charlie said, and he meant it. Part of him longed to believe that powerful decisions were made by people smarter and wiser than him, but Charlie looked at the contractor and realized that one man's indigestion could cause the deaths of thousands as he hastily signed documents in a rush to get out of the office. His eyes rapidly traversed the room. He frowned, furrowing his brows at little details. He looked more carefully. He leaned his elbow on the table and ran a hand across his mouth, thinking.

"Zadie?" he finally asked. "Why are they so tense?"

"They're not," she assured him. "They're relaxing."

"No, they're not," he insisted. "Maybe some of the women,

but look at the guys, and the women wearing suits instead of dresses. They're uneasy about something."

He leaned in toward Zadie, pointing out the quick flick of eyes, the wrists that turned gold watches over, the stiff expressions, and the obvious lapses in attention. Zadie frowned.

"Yeah," she agreed. "Something's up."

She scoured her memory for names and positions, putting together the connections. She grabbed the maître 'd by the elbow as he passed.

"Louis, who's the guy walking over to table nine?" she asked, tilting her head to where *the Butcher* sat.

"Chief of Special Operations," the man replied, craning to look. "He's running late, though. That's odd. He's usually quite punctual." Louis frowned and continued on.

Charlie felt a chill creeping up his back.

"Zadie, I've got this feeling . . ."

She nodded.

"Me too, Charlie. Me too."

# CHAPTER SEVEN

. . . . .

## *The Greatest Terrorist On Earth*

Charlie woke in the dark hours of morning and rolled over on the couch. A streak of leaden light slipped under the curtains of Aubrey's apartment. Unfamiliar noises prickled his ears. The city never rested. It groaned and wailed all night long. Charlie had lain awake for hours listening to the moaning of its steel and concrete language until exhaustion finally deafened his ears and he slept. A sudden fall-off of the city's noise had woken him. He blinked twice in the unexpected quiet. Then the clank of garbage trucks bashed in the dark street below. Charlie swung his legs off the couch and sat up. A cool breeze wafted through a sliding door that opened onto the tiny balcony where Aubrey grew fresh herbs. Charlie saw the man outlined against the patchwork squares of light from the apartments across the street.

"Come out and sit with me, if you would like," Aubrey invited in a low voice, not turning.

Charlie stepped out onto the cool cement in his bare feet and sat on a small wooden bench beside the other man. He threaded his feet between the slats of the iron railing. He peered down. The ground was nothing more than small swaths of headlight beams and the orange pools of streetlights. Aubrey's chiseled face reflected the barest gleams of humanity's desperate electric battle against the night.

For a moment, they sat quietly together, saying nothing. Charlie stared out at the city. He sensed it waiting, eerie and heavy. The towering buildings seemed tensed, poised like dominoes for the first blow. Unease prickled between his shoulder blades.

"Aubrey," Charlie asked, "do you know what is happening?"

From the darkness, the older man replied wearily.

"Let's not talk about it now. There is so little time left."

A chill ran down Charlie's spine.

"What is it? What - "

Aubrey raised a hand, silencing him.

"In a little while, there will be talk of nothing else. Let us just sit together and savor the peace that we have."

Charlie started to object.

"Please," Aubrey begged. His voice split with the anguish of a man carrying a secret. "I will tell you at dawn. It is only an hour or so away. I beg you, let us talk of other things; things we may not talk about for many years to come. Let us talk of beauty, perhaps, or hope. No . . . let us talk of love."

Charlie heard Aubrey rake his fingers through his thick hair. The wind echoed the sound as it slid between the buildings. Aubrey's voice came out in a gentle sorrow as if he were a lover of love itself, holding it one last time.

"*Sans amour,*" he said in French, "*la vie ne vaut pa la peine.*"

*Without love, life is not worth the pain.* Charlie smiled in the dark, leaning his head back against the hardness of the wall behind them.

"Charlie, you love her, yes?"

"Zadie?" he answered, startled.

"Of course. Who else?"

Charlie did not reply. It was no secret. His heart was a match flaring up in the dark. Everyone but Zadie saw the burst of light.

"You have loved her for a long time?" Aubrey asked.

"Yes. How did you know?"

The other man shrugged.

"When one has loved many times, you begin to learn the signs." Aubrey leaned back against the wall, his sharp nose and cheekbones prominent against the gleam of city lights. His pale, angular face turned thick with rumination. Aubrey rolled the notion over in his mind . . . this young man for that girl? His thin lips twitched. He snuffed his nose on a sharp thought. Twice, the black holes of his eyes flicked to Charlie, measuring him. Charlie waited, saying nothing. His heart knew that only one person could decide his fate . . . and she would make her own decision. Charlie shrugged all other opinions off like water. He was not an adolescent, insecure in the understanding of his heart. He had tempered his feelings against the blade of time. He had attempted to drown what burned within him in the stream of other women. He had tried to machete the jungle of his emotions down. His love persisted in springing back, undaunted.

Aubrey, immersed in his own flow of thoughts, began to murmur to himself in the style of men accustomed to their solitude. His mumblings twined with the constant conversation of the city, becoming another strand within the great beast's throat. The quiet whispers grew as the man spoke his thoughts. His voice ran like water, a trickle that swelled in strength and volume, desiring no interruption as it flowed toward the great ocean of understanding.

"*Un Acadian, eh?*" Aubrey said to the night. "That would be good for my little bird. He has family, roots. She needs a place to come to roost."

Charlie silently countered the assumption. *Un Acadian*, yes, but also a Rider, the son of a family lost to the madness of the continent; prodigy of broken homes and pipedreams, always moving on in search of paradise, never settling down, dying too young, too quickly, leaving legends and ghosts behind them, one solitary son after another. Charlie remembered his father's joking warning, *we're cursed, you know. The Riders have a son and poof! We vanish.* Charlie's father survived long enough to see his son push the edge of adolescence, and then one night, driving back from downstate work, Scott Rider taunted Death too carelessly and crashed.

*Those were the bad years*, Charlie remembered. The Rider curse slipped onto his shoulders along with his Dad's leather jacket. He became a ten-year old with a death warrant on his back. He was going to die. The curse would get him, too. By eighth grade, the sting of fear had faded, but the devil-may-care attitude had slammed Charlie into constant trouble. Thank God for Zadie. It took that precocious twelve-year old one imperious foot stamp to set his whole world on edge. *If you've got a death curse on you*, she demanded, *why don't you just LIVE, bigger and bolder than anybody else? You've got nothing to lose, so you might as well risk everything to do something amazing!*

Years later, on a balcony overlooking Manhattan, Charlie let out an incredulous snort of breath; *here we are, Zadie, doing it.* He leaned back against the cool concrete wall with a whoosh of amazement. Aubrey's murmurings stopped in a sudden halt of silence. The sighs and grumbles of the city rushed into their ears, filling the quiet vacancy of thought like eager, noisy tenants. Aubrey cleared his throat and evicted the rumbling city with his speech.

"It is a night of many thoughts," he sighed. "Soon, everything will change, so tonight, I look back wondering how we came to this. Charlie, I came to the United States as a young man, hardly a man at all, just graduated at the top of my class in culinary school, already offered the dream of America: wealth, status, freedom. On my first day in this city, I went to the

Statue of Liberty. I am a great devotee of Lady Liberty. *Give me
your tired, your hungry, your poor.* She is a gift from the French
people, did you know? Well, I circled her feet and looked back
at the city. Do you know what I saw?"

Charlie shook his head.

"Two planes crashed into a set of towers and this country
went insane. Fear. Hatred. Anger. Lies. Nationalism frothing at
the mouth. People rabid with militarism. Violence. Sorrow.
Terror. I came for a dream and arrived in a nightmare."

Aubrey shifted uncomfortably on the cold bench. The dark
morning air pulled goose bumps up on his arms. A shiver ran
through his spine.

"Now, all these years later, I hear some people say it was the
government that did it. Others maintain that it was extremists.
A third faction claims it was both. I say it hardly matters now,
because those terrorists succeeded in creating even greater
terrorists of the people in this country."

He spat on the corner of the balcony in disgust. Charlie
stayed silent, not knowing what to say. He could not remember
a time before the war on terror swallowed the whole world and
came home to roost on the shoulders of U.S. citizens. But, even
still, Charlie knew the wars to end terrorism were phony
crusades. He knew the threats of attacks were trumped up to
achieve hidden political and economic aims. He knew millions
had died because of the lies of politicians, but none of those
high-ranking mass murderers had ever been tried for their war
crimes, and many enjoyed exalted footnotes in the annals of
history. The war on terror had become a war on freedom, and
the basic principles of democracy were being crushed by the
rabid power of fear. International standards of human rights
had been ripped to shreds by the American frenzy for
assassinations, drone warfare, torture, and indefinite detention.

The United States had used the tragedy of the towers to become the greatest terrorist the world had ever known.

"For many years," Aubrey told Charlie, "I lived in confused shock. I could not even fathom what your people were doing. . . all the money was sucked right up into death and destruction. The business of killing boomed. Life died. Hearts shriveled and disappeared. All this time, I was cooking foie gras, filet mignon, and tiramisu for wealthy warmongers. Behind the restaurant, I saw children raiding the dumpsters for food. People told me to lock the garbage, but I said, what does that do except starve children? They called me a socialist frog. My heart broke for the people of this country, so full of hatred that they would not even feed their own children. I prayed to Lady Liberty, saying, please, please, you must send me aid. Send someone to help me."

Aubrey paused and looked out in the direction of the harbor.

"That is how I met Zadie."

"Zadie?" Charlie responded, surprised.

"*Oui.* She showed up looking for a job . . . maybe she was sixteen. I remember, my first thought was, *look at this girl! She deserves to be Queen of America!*"

"So, you gave her a job?" Charlie asked.

"No, no, I was not hiring children. I told mademoiselle that she was bound for greatness and she should be walking in on the red carpet, not begging at the back door."

"What did Zadie say?"

"*Merci beaucoup, thank you very much, if I do not freeze to death tonight, maybe destiny will hire me tomorrow.* What could I do? I took her in, gave her a job, and taught her decent French."

"Zadie speaks better French than I do," Charlie put in defensively.

"*Oui*, now she does. Back then she spoke the same butchered dialect as you - " he broke off laughing as Charlie bristled at the linguistic snobbery.

"It was a fortunate encounter," Aubrey continued. "One for which I have always thanked my saint, Lady Liberty. Zadie helped me get food to the hungry and money to those in need. She knew hunger, that girl," he sighed, remembering. "In a few months, the President was coming in the front door while the Food Not Bombs group was going out the back. They called me the Robin Hood of restaurants; taking from the rich, giving to the poor." He chuckled, but the sound shriveled into a sad sigh. "Over the years, I have learned that Americans are the fattest and richest people on earth, but they are all starving for kindness. It is a tragedy. There is so much goodness locked in the hearts of the Americans. The people of this country could truly make this the greatest nation on earth . . . if only they were not caged with fear."

He sighed again. The first hint of light shifted in the east. The silhouettes of the buildings stood up and stretched. The city began to groan as it awakened. The sun licked the eastern skyscrapers. Dawn rose.

"It's time," Charlie said, reminding Aubrey of his promise. "Tell me what's going on."

Aubrey pressed his lips together and bowed his head - whether in thought or prayer, Charlie could not discern. The man's black eyes rolled up to heaven in supplication.

"There will be an attack on the power grid," he said. "Terrorists."

"Jesus," Charlie swore. "When?"

"Tonight."

"How do you know?"

"The Chief of Special Operations told me."

"How does he know? Why doesn't he stop it?"

"He has no reason to stop it . . . and many reasons to pretend he knows nothing."

"Is it the government doing it?"

Aubrey shrugged. "I doubt we will ever know for sure." He reached into his breast pocket and pulled out two slips of paper.

"Military passes," he explained. "The city will be locked down. You, of all people, should not be here when they begin demanding papers."

"You know who I am?" Charlie asked.

"*Mais oui*," Aubrey answered. "A little bird told me in a burst of excitement. I told her that I am a man who can keep a secret, but that is as rare as a fearless American."

"Courage is returning," Charlie said passionately.

"Yes, of course, and the powerful ones know this," Aubrey warned. "Why else would terrorism strike now?"

He handed Charlie the two military passes.

"Take Zadie and get out of the city."

"But what about you?"

"Bah!" Aubrey waved his hand. "I am an institution here. No one kills the cook." He looked sadly out at the city. "Besides, there is too much to be done here."

"We'll help - "

"No!" Aubrey cut him off. "Whatever happens, Charlie, you must keep writing! We need this *Insurrection Dent-de-lion!* Every day, the people rise up to go to work, but someday soon, tomorrow even, they must rise up to restore their country to the people! Your words must resound in every heart! *Écouter!* Listen! You hear this city?"

Charlie nodded. The roar of awakening people was growing.

"If you were going to silence it, where would you start?"

"I -I couldn't," he stammered. "It's everywhere; thousands of voices, the sound of people, radios, cars, bicycles, garbage trucks."

"See Charlie? You must get the people to rise up roaring like life itself! Listen to it! Listen! You cannot silence it."

Aubrey stood and put his hands on the railing, leaning out so the sun touched his cheek.

"Once, I saw the sun ignite the torch of Lady Liberty. I thought, someday, this country will wake up with a song in its throat. Not the choke of fear, not the roar of anger - a song of compassion! Imagine! A song that reminds us that this nation can break free of the cage of fear and find its freedom through kindness."

He gripped the railing.

"There is nothing I can do to stop darkness from falling, but, I promise you, when the sun rises, I will be here singing!"

*Rivera Sun*

# CHAPTER EIGHT

· · · · ·

*Inez Hernandez*


Urgency haunted them like a hungry ghost. Its edgy howl deafened Charlie and Zadie to the honks and grumbles of the city's midday mayhem. Battered by invisible anxiety to get out of the city, they ran back down the long blocks to where they had left the car last night. Police officers asked to see their military passes three times between Aubrey's apartment and the neighborhood near the bike co-op. They wove through pedestrians and dove between traffic signals as the rest of the populace groaned its way through another ordinary day in the city.

"I just want to scream, *get out! Get out!*" Zadie whispered with a shudder.

"Panicking is not an option for any - "

Zadie stopped so fast that Charlie ran into her. A line of people stood wearily outside the Catholic Church's soup kitchen waiting for noon. A wiry, short woman spoke rapidly in Spanish to the people in the line, gesturing up the street and making swinging motions with her muscular arms.

"*¡Sí, sí!* Tomorrow, *mañana. ¿Claro?*" she asked in a stubborn, determined tone. The man vacillated and the woman put her hands on her narrow hips. "*¡Pendejo!*" she swore at him then switched to English. "They have closed the doors to the Food Assistance Program. If we don't break apart the concrete for the garden, who do you think is going to feed our families?"

The man muttered something about God provides and the little woman whacked him on the back.

"*Sí, Díos* provided you with a strong back and arms."

The other people in line snickered and the woman whirled upon them.

"And you all? God gave you strong sons and daughters, why are you letting them die in the military? Don't send them to war! If it is poverty that drafts them, send them to me! I'll put them to work feeding their families!"

She straightened up every inch of her formidable four and a half feet. She stuck strong calloused thumbs through her belt loops.

"I am breaking open the concrete in front of the Food Assistance office even if I have to do it myself!" she swore.

"Don't test her on that," Zadie warned with a laugh. "We all know Inez Hernandez would truly do it!"

She whirled around.

"ZADIE?" the woman cried out.

A shriek worthy of a fire alarm issued from both women. The dark-haired woman threw her arms around Zadie. Even without her heels, Zadie would have towered over her short friend. Inez stepped back and straightened her hair with one hand. A smile stretched across her strong chin and brightened her brown eyes.

"Zadie Byrd Gray! What are you doing in the city?"

"Getting out of it," she answered honestly.

"*Chica*, don't say that. I could use your help," Inez coerced.

"Breaking concrete?" Zadie teased.

"*¡Sí!*" Inez answered. "You're strong and you know how to grow vegetables! You heard about the Food Assistance Program ending, right? Well, someone has to feed the people. We can't just lie down and starve! So, we're going to go plant a garden in front of the old office if any of these people have *huevos* enough to do it! This year, I've got work for the whole community growing food; wages in corn, tomatoes, and beans. I have three times as many community gardens going as I did two years ago, and I want to triple it again this year." Inez drew a breath to continue, shining with enthusiasm, but Charlie interrupted.

"We really don't have time - "

"Charlie!" Zadie hissed.

"This is not the time for chitchat!" he said through clenched teeth.

"One moment," Zadie said to Inez. She pulled Charlie aside. "Inez Hernandez is the foremost organizer of community groups on this side of the Hudson River! If the Dandelion Insurrection is known at all in these neighborhoods, it's because Inez has local troublemakers running underground newspaper routes, giving them something useful to do with their penchant for illegal activities! Not only is she beyond trustworthy, she also has the skills and resources to take Aubrey's warning and put it to good use. Of course we don't have time . . . but we're going to *make* the time. Got that?"

He looked unconvinced.

"Look," Zadie said in exasperation, "nothing is going to happen until tonight, and Inez, more than anyone, should be warned!"

"Warned about what?" Inez asked sharply. She had been trying not to eavesdrop as their argument increased in volume, but at those last words every fiber of her muscular body went on alert. Inez pinned them with her eyes, suddenly tough as steel.

"Spit it out," she ordered. "I know something is up. The police are enforcing curfew even though it's supposed to end at sunrise. The Internet is cut off, though the cellphones are still working. Tell me what's going on."

"There have been rumors of terrorist attacks tonight," Zadie said as quietly as possible.

Inez's eyes widened.

"*¡Madre de Díos!*" she cried. "For real?"

"Uh . . . " Charlie floundered for an answer. "It depends what you mean by real."

Inez rolled her eyes to the heavens.

"*¡Aii, Díos!* Just what we need. Come with me," she ordered, dragging them past the curious eyes in the soup kitchen line, up the church steps, and through the chapel. Inez crossed herself before taking them behind the altar, out the backdoor of the church, and into the yard.

"My first community garden," Inez said, gesturing to the large tumbles of plots boasting last year's dried husks. "An accident in city planning turned into the salvation of the people." She paused in the center of the garden, looking around, but spring was newly on the city's doorstep, and no one was in sight.

"So," Inez asked directly, "what's going on?"

"We're not sure," Charlie said. "We heard a fairly official rumor about terrorist attacks on the power grid."

"When are the attacks?"

"Tonight."

"Shit," Inez swore.

"What's worse," Zadie added, "is that we're pretty sure the government knows about the attacks and isn't doing anything to prevent them."

"*¡Pinche* government!" Inez cried. She let loose a stream of obscenities in Spanish, then glanced at the Mother Mary statue that presided over the garden and muttered, "*¡Lo siento, Señora,* but you understand!"

She turned back to Charlie and Zadie with a severe look on her face.

"We have been clinging to survival in the poorest areas,

waiting for spring, preparing to triple our gardens because no one else cares about keeping poor people alive. During the winter, the church had to scrape the altars clean to raise money to keep the heat on in certain neighborhoods. The children are going hungry while Congress destroys the welfare programs to pay for their wars! The police have been arresting us for breaking curfew when we try to get to what little work exists! And now this?!"

"As far as we know, it's only a power failure," Charlie answered, trying to be reassuring.

"Hah!" Inez barked out. "As far as I understand, it is yet another attempt to destroy poor people simply for being poor."

"I doubt this is a direct attack on the poor," Charlie argued.

Inez shook her head, her temper hot and biting.

"Whether they shoot you in the back or the front, it kills you just the same. Only God knows why the government is involved in terrorizing its own people . . . but you can be sure *someone* is going to make a lot of money."

"I suspect it's more about controlling people," Charlie reasoned. "There have been threats of riots."

Inez slapped her fist in her palm.

"Don't believe everything you hear on TV," she snapped. "The middle and upper classes are terrified about *the anger of the poor*. There have been plenty of advertisements about what to do in times of unrest; how to call the police to report people, how to barricade your door, board over your storefront quickly, hide from the drug-crazed violence of the lower classes. Hah! When was the last time *anyone* came into my neighborhood, huh? No one comes down here. They are all scared. They think we're huddled on the street corners ready to attack. They imagine that we walk by their grocery stores with rocks in our fists, ready to smash in the windows and loot the shelves. They have nightmares of us raping them, kidnapping their children, stealing all their money."

Inez's laughter scraped out of her throat, harsh and humorless.

"But no one comes down here to find out the truth. I have worked harder than I have ever worked in my life breaking open the concrete in people's hearts and strengthening these communities. Everyone is saying the closure of the Food Assistance Program is the start of a crisis. It's not. The people were ready to riot six months ago, when the new president stole the election. People wanted to smash storefronts when we could no longer buy bread, but we did not. We smashed the pavement of an abandoned lot in the middle of winter and said our greatest revenge would be to *live*. And not just to live, but to organize."

Inez began to pace the garden.

"You see, the rich treat the poor like cattle in their stockyards. They keep us alive only as long as we continue to bring them profit. They starve us out for jobs, so our sons and daughters are conscripted by the poverty draft and sent to die as soldiers in their wars. They poison us with their cheap food, so then we must slave in their debt-camps to pay for their expensive medical care. They convict us for crimes of survival and then tax us double to lock our brothers and sisters into privatized prisons! Too much money is made from the suffering of the poor!"

Charlie watched the passionate storm of words erupt from the tiny woman. Her body reverberated with intensity. Inez Hernandez was a vessel for the power of her God. His strength poured through her. She distributed it among the community, a water bearer in the trenches of life.

"The days of profiting from the poor are numbered," she

continued. "The wealthy are sucking us dry, just like they do with everything." Inez looked up fiercely. "It is foolish. When people would rather lie down and die than get up and live, then the wealthy will collapse from their own greed. But it won't come to that if I can help it. Before the people are crushed to extinction, I am determined to see them rise up to live! Just a few weeks ago, it seemed that every church resounded with the message that we will not empower them with our desperation. They want us to die? We refuse. We will risk everything to change injustice! There is a man from the north," Inez said. Charlie and Zadie exchanged glances. "*Be like the dandelions,* he says, *rise up in the most inhospitable of soils.* There may be a lot of concrete in this city, but . . . "

Inez pointed down the garden's footpath. They craned to look. A patch of dandelions braved the elements and one yellow orb had burst open.

"We are breaking through. If the government intends to frighten the people and use our fear to control us . . . "

Inez blazed at them.

" . . . then we must show them who is truly in control!"

Charlie's soul felt humbled by this woman's fearless determination.

"I will prepare the churches," she said. "By the time the power fails, we will have the people assembled. We will tell them what little we know, and plant the seed of suspicion by alerting them beforehand. We will prevent panic, keep people connected, and set up support systems for this time of crisis."

"Be kind, be connected, be unafraid," Charlie said. "That's the slogan of the Dandelion Insurrection. Pass it on, repeat it like a prayer: Be kind. Be connected. Be unafraid."

"And get Zipper down here to shoot footage of the meetings," Zadie urged. "You'll want to get the truth out."

"*Bueno*. I will," she assured them. "Where are you going from here?"

"We don't know," Zadie said. "Aubrey got us military passes out of the city because Charlie - "

"Don't tell me," Inez interrupted, waving her hand. "I have enough secrets."

"We're going to try to get clear of the city and get the word out," Zadie amended.

"*¡Aiii!*" Inez exclaimed. "I know where you should go!" She pulled an old flier from her bag and scribbled an address and phone number on the back, handing it to Zadie. "Go to my sister's house. It's about forty minutes outside the city."

Zadie's face lit up in a smile.

"That's perfect!" Zadie exclaimed, turning to Charlie. "Inez's sister, Lupe, has organized what the anarchists call *the largest subversion of the dominant paradigm in American history.*"

Charlie's eyes flew wide.

"No!"

"Yes," Zadie answered.

"Lupe runs - "

Inez finished the sentence with a proud smirk.

" - the Suburban Renaissance."

# CHAPTER NINE

· · · · ·

## *The Suburban Renaissance*

A sense of surrealism hit Charlie as they drove into the quiet complacency of the suburbs. The rows of orderly lawns and evenly spaced lots scoffed at the notion of terrorist attacks. The similar style houses gleamed with promises that nothing bad ever happened here. Charlie fought off his sense of foreboding as he cruised through the grid of streets, squinting at street signs that were half-hidden under the budding foliage.

"This might be the first time I've ever actually been in a suburb," he admitted to Zadie.

She stared at him.

"You're joking, right?"

Charlie shook his head. He had seen them on television, of course, but the towns of the St. John Valley had been developed long before the notion of suburban communities took hold. Besides, the nearest urban center was four hours away, north or south; you could take your pick. He thought about Inez saying, *no one ever comes down here,* and wondered how often people - of any type - got out of their own little niches of reality.

"There's the street," Zadie pointed out. He pulled over under the shadows of a large oak tree. The branches swooped down and rustled above the car roof. He shut off the engine. Inez had said to park at the bottom of a gulley between two roads and Lupe would meet them.

A shriek of sound jolted him. He twisted in his seat just as a horde of kids raced down a narrow path between the houses and engulfed their car. Palms slapped against the windows.

93

Children clamored and called out unintelligible greetings. A woman who was undeniably related to Inez waded through with a baby on her hip. She hollered through the window to Zadie.

"Sorry! Inez phoned and somehow the kids got the idea that a reporter was coming." She rolled her eyes, but Charlie caught the quick anxiety that skittered across her face. Lupe licked her lips nervously. *She knows about the attacks,* he thought.

Zadie rolled down her window.

"First one to that tree gets the first photo!" she hollered.

Instantly, the kids vanished. Zadie got out of the car.

"There is big news," she said in a hushed voice.

"I heard," Lupe grimaced. "Let's not talk about it in front of the kids." She wrapped her free arm around Zadie. Her face was rounder than Inez's, but her deep brown eyes echoed her sister's. Her long hair was twisted up out of the baby's reach, but a few curls escaped to tease the little boy. Lupe shifted the baby to her other hip and held out her hand to Charlie.

"Lupe Hernandez-Booker."

"Charlie Rider."

"Nice to meet you." She turned to the children and called, "*¡Ándele niños!* Let's go to the house!"

"Are these all your kids?" Charlie asked tentatively as the children raced off. Large Catholic families were common in Charlie's French Acadian family, but the ages of this pack implied twins, or even multiple sets of triplets, not to mention a diverse gene pool of ethnicity.

"*¡Aii Díos, no!*" Lupe exclaimed dramatically. "They belong to the whole neighborhood. I watch them on Fridays until their parents get home."

Lupe rattled on nervously. They traveled up the footpath that ran along the gulley in a carefully negotiated common area between the backyards of the houses. Fences narrowed it in some places; other sections expanded right up to back porches, but by using the individually owned property collectively, the neighborhood provided their kids with a car-free run of an entire street. Zadie reached for the baby as they strolled up the trail.

"Oh, please take him," Lupe sighed gratefully. "That one came out like a bowling ball!"

Charlie scrutinized the yards.

"So, this is part of the Suburban Renaissance?" he asked.

Lupe nodded.

"When I lived in the city, Inez and I worked with the Urban Renaissance group in our family's neighborhood in New York. Then I moved out here with my husband, and I hated it. My mama's relatives in Mexico call the United States, *la tierra de los muertos en vida*, Land of the Living Dead, and that's what it seemed like. No heart, no caring, no friendships. I was about to move back to the city, but Inez said, *don't run from it . . . change it!*"

Zadie laughed.

"That's always been her motto!"

"*Sí*," Lupe smiled. "She insisted that there was nothing we had done in the city that couldn't happen out here twice as easy. Tool co-ops, daycare, ride-shares, block parties, toy libraries, garden projects; you name it! Soon, I started getting calls from other suburbs. Ten years later, there are groups all over the country!"

Charlie whistled appreciatively. The Suburban Renaissance resurrected the shell-shocked communities that had been reeling from foreclosure scandals and layoffs. The remnants of America's middle class were derisively called *roof rich*; they had a roof over their heads, but no food on the table. Their gas tanks guzzled their salaries and their children went to bed hungry. At the end of the day, many of them went bottom up on their mortgages and landed back out on the street, still owing money on a house they had never really owned.

The Suburban Renaissance pooled the resources of its troubled communities, offering childcare, carpools, and community gardens as a strategy for mitigating the expensive effects of isolation. They combated the consumer culture with connection, organized social events, and offered assistance in an old-fashioned way. The *largest subversion of the dominant paradigm in American history* turned out to be something as ordinary as apple pie . . . people helping people.

By the time Lupe's husband arrived home from work, the pack of children had been dispersed to their respective homes, her older kids were happily shrieking upstairs, and she was listening gravely to Inez's plans to get the truth out to people before the attacks even started. Lupe reached over and tuned the radio to a low volume.

"Uh-oh," Todd commented as he came in the room. "We got the Che Guevara on, huh?"

"That's what we call the guerilla radio," Lupe explained with a sigh. "Inez insists that we listen to the underground stations, but it makes me nervous. What if the police find out?"

Her husband shrugged.

"We'll be screwed, sweetheart. The computer's named Cesar Chavez and the cellphone is Dr. King." He introduced himself to Charlie and Zadie. Todd Booker was a broad, black man whose voice boomed out heartily and made the kids come pounding down the stairs. He scooped up the girl and tickled her.

"Marcos, little man, come help me!" he called to the boy.

The kids ganged up on their father instead and launched into a riotous chase around the kitchen.

"*¡Shhh, mi amor!*" Lupe called out. "I can't hear the radio."

Todd straightened up and held out his hands for truce. The shrieks quieted to giggles. The kids started to tussle with each other, but Todd pulled them apart.

"Nope, you guys gotta cool it. You can go upstairs and play, or you can sit around with us boring old folks and keep quiet. Your choice."

Evita crawled into her daddy's lap. Marcos swung around the edge of the table toward Charlie.

"Hey mister," he demanded. "Are you really a reporter? *¿El Hombre del Norte?*"

"Spanish?" Charlie gasped. "I'm in Spanish?"

"You're him?" Lupe exclaimed, eyes flying wide open.

"Uh," Charlie stammered in consternation. "That's not public knowledge."

Lupe's eyes turned dark with worry. She bit her lip and looked at Todd, then down at the kids.

"I don't know how to say this - we can't - it's not safe for us to have you in our house! If the police find out, what will we do?! We can't take this kind of risk with the children. I had no idea who you were! Inez should have told me!"

"Inez didn't know," Zadie said softly.

Lupe's face turned red with embarrassment. Discomfort flushed hot in Charlie's cheeks. He stammered out an apology that crumbled into awkward silence. Todd cleared his throat.

"Lupe, baby, maybe - "

She cut him off with a gasp of disbelief. Irritation, fear, and anger executed a complicated contortion act through her expression, ending in a tight-lipped look that pressured her husband to escort Charlie and Zadie out the front door.

The radio interrupted them with a crackle of sound.

"We have been issued a warning about a possible terrorist

attack on the city's power grid tonight. Please remain calm. As you know, the Internet has been dead in the city since this morning, but so far, cellphones are still working. Information hotline numbers are as follows . . . " the underground radio rattled off a list of phone numbers, quickly informing the listeners not to panic, but to activate all phone trees and communication networks.

"What is this?" Todd demanded to know.

"Charlie and Zadie received a warning and passed it on to Inez," Lupe explained. "Inez sent them out here."

"The police hadn't lifted the neighborhood curfews when we left this morning. We needed military passes to leave the city," Charlie mentioned.

"Interesting," Todd commented. "For a surprise terrorist attack, the police sure had everything planned out, didn't they?"

"Apparently, they had a warning."

"Uh-huh. The original version probably came straight from the CIA."

Todd Booker was not a great fan of government. He had been spinning on this planet long enough to watch plenty of false flag operations, scandals, scams, and lies come pouring out of politicians' mouths. He had a mile-wide cynical streak that could choke his spirit like a weed, but Todd made sure a tender sprout of hope had room to grow within him. The future of his kids depended on it.

Todd turned on the television at a low volume.

"That won't give you any real news," Charlie snorted.

"No," Todd agreed, "but it's always good to know what lies they're telling."

The television snapped suddenly to the official news station.

"Whoa, whoa, there it is," Todd exclaimed, "special news report."

He turned up the volume as the frantic announcer screeched.

" . . . seven major cities left without power or Internet! New York, Los Angeles, Chicago, Houston, Seattle, Atlanta, and Philadelphia! Hit by international cyber terrorist groups and domestic terrorists - "

"They sure figured out who was doing it real quick, didn't they?" Todd pointed out.

"Uh-huh," Charlie muttered, staring at the map of the United States that flashed on the screen. Red lights blared on the seven cities and a siren-like sound wailed over the announcer's voice. Charlie tuned them out and forced his mind to focus. "They left the lights on in Washington D.C. How convenient."

"Shhh!" Zadie hissed as the screen switched to the announcer again.

" . . . authorities are working rapidly to deal with this. Citizens are advised to stay calm, stay inside. Please do not leave your homes at this point. Leave the roads open for the officials. Do not panic . . ."

"*¡Madre de Díos!*" Lupe cried, pointing as the television ran an aerial shot of the blackened New York City against the midnight blue skyline.

"Look at that!" Zadie exploded. "The lights are on at Greenback Street!"

The oasis of the wealthy gleamed in a thin strip of light amidst a sea of darkness. Charlie's stomach dropped with a sickening jolt. How could they be so blatant?

"How nice of those alleged cyber-hackers to make sure the elite always have power at their fingertips," he muttered.

The television announcer, who seemed ready to bolt from the studio, wiped his sweating brow dramatically. The siren screamed in the background. *Nice touch*, Charlie thought bitterly. There was no real need for air raid sirens in a television studio. It was a fear-mongering media tactic. Charlie had no doubt that it was working on the majority of the populace. The television announcer took a gulp of water with an obviously shaking hand.

"The cyber-terrorists struck emergency generators at hospitals, police stations, schools, water lines, subways, sewer treatment plants, and senior care centers. The cities are being crippled! Authorities are urging people not to panic. If the attacks continue, evacuations will begin."

"Evacuations? To where?" Charlie asked.

Todd scowled. "They've got those camps."

He lifted the little girl out of his lap. "Evita, go upstairs with your brother."

"Are the terrorists coming here?" she asked, wide-eyed.

"No, sweetie," Todd answered with a sardonic sigh. "Everything's going to be just fine here in suburbia. Now, go upstairs 'til dinner, alright?"

She nodded and ran off with her brother. Todd's eyes followed them as they left, waiting until they were out of earshot. As soon as he and Lupe had learned they were expecting, Todd Booker had vowed to keep his kids out of the cities, out of the range of police, drugs, early deaths, and arrests. His kids weren't going to grow up in terror of the camps . . . not like him.

"Those camps," Todd told Charlie and Zadie, "are the nightmare of the urban poor. Prison camps, debt-labor camps, and the camps you don't come back from."

"I thought those were just urban legends," Charlie frowned skeptically.

"No. I swear on my father who died there, on my uncle

100

who'll die before his debt wears out, on my cousin who disappeared after talking smart with a cop, on my best friend who's locked away, and many more. The media pretends they don't exist. They talk about the evacuation centers as if they're just for emergencies. That's a lie. The prison system overflowed into them. The debt-labor programs turned them into work camps. All hush-hush, you know? No one talked about the way that the bankruptcy fees increased so that only the rich could afford to go bankrupt. There were no reports on how debt became hereditary and passed through families. The official reports don't even talk about how you can't work your way out of the debt-camps. You die there. Outside the cities, nobody's heard this, but if you're like me and Lupe, you grew up terrified of the camps."

Lupe confirmed it.

"My mama always threatened us, *be good or you'll get sent to the camps.*"

"And it's true," Todd agreed. "My mom screamed at us, stay away from the cops, don't get caught, sell your car, sell your body, sell anything but don't get thrown into a camp like your father."

"Todd," Lupe shushed him.

"What? They gotta know. When the people in the city realize that they're being shipped to the camps, they're gonna go crazy. They won't go, not for anything."

"It's just for emergency shelter," Charlie argued. "They can't stay in the city without electricity. There's no refrigeration, no water, the sewer won't work, no lights, no security systems . . . "

Todd cut him off with a shake of his head. Lupe bit her lip.

"They'll try to stay anyway, Charlie. You don't understand," she said.

Todd pointed to the television as it flashed aerial shots of the blackened cities. Like New York, each city had strips of light surrounded by dark blocks.

"Those blacked out areas," he asked them, "do you know where they are?"

Charlie shook his head.

"Same places already under curfew. When the power comes back, it'll light up right along the streets where the rich people live. It won't come back in the poor neighborhoods. It won't come back in the university districts where the radical professors and students hang out. Reminds me of Jews in Nazi Germany: fear, hate, propaganda, ghettos, curfews, and now, the camps."

"No," Zadie objected. "They wouldn't be that obvious. Americans would never let that happen here!"

"It has happened here," Charlie pointed out grimly. "The genocide of the native tribes, the internment of the Japanese, the deportation of the Acadians, the enslavement of Africans; this continent has a long tradition of brutality. Atrocity has happened here before; it can happen here again."

"You'll see," Todd added darkly. "The attacks won't stop. Evacuations will begin. Martial law will be declared and it won't be lifted anytime soon. There's a media blackout on those camps, so what goes on in the camps, stays in the camps."

Zadie's face contorted.

"You don't think . . . they couldn't . . . they wouldn't kill them?" she asked.

Todd shrugged and said nothing more. The proof was in the pudding, as the saying went. Camps were camps. Plenty had died in them already. They wouldn't kill them right off, though. First they'd work them to death. Then there would be disease, yeah, that'd be convenient. Todd had seen it before: viruses running rampant in poor districts, people quarantined inside, no medical aid coming in, no one going out . . . unless they could pay for vaccines. A lot of money was made off vaccines. His pop had bought his kids' life with the price of his own. His older brother now worked to pay off that debt. That's how it went in America these days. The debts of the parents passed on to the children, but only for the poor people. That was the law. The corporate media and the politicians claimed that people like him were lazy, no-good druggies, and, with the consent of the unwitting majority, managed to legislate the poor into a life of debt slavery. Todd Booker had paid a black market broker to change his name, forge documents, and break him free of the city. He bid his past and his family goodbye, and didn't look back. There was only death there. His kids deserved better. Lupe deserved better. He tried to get his wife to ditch the anchor of her family, but Lupe dug in her heels and drew the line. Family was sacred to her, for better or worse; you simply did not give up on them, not ever!

Now Lupe held the baby to her tightly. Her round face grew grave and deeply disturbed.

"Inez has been concerned about something like this," she said hesitantly. "I discounted it for a long time, but Inez has been insisting that when the poor are no longer of any use to the powerful, they will be slaughtered like sick cattle and thrown into mass graves."

"Inez can be dramatic," Zadie conceded.

"Inez also knows what she talks about," Lupe said shortly.

"But it makes no sense," Zadie said. "Why now? What are they getting out of it?"

Lupe closed her eyes in silent prayer. Then she spoke almost in a whisper.

"Inez said that the only thing that would force the powerful to act quickly would be the threat of a poor people's uprising. If they fought back before they were crushed, then the power elite would be forced to stop it."

"But that's crazy! It's an insane thing to do!" Zadie exclaimed.

"But don't you see?" Lupe insisted, eyes wide with alarm. "This is exactly how genocides happen. Everyone sits around saying, *this is crazy! They wouldn't do it!* Then they make excuses - oh, those people died from disease, cold, overwork, hunger - until one day, we look back and realize that millions of people have died!"

"We can't let them be evacuated," Zadie swore. "Lupe, that's everybody you know; your mom, Inez, the whole neighborhood, all my friends, Zipper, Hawlings. We've got to do something!"

She turned to Charlie. Her eyes begged him to think of an answer. Charlie laid his head on his hands. *Think,* he commanded himself, *for Zadie's sake, think!* His mind churned its gears, aching and sweating as it labored for solutions. His neurons overheated as a million ideas shot through his consciousness. He scrutinized them rapid-fire and cast them all aside. *Too weak. Too unwieldy. Takes too much time!* He stood up, lifting a hand to forestall their questions.

"I'm just trying to think. Give me a moment."

He stepped out onto the porch and sat on the stoop. The cool spring night rushed up to prickle his skin. The street hung between the last shade dusk and total darkness. Millions of lives pressed their weight upon his shoulders. The answer was so close . . . he could feel it . . . it was right before his eyes, on the tip of his awareness, itching him, driving him nuts, it was like he was practically on top of it -

"That's it!" he shouted. "Jesus! That's it!"

He jumped to his feet. Beautiful! It was a perfect equation blooming in the mind of a mathematician! A symphony harmonizing within the imagination of the composer! It was so elegant, so incredible! Charlie burst back into the kitchen.

"They're not going to evacuate the cities!" he exclaimed.

"They're not?!" they cried.

"No," he answered. "We are."

# CHAPTER TEN

. . . . .

## Operation Urban Evacuation

Lupe's phone call reached Inez as she navigated the storm of confusion. A battering of panicking updrafts flung her into rapid action, beating furiously to organize the people as fear of the camps spread. Over the clamor of voices at the church, Inez plugged her ear with one finger and barely caught Lupe's breathless message.

"I still have to call around to be sure, but why wouldn't they do it? It's so noble to give shelter to people in a crisis, and so patriotic to take our fellow citizens into our homes! I'll call you back in an hour."

That was at eight o'clock. The adrenaline of *maybe* invigorated Inez . . . maybe the suburbs would help them . . . maybe families across the country would offer to take in the people from the cities . . . maybe salvation would reach out its hand. Inez dove back into the streets with the news. She tracked down organizers and community leaders. She hollered frightened crowds into submission. She scaled streetlights to get people's attention. Her voice spluttered into a rasping croak of reason as people screamed about death camps and terrorists, police raids, and the apocalypse. She urged families to stay calm, told young people to stop milling around like cows in the street, pounded on old people's doors to make sure they were still living, spreading the possibility of Charlie's idea like a contagious infection of hope.

At midnight, martial law was declared. Lupe had not called. Soldiers in trucks crawled the streets, blaring on bullhorns that people should stay calm, it was under control, evacuations to the camps would begin in the morning. Stay calm. Stay calm. Stay -

Panic burst into flame through the firetrap of tenement rows. Paper-thin walls buzzed with the fear of the camps. Wailing could be heard in the gaps of the sirens. In desperation, Inez traded lies for a fraction of time.

"We are not going to the camps," she repeated over and over. "There is another plan."

*What plan?* people asked.

"You'll hear soon," Inez promised, praying that it was true. *Lupe, hurry!* Inez scurried through the side alleys as the soldiers moved in. She raced to clear people off the streets in case the army rounded them up. At one a.m., her cellphone battery died. *Never give up your landline!* Inez told herself. Only Father Ramon and her mother still bothered with the old fashioned phones that drew their power through the telephone lines. Inez wove her way back to the church. She rounded the corner and gasped. The nuns had been cast onto the street. The soldiers mounted the steps. Father Ramon blocked the door with his body.

"You can't take over our church!" Inez shouted as the soldiers shoved Father Ramon aside and entered. She ran up to a soldier who leaned insolently on the statue of the Virgin that guarded the door. "You can't commandeer our church like this!"

He cracked a backhanded blow so strong that she crashed against the hard granite wall. For a moment, she thought the lights of the city had returned, winking and swimming in front of her eyes. Father Ramon pulled her down the steps and told her to go home, check on her mother, there was nothing to be done here . . . Inez protested deliriously that she didn't need to check on her mother, she was fine. Pilar Maria would survive the Armageddon with black market chocolate to spare, the old *bruja* grew fat during famines, *su madre* dealt deals that put stockbrokers to shame, undoubtedly she would outlive taxes and cockroaches . . . the litany carried Inez home like Hail Mary's. She tumbled in the door with a cheek so swollen she couldn't see out of one eye and was sideswiped by the shrill ring of the telephone. She dove for it.

"Lupe!?"

Her sister hit her with news that hurt worse than the soldier's blow.

"I'm sorry, Inez, *lo siento!*" Lupe cried. "I tried everything. They won't do it."

The suburban families had lynched hope and hung it from the tree of their fear. They slammed down their telephones and locked their front doors as the television news screamed about riots in Chicago, fires in Houston, lootings in Los Angeles, murders and violence in Atlanta; the panicked poor, the pandemonium, the depravity of the lower classes.

*They're criminals, prostitutes, druggies; they'll rob us, molest our children, cause problems,* Lupe's friends in the Suburban Renaissance protested. *Send them to the evacuation centers. This type of crisis is what those places were built for. The government knows what it's doing.*

"They don't know, Inez," Lupe apologized for the insulated prejudice of the suburbanites. "They don't know about the prison camps or the debt-labor camps. All they see is ribbon-cutting ceremonies on television."

"Well, tell them!" Inez screamed to her sister. In the street below her apartment, a line of empty army trucks rolled toward the church. She spat out to Lupe that their last place of refuge was now occupied.

"Holy Cross?" Lupe gasped. "They actually took over the church?"

In Lupe's kitchen, Charlie bolted upright as memory stabbed him like a knife. A generations-old shudder snapped through his spine. His grandfather's gravelly voice grated in his ears.

*In the time of Le Grand Derangement, when the English deported the Acadians, the soldiers lured us to the churches and locked us inside. Then they marched us out at gunpoint, put us on ships, and sent thousands to their deaths.*

"Don't go, Inez!" Charlie gasped out as he snatched the phone from Lupe. "If they send word of a meeting at the church, don't go. They'll force the priests to lie to you and round you up that way."

Inez's faith in the goodness of humanity withered in her gut.

"I've got to warn people. Tell Lupe to keep trying, please!"

Inez hung up and started to dial another number when the magnitude of failure knocked her knees out from under her. She crumpled to the floor and wrapped her arms around her shins in a tight ball of betrayal. Pilar Maria grabbed her eldest daughter and rocked the clenched curl of muscles as the implacable plaster face of the Virgin watched them from the altar above.

"Why?" Inez wailed out in an agonized appeal to God as the matchstick of hope burnt out. The candlewicks spluttered in their pools of wax. An extinguished flame released a bitter curl of smoke. Pilar looked to the Virgin as Inez begged to know why the suburbs, the heavenly father, and the whole of humanity had forsaken them in an hour of crisis. Why? Pilar asked the mother of a crucified son. Why do our children cry to the holy father while their mothers listen in anguish, having never forsaken them, not for a moment?!

"Inez," she complained for the five thousandth time, "you expect too much of people. They are not saints." They were not even courageous, or kind, or intelligent, Pilar thought pragmatically. They were people. You had to get down and dirty with them. You had to roll in their grime and appeal to their guts. You had to lie, cheat, steal, beg, and grovel. Pilar had done it all.

She rocked her holy daughter, the pure one, the righteous saint, the mortal pain-in-the-ass, her wiry steel-hardened thirty-five year old child. Inez, she thought, you burn so bright inside that you cannot see darkness for what it truly is . . . darkness. Failure and misery cannot always be washed clean by the light of the soul. Welcome to the world, *hija, el mundo armago lleno de dolores,* the bitter world full of sorrows.

Inez cursed Lupe's failure, condemning her sister to a thousand years of agony for letting them down like this.

"Don't curse your sister," Pilar chastised her even as she burst into laughter.

"She gave up on us! She let *las putas en los suburbios* walk away from us into the perfect little world where nothing bad ever happens. May her lawn swallow her soul and her SUV drive her straight to Hell!"

"One more word and you'll find yourself tied to her fender on the bumpy road to the Devil's!" Pilar croaked, torn between laughter and concern. A peal of obscenity streamed out of Inez and Pilar gave up on scolding and looked at her daughter with vindicated pride.

"Ah, see? You were listening to me all these years!"

The fire of outrage pulled Inez out of the quagmire of despair. Her black eyes evaporated her tears in a hiss of steam and her irises blazed with fury. Pilar nodded approvingly. Now, Inez was ready. She met her daughter's eyes with determination. She had not crossed illegally into this country and survived all these years without learning a few tricks.

"A lie told often enough becomes the truth," she quoted to Inez, "and I say, the suburbs will open their doors to anyone who shows up."

"No, Mama, Lupe said they're too scared of us to help - "

"Guadalupe Dolores doesn't know everything," Pilar claimed haughtily. "Lock the doors, barricade the windows, then get on the phone and tell everyone to do the same."

"But, Mama! We can't stay here forever!"

"I never said we were going to," Pilar sniffed as she gathered her coat and satchel. "You'll see. When a crisis arrives on one's doorstep, fear gets kicked off the couch."

"Where are you going?" Inez demanded.

"To deliver a crisis to the doorstep of your sister."

Inez looked at Pilar with dawning understanding.

"The government isn't evacuating the cities. The suburbs aren't evacuating the cities . . . "

"No," Pilar confirmed. "We are."

*        *        *

Two hunched silhouettes sat side by side on the porch as the sun rose. Zadie rubbed her reddened eyes. Charlie's hands curled and uncurled a battered sheaf of paper. His furious scrawl of handwriting raged across the sheets, denouncing the fearful hesitancy of the populace. He sighed and let the useless words fall to the porch step between his feet. The splat of dead paper silenced the lone bird that cried in the overhanging trees.

"We can't take the risk, Charlie," Zadie repeated. "If you send that article through the Internet to the suburbs and the cities that still have access, the Feds will track you down. We've got to use the old distribution network - "

"It's too slow, Zadie," he argued. "We've got to tell people what's going on *now*. Besides, who are we going to reach? A couple thousand insurrectionists? We've got to send this out publicly to everyone."

"It's no good, Charlie, you know that. The Internet Censors will just delete it as soon as they catch it posted anywhere."

"If we could just deliver it straight to the people," he complained, sweeping an arm to the vast suburbs that stretched across the nation. His frustration had smoldered as hot as Lupe's as the night wore on and the Suburban Renaissance organizers refused to help the masses of the urban poor. At three in the morning, unable to sleep, *the Man From the North* scripted a fiery letter of condemnation that incinerated itself as he wrote. Charlie left it smoldering and tempered his words to hardened steel and cut through the lies that vilified the poor. By four a.m., the warm embers of his heart were urging the Suburban Renaissance to reconsider their stance and to reach out to those in need. At five a.m. in the cool clarity before dawn, he revised his writing into a cry for the awakening of the heart. Zadie's eyes grew moist as she read the final draft, but she shook her head at his desire to post it on the web. They argued as the sun rose, the house lights snapped on, and the smell of coffee touched the morning.

"It takes the Internet Censors a few days to go through emails. Maybe we could start a chain letter," he suggested.

"They'll track it back through and interrogate everyone who receives it," she pointed out.

"Yeah, but if we could send it quick enough . . . "

"You'd need a list of thousands, a bulk email list."

The screech of the screen door silenced them.

"Use the Suburban Renaissance's," Lupe said. "Send it anonymously, and if we're found out, I'll say you hacked the system."

Lupe stepped out barefoot onto the cool paint of the porch. Tear streaks aged her face like wrinkles. Her sleepless eyes ached. Her throat had cracked into hoarse strands of overuse, splintering on the shards of her broken promise to Inez. She did not sit down, but stood above them, coldly staring out at the suburban houses.

"My mother's phone rings unanswered in the city," she said, starkly hinting that their efforts were too little, too late. She shrugged. As long as the cry for shelter continued, she intended to keep trying. "Give me the article of *the Man From the North*. I'll send it. If Charlie is courageous enough to take risks, so am I."

Her features stiffened granite-like against the cruelties of the world. Her bare feet rooted firmly to the porch. Zadie and Charlie stared up at the hard-carved woman as she gazed at the overcast sky. No one noticed the solitary figure walking steadily up the street until a thick roll of Spanish shattered the stillness of the morning.

"*Madre de Dios! Hija*, don't stand there doing nothing. Help your mama up the steps, I swear I've walked the very soles off my feet!"

\*    \*    \*

Pilar Maria Ignacia Hernandez held court in the suburban kitchen, organizing a black market evacuation on the one breath, and ordering Lupe around imperiously on the other.

"Make the coffee as black as your husband, Guadalupe! My eyelids are as heavy as rocks! *Sí*, of course I walked out of the city. What, you think the *pinche* soldiers gave me a ride? Ach, don't scold me for my foul mouth, *hija*, you survived it, and so will my grandchildren. Now listen, there will be a truckload of children arriving in a few hours. *Mis socios* on the black market will bring them out of the city. They'll go back with bottled water, flashlights, food - eh? No, no, not for the poor people. They plan to sell it to the university students for triple the price. The trucks will run all day. *Sí*, of course they've got military passes. What do you think bribes are for? There will be a second truck at noon, a third at three, and - "

"But Mama!" Lupe cried. "What are we going to do with them all?"

"When a crisis arrives on the doorstep, fear gets kicked off the couch," Pilar repeated. "The suburbs will open their doors to anyone who shows up. You'll see. The beds will be found."

And they were. Lupe's neighbors saw the wide-eyed, terrified children climb out of the back of the first truck and felt a twinge of guilt bite their hearts. Casseroles made their way over to Lupe's house, along with extra sweatshirts and socks, blankets, and finally, offers of help. Pilar waded through the chaos like a broker on Wall St, calculating each move like a wolf.

"Alma," she told a charming girl, "tell Mrs. Blackburn about the soldiers coming to take you away."

The six year old solemnly recounted the events of the night before to Mrs. Blackburn and a bevy of other neighborhood women.

"Miguel," the crafty woman hinted, "maybe Mr. Edmonds can play catch with you and Carlos and the others. Tell them about the camps. He has never heard of them."

Stories poured out of cops and arrests, hunger, hard work, loving parents, despair, daydreams and heartbreak, flowers growing in sidewalks and late nights on the rooftops, barricades, curfews; a thousand true stories of life in the neighborhoods, children's stories, love stories, people stories; stories that ripped all words from the throat, stories that dropped mouths into the round shape of *wow;* stories that stung eyes, opened doors, and sparked miracles.

By nightfall, the children had climbed into their listeners' hearts.

Pilar sucked her gold tooth. *Bueno,* she thought, *it's working.* The next morning, she stalked the suburbs like a pushcart seller vending her wares, knocking brazenly on doors, and taking only yes for an answer. She enlisted her grandchildren, sending them up to the door with some urban cohorts in tow, shuffling behind them like a sweet *abuelita,* leaning on Zadie's pale-skinned security as she cajoled total strangers into helping them all.

"It's all business," she muttered to Zadie. "I've got a cart full of lemons and no one likes lemonade. So, what do I do? I give away free recipes for my *abuela's* irresistible lemon meringue pie - for free! All they need to do is bring home a lemon or two."

"My mama is the Devil incarnate," Lupe told Charlie in a disgusted aside. "She's devious as hell, but somehow, she manages to work miracles."

Pilar Maria contacted her *socios en el mercado negro* and initiated similar underground evacuations in the other six cities. Charlie's article swept through the Suburban Renaissance email list paired with testimonies about the visitors. Across the country, Lupe's fellow organizers found their email accounts flooded with true stories from the cities, photos of children, and requests for assistance. Phone calls started to bounce back.

"How can we help?"

"Is there a Chicago contact?"

"We have homes ready."

Despite the good intentions of the people, the authorities laid down a wall of resistance, reinforced by the stranglehold of martial law. The evacuation was constricted to a trickle that slipped through the cracks of control. Instead of aiding the citizen-based evacuation, the authorities ignored the offer of assistance. The underground radio was willing to broadcast the information, but only a few people at a time could be smuggled out successfully. Pilar scowled darkly.

"The wall of barricades and restricted travel must fall," she said. "There is no reason for it to stand."

Lupe told her families to contact the authorities. Inez asked her people to lodge formal complaints.

"That's it, my girls," Pilar encouraged them. "The one-two punch, call those officials to task from within and without, give the scoundrels no rest! Tell them the poor are barricading themselves in their apartments for fear of the camps, there are houses waiting to help, have the officials no sense? Let down the restrictions on travel. Let the people come to good homes. We will keep families together and find medical care for the elderly. At the very least, tell the authorities to let the supply trucks through to bring fresh water to those waiting inside! The whole situation is a mess! Tell them they are mishandling everything, they are incompetent, just let the people out of the city until the power is restored . . . "

Lupe handed the phone to her mother.

"Mama, if you're going to nag . . . "

Pilar shrugged and put her skills to good use. She harangued, badgered, wheedled, coerced, pleaded, flattered, manipulated, cajoled. She enlisted an army of helpers; old ladies, young mamas, preachers, children; every evacuee took a turn on the phone. One reluctant stone at a time, they chipped away until finally Inez called.

"Turn on the radio," she cried. "We've done it!"

It was the secretary for the head of the local National Guard who finally listened and was moved enough to ensure that the radio stations across the country started broadcasting the news. The secretary believed in a time of crisis, all options should be utilized to keep people safe.

"One person," Inez kept saying, "one person makes miracles possible."

A crowd gathered around the radio for the official announcement. Lupe, the children, Pilar, Zadie, several neighbors, and Charlie sucked their cheers into their chests as the largest radio show in the area informed listeners of the news.

" . . . in the face of these continued power failures, for the good and safety of the people, suburban families around the country are offering up their spare bedrooms, churches, community centers, and gymnasiums to provide refuge for their urban counterparts. The authorities have expressed unease about this offer."

The program cut to the Mayor of New York City.

"We're convinced that government agencies are best equipped to handle mass evacuations," he said.

"But," the radio host continued, "in light of the breaking news that the urban poor are barricading themselves inside their homes due to superstitious fears of the evacuation centers, the suburban communities' offer has been applauded as a sensible resolution. The mayors of Philadelphia, New York, and Los Angeles voiced approval of the unconventional solution and have given their permission for the people to evacuate to suburban neighborhoods. Officials from the other affected cities have reluctantly agreed to the notion as well. Meanwhile," the announcer continued, "the authorities are putting every effort into getting power back into peoples' hands."

Charlie shook his head.

"There's a little switch called democracy," he muttered. "All they need to do is use it."

The floodgates released and the people came streaming out. The suburbs channeled people through the streets like water irrigating the fields, tempering the massive force into manageable canals. As Pilar predicted, the suburbs rose to the crisis. Church groups stepped forward. Schools opened their gymnasiums.

Later that day, Inez arrived in Lupe's neighborhood at dusk, weary to the bone. Lights glowed from the windows of her sister's house and the clamor of children mingled with the clink of dishwashing. Inez shivered in the cool twilight. She stood outside the bottled up comfort of the house, feeling like an outcast in a world sliding toward darkness. Her body had made the trip from the city, but her soul still wandered the empty streets, hearing voices crying for her to return.

*Mañana,* she promised to those still trapped in the city, *give me one night of rest.* She leaned toward the house, but her feet cemented to the hard sidewalk as a host of images rose from the tomb of her memory: concrete and blockades, black helmets of cops, a punch to her cheekbone, the jab of her hunger, the echoes of *no!,* the slam of the door, the endless throb of the ring tone, sudden truncated silences, megaphone orders, soldiers on church steps, the shout of anger, the tremor of desperation.

Inez shook with exhaustion from days of hammering at the concrete wall of human stupidity. Her lips curled in derision, pulling moisture from the parched cave of her mouth, and spitting to the side with a sharp twist of her head. The grass swallowed it up, robbing her of the satisfaction of a hard splat on cement.

A choke of laughter aborted in her throat. Humans had invented many flavors of stupidity: greed, hatred, anger, despair, violence, apathy . . . but hope was the greatest stupidity of all. Hope was the sort of idiocy that drove Inez, a woman not five feet tall, to pick up a sledgehammer and try to crack open layers of concrete so thick that they held up whole skyscrapers. Hope was the kind of stupidity that led women to put seeds in the ground, bread in the oven, and bring children to life; when day after day, frosts withered the sprouts, rats gnawed on the loaf, and small coffins slid starved children into graves. Hope demanded one's faith. Hope denied all the facts. Hope was a madness that kept us alive.

Inez stepped off the sidewalk to cross the lawn up to the house. Her shoes sank into the soft welcome of the grass. She staggered in a burst of understanding. Inez fell to her knees and dug her fingers into the soil. She looked up and down the street in the last traces of daylight.

"Forget hope," she groaned. The greatest stupidity of all was the idiocy of a woman who broke open concrete when the old farmland of the city lay under the lawn of her sister!

\*       \*       \*

The shovel punched through the grass with a satisfying crunch. Charlie rocked it loose and unwound his shoulders from the slouch of writing. Zadie leaned on her shovel animatedly telling some story about housesitting while the others dug up the lawn. Charlie smiled to himself. Zadie worked like a bird, pecking here, scratching there, stopping to warble out some new joke or thought or story; not turning much soil, but making the hours fly by.

"So then," she laughed, "the president of the homeowners' association showed up with a yardstick and told me the lawn was over the regulatory three inches and I needed to take care of the problem. I didn't consider a meadow in front of the house to be a problem, so I ignored it until at twelve inches they came back with two teenagers and a lawnmower in tow. I told them the neighborhood rulebook contained no restrictions on wildlife preserves. They insisted I cut the grass, and I took one look at the butterflies and wildflowers and said, *Hell no, I won't mow!* Two days later those teenagers tagged every car in the neighborhood with a bumper sticker containing the phrase and launched the Lawnmower Liberation Front! The adults blamed me, of course, called my aunt on her vacation, and asked me to leave, which I did . . . but not before dumping a fifty pound sack of dandelion seeds onto their front lawns." Zadie concluded with a sweeping gesture, pretending to fling seeds like a parading queen throwing coins to the crowd.

The laughter mingled with the rototiller's rumble. Pilar's sharp rattle of Spanish erupted from the house as she organized another supply run to the city. Three more powerless days had sent waves of people into the suburbs. Lupe put them to work tearing up lawns to plant gardens. Stories flew along with clods of dirt. Misconceptions and lies rose like a cloud of dust and were hosed by the clear water of truth. The few neighborhoods that had been taken to the evacuation centers were being carefully watched and the bulk of the populace that was stubbornly hunkering down in the cities had been left alone by the authorities. Bill and Ellen sent a message down to the suburbs. They were growing dandelions this year, if anyone wanted to come north. A wave of students and activists traveled up to the farm and began training in nonviolent struggle. Aubrey gave Zadie's parents the money to double their production . . . there were a lot of hardworking dandelions that would need to be fed. He offered Lupe and Inez capital to buy seed for the urban and suburban gardens, and promised to seek out more donors, as well.

Charlie smiled to himself as he looked at the long garden. This was their Victory Garden, not for soldiers at war, but for people at peace. The electricity had not been restored, but the wires of human connection were being laid. One day soon, Charlie knew, the switch of the heart would be thrown, and the country would rise up with power. He lifted the shovel to plunge it back into the earth. Lupe's shout leapt off the porch.

"The electricity's back!"

A cheer burst out. A flurry of speculative clamor scuffled to explain what had happened. Sensible rationalizations and conspiracy theories vied with each other. Charlie slung his spade up onto his shoulder. It didn't matter much to him. *The Man From the North* understood; true power lay within people. The authorities had tried to grab hold of it, but it slipped from their grasp, refused to be rounded up, snuck out of the city, knocked on doors, opened hearts, and survived. Charlie left the patch of yellow flowers in front of him undisturbed. Up and down the street, the lawns had been turned over by crisis and change, and the indomitable dandelions endured.

# CHAPTER ELEVEN

. . . . .

## *Fuel For Change*


Despite the restoration of power, nationwide martial law continued. Authorities claimed that the threat of new terrorist attacks was still high. Zadie spent hours trying to track down the real reasons. Inez maintained that the elite feared the uprising of the poor. Aubrey had no answers. The lips of the powerful were sealed tighter than their private vaults. Charlie kept his suspicions smoldering inside his chest, and watched bitterly as they were confirmed, one-by-one.

The fist of the government tightened. Soldiers set up regular patrols through the cities. Papers were checked at the street corners. Radicals disappeared. Institutions that criticized the government were shut down. Lenient local officials were replaced with ex-military commanders. Tanks and guns became commonplace. Citizens got used to the sight of soldiers. Curfews were rigorously enforced. Gatherings over twenty were strictly forbidden. Under the guise of security, militarism invaded further into the mindset of the nation. Martial law crept closer toward normal.

Charlie's mind spun in endless circles of *why?* It was clear that the high-ranking politicians feared unrest. The evacuation plan had backfired. The poor returned to the cities armed with social connections, knowledge, and gardens to keep them alive. Inez reported that attempts to organize people were closely watched and often undermined by agents . . . and not just government agents, she warned. The corporations employed a bevy of spies, infiltrators, and informants to stamp out any resistance to their control.

Charlie watched the shifting crosswinds like a hawk, plagued by a suspicion that he was overlooking some crucial detail. The mainstream media kept to its barrage of phrases about cyber-hackers and domestic terrorists, claiming that nothing could be proven definitively about the identities of the perpetrators, but people could be assured that the authorities were working on it.

"They're working on covering their tracks," Charlie scoffed.

A barrage of new laws swept out of Congress, including something called the *Freedom of Defense Act*. Charlie's gut shriveled when he read it. The act reinforced the trend that criminalized protests, demonstrations, and many forms of dissent. It erased the nation's last nod toward international standards of human rights. Fair trials were replaced with some new kind of court that no one knew anything about. The vague term *domestic terrorist* was defined by a set of clauses that allowed law enforcement to stop and detain, without warrant or trial, anyone suspected of being involved with groups that undermined the safety and wellbeing of the United States of America.

*In other words,* Charlie wrote in a heavy sardonic tone, *the term domestic terrorist applies to anyone who questions or resists the tyranny of the current corporate-political regime.*

Resentment over the presence of soldiers peaked. A kid threw a rock and was shot. Animosity flared between citizens and soldiers. People chafed under the restrictions. Frustration boiled beneath the surface of quiet streets. Building tensions were palpable nationwide.

"There's something going on that we're not seeing," Charlie muttered. He shook his head. "They're after something besides control. Somebody is profiting from this."

One night, Zadie got a call from her father.

"Charlie," she said as she hung up, "I think I just found out."

*     *     *

Charlie and Zadie drove down the main street of the rural Pennsylvanian town. The locals stood in the doorways, frowns carving their faces as they stared at the teeming soldiers. The waitresses at the diner peered through the windows with their arms folded tightly over their aproned bosoms. Behind the backs of the passing soldiers, men spat onto the asphalt. Surveillance drones hovered overhead. Tanks idled in front of the small town's post office. Gas drilling equipment rolled down the street. Soldiers barked out orders. Military law had superseded local and state regulation and was escorting the extractive energy industry right into people's backyards.

Charlie swallowed hard and sent a silent apology to Zadie's father for doubting him all this time. Operation American Extraction was definitely *not* a conspiracy theory. The continent was being raped for fossil fuel export. In his mind, Charlie heard Bill's humorless laugh.

"Conspiracy theory is a neat little label that the government uses to fool people into discounting the truth," Bill had once argued, "but pipelines don't lie. Twenty new coal shipping terminals on the west coast, refinery upgrades, permits, licenses . . . the evidence is all part of the public record for those that have the persistence to track it down and put the pieces together."

The once-peaceful streets of the town seethed with infuriation. Tension twanged metallic on the air. Animosity fumed from the people like churning smokestacks. Everyone knew fossil fuels were a death sentence for the entire planet. The carbon emissions, global warming, climate change, even the extraction processes for oil, natural gas, and coal destroyed the earth and poisoned the water . . . but as long as export to China, India, and global industry remained an option, *the Butcher, the Banker,* and *the Candlestick Maker* continued to move full-steam ahead toward destruction.

For a long time, everyone thought the threat of climate change would stop this madness, but the corporate-controlled media created a complete obstruction of common sense and scientific truth. The United States was playing a sinister blend of make-believe and monopoly at the cost of human extinction. The landscape of the immediate future was choked with oily rivers, cracked deserts instead of fertile farmland, toxins leaching through watersheds, mountains blown apart, and radiation left to blow on the wind.

"People won't stand for it," Charlie had once argued with Bill, "they'll revolt."

"You think those in power don't know this?" Bill had replied. "They've got the laws in place for mass arrests, civilian murder, indefinite detention, military tribunals, and martial law. The people, for the most part, are clueless." He swept a gesture to the nation. "Lambs at the slaughterhouse! Jews on the way to the Holocaust!"

The people just didn't want to believe it was happening. They would sit around chewing on the cud of rumors for endless hours while the machinery of extraction crept closer to their doorsteps. They would bicker and argue themselves to death, not wanting to believe the horror of the truth. Charlie's heart turned sad as he pictured his cousins sickened with toxins, his mother weary and rundown. He pictured his grand-père's eyes, so often laced with mischief. He heard the old man's words, *life, liberty, and love? Who will stand up for it?*

*I will,* Charlie thought as he drove past a row of soldiers.

"This is insanity!" Zadie protested. "They're using martial law to march the corporations right in and poison the watersheds! How can they destroy all of life for the greed of a few?"

"Why should they care?" Charlie questioned bitterly. "They've got enough money to buy the last pristine places, purify their private homes, and live out the remainder of their days in relative comfort while the rest of the world dies in agony."

"But how can they? They have no right!" Zadie argued.

"They had no right to enslave Africans," Charlie mentioned, "or to take this land from the native tribes, but that didn't stop the powerful from insisting on their right to profit from their *property.*"

Zadie's expressive eyes glowed like burnt embers.

"This is it, Charlie. This is the final showdown between the force of greed and the power of love. Either we're going to stop this extraction, or we are going to perish."

They swung into the parking lot behind the public library. Bill had heard the news of the gas company's military escort from a local man named Rudy and had arranged for Charlie and Zadie to drive down from New York and meet with him. The stocky fellow was found leaning on the circulation desk talking in hushed tones with the head librarian. She caught sight of the two newcomers and nudged his shoulder. Rudy turned, shook Charlie's hand, and doffed his baseball cap to Zadie.

"Glad you could make it. We're in a real sight of trouble, oh Lord, let me tell you." His eyes flicked outside to where the soldiers idled in the street. Rudy led them down into the partially renovated basement of the library, between some rolling bookcases, and into a small musty side room made of stone. There were no windows. Water ran down the old granite walls. The lamp overhead struggled vainly to shove out a dim patch of light. Zadie shivered at the chill, pulling her sweater coat tightly around her torso and wishing she'd worn thick pants instead of thin leggings under a skirt. She ran her fingers up and down the goose bumps on her arms. She had been uneasy about driving down, but Rudy was desperate for advice, and Charlie wanted to see the situation firsthand. Rudy pulled out three folding chairs from a stack against the wall.

"This old storage room dates back to the Revolutionary War. I'd have taken you to my place," he explained apologetically, "but they're watching it 'cause I told those soldiers to get the hell out of my town."

Rudy looked unrepentant. There was a time and a place for soldiers . . . and his rural little town in Pennsylvania wasn't it! He tolerated their shenanigans on the Fourth of July, but that's as far as his patience went. He was a God-fearing, flag-waving American citizen, but soldiers were for defending this country - not for protecting a bunch of greedy corporations as they extracted fossil fuels against the will of the people.

Rudy whipped off his baseball cap and smacked it across his knee.

"The army rolled the tanks right down Main Street with the gas company machines in the middle and soldiers marching behind! I couldn't believe my eyes. I asked 'em what the hell they were doing. They told me they were enforcing the Constitution."

Charlie gaped.

"Uh-huh," Rudy nodded, "they said the gas company's got mineral rights, and they're here to make sure those rights get upheld. Told me that we passed some unconstitutional laws, so

they're here to make justice. Well, I have to confess to losing
my temper."

Rudy had plunked himself down smack in front of the tanks
and let loose a spew of outrage that gathered half the town as he
ranted about crooked politicians over in D.C. who passed
unconstitutional laws faster than beans passed gas! And
speaking of gas, the military had no right to escort the gas
company in here. Ain't nowhere in the law book did it say the
military got to decide on justice! That's what the justice
department was for - at which point the soldiers informed him
of the nuances of justice in times of martial law - to which he
roared out, martial law my ass! Get your thievin' conniving
tank-wielding hides out of my town!

"See," Rudy informed Charlie and Zadie, "a long time back,
this town passed a Community Rights Ordinance to ban
fracking for natural gas and to protect the rights of nature. We
all risked sounding like tree huggers 'cause we had to do
something to keep the gas company from poisoning our wells.
The scumbags up at the state and federal levels will allow
nuclear testing at your dinner table if someone pays 'em enough.
So, we passed the darn thing 'cause we didn't have much other
choice. There was talk of lawsuits, but I dunno, it just stopped
all of a sudden. I thought we were off scott-free . . . until now."

Rudy shuddered and rubbed his rough palm across his two-
day stubble.

"Anybody with two bits of common sense to rub together
can see that what's going on is just plain *wrong*," Rudy said.
"Those soldiers out there should be protecting the people from
being poisoned, not escorting the corporations right into our
backyards!"

He snorted in outrage.

"The troops got real nasty about my li'l sermon. They

threatened to court-martial me, but settled for simply reading the town the riot act."

The commanding officer had told the people in no uncertain terms that he expected compliance with orders and obedience of curfews at dusk. He wanted no backtalk, and demanded full cooperation with the troops as they settled this matter with the gas company.

"Essentially, we were supposed to lie down like a bunch of cowering dogs! We broke curfew right off - no sense in obeying that - and held a meeting that night. Folks were all up in arms, crying foul and reaching for their guns, but I said, you're all a bunch of damn fools. What's your shotgun gonna do to a tank?"

"That was quick thinking, Rudy," Charlie sighed in relief.

"Just common sense," the man shrugged. "I told 'em, if we wage war, we're just gonna get butchered. We gotta wage peace until we send 'em all packing! So, I got folks cooled down, but I can't claim to be no Gandhi, you know? I need advice 'cause there ain't no way in hell we can let 'em frack this town. We only got one watershed and if that's poisoned, that's it." He made a choking sound in his throat. "The whole town'll go. I've seen it in other places."

"Have you been in touch with the other towns in the area?"

"Yeah, they got soldiers, too, same as us and every other place that passed laws to keep the extractive energy industry out. They expect resistance."

"Well, they're going to get it," Charlie promised. "First of all, where do the local police stand?"

"They're pissed off and squirming under the thumb of the army. So far as they're concerned, they swore an oath to protect the people. We passed a law banning fracking, fair and square. Their job is to enforce the laws."

"Wow. You've got some good cops here."

"Yep. We do," Rudy said proudly.

"And how about the people? Are they just blowing hot air and waving shotguns, or are they ready to act?"

Rudy gave him a look. He knew his people. They'd bluster and procrastinate to high heaven, but dammit, when something had to be done, it got done. They were working folks. They drove trucks, dug ditches, poured asphalt, hammered steel, cut lumber, baled hay, loaded freight . . . they weren't afraid of hard work and you couldn't call any one of them a coward. He nodded.

"Alright," Charlie said, running his fingers through his hair. "If we weren't in martial law, there'd be a lot of ways to slow the gas industry down and make this hard on them. Even as it is, they may still need certain permits, road clearances, and licenses. If you insist on those things, you've at least got a place to dig your heels in and resist to the fullest extent of the law. Just because they've got an army guarding them doesn't mean the town clerk can't make their life miserable. Can he or she misplace some files for a while?"

"Cathy?" Rudy snorted. "That's her specialty."

"Perfect, try to slow them down with paperwork. If the military waives it all, well, then there are other options. Have they got their rigs completely in yet?"

"No. That's what they're trying to do now, but the mud's too soft."

"Good. Slow them down, maybe dig some large ditches for culvert replacements on the roads that go out to the wells."

"But we don't need any culvert - " Rudy truncated his words as he suddenly got what Charlie was driving at. "Mmm-hmm, I know the guy who owns the backhoe. He'd be happy to dig some deep, wide ditches in those back roads."

"Exactly. It takes a long time for culverts to come in,

especially if they never got ordered. Where are they getting their water from?"

"John Payton's cow pond."

"Can you get him to drain it?"

"Sure. He's been fuming 'bout breaking the dam since they marched in with the army. He said he ain't never given them no permit to take his water. They got his family's mineral rights back in the Depression . . . but this whole nonsense about building a road smack on top of his wife's petunia garden and suckin' his cow pond dry is just plain too much! A man has got to draw a line."

"Great," Charlie encouraged him. "Also, those soldiers and the gas company workers are going to need services while they're here - "

"Well, I'll be damned if they get it!" Rudy cried. "My sister's got the best diner in town and she says she just plain won't serve them. If they make her at gunpoint, she swears that she'll piss in the soup."

"Good for her," Charlie chuckled. "Talk with the other shop owners and especially the gas stations. Some folks will be too scared to resist, but let's get the others on board. They can close down for a while, maybe put up a sign; *closed for death in the family.*"

"Gone fishin'," Rudy wisecracked.

"Okay, you get it," Charlie said. "Be creative about it, but be careful, too. Get the other towns around here to follow suit. Hunker down and hold on. Keep your ear to the ground for friends or neighbors who are getting too pissed off and simmer them down. Don't monkey wrench or destroy gas company property, either. It's grounds for arrest and makes the company men feel like they have a right to beat people up. You've got to make it clear to everybody that the government is out of line to send in troops when they ought to be fighting laws in court."

"The community rights ordinances have held up in court more than once," Rudy mentioned.

"Yeah, that's why this is all happening. The rights of nature are one and the same as human rights, and the oil, gas, and coal industry has been tromping on them both for far too long. Now that we're facing major environmental crisis, the handwriting is on the wall for fossil fuels, but they just don't want to lay down and die."

"Hell," Rudy snorted, "neither do we."

"We won't," Charlie assured him firmly. He paused and thought for a moment. "There's only so long the President can continue martial law . . . the people are already blowing steam out their ears because of it, and the morale of the troops in the city is sinking lower every day. If you can hold out and resist long enough, we can work on ending martial law and getting the military out of the equation."

"We're gonna need some support with basic things," Rudy pointed out. "If our stores close down, we still need groceries and the like."

"Yeah," Charlie sighed, "and it's not just you guys. Every town that has a pipeline, coal mine, a shipping port, or an oil refinery is probably also looking at soldiers and tanks right now. We need to get some infrastructure in place for basic necessities for all the resistors. Zadie? Do you know anybody who likes to be a switchboard operator?"

"Yeah, Charlie, but - "

"Good. Let's get ahold of them and start planning some resource strategy."

"My wife runs the local branch of thrift stores," Rudy offered.

"Really?!" Charlie's eyes lit up.

"Yeah, they got trucks and delivery routes into two other states, too. They're a real regular thing. Folks drop off their junk, and my wife's team sorts it and sends it out. They got networks with other chains, too. I'll talk to her 'bout it." Rudy promised.

"That could make all the difference in the world. You're going to have to try to outlast this martial law."

"Charlie," Zadie interrupted anxiously, "we gotta go. I have a feeling - "

Charlie glanced at her. She was already on her feet, eyes flicking around in alarm, worry written all over her face. They heard a rustle coming through the basement. The head librarian rushed through the narrow passageway of the rolling stacks.

"Rudy," she hissed, "there's a cop upstairs! He says he's looking for a terrorist. Some guy known as *the Man From the North* and he's got a photo of - " she broke off. Her eyes widened in recognition as she pointed at Charlie.

" . . . him!"

# CHAPTER TWELVE

. . . . .

## *Blue Ridge Run*

Before they could register what happened, Charlie and Zadie found themselves out of the library and hurtling down the interstate in Rudy's old pickup.

"Take it, take it!" he had insisted. "I got two more in the yard. I'll pull the plates off your car and hide it in the junkyard where all the abandoned vehicles get towed. Just go!"

Zadie drove out of town with Charlie hiding down on the floor of the cab. Charlie thought he would die of cramped anxiety as the truck rumbled slowly through the twenty-five mph section of town. His heart flopped in a mantra repeating, *it was just routine, just a routine search, they didn't know I was there, it was just one cop doing a basic sweep.* No swarms of police officers surrounded them. No checkpoints stopped them. Finally, Zadie floored the gas and shifted gears as she climbed up onto the freeway. She looked around anxiously for surveillance drones. Nothing. She checked the rearview mirror in case they were being followed. Nothing. She stayed just under the speed limit and was reassured as the other cars sped past. Charlie rolled out and buckled up as the steady speed of traffic settled their pounding hearts.

Zadie let her breath out in a whoosh. Her fingers laced with his and squeezed them before letting go. Both of them were shaking slightly. Her heart thudded in her chest. Her blood raced in her veins. Wild disbelief rose up in her.

"Did we really just evade arrest?" she blurted out.

They exploded into laughter at the same time, wheezing in

huge fat howls of surreal humor, choking on shock.

"It's . . . not . . . funny!" he tried to say.

"N-no," she howled, but neither could stop. Finally, the truck wove a little and they sobered up.

"They're really looking for me," he said, swallowing hard. Until now, it had only been rumors and unease, but now the authorities had pinned his identity down.

"Are you having second thoughts?" she asked.

"No," he answered. "I'm already thinking of all the work we have to do next."

Their eyes shot up and tackled each other, shaken, but still determined.

They filled up the gas tank in Virginia. Zadie went in to use the restroom and came running back out a minute later.

"You're all over the news. They're running ads about the terrorist Charlie Rider, *the Man From the North!* The government is enlisting the people's assistance in tracking you down."

"Well, that's the first thing I'll have to write about," Charlie said furiously as they hastily pulled out. "Until the government has a better track record in the processes of justice, the populace shouldn't be aiding and abetting them in destroying citizens' lives!"

The next gas station had a poster hung on the bulletin board outside: Charlie Rider WANTED TERRORIST. Zadie indignantly pulled it down.

"Don't do that," a woman snapped at her.

Zadie refrained from saying that she was a big fan of Charlie Rider's work and intended to get the poster signed.

"Why not?" she asked instead.

"He's a terrorist!" the woman practically shrieked.

"Oh?" Zadie responded evenly. "What has he done?"

The woman looked at her like she was from Mars.

"He's all over the news."

"So are the latest celebrities," Zadie pointed out.

"No," the woman said in exasperation. "He's on the news as a terrorist!"

"But what did he do?" Zadie repeated.

The woman looked at her in confusion. Zadie clarified.

"Did he blow up a building? Attack somebody? Destroy the government's computer system?"

"No . . . but he must have done *something* to get on the news like that."

"Wouldn't the news tell you what he had done?"

"Maybe it's classified," the woman said stubbornly.

"Or maybe it's nonexistent," Zadie answered back. "Maybe he hasn't done anything."

The woman paused and frowned. Then a gleam of satisfaction broke over her face.

"He wrote those articles!" she cried triumphantly. "That's what he did! He's *the Man from the North.*"

"Have you ever read those articles?" Zadie asked her.

"Of course not!" she denied emphatically. "Do I look like a terrorist?"

"Does he?" she asked, looking down at the poster of Charlie.

"Well, you never can tell," the other woman sniffed.

"His articles would tell you, if you read them," Zadie muttered.

"Oh! I wouldn't do that. They're banned!" she hissed. She looked fearfully around in case they had been overheard and then rushed into the convenience store.

"They've got a lot of nerve to label me as a terrorist," Charlie complained as they drove away. "All I've ever done is urge nonviolence!"

"That nuance is probably lost on them," Zadie pointed out. "You're urging insurrection and they've got to stop you. We need to hide, Charlie. Your picture is everywhere."

"They're using me to distract everyone from martial law," Charlie muttered.

"Or as an excuse to prolong it," Zadie added thoughtfully. "The Search for Charlie Rider will be primetime news until they catch you. Martial law will be touted as a great aid to tracking you down. The military will get involved. The cops will throw up roadblocks and mount search parties without warrants. The armed forces will conduct interrogations . . . and I bet that the people will scramble to help them, too."

He sighed in agreement and looked out the window. Crawling across the American landscape were thousands of people who went about their business, swallowed the television's lies without blinking, and showed up to work day after day. Jesus called them *lambs*; the anarchists labeled them *sheeple*; both terms described the great flock of followers that huddled in a frightened cluster while the wolves picked off the sick, the oddballs, and the weak. Charlie felt such frustrated affection for them. On their plump and wooly backs grew the comforts of society. They fed the nation. They clothed the people. They were kind to their own. They respected their leaders, maintained order, and brought up wonderful children.

For *the Man From the North*, they were more dangerous than wolves.

They were so frightened of stepping out of line that they would trot to the slaughterhouse with a self-satisfied *baaahh*. If you tried to warn them, they kicked with their hooves and butted their stubborn heads. They feared the unusual more than familiar tyranny. Charlie shook his head at such folly. Couldn't they see that the shepherds trained the dogs that nipped them into line? Couldn't they understand that the wolves were at the door because the shepherds let them in the gate? Charlie sighed. Couldn't they see that shepherds raised sheep for the butchers?

*Come on,* he urged silently to the invisible masses. Before fences and shepherds, leaders of flocks came from the flock. They led toward better pastures, toward safety, toward life. *Even the tender shepherds want to eat you,* he told the people silently, *and the cruel ones abuse you until you are roasted.*

Charlie laid his forehead on the truck window and tried to picture this unimaginable flock as a collection of distinct human beings. He had seen them in the supermarket, at the bank, the gas station. He could picture them, one by one: the fat man on the treadmill, the pair of bony legs at the coffee shop, a sweating brow under a hardhat, that pudgy baby clutching his mother, the teenager with acne . . . one of them would be the death of him.

"The well-intentioned do-gooder," he said to Zadie, "is our greatest danger."

She nodded in agreement.

"Especially now that the televisions are blaring out that you're a terrorist. Most of the country is frothing at the mouth from the latest attacks."

"But I didn't do those," Charlie protested.

"People don't care," Zadie groaned. "They hear the word *terrorist* and stop thinking straight."

Charlie swore.

"I can't just drop out of sight. I've got to write something about the soldiers in Pennsylvania and the continuation of martial law."

"They'll be watching the Internet like gamblers at a slot

machine," she told him. "You put out an article and they'll be surrounding us in minutes. Lupe is going to be in hot water over this."

Charlie groaned as the knife of worry split him open and salted the wound with guilt. Hundreds, if not thousands, of people had seen him at Lupe's during the evacuations.

"She'll get through it," Zadie said, trying to convince herself that it was true. "She may look like an innocent suburban mom, but Lupe is as crafty as her mother and twice the liar. She'll claim she didn't know . . . you seemed so nice . . . who would have guessed?"

"What I want to know is who tipped the Feds off?" Charlie asked.

"Good question," Zadie agreed. "Your family would never have revealed that you're *the Man From the North*. Zipper wouldn't have done it. Aubrey takes secrets to the grave. Who else knows?"

Spark Plug. If that punk had been arrested, he would spill the connection to get his own hide out of jail. But then again, Charlie rationalized, Spark Plug didn't know his name was Charlie Rider - none of the anarchists did. He tucked his suspicions away and turned the conversation back to strategizing.

"We have to find out if the Feds suspect you're with me, Zadie," Charlie mentioned. "They'll track us both using your - "

"My phone!" Zadie exclaimed. "I left it in the back of your car!"

"Should we risk trying to get it?"

"No - I mean, yes - oooh," Zadie moaned. "I don't know. They can track those phones even when they're off. It's not in my name - not my real one, anyway - but if they figure out the connection, they'll be crawling all over Rudy's junkyard by tomorrow."

"We could call Rudy from a payphone and find out. I've got his number scribbled down in my wallet," Charlie suggested. "We could tell him to smash the phone."

"No!" Zadie exclaimed. "All my contact numbers are in there! We can't destroy it without getting those, Charlie."

Charlie groaned. Without those numbers, they had no place to hole up and no way to send out articles to the underground network. He suggested calling Bill or Aubrey to get them, but Zadie thought it would be risky to contact anyone in the Dandelion Insurrection right now. They had to find out if the Feds were tracking Zadie. They strategized in dizzying circles as they crossed the northern farmlands of the Shenandoah Valley and climbed up onto the Blue Ridge Parkway. They figured the winding, forested road was out-of-sight, out-of-mind. Adrenaline dissipated from their bloodstreams, leaving them wrung out and weary.

"Thunderheads," Zadie pointed out. In the distance, a cloud mass rolled toward them, black and thick. A solid sheet of rain curtained the road to the south.

"So much for camping," Charlie sighed.

"There's bound to be a motel along the way."

"We don't have any money, Zadie," he reminded her. "The minute I use my debit card, they'll be on our backs."

"I've got my card."

"What if they know we're together?"

She thought about that for a moment.

"Well, I've got enough cash for a room and some food, but I'll have to get more."

"How?"

She shrugged and didn't answer. The gray hanging clouds pulled shadows down across the land as they drove south. The sun dipped through a westerly split in the clouds, blinding them with an arrow of light just as the first smack of rain whacked the windshield. By the time they reached the first rural route that crawled down the mountainside into a town, the rain was pummeling them in relentless torrents. The tiny hotel was a welcome sight.

Zadie paid for the room while Charlie slouched low in the truck with a ball cap shoved down over his face. She kept one eye on the lobby television. The search for *the Man From the North* did not include any mention of her. Zadie breathed a sigh of relief. Their room was cramped, but clean. Chilled and hungry, Charlie started making notes for the next article on some blank paper, even though he had no idea how or when they could release it. Zadie hopped in the shower to warm up. She sniffed her clothes. They reeked of adrenaline and sweat. She sighed and put them on anyway, telling Charlie she was going to go rustle up some food.

"It might take me a while," she said, catching her lip.

"Don't worry," he answered absently, trying to hold onto the teasing thought he was jotting down. "I'll just be here writing."

"Okay."

She left. Charlie hunkered down to write. He wrestled with long and complicated thoughts, compressed them into succinct sentences, and racked his brain for important angles to explore. It was close to two in the morning when Charlie heard the truck cough to a stop outside the hotel. He blinked and rubbed his hand across his eyes as the numbers on the digital clock swam. His stomach stabbed him as Zadie jostled the key in the lock and came in.

"What took so long?" he asked. She looked exhausted.

"No grocery store for thirty miles," she complained, "and

then it was closed. I had to drive to the next town over, but I got food."

They laid out a small picnic on the bed, eating with their hands. Zadie wasn't in the mood for talking, nor could they hear each other over the rat-a-tat-tat racket of the rain on the roof. Charlie's mind kept fussing with words in the article. He looked up from his scribbles to see Zadie had fallen sound asleep, awkwardly curled in the narrow strip of bed above the remnants of their dinner. He cleared off the bed and convinced her to wake up long enough to get under the covers. Then exhaustion grabbed him. As he drifted off, he noticed the gray light of dawn was already kicking at the window.

Eleven o'clock checkout came far too soon. They wearily chugged up the ridge again. They drove hard the whole day, feeling an itchy need to put the miles behind them. The second day blended into the third. One night, they slept in the cramped cab of the truck, waking stiff and irritable the next morning. The curves of the road and constant trees became monotonous. The meals of bread and hummus grew stale. They pulled into a hotel parking lot under another sheet of rain. Charlie unlocked the room and snapped on the lights. Zadie paused in the doorway.

"Are you going to write tonight, Charlie?" she asked.

"I should. We can use the articles if we could find some way to get them to Bill or Aubrey or somebody," he said, looking at a handwritten notice taped to the phone. The room had no long distance calling. There was a payphone outside that he could use to call Rudy and find out if the Feds had been looking for them. He sighed. He dreaded standing in the cold rain that long. The booth would provide little relief from the slant of the wind-blown torrents, but at least people wouldn't be looking at him too closely as they hustled in from their cars. Zadie nodded. She seemed equally disheartened.

"I'll go get another load of supplies," she sighed. "We're running short on everything."

"Alright," Charlie answered. They ducked in opposite directions through the rain. He waved as she pulled out. She didn't wave back. He dialed Rudy's number and waited while it rang. Charlie squinted, trying to hear over the storm. Water squeezed in the cracked rubber soles of his sneakers. On the fifth ring, the message machine picked up, but he didn't dare say anything. He hung up and dodged back through the rain. Charlie paced the cramped hotel room, feeling hampered at every turn. His mind chewed doggedly at their situation, going over every option again in his mind. *What we need is a secure encrypted web system*, he griped to himself. Such things existed. The government hadn't made them illegal; the corporations simply made them unaffordable. Privacy was a privilege of the wealthy. Everyone else had to resign to being read like a book. *There must be pirated software out there*, he thought, but Zadie had never mentioned it. Maybe the government tracked it. Or maybe it just cost too much. Charlie's mind ran around in circles. He tried to write, but the words drowned in the depressing onslaught of the rain. At some point, he crashed into sleep. He woke the next morning with his cheek pressed against the pages and a painful crick in his neck. Zadie sat slumped in a chair, staring out the hotel window. Dark circles had formed under her eyes. Her shoulders sagged. The fire had gone out of her, extinguished by damp weather and late nights.

"Are you alright, Zadie?" he asked, rubbing his eyes.

She turned her face away until her profile was etched in the morning sunlight that pushed through the window. He could see the quiver in her lip as she tried to bite it back.

"What is it?" he pressed.

"I'm just tired, Charlie," she answered dully.

"What if we slow down today?" he offered. "They're not on our tail at this moment. Maybe we could go sit with some of those trees we've been racing through."

"Yeah," she said in a small voice. "That'd be nice."

He reached for her hand and squeezed it.

"C'mon, let's drive up the ridge and pretend like the country isn't crazy."

She laughed sadly, but agreed.

She climbed into the truck and Charlie fought with the sticky transmission as they climbed back up onto the parkway. He drove until he saw a pullout that dipped out of view. They climbed out of the car and sat in the thick meadow grasses, leaning their backs against a sun-warmed rock. The trees parted into a wide vista of hazy mountains. The wind ruffled spring's tender leaves. The sounds of the forest slipped around them. Songbirds serenaded. Squirrels scolded. Twigs cracked under the footsteps of an unseen animal down below. Zadie quietly spoke.

"The hero stories don't tell you about the part where you're scared, tired to the bone, not eating right, sleeping at odd hours, and wearing the same old clothes because you can't take the risk to go shopping."

She dropped her head and looked down at herself.

"I'm *dirty*, Charlie. Not with good healthy soil, but with the grime of humanity, like the worst human behaviors are leaving a film of exhaustion and fearful sweat on me that I can't scrape off no matter how many showers I take."

"Nah," he disagreed, nudging her shoulder with his. "They can't weigh you down with their grime. Look at that." He pointed out into the clouds above the mountain ridges where a little bird was struggling in a strong updraft. "You're like that bird. Inside you, there's a heart that refuses to stop trying even when the rest of you is bone-weary."

She smiled slightly, grateful for his kind words.

"You're such a good friend to me, Charlie."

"I know," he answered happily. "I'm the best friend you've got."

"You always have been, you know?"

"Mmm-hmm," he replied. "You've been a good friend to me, too."

"Me?" she scoffed. "What have I ever done for you except ruin your life?"

"Well, aside from that," he wisecracked, thinking about the FBI agents tracking him. Then he saw her crestfallen expression and groaned. "Zadie, I'm joking."

"I wasn't."

"Well, maybe my life was meant to be ruined by you. Ever think of that? Maybe I wasn't supposed to do things normally and you were meant to come and make sure of that." He glanced at her solemn expression. She wasn't thrilled by this concept. He shrugged. He didn't mind . . . too much.

"Come on, Zadie. What would I have done without you?"

"Oh, I don't know," she sighed. "Maybe you would have lived a nice quiet life."

"Fat chance in this world," he replied. "I mean whoever gets to live the American Dream, huh? House, car, two kids, a dog-"

"A wife in a 1950's house dress," Zadie reminded him.

"With an apron."

"And a perm."

They both smiled.

"What a crock of shit!" Charlie snorted.

Humor conquered weariness. The sun and stillness settled both of them, drying out their anxiety, and relaxing their bodies slowly. Zadie rolled her head sideways on the rock, a smile spreading across her lips.

"I'm picturing you in penny loafers," she said, "reading the Sunday paper."

"In a bathrobe," he put in, "over plaid pajamas."

"With the kids on the floor reading the comics . . . one adorable little girl."

"And one strapping young boy," he added.

"Blonde hair and brown eyes?"

"Blue-grey. Like their mom," Charlie said.

Zadie stiffened. The smile vanished. Charlie's heart sank. He had carried the joke too far. They were perched on the precipice of truth, hearts pounding, looking down at the jagged rocks of unrequited love. Charlie cursed himself for the slip. Zadie looked down at the ground.

"Some dreams aren't meant to come true, Charlie."

Time froze. Charlie looked away awkwardly. Neither said anything. *She's practically told you this a thousand times,* Charlie chided himself. *She's not interested.* The world turned sharp before his gaze. Each leaf, each stone, each swaying blade of grass mocked him. The sky's blueness took on an edge of bitterness. His thoughts turned darker than a mountain storm.

This whole country was built on dreamers and speculators, Charlie thought, a bunch of suckers seduced by glossy images of flat, fertile farmlands, mountains of gold, and an entire continent full of nothing but freedom. Must have been heartbreaking when they got here and found rocky coasts, dense trees, biting insects, ice, cold . . . not to mention thousands of native people already turned against them from earlier massacres. Should have been a real wake-up call, Charlie thought, but instead, we just kept insisting on *our* dream, butchering natives, enslaving Africans, grabbing land as if it were free for the taking . . . and we're still doing it, turning the dream into a nightmare by refusing to wake up, condemning every man, woman, and child in this country to the butcher's knife of export, extraction, and greed.

Charlie's eyes turned bitter. Twelve years of dreams evaporated faster than mist from the mountain ridges; Zadie, house, kids, and that grand dream of the American culture, the one that promised; *if you work hard enough, you get to live in blissful perfection.* All fall, he'd been grappling with the truth that the country faced nothing but a long uphill struggle to maintain sanity and democracy. He was never going to live the American Dream, no one was, but he had been refusing to rouse himself to complete wakefulness. The whole government, the corporations, rich people, poor people; everybody was living a lie, buying into a dream that wasn't ever going to come true.

"Come on," he muttered, "wake up."

"What?" Zadie asked.

He startled, not realizing he had spoken aloud. She looked dazed, as if his words had pulled her from her own dream-turned-into-a-nightmare.

"Nothing," he said, running his hands across his face. "I'm just telling myself to wake up."

"Are you tired? You were writing all night," she said.

"No, not from writing," he sighed. "I'm *weary* of all the stupid things people do. I'm tired of our folly and our inability to just love each other and take care of each other." Charlie's eyes turned hot with conviction. He stood up from the rock. "We can't keep lusting after a dream. We've got to wake up! We've got to become aware . . . active . . . "

"Alive," Zadie said. Her eyes shot out and pierced the forested ridges. The day pulsed around them in the slow heartbeat of the world. The whir of insects filled the air. A tumble of wind shook the meadow grasses. The itch of pollen tickled their noses. Sunshine poured its liquid warmth down their faces. The buzz of bees vibrated in their blood veins.

"Look at this Earth, Charlie," she said slowly, gesturing to the great expanse of cloud-swept mountains. "Life wants to live, but, more than that, it wants to love. It must love. Survival is not enough. Despair and hatred, loneliness and cruelty - those are the calling cards of death. Life turns tenderly toward itself, embracing and enveloping. But now, life is struggling to live and there's nowhere left to run. We're all going to live or die according to what happens with the Dandelion Insurrection. Not just us, but the whole planet."

He nodded. He felt it, too.

"Zadie, I have to ask you something."

"Yes?"

His heart was breaking as he searched for the words. There was only one thing in his life that he had wanted more than the success of the Dandelion Insurrection . . . and she had just told him it was all a dream. He stood in the grass, looking out at the vacant blue of the sky, feeling empty as a mirror, vast and unafraid. He had no dreams left. Just a reality etched sharply before his eyes. He was ready to fight for life, even to his own death.

"I think we should part ways here, Zadie," he said. Her mouth dropped open. He held up his hand as she started to protest. "I'm not running anymore. There's work to do and it's going to be dangerous. The agents are already hunting me," he shrugged, "but they aren't hunting you. You'd be better off without me - "

Zadie shot out of the grass so fast that he jumped back in alarm. She jabbed him in the chest, on fire with indignation.

"Are you saying you want to ditch me? Now? After all we've

been through?!" she exclaimed.

"Aw, no, Zadie!" he stammered. "I would never *want* to ditch you. It's just - "

"Shove it, Charlie Rider," she told him, spinning on her heel. "You're stuck with me. Get in the truck." She pounded across the grass. He jogged after her and passed her at the parking lot. She halted abruptly as he reached for the passenger side door.

"What do you think you're doing?" she demanded. "We had a deal, remember?"

She pushed him toward the driver's side.

"You drive. I tell you where to go."

# CHAPTER THIRTEEN

. . . . .

*Resist!*

Zadie navigated them through the narrow capillaries of the great vascular system of American highways. They traversed back roads so tiny that no one bothered to put up names or finish paving them. She didn't consult a map. She headed north in an intuitive migration that meandered back toward Rudy's town. They didn't see a single roadblock, soldier, cop, or any other living soul. Just before they arrived, Zadie pulled into a gas station to call Rudy.

"Is that my niece?" Rudy exclaimed, speaking in code, knowing that every phone call would be recorded and reviewed. "Shoot! Young lady, I've been waiting for you to call. Thinkin' of visiting soon?"

"Yeah, actually. I left my phone - "

"'Course you did. Sorry to say my neighbor's kid got ahold of it, hacked into your info, and then ended up breaking the whole thing. I'll pay for a new one, but I did manage to wrangle your phone numbers out of the little horror."

"Thanks!" Zadie exclaimed in relief. "Uh, have any friends of mine been around lately?"

"Naw, it's too boring out here. You should come visit. It's a good place for rest and relaxation, even if the soldiers are still camped out downtown. I'll fix up my mother's place. What do you say?"

Zadie said she'd be there in half an hour, hung up, and backtracked along the route they had taken out of Rudy's town a week ago. The tanks were still parked in front of the post office. The shops were now closed up. The diner had a sign that read: *Cook your own damn dinner!*

Rudy hid Charlie up in his mother's attic. The venerable old lady lived in a farmhouse on the outskirts of town. Charlie used the contact information recovered from Zadie's phone to begin circulating articles again. Zadie ascertained that the Feds weren't looking for her, as far as anyone knew. She stayed low profile as she showed up at meetings as Rudy's niece and helped the besieged townspeople slow the processes of extraction. Zadie encouraged a campaign of courteous noncooperation intended to earn the respect of the soldiers while sending them a clear message that their protection of the corporations was out of line.

"They've got enough guns to wipe out the world. Let's make sure they think twice about using them . . . not through fear, but through love."

It was a tough position to take as the first gas tower rose up in their pastures. Irritation flared and patience snapped. Zadie talked down violence one angry farmer at a time.

"Look," she explained, "there's a silver lining to having soldiers on your doorstep. We can use this time to tell the troops that we want them on our side! As soon as the soldiers are sent back to their base, we've lost our chance to communicate with them. We've got to make sure the soldiers know why they should disobey the orders of their commanders and help the citizens protect their own country!"

They looked at her skeptically as she explained that, in the long run, their strength rested on connecting to the military and persuading them to lay down their guns or stand aside.

"Someday," she promised, "those soldiers are going to stick up for us . . . but not if we start throwing rocks at them."

*Underneath every uniform is someone's son or daughter who is being used as a pawn for politics,* Charlie wrote for his next article. *Kindness is the Dandelion Insurrection's greatest strength. It can erase divisions that are being used against us. We must remind the soldiers of their humanity, their connection to this land, and their kinship with the people.*

In response, people began to post signs along the roads for the soldiers.

*Don't allow profit to poison the country you swore to defend!*

When the gas company tore the signs down, Zadie encouraged the people to stand on the crossroads and street corners with posters that reminded the soldiers that their own hometowns were affected by extraction as well. Rudy rallied the townspeople to walk around with signs that read,

*Your mother.*

*Your father.*

*Your sister.*

*Your brother.*

*Your home.*

*Your farm.*

*Your well.*

Rudy's sister brought them cookies and lemonade, apologizing that she couldn't serve them at the diner.

"You men and women are fine folks, I can tell. So are the workers, for the most part. It's just the fracking, itself, and the gas company, you see. We've got to be clear that they're not welcome in our town. I'm sure you understand. You come back sometime . . . and I'll show you a real small town welcome!"

Rudy, having a penchant for monologues, spent hours standing around with the soldiers arguing about the immorality of classifying civilians as the enemy and the challenges of meeting one's *true call of duty.* He urged the soldiers to disobey unethical orders. The Nuremburg trials set a precedent that shouldn't be ignored. *Just following orders* was not an excuse accepted by posterity.

"If your general told you to drop the atomic bomb, would you do it? I wouldn't!" Rudy exclaimed.

The soldiers told him to go home.

He returned the next day with a retired veteran who went straight up to the troops and commiserated about the state of the world.

"Why are they sending good soldiers like you in to frack wells and put in pipelines, huh? Corruption, that's what's going on. What politicians and corporations can't achieve through law, they do through force! It's a shame - a crying shame - to see the armed forces used this way."

*The Man From the North* sent out essays on the low morale of the troops and the sorrow of men and women who had sworn to defend the country and now found themselves threatening civilians. Soldier suicides had been an issue for decades and concern peaked again. Charlie wrote a second article, urging citizens to do everything they could to support the people underneath the uniforms. People began to send sympathy cards, delivering them in person to ensure the soldiers received them.

*We're sorry you have to do this, too!*

*My son is fracking your mother's well. Let's stop this together!*

*Working with you to end this situation.*

It was hard to tell if the strategy was having any effect until one night Rudy came to his mother's house long after curfew, shaking from head to toe, but with a huge grin on his ruddy face.

"My God, they coulda had me! I had the wire snips in hand from cutting the phone lines to the gas company's office - I know you said no monkey wrenching, but I laid those wires last year and I'll be damned if they're gonna use 'em to poison me! If they sue me for failure of services, I'll sue them for crimes against humanity! Anyhow, I was getting out of there when I ran smack into the soldiers who were sent to investigate. They looked at me for a minute, kinda surprised. Then this one fella I been talking to just yesterday hissed, *get out of here*, and I scampered. He musta known. He musta!"

All week long, Charlie and Zadie were engaged in a frantic race to make sure the people kept their tempers and frustration in control. Rudy's town was fairly unified against the gas company, but in other places deep-seated animosity over the extraction-export scheme cut communities like a knife. People were starving for work and desperate for jobs. The evening news claimed that the eco-freaks would starve the children to save the whales. Charlie gritted his teeth at the enormous capacities of the corporations' propaganda machine.

"We just have to be twice as clever," Zadie sighed. "We've got to tell people that extraction is the quickest way to kill the economy . . . and ourselves. Let's circulate that; *we're not against the economy, we're against extinction.*"

Economics held the lynchpin to the whole equation. Fear of an empty belly fueled the destruction of the environment. *The Man From the North* put out an article on the myriad ways the corporate cronies of the power elite had destroyed the economy and suppressed the growth of renewable energy.

*Almost everything you've ever heard about economics is a lie,* he wrote; *trickle-down, corporate tax breaks, austerity measures, work harder and you'll get ahead; these are all lies. The economy is a living system, like our bodies, and like the earth. It works best when we support each other. The exchange of money is what creates a healthy economy, not the control and amassing of wealth by the people at the top.*

Great clouds of misinformation obscured the constellations

of truth. Zadie and Charlie had no way of gauging if people were waking up or sinking further into the quagmire of fear. Rudy's town was just one of thousands that were confronting armed soldiers on a daily basis. Clashes occurred constantly. Arrests were made. Houses were raided. People were threatened. As the nation completed its third week of martial law, the frayed patience of the people began to wear out. Charlie watched it carefully, waiting for the exact moment when the smoldering embers would catch on fire.

# CHAPTER FOURTEEN

· · · · ·

## *Cazerolazo Countdown*

*It's time! It's time!* the bird sang outside the attic window. Hidden in Rudy's mother's farmhouse, Charlie looked up from his writing. One by one, the birds had left their huddles on the telephone lines and begun to challenge the stubborn edge of spring. Orioles and chickadees, the starlings, jays, and swallows, the thrushes, finches, and the meadowlarks; all the birds had taken to wing. Warbles sang out from farmyard fences, backyard gardens, and city parks.

*It's time!* the little bird chirped. *The shift in seasons is upon us! It's time! It's time! It's time!*

Charlie scratched his growing stubble and looked longingly out at the bird in the leafing maple tree. He had consoled his itching impatience with a steady stream of writing. That was one thing, at least. The terrorist charges had him cooped up and caged up with clipped wings and chained feet . . . but they hadn't stopped him from writing. He touched his pen to the page.

*It's time!* the bird shrilled from the maple tree.

*I know,* Charlie thought, *it's time for martial law to end . . . but how?*

A stray cow bellowed from the flowerbed. Rudy's mother leaned out the window and banged a copper-bottomed pan with a wooden spoon.

"Go on," she cried. "Git!"

Charlie looked up sharply. The clang of the pan rang in his thoughts. He scrawled an idea down and sent it flying.

157

On the following Monday, people across the country stepped out onto their porches and front stoops with solemn expressions. Arms crossed stubbornly over chests. Twilight turned gray. Curfew fell. They didn't move. Soldiers ordered them inside. Feet stayed planted. *It's time*, they said, *the power's back. The attacks are over. It's time for martial law to end.* The soldiers told them it could only be lifted on the President's orders. The people shrugged. *Consider yourselves warned*, they said. The sun vanished. The people went indoors.

They reappeared in the windows with pots in hands. All across the country, the sound walked where their bodies couldn't. Pots banged out their protest. Rhythm stepped across police blockades. Human spirit connected through the beat. The cacerolazo demonstration came from the Spanish speakers and the French. It passed like wildfire from city to suburb to town, igniting from the frustration of the people.

On Tuesday, the pots and pans rang out at dawn, calling the neighbors out of slumber. *It's time! It's time!* the clatter-racket rhythm insisted. The sharp retorts reverberated into tanks, rattled politicians' offices, drove concentration out the window, disrupted meals, disturbed the peace, and drove officials crazy.

On Wednesday, the people in Rudy's town were banned from banging on pots and pans. They pounded on their tractors and car hoods, instead. The local police were ordered to enforce noise ordinances. They refused. The military banned all drumming. Silence fell.

On Thursday, Inez Hernandez sent a message to Rudy.

"Turn on the radios. We'll broadcast the racket from the city."

Boom boxes appeared in windows. The shops put radios on the roofs. The local musicians hooked up their amplifiers and rang out the rhythms that were reverberating the city.

"Keep drumming!" Inez told her people. "The nation is listening!"

New York City had never pounded so hard.

On Friday night, the city shook. The suburbs shuddered. The rural regions roared. The racket connected cities to towns to countryside. Solidarity united the people. The sound grew monstrous and wild. It thrilled the soul with its thunderous cacophony. The people leaned out their windows, shocked by the uproar they had unleashed, stunned by the magnitude of the protest, awed by the volume of the masses.

On Saturday, the nation was ordered to desist. The response ricocheted back undeniably. There would be no quiet until martial law was ended! *The Man From the North's* last article echoed in their ears: *bang to end curfews! Pound to halt pipelines! Strike to stop gas wells! Hammer to get soldiers off our streets! Whatever your reason, get out your pans. We will not live under the thumb of tyranny!*

On Sunday, the drumming fell into the rhythm of prayer. Hail Mary's wafted with the ping-panging of pots. Churchgoers were told to strike three times in penance, four more in contrition, five times for their souls, and six for a miracle. That night, people swore the Devil got involved. Only Satan could have raised such a ruckus! No one slept, not in heaven, not in hell, and certainly not down here on earth. It was rumored that God or the Devil - or possibly both - twisted the ear of the Commander-in-Chief and told him that his mortal soul was at stake - not to mention his sanity, his sleep, his position, his authority, and his command of the troops - if he did not yield to the demands of his people!

Others proffered more secular causes: the atheists swore the stock market's nosedive did the trick, the anarchists claimed the threat of societal collapse swayed the decision, the psychoanalysts swore the First Lady had threatened divorce, *the Banker* said it had been statistically inevitable, *the Butcher* blamed *the Man From the North*, *the Candlestick Maker* grumbled that the President had no balls, the people shook their heads at the lunacy of the others - any idiot could *hear* the real cause was the hammering - but all explanations aside, everyone agreed, on Monday a miracle occurred.

Martial law was finally repealed.

# CHAPTER FIFTEEN

· · · · ·

## *Close Call*

It began as a whisper, a rumble of sound.

A cry broke loose.

A shout.

A whoop of excitement.

The news tumbled over itself and roared until it crashed over the townspeople like a tsunami.

"They're gone! They're gone!"

*Gone! Gone! Gone!*

The cry rang out like bells, striking this moment of triumph. Relief broke through tense shoulders. Tears spilled from eyes. Hands jumped to mouths. The last tanks rolled out of Rudy's town and Zadie threw her arms around a stranger.

"Congratulations," he said, lifting the brim of his baseball cap.

Zadie's eyes flew wide open.

"Charlie!" she hissed. "What are you doing here?!"

"Couldn't miss out on *this*," he answered, gesturing to the jubilant townspeople. He had been cooped up all week while the nation hammered for freedom. A thick stubble covered his chin. He was well hidden in the crowd of shoulders that had amassed along the sidewalks of the town to watch the official withdrawal of the troops. His heart pressured his chest as the retreating backs of the soldiers turned around the bend. They had done it! The people had ended martial law through peaceful means. Zadie hugged Charlie in a surge of excitement and his heart thrilled with an emotion that had nothing to do with the departure of the soldiers.

"I love you!" he said, but the roar of the crowd swallowed his words.

"What?!" she hollered back.

"I just said - " he broke off. He grabbed Zadie's arm and turned her, pointing. Her mouth dropped. She yelled, but no one could hear her. Frantically, they shook the people next to them, but it was too late.

Without warning, a wave of police officers crashed over them.

\*     \*     \*

"What are you arresting us for?!" the bushy bearded guy yelled at the officer. Zadie tried to nudge him to pipe down. He was one of the activists that had come to help the town. *Please,* she urged silently, *don't make a big stink and bring the head honchos over . . . not with Charlie right here.* Zadie prayed the police wouldn't recognize him. She eyed the special task force officer who was pushing them toward the riot van. The local police were nowhere in sight.

"You're being arrested for congregating without a permit, Freedom of Defense Act, Section 326B," the cop answered flatly.

"Oh, right," the activist grumbled. "I forgot about that unconstitutional bit of nastiness." The burly man wheezed as he sat down. His belly rolled over his belt. His face was flushed red. He nodded at Zadie and glanced at Charlie, but didn't recognize him with a full beard and long hair. The fellow looked up at the police officer.

"End of martial law and back to our good old police state, eh?"

The cop shot him an irritated look before he walked away, leaving the three handcuffed in the van. The guy nodded at Charlie. "You look familiar. Got a name?"

"I'd rather not say," Charlie replied shortly.

"Barnabus . . . Mortimer . . . Horatio?" the guy teased. "Did your mom name you after Uncle Phineas?"

"Something like that," Charlie answered, tense and nervous about their current situation as the cop returned to the van door with the driver. Charlie blinked. The driver was an army guy, not a cop. What was going on here?

"I.D.'s!" the cop barked.

"Gotta feel up my crotch to get it," the activist told him. "Front right pocket."

The police officer glared at him and turned sharply to Zadie.

"You."

"Lost mine. It's in my purse, out there." Zadie jerked her head back to the sidewalk. Through the doors of the van, they could see that the crowd had been dispersed through flight or arrest. The cop turned to question Charlie.

"How many democratic civilians did you nab?" their bearded companion interrupted.

The policeman narrowed his eyes, but didn't answer.

"This has got to be the biggest arrest since you all decided tear gas was more fun," the activist mocked the cop.

"You have a right to remain silent. I suggest you do so."

"Well," he exclaimed, "isn't this a rare day in protesting history! I have a right to something and you actually informed me of it?"

The officer gave him a disgusted look and shut the van door. He spoke with the army guy briefly, telling him to collect identification, fingerprints, and names down at the station. The young soldier squinted at them with a very odd look on his face. Then he nodded briskly to the cop and walked to the front of the van.

"Still got your ID's, dontcha?" the activist asked with a satisfied grin.

"Yeah, thanks," Charlie replied gratefully as he realized the tactic behind the man's flippancy.

"Don't mention it. My name's Mack. Telling him you dropped your purse was fast thinking," Mack complimented Zadie. "You been through a few protests?"

"A few too many to count," she replied tersely.

"We've got to ditch our ID's," Charlie muttered to Zadie.

"Oooooh, you must be named Weiner," Mack chuckled. "Don't sweat it. So long as you're not a suspected terrorist you'll get out - " he stopped, looking at Charlie curiously. "Wait a minute," he dropped his voice, "are you what's-his-name?"

Charlie said nothing. Mack sat back stunned as he recognized *the Man From the North*.

"Your beard - the longer hair - the melee out there - that's why I didn't recognize you from the television ads." His eyes flicked to Zadie. "If I was you, I'd pretend you didn't know him. As for you, kid, you should have dropped that ID of yours like it was a burning poker. I suggest you lie through your teeth at the station. What the hell were you thinking coming into the viper's nest?"

"Curiosity killed the cat."

"Well, I hope you're satisfied," Mack groaned, "because for a fellow like you, there ain't no coming back from where they'll take you."

The van lurched to a stop. Zadie toppled onto Charlie. Mack frowned.

"What's the driver up to? We're not at the station yet."

The soldier flung the back door open.

"Out."

They scrambled out awkwardly in their plastic handcuffs. They were in a deserted alley, pulled out of view of the street. The army guy had a gun on his back and another on his hip. He glanced tensely over his shoulder. Mack swallowed.

"You know, martial law was lifted a couple days ago," he said nervously, "and, uh, executions in alleyways are really not in vogue right now."

The soldier spun Mack around and pushed him up against the van, grabbing his handcuffed wrists.

"Today is your lucky day, chubs."

Click.

The soldier cut the plastic handcuffs.

"Don't jump me," he warned Mack. He gestured for Zadie to turn around as he cut her free.

"Not that I'm complaining," Mack said, "but what the hell are you doing?"

"I signed up to defend the American people and protect the Constitution," the young soldier growled out, "not to book people into indefinite detention for exercising their rights."

Zadie's eyes flew open. Her hands jumped to her mouth.

"Bless you! Bless you!" she cried. "You're a miracle."

"Ma'am, it would be more of a miracle if you could keep your voice low."

Zadie shut up. Charlie was still frowning, trying to figure out what was going on when the soldier twisted him around. He spoke almost inaudibly to Charlie as he cut the plastic ties that held his hands.

"I know who you are. I know what you're doing. Don't write about me. I just want to say . . . thanks." He stuck out a hand. Charlie shook it, still utterly bewildered. "Keep defending our democracy."

He walked tensely to the front of the van and drove off. Mack slapped Charlie on the back so hard that he nearly fell over.

"Charlie-fucking-Rider! You are one lucky son-of-a-gun. Out of all the brainwashed cops 'n' soldiers," Mack paused to shake his head in awe, "you got an Oath Guardian."

"Two questions," Charlie interjected. "One, how do we get out of here? And two, what on earth is an Oath Guardian?"

Mack clapped him on the shoulder.

"I got answers to both. C'mon."

\*       \*       \*

Mack boomed out his explanation of the Oath Guardians as they sat squeezed like sardines in the front seat of his tiny car. The backseat was crammed to the roof with his belongings. Charlie slouched low in the passenger seat, one of Mack's grimy old ski hats shoved down almost to his eyes. Zadie straddled the stick shift, and Mack apologized every time he had to change gears.

"An Oath Guardian," Mack told them, "is a soldier, a cop, or any other security officer who refuses to enforce unconstitutional laws. They took an oath to defend the Constitution of the United States and they aren't about to let scumbag politicians use them as pawns in their power games. Not against their own people."

"They started out as right-wing second amendment fanatics," Zadie put in, "but the laws have gotten so out of hand that more and more officers and soldiers started joining."

"How many of them are there?" Charlie asked.

"They say there's something around thirty thousand of

them, but who knows? It's not exactly something they broadcast to their superiors," Mack said.

"I've heard that there are more joining every day," Zadie added.

"Isn't it considered total insubordination?"

"Yeah, more or less," Mack shrugged. "But it depends on the chain of command. Rumor has it that there are Oath Guardians all the way up, now. I heard it was one of the top generals who pushed for the end of martial law."

Charlie's mind spun. It was crazy. The Dandelion Insurrection was sprouting in the heart of the military itself! He itched to write about it, but he saw the danger for those involved.

"Wow," he said, reaching across Zadie to squeeze Mack's shoulder. "Thank you. If that first cop had gotten ahold of my identification, I'd be spending the rest of my life in solitary confinement."

"Well, I'd probably be rotting in jail along with you," Mack pointed out.

Zadie frowned.

"What about the other people who got arrested today? Do you think they'll enforce indefinite detention on them?"

Mack nodded decisively.

"Absolutely. This crackdown is meant to be a lesson to overshadow the fact that we just forced the government to end its own martial law!" Mack cheered for a brief moment, then turned sober quickly. "It's no joke what those people are facing. These arrests are a warning that opposition to authority will not be tolerated. Dissenters will rot in jail like all the other alleged terrorists."

"Democracy is now considered terrorism?" Charlie spat out dryly.

"Sure," Mack said without apparent concern. "It has always been a threat to the elitist power structure." He laughed without humor. "Let's get you two a pair of wheels and get you out of here. Give 'em hell, Charlie Rider. For the sake of the citizens who are now locked in prisons right where we should be, let's bring this corporate dictatorship down!"

# CHAPTER SIXTEEN

· · · · ·

## *Westward!*

The tenor of the country shifted like the spring winds. At the ball games, the bars, the church suppers, and the hairdresser's, people could talk of nothing but the cazerolazo's success. Eyes challenged police and soldiers boldly. The people had flexed their muscles of resistance . . . and won. The Dandelion Insurrection gained a toehold of respect in the cynical hearts of the nation. Ordinary people heard it mentioned that the terrorist kid, the one on television, was behind the cazerolazo. They looked over their shoulders and hissed, *Charlie Rider? Are you sure?* Some worried that they would be charged for aiding the enemy by having banged on a pan. Others scowled at the WANTED posters and wondered if this kid was really the enemy of the people as the ads claimed. Articles from *the Man From the North* proliferated. Mack headed up to Maine carrying greetings from Zadie to her parents. Meanwhile, Charlie and Zadie traveled westward in an unreliable hatchback that Mack had been piecing together from his junkyard.

"If she dies on you, pop the clutch, hit the gas, and that'll spark her back to life," he told them cheerfully. "She isn't much to look at, but she gets good mileage, and if the Feds pump you full of bullet holes, it won't show much between the rust spots."

None of that was particularly reassuring. It was rumored that the corporate elite had demanded Charlie's assassination and that the President had signed the order. Charlie and Zadie kept one eye on the sky for killer drones and the other scanning their surroundings for snipers. A checkpoint at the Mississippi River had sweat rolling down Charlie's back, but Zadie whipped out their old military passes and flirted so hard with the young officer that it was a miracle he didn't climb into the back of the car to ride off into the sunset with them. The river flowed sullenly under the bridge, brown and belligerent. The fields of Kansas stretched in front of them, flat and open after a short space of rolling hills. Charlie breathed in the expanse of the West for the first time in his life.

They avoided the urban centers and drove through deserted little towns with closed up main streets. Miles of corn and wheat stretched in all directions. The beat up car was perfect camouflage in this area. Charlie wrote in the passenger seat while Zadie gave him a break at the wheel. The vibrations of the American back roads lifted his pen as it traversed the page; *we are the ink scrawling across this country, the story of its revival or demise.*

That evening as they pulled into a dismal Kansas town, their car spluttered and died. Charlie cranked the starter, pumped the gas, lifted the hood, and fiddled with the engine's innards. Nothing. He slid down the rusted side of the car and sat next to Zadie on the ground.

"We've got to call a mechanic."

"We need money," she pointed out.

"Yeah," he agreed.

"Well, every town has a bar," she sighed. She moved to stand. Charlie looked up sharply and grabbed her arm.

"What do you mean by that?"

"Bars hire strippers, Charlie," she answered, avoiding his eyes. He dropped her arm like it had just burned him.

"When we were going through the Blue Ridge Mountains is that how you were getting money?" he asked her.

"Well, it doesn't grow on trees," she answered defensively. She stood up. "It's Saturday. There's money to be made tonight. Tomorrow, all that's holy takes over, and then Monday will kick off the work week, and that will leave us shit out of luck." She started striding down Main Street. Charlie jumped up and followed.

"Zadie, don't do this . . ."

She spun around.

"You got any other bright ideas?" she retorted.

He didn't.

"I've been doing this since I was sixteen, Charlie," she said fiercely. "It's not like anything new." Something hot and metallic hit her voice. Sharp edges of the past showed up tight in her shoulders. She crossed her arms over her chest, defensive against his reaction. He stared at her like he had just ripped the husks off the sweet corn and found it full of worms.

"Sixteen, Zadie?"

"Had to eat," she said shortly. "And then I had debts to pay off."

"What kind of debts does a sixteen year old have?" he jabbed at her.

"Abortion."

He hit a dead stillness. The town froze around that one word. Charlie's ears rang.

"That's why I skipped out, Charlie," Zadie said, her voice burning like a hot iron brand. "I freaked and ran away from the valley because I didn't dare tell my folks."

Jagged memories of Zadie's raging fights with Bill stabbed through Charlie's memory. Back then, hanging around Zadie and her parents felt like sticking your hand into a meat chopper. The wicked lash of Zadie's adolescent tongue had knifed her relationship with Ellen and Bill. Time heals all wounds, they

171

say, but it had been an arduous recovery. Zadie hadn't been in the habit of telling her parents what she ate for lunch, let alone confiding in them about unwanted pregnancies.

"I took a pill. It wasn't so bad. It was over," she shrugged.

Charlie shook his head. His temper rose.

"Don't lie to me," he snapped.

"I'm not!" she exploded.

"Pills don't cost much," he jabbed at her.

"No," she agreed. Suddenly, she tilted her head back, blinking ferociously up at the sky. Charlie felt a sinking feeling as she swallowed hard.

" . . . the second abortion did."

Every fiber of his body screamed *what?* but his jaw was locked tight.

"When you fly high in life, sometimes you take more than one crash," she said. Her show of toughness didn't fool Charlie at all.

"Zadie, whatever secrets you haven't told me, you best spit out right now. We've come a long way since we were twelve, but I'm not going another half mile with you if we can't be honest with each other."

She dropped her head and her hair veiled her expression. She scuffed the sandy grit on the asphalt with the toe of her boot. She swallowed again and looked up.

"I had two abortions, Charlie. The first one was when the government still handed out free pills. The second time around, I was nineteen, traveling with a guy that Aubrey told me a thousand times was no good, but - " She stopped again.

"But what?"

"I guess I wanted the dream, Charlie; marriage, kids, house, normality."

"You're joking," Charlie scoffed. "You?"

She shrugged.

"Were you out of your gourd?" he burst out. "How many times have you said, marriage and Zadie don't go together in the same sentence?"

"See, I knew you would have talked me out of it," she sighed.

"Then why didn't you call me, stupid?" he snapped back.

"Well, I wasn't real strong on good judgment back then!" she protested.

"Apparently not!"

They glared at each other in silence for a few moments. Zadie broke her gaze and shifted awkwardly from foot to foot.

"So?" he muttered. "What happened?"

"I waited a couple months to tell the guy, hoping he would want the kid and marry me," she replied. "Instead, he beat me up and disappeared."

Charlie's anger died in his gut.

"Jesus, Zadie, I'm sorry."

"Yeah, me too," she said bitterly. "By then, the conservative government had cracked down on abortions and put the clinics out of business. Not that it mattered, since I didn't have much besides saltine crackers in my pocketbook."

"Your parents would have helped you. Jesus, Aubrey would have flown you to France to get it done," he told her.

"I know. *Now*, I know that. Back then, I was trying to fix my fucked-up self all on my own, and just screwing up even more. I found a back alley doctor straight out of the Christian horror flicks, and, yeah, it was awful. I bled my insides out, Charlie, out here in a goddamn town that looked just as straight-laced as this," she kicked angrily at the curb, "because I couldn't get the pill that the government used to give away to girls like me who were too young to take care of themselves, let alone an unwanted kid!"

She looked up with both fury and heartbreak cracking over her face. Zadie bit back a hot rush of tears as the past flooded into the present. She sat down on the curb, looking like the lost, hurt, teenager she had once been. Charlie sank down next to her. He hesitated for a moment, then reached out and put his arm around her.

"I'm sorry." He didn't know what else to say; all the poetry in his soul had shriveled up. "You could have told me."

"It isn't the kind of stuff you write on postcards," she sniffled over a small smile. "And what could you have done?"

"I'd have dropped out of school and worked my ass off to help you out."

"Really?"

She swiveled on the curb to study him. He stared back.

"Zadie, I would have done anything for you. Anything. Still would. I'll be the best man at your wedding, babysit your kids, whatever you need."

"I can't have kids, Charlie. I told you that."

He stared at her.

"No, you never told me that."

"Yes, I did, up on the Blue Ridge Mountains."

He looked at her like she was crazy.

"You were joking about my kids," she insisted. "I said that some dreams aren't meant to come true."

Charlie choked.

"I thought you were talking about . . . weren't we talking about my kids?" His tongue spluttered and died like a beat up car engine.

Zadie shot up from the curb, flustered.

"Well, we were just joking around," she stammered, turning red, "but I thought I had to tell you that it wasn't going to be like that."

He rose, feeling a little shaky.

"What wasn't going to be like that?"

She started pacing.

"Well . . . if it ever happened . . . if you felt . . . "

She froze. He froze. The three feet of pavement between them seemed as vast as the Grand Canyon. The edge of truth loomed perilously close. Charlie swallowed. His heart jumped into his throat, threatening to croak out and flop to the ground if he said anything. She stared at him with startled deer eyes. Every fiber of her body seemed poised to bolt. She blinked and wet her lips.

"Charlie? I'm going to ask you something, and if I'm dead off my rocker, we can just forget I ever mentioned it and go on as we always have - "

"Zadie, I love you," he cut her off.

It was out. The truth stretched between them like a tightrope.

"You do?" she said.

He nodded.

"Really?"

He nodded again.

"You mean it?"

He exploded.

"Yes, Zadie! Yes! I've been in love with you since eighth grade. If I had known what you were going through, I'd have robbed the church collection basket, hot-wired my grandfather's car, and gone after you. It drove me nuts to listen to you rattle on about the adventures you were having, the guys you were dating - "

"I was trying to impress you," she confessed suddenly.

"Zadie, don't tease me, okay?" The world was heaving

under his feet and truth was a thin little wire stretched across a canyon of hard feelings. "If you want to break my heart, it's right here on the sidewalk. Just smash it once and for all, okay?"

"Charlie?" she said, licking her lips nervously.

Charlie suspected his heartbreak was on the tip of her tongue.

"Just say it, Zadie," he urged her. He closed his eyes like a man awaiting his execution.

"I love you."

He opened one eye. She had crossed the gulf. Her nose was inches from his. A smile teased her lips.

"You do?"

"Yes."

"But - but - why - how come you never said anything?" he stuttered in astonishment.

"I thought you'd settle down with someone really great."

"You're joking. *Me?*" Charlie choked. He couldn't believe it. "All I've ever wanted to do was *not* settle down, or ride off into the sunset, or whatever . . . just do it with *you*. Zadie, didn't you know? I'd have jumped off the border bridge for you! I've tackled the government for you. Everything I'm doing is . . . because . . . of . . . you!"

"Charlie?"

"Yeah?"

"Shut up."

She kissed him.

Did the earth tremble? Did his knees give out? Did the universe explode and reconfigure? Charlie didn't know and didn't care. A car of kids hooted at them as they drove by. The streetlights snapped on overhead. A fire truck blared through the intersection two blocks down. The heavens split open and the angels strummed their violins. Charlie didn't notice. He had dissolved into a tiny patch of passion, oblivious to anything else. Their lips parted, lingered, panted . . . breath gasped back into his lungs, but she stole it away as fast as it could rush in. Time left them on the curb as the town hurtled home to dinner. The nation passed them by in pursuit of mashed potatoes. The evening news forgot to mention the momentous event that was taking place on a dusty Kansas sidewalk. The textbooks would never report the moment that changed the course of history.

Night gathered her dark skirts around them like a fussy old woman and they looked up when her cool fingers prodded them. Zadie stared at the hatchback and sighed. The sudden shock of love hadn't pulled any miracles down from the sky.

"Charlie, I hate to say it, but we still need to get the car fixed."

He shrugged. He was content to spend the weekend sleeping on the sidewalk, go to church on Sunday to thank God for Zadie, and figure everything else out on Monday. He was so high on love that -

A cop car rounded the corner. Zadie twisted his head toward her and hid his face in her hair. Her heart thudded in her chest, startled and sobered cold. Charlie might think he was living in paradise, but she knew his body was still here on earth and heaven was a short ride on a sniper's bullet. The car crawled past. It turned the corner and she exhaled in a whoosh. They were just two kids necking on the sidewalk.

"Charlie?" Zadie said softly. "We're being honest, right?"

"Mmm-hmm," he replied, running a line up her neck with his lips.

"There's something else I should tell you."

"Mmmph," he mumbled.

She pulled back and caught his cheeks in her palms.

"I made the Dandelion Insurrection up."

177

His eyes tried to focus on her face, but he was dizzy from love, shortsighted in the darkness, and her words just didn't make sense.

"You what?"

"I made it up last autumn. I was driving north to visit, trying to think of some cool story to tell you, and - bam - I invented the Dandelion Insurrection."

The pavement cracked under him. Reality staggered.

"You mean it's not real?" he choked.

"Oh no," she said, deadly quiet, "there's a real insurrection going on . . . only, we're the ones fomenting it."

Charlie felt the cool air sweep across his back. He shivered in his thin tee shirt.

"The stories - " he croaked.

"They were already happening, but once you started writing about the Dandelion Insurrection, it all took off," she said, waving her hand at the roiling tumult of the nation.

Charlie's thoughts raced back over the number of times he had called for resistance to the government's tyranny, the Suburban Renaissance's evacuation, the detailing of direct action strategy to Rudy, the cacerolazo, and this latest escape from arrest.

"Holy shit," his voice cracked. "The government is right . . . I started an insurrection."

"Um, technically, yes."

He exploded from the curb.

"*ZADIE!*" he cried. "How could you?"

"I didn't know this would happen!" she exclaimed. "At the time, I thought it would be a good joke!"

"Being a wanted terrorist isn't a joke!" he snapped.

"What were you going to do, write about soccer matches your whole life?" she retorted.

"Sounds nice compared to being stranded in Kansas with the FBI on my tail!" he yelled.

"Well, tell the whole country, why don't you?!" she hollered at him. She spun on her heel and marched in the other direction.

"Where are you going?" he called after her.

"To get you some money before the Feds show up!" she shouted back.

"Why not just leave me as target practice?" he suggested furiously.

"Because I love you, you moron!" she screamed over her shoulder.

Charlie swore. He kicked the car. It let out an unsympathetic thump. He stared at Zadie's fast twitching stride as she stalked down Main Street.

"If I were you," a man's voice said, "I'd go after her."

Charlie jumped a mile out of his skin. A thin little man with wild spiky hair leaned nonchalantly against a telephone pole surrounded by a pool of streetlight. Charlie scowled moodily at him.

"Why's that?"

"One, because you love her," the man pointed out. "And two . . . "

He slowly turned his thumb at the bumper of his car, which was parked behind their rusted clunker. Charlie's eyes squinted at the symbol. White, green, yellow, with red letters -

"ZADIE!" he yelled. "Zadie, come back!" He sprinted down the street after her, his legs pounding the pavement and his voice whooping with surprise.

"ZADIE!! The Dandelion Insurrection is here!!!!!"

*Rivera Sun*

# CHAPTER SEVENTEEN

. . . . .

## *Cybermonk Extraordinaire*

The signs were everywhere! Bumper stickers, round decals stuck behind stop signs, discreet emblems on the corners of fliers; images of a scraggly leafed plant with a shining gold blossom and, occasionally, in the most tucked away places, the words in bold red: *The Dandelion Insurrection is here!*

Tucker Jones cavorted like a thin imp set down in the midst of the cornfields. Mischief gleamed in his brown eyes. He had walked out from his print shop downtown and overheard the whole argument. Counting his lucky stars - and theirs - Tucker Jones kicked his heels to have found them before anyone else. Even with the beard and shaggy hair, Tucker had no problems recognizing *the Man From the North.*

"Of all the places for you to break down!" he cried to the now infamous Charlie Rider. "This sleepy little Kansas town isn't exactly a hotbed of insurrection, but there's a few of us. The TV said a terrorist named Charlie Rider was on the loose, so I whipped out some decals and snuck around at midnight putting out the welcome mat."

Tucker Jones rubbed both hands across his nest of hair. He ran the only print shop around and had been reprinting and circulating Charlie's articles for months, aided by his underground railroad of paperboys, as he called them.

"You!" Zadie exclaimed. "It was you!"

Somewhere in the country, Zadie knew an anonymous link in her network had been massively bumping up the distribution of Charlie's articles. She had tried to trace it and make contact,

181

but it was risky. Her search alone could alert the authorities.

"Well, yes, it was me," Tucker Jones admitted humbly.

He scooted around opening the car doors for them like they were visiting royalty. Charlie took an appreciative look at the bumper sticker that had brought them together. Tucker laughed.

"I print a lot of *My Kid Made Honor Roll* bumper stickers. It was only a short hop of imagination to come up with *The Dandelion Insurrection Is Here.*"

"Aren't you worried about the police?" Zadie asked him.

Tucker shrugged. "We've only got six cops in this town, and so long as nothing's exploding, they mostly ignore it. I was worried about the local folks, but after the success of the cazerolazo, I swear the whole sentiment about *the Man From the North* changed. No one liked living under the thumb of the soldiers, even if they weren't in the path of an oil pipeline. I can't say that people are *for* the Dandelion Insurrection . . . but they aren't against it, either. Mostly, they just don't want to get in trouble."

"Well, trouble's on their doorstep. They don't have a choice about that," Charlie pointed out.

"I know, I know," Tucker sighed. "The local sheriff popped into the print shop this morning. I nearly died; the proofs for the stickers were in plain sight, but he just wanted to warn me not to get in any trouble he couldn't ignore." Tucker laughed. "Now that you're here, though, I guess I shouldn't test his eyesight - or his patience - any further."

Tucker peeled the bumper sticker off his fender and slapped it out of sight under the steering column. He drove them to his house, which was backed up to a sea of cornfields. Tucker was full of fire and humor, talking a blue streak in the manner of bachelors who enjoy company, but spend too much time in solitude. He snapped on the kitchen lights, drew the shades across the windows, and dragged out a bachelor's assortment of dinner makings, apologizing to his guests for the lean pickings.

"I never did get married or learn to cook, and some days I regret both. Most of the time, though, solitude and frozen pizza do me fine."

The slight, cerebral man spent his days printing and his nights programming, describing himself as a quiet little cybermonk, praying for world peace, and doing his part however he could. He joked about being one part revolutionary, one part tech geek, and one part Kansas farm boy. People thought farming was all tractors and cows, but computers and Tucker had come of age together like a couple of twins. He had been troubleshooting the agricultural industry's laser controlled planters and tillers since childhood. For Tucker, a world of worlds unfolded, flourished, and destroyed itself in the void of ones and zeros. The realms of programming offered up a model of the Universe, creating a refraction of reality that revealed the infinite permutations of life. Occasionally, Tucker told them, he peered into a stream of numbers and stumbled upon the inner workings of the soul.

"Computers can be as great and as evil as humans themselves," Tucker said with a wry look, "which is a scary thought given the vicious and inane behaviors that go on, not only by average people, but by every level of the society."

Tucker described how corporate and political leaders were currently replicating their own worst qualities by using computers to hunt, murder, destroy, fear-monger, and control people.

"The things our government and the corporations are choosing to do with technology turn my stomach," Tucker said. He stared at the ceiling in thought for a moment, scratching his bird's nest of hair. "But, then again, it's no different than what they're doing to the natural world."

Zadie stared at him, holding her breath, *did he see it too?*

"It's alive," he said. "I swear to you, the Internet is a living system as surely as the atmosphere, the ocean, and the layers of the Earth. People don't get it. The quest for artificial intelligence is a mistaken folly of our human snobbery about sentience. The rocks, the trees, the clouds - they are all beings that contain their own forms of intelligence. We don't need to make computers in our image. We need to acknowledge that we have created another form of being on the planet that lives in interconnection with us, evolves, requires resources, and must exist in balance with the rest of creation."

Zadie felt the curl of a smile blossom in her cheeks. He got it. The lean little cybermonk understood the sanctity of life, right down to the rights - and responsibilities - of a jumble of wires. Zadie stared at Tucker, suddenly imagining the childhood journey of this man, too small for football, too smart for his own good, and a few years too old to have hit the computer-geeks-are-sexy fad. In New York or San Francisco, the young Tucker Jones might have found himself in the center of a creative and radical group of friends. Zadie shrugged. The man possessed an earnest humility that she appreciated. All these quiet years out in the cornfields may have served as the mountain hermitage to a Midwest cybermonk in the making.

"The Internet should be free, open, uncensored, and self-governing," Tucker declared, his face shining with passion. "No one should have the right to control it, corporatize it, manipulate its truth, or own it. It is a being. And, like people, like animals, like plants, and like the Earth itself, this *being* has rights."

Zadie leaned her elbow on the table and toyed with the

crust of her toast. *We're a long way from that vision,* she thought. Humans hadn't even fully acknowledged the equal rights of each other, let alone those of animals or the planet. Animal slavery was as common as housecats and feedlots. Subjugation of ecosystems for natural resources ran as rampant as the rape and abuse of women. The same mentality that sought to possess and extract from the land also sought absolute dominance over the Internet and computers. And now this current corporate-political regime strove to shove humanity back into the dark ages just when our survival depended on recognizing the equal rights of all creation. A sigh slipped out of her. Tucker heard and grinned as if he had the answer to all of life's conundrums.

"Fortunately, we've got the Alternet."

"The what?" Charlie and Zadie asked, together. Their eyes met. Zadie's heart gave a hopeful little leap. Charlie winked and a small sunburst exploded in her chest.

"What's the Alternet?" Charlie asked.

Tucker waggled his eyebrows and led them down the steps into the basement. He flicked on the lights. A dizzying tangle of wires and circuit boards popped into view.

"That is junk," Tucker snorted, leading them around the racks. Behind the chaos was an orderly corner, comfortably situated with a rug and a side table that held a small teapot and an electric kettle. Tucker pulled out a couple of milk crates for them to sit on and waved at the computer. "This is the Alternet, a multi-nodal, uncensored, encrypted interactive online alternative system to the governmentally manipulated, corporate-controlled Internet."

Charlie scratched his head.

"Internet for the people, by the people," Tucker simplified. "And with privacy." He snorted. Privacy was an idea long overdue in the online world.

Charlie bolted upright. If only they had known about this months ago!

"How does it work?" Charlie asked eagerly.

"Encryption," Tucker answered. "It's not perfect, but it's a heck of a lot better than what people are using currently. There's also coding that hides the location of the originating message. Very important. With your articles, I can click right here and send them to thousands of originating locations all over the globe . . . which means you can write from Kansas, but the Feds will think you're in Maui."

"I'd rather write in Maui and send the articles to Kansas," Charlie joked.

Tucker poked his shoulder.

"Yep, but then I'd miss out on meeting you."

"Bah, I'm nothing. This, though," Charlie gestured to the computer with sincere appreciation, "this takes some intelligence."

"Well, someone had to do it," Tucker answered. "The corporations started building the hardware of the computer phones in such a way that allowed the government to track people. Pair that with a killer drone and you're basically a walking target. They talked about microchips for years, but when people got cellphones, there wasn't much need to implant chips in people. We carried them with us."

"Well, sometimes."

"*All* the time," Tucker argued. "The corporate business world shifted pace to the point where the whole world was on call. We started navigating, shopping, and communicating in ways that necessitated an addictive relationship to our phones and computers. It was all economics. You couldn't succeed in life if you didn't have a computer phone. And every one of those phones was hardwired to reveal your whereabouts, your actions, and your political views to the government."

"Which people thought wasn't a problem," Charlie commented, "except for a few of us who had an inkling of the madness that was unfolding. I never got a cellphone. Zadie called me old fashioned, but . . . " he trailed off, laughing and looking over his shoulder at her.

"Well," she conceded, "given your career choice, it turned out to be a smart move."

"Don't knock old fashioned notions. They may have saved your life," Tucker said bluntly. "They might save us all. We borrowed from the early days of the Internet, creating a distributive processing framework where each unit in the matrix acts like a mini-server, augmenting and replacing parts of the regular Internet. We're about communication, energy flow, interconnection, and privacy. The Alternet has been a race against time for my colleagues and I. We've been trying to develop this alternative system before the repressive corporate state really seized hold of the nation. I just hope we're not too late."

"How many participants does the system have?" Charlie asked.

Tucker shrugged.

"Around a couple hundred, I'd say."

"Shoot, really?"

"Ah, that's nothing. Peanuts," Tucker scoffed. "We're about to take a big step if my colleagues ever screw up their courage."

"What do you mean?" Charlie asked.

"Thus far, the Alternet has been a well-kept alternative secret for conspiracy theorists, activists, and whistleblowers, but now we've got a software version that anybody can download and link their hardware into the Alternet, restoring privacy and liberating people from the government's data fascism."

"How?" Charlie asked.

"Well, lots of ways. We use encryption, of course, but the important aspect of the Alternet is that the software hunts down the government's surveillance viruses. Most people don't understand this, but one of the ways they're reading our files is through infecting our computers with their snooping bugs. So, the Alternet tracks them down and sits on top of them like a sentinel. Whenever a message arrives or departs, it asks, *what are you?* Depending on the answer, it scrambles the code differently. So Mom gets an encryption that only Mom's computer understands. And the government? Well, they get whatever we want them to see; recipes, love letters, a bunch of gobbly-gook."

Tucker's face lit up in a wild grin.

"Here's the kicker: just having a small number of Alternet users creates an anomaly that is easy for the government to attack, but if a huge part of the country picked up the Alternet at the same time, the Feds wouldn't know what hit them. Gobbly-gook, constant gobbly-gook. Meanwhile, life goes on for the rest of us."

Charlie whistled, thinking of the Suburban Renaissance, and realizing the implications suddenly.

"Wow. Goodbye Internet," he exclaimed.

"Hello Alternet," finished Tucker, "the new, un-corporatized, uncontrolled alternative system."

"So, why aren't you doing it?" Charlie demanded.

"Oh, fear, mostly," Tucker said in exasperation. "We're spooked of the federal boogie men."

"That's justified," Charlie conceded. "I've had agents on my tail for months now."

"Yeah, but at some point, guerilla tactics cease to be strategic," Tucker pointed out. "We're ready. The Dandelion

Insurrection is ready. We need the Alternet!"

Charlie couldn't see why Tucker didn't just release it himself.

"Respect for the democratic process." He laughed at Charlie's confusion. "Means and ends, Charlie. You, yourself, wrote about it. *We can't grow an apple from a pricker bush.* If we're going to build a true democracy, I can't just steal my colleagues' work and act autocratically. I've got to *convince* them, one-by-one." He groaned. "I've been working on it all month. Now that you're squatting under my roof, though, that might tip the scale of things."

"How do you mean?"

"Well, you're the living embodiment of our exact pickle. Run and hide? Or stand and fight? It's all strategic. Sometimes, you gotta go underground, work small, resist symbolically. People discount that stuff, but it's really important. Think about my bumper stickers, huh? They connected us without a word, right? A symbol. But then a moment comes when it's not time to hide anymore. It's time to bust out and shake the world by its britches."

"You think that time has come?"

"I think it's coming quickly, and I think the Alternet can help it come even faster."

"But you're not sure?"

"No, I'm not. I don't have my finger on the pulse of the whole insurrection. I keep trying, but - "

"It's as slippery as a greased pig," Charlie grinned.

Tucker laughed and agreed.

"I'll tell you something, though, your little insurrection is gaining popularity faster than dandelions pop up in the spring. Those civilian evacuations gave the Dandelion Insurrection a great public image."

"Oh, we weren't behind those, technically," Charlie demurred.

Tucker raised an eyebrow.

"That's not what Guadalupe Hernandez-Booker told the cops."

"You've heard from Lupe?" Zadie cried.

Tucker grinned.

"Everyone has heard from her. She was on primetime news saying that Charlie Rider, the infamous *Man From the North*, concealed his identity and tricked her into organizing the citizen evacuations. By the time she was done, the cops were convinced Lupe had been held hostage by Charlie and everyone knew that the Dandelion Insurrection was responsible for saving millions of lives! And now, with insurrectionists showing up in every town resisting extraction and the cazerolazo's success in ending martial law, the Dandelion Insurrection is thoroughly trouncing the government in popularity!"

Charlie and Zadie exchanged looks of incredulous surprise. Zadie started to laugh, but a yawn swallowed it up. Tucker glanced at the clock. It was nearly midnight.

"My friends," he suggested, "we best get some sleep. Tomorrow, things are going to get really exciting!"

\*       \*       \*

Alone in the spare bedroom, Charlie and Zadie looked shyly at each other. Their discovery of love on the sidewalk that afternoon seemed like a distant mirage. She sat on the edge of the bed, staring at the worn fibers of Charlie's shirt. Her fingers twitched, aching to touch his ribs through the torn hole. The fabric rippled with his breath. Her left hand moved. The opening darted away. The bed dipped with his weight.

"Are you still mad at me about the Dandelion

Insurrection?" Zadie asked him quietly.

He shook his head, a small smile spreading for his foolishness, her wild ideas, and for the hope that they hadn't ruined everything. He held out his hand, palm up and open in a sign of truce. She traced his long lifeline with her finger then slid her palm into his. She smiled. Their pulses matched.

*Zadie Byrd Gray,* he thought. His eyes ran the length of her body; long limbs, scarred knees from rough playing, that funny crook where her elbow jutted out, the strong muscular build of her arms, those fingers, the press of her breasts against her shirt. His eyes traced the line of her collarbone, the hollow of her throat, the tilt in her head, her cheekbones. Her blue-grey eyes grabbed his and held him hostage. A smile teased her mouth. Charlie couldn't move.

The syncopated heartbeats of alternating questions: *does he love me? does she love me?* slipped into rhythm together; *you love me! you love me!* In the vast night of loving, lonesome uncertainty vanished. The bass drum of recognition thudded in their chests, achingly strong, sending reverberations of tingling excitement up and down their almost touching bodies. They hung suspended in the last inch of distance.

He froze on the threshold he had waited twelve years to cross. Without hesitation, Zadie laughed and pulled him beyond it.

*     *     *

Tucker took off his black-framed glasses the next morning and smiled. *Finally,* he thought, as if he had been watching their love orbits creep toward each other for twenty years, not just the few hours that he had known them. The whole world seemed to have shifted into alignment. Today, he felt *everything* was possible!

After a quick breakfast, they tromped down to the basement, buzzing with excitement at the thought of reaching people on a secure connection. They infiltrated Bill's webcam first, which he had a distracted habit of forgetting to disconnect. When they heard him grumbling, Zadie shouted to him, telling him she was calling on a secure system and for heaven's sake turn the webcam viewer on. A moment later his face popped up onto their screen. He caught sight of his daughter and burst into a smile. Then tears reddened up his eyes and he lowered his head for a minute, overcome.

"Dad, don't cry. I'm alright," Zadie assured him.

"Your mom and I started watching the news reports in case they caught you or Charlie," Bill said, his voice raspy with worry. "Is Charlie there?"

"Yeah, Bill, I'm here," Charlie squeezed in next to Zadie. Bill rubbed both palms up and down the length of his face. Zadie saw several new grey streaks in his hair.

"It's been intense up here," he admitted. "They frightened Charlie's mother half to death, showing up in the middle of the night and tearing the place apart looking for you. We've got federal agents sniffing around the farm. The Feds are suspicious of all the students who showed up last week. They reek of rebellion, I'm afraid." A tired frown flitted across his expression. "Oh, a friend of yours, Mack, arrived. He's a godsend. He has been training the activists while pulling weeds. Ellen and I have never had so much help on the farm, which is a blessing, since Aubrey set up a supply run down through the East Coast."

"Where's Mom?" Zadie asked.

"Over with Charlie's mother. They're watching her like a bug under a jar. I wouldn't contact her, even with this secure system of yours. The Feds have been interrogating heavily, but they haven't been getting very far."

"Why?" Charlie asked. "What are my relatives doing?"

"Oh," Bill replied with a chuckle, "they've been trying to be as helpful as possible, but unfortunately, it appears they're either deaf like old Mathieu, or monolingual like Valier. He told me that no one had the right to question him but God! If they wanted to badger him with questions, they would have to do it *en français!*"

Charlie started to smile.

"So, the Feds brought in some Québecois translators for that thick dialect, but it appears that the whole family is extremely misinformed about your whereabouts," Bill went on with a slight smile. "They keep saying you're in Quebec, Montreal, Paris, Mexico . . . your aunt told them straight-faced that you had been an altar boy growing up and she was sure you ran off to Rome to meet the Pope."

"Wow," Charlie whistled. "I've always wanted to travel the world."

Tucker suddenly shot up in the air.

"That's it!" he shook Charlie's shoulder. "We'll make a cyber-smokescreen for you using the Alternet *and* the Internet. We'll get folks to mention you in emails, phone calls, online posts. We'll fake a million Charlie Rider sightings all across the country!"

"Kilroy was here?" Charlie chuckled.

"Yeah, Charlie Rider was here!" Tucker crowed. "We'll keep the federal paparazzi chasing ghosts!"

They wrapped up the phone call quickly, promising a longer chat as soon as they got this idea rolling. Tucker immediately jumped into action, reinforcing Bill's Alternet connection and contacting his cohorts about Charlie's smokescreen project.

Connection electrified the Dandelion Insurrection. Tucker and Charlie took to each other like Huck Finn and Tom

Sawyer, ricocheting off each other's excitement. Zipper had videos from the cacerolazo. Aubrey relayed exciting news about inside fighting among the power elite. Inez chuckled wickedly as she told them the poor had decided the curfews and police blockades were an excuse to use democratic processes to establish local governments for what were becoming autonomous neighborhoods. Lupe let loose a stream of Spanish at the news of the Alternet and begged Tucker to convince his partners to release the software version to the Suburban Renaissance.

"*¡Madre de Díos!* Do you know what we could do with that?!"

Tucker contacted his associates. He leaned. Charlie pulled. Lupe pushed. Zadie persuaded. The dam of reluctance broke. The Alternet went viral.

The FBI panicked. They labeled it another terrorist attack by Charlie Rider and the Dandelion Insurrectionists. *The Man From the North* laughed, hit the send button, and delivered an article that countered the allegations straight to everyone's inbox.

*Calling the rise of Alternet usage a terrorist attack,* Charlie wrote, *is like claiming the invention of the toaster oven threatened national security. It is a technology, nothing more. If the government is afraid of the Alternet, it is because they are, in truth, afraid of the people.*

The nation hummed with news and information. Words flocked like birds. People used Zadie's concepts of *create, copy, improve, share* to proliferate each other's ideas. The slogan of the Dandelion Insurrection passed from person to person; *be kind, be connected, be unafraid.* Tucker's smokescreen caught like wildfire. The *Kilroy Was Here* humor of it tickled the American funny bone and Charlie Rider sightings were soon reported nationwide. Folk tales and urban legends began to circulate about his adventures. Cyber hacktivists mischievously sent his online persona running through the halls of the Pentagon. Another person circulated a rumor that Charlie Rider had climbed to the top of the Golden Gate Bridge, slid down the arching support wires, and dove off into the ocean. A third story claimed Charlie Rider had snuck into the White House and blown dandelion seeds into the face of the President. *The Man From the North* grew into a legend of rebellion.

One afternoon, Zadie was scrubbing the bachelor's kitchen, scouring out the sink with yellow gloves as she hummed along with the radio. Charlie and Tucker were in the basement working on strategies when Zadie shattered their focus with a shriek.

"*CHARLIE! TUCKER!* Come here!!!"

The two men tumbled up the stairs, fell through the kitchen door, and landed in a heap over one of the chairs.

"What is it?"

"Shhhh!" she ordered them.

The radio blared out a message from Silas Black, the self-styled King of Rock 'n' Rebel, an underground radio legend so popular that he had broken through the surface of mainstream music. He had grown up as a black 'n' blues man who had been knocked down so low there was nothing he could do but rise up singing. The rabble-rouser had managed to skate by on mass popularity even as the airways had become increasingly constricted. Silas often wisecracked that he was the token rebel on the radio; the industry kept him around because he made everyone else look like good old apple-pie eating, corn-on-the-cob munching, patriotic flag wavers. Today, the station was broadcasting a live show out of Chicago.

"Well now," Silas Black began in his characteristic low

drawl, "I think I ought to tell y'all a little story 'bout getting stopped by the Feds." He paused and tuned his guitar, letting his fans wonder what he had done this time. "They asked me if I had seen that terrorist, Charlie Rider. I said, terrorist? What terrorist? Ain't nobody been terrorized by *the Man From the North* 'cept for the crooks in Washington." Silas Black plucked a quick jingle on his guitar as the audience laughed.

"Well folks, I told them the only truth I heard . . . Charlie's riding around in Georgia someplace . . . unless he's hiding under an umbrella up in rainy Seattle . . . but then again I also heard tell that he's sun tanning down in the desert. You know, now that I think of it, everybody has seen Charlie Rider 'cept for the Feds!"

He ran his fingers up and down the strings, chasing an elusive tune as he spoke. Zadie bit her lip in merriment as Charlie's jaw dropped. Tucker turned up the volume.

"I told them, maybe if they stop calling him a terrorist, he'll bake 'em some cookies and come visit."

Silas riffed a guitar solo, chuckling to himself. Then he broke off and cut the humming strings into silence.

"You know what I say?"

They could hear him leaning into the microphone. They could almost feel the suspense of his audience, hanging on his next words.

"Ride on, Charlie Rider, ride on," Silas growled. "The King of Rock 'n' Rebel sends you this song . . . "

The band flared up.

*"All you wanna do is ride around, Charlie . . .*
*Ride, Charlie, ride!"*

The old soul song burst out the musicians. Cheers erupted from the audience. Laughter exploded from Tucker's nose. Zadie started lip-synching with the scrub brush.

*"All you wanna do is ride around, Charlie . . .*
*Ride, Charlie, ride!"*

Tucker howled with laughter. Charlie was stunned. Silas Black had reworked every line of the lyrics. The crowd sang along to the refrain. Charlie stared at the radio as if he couldn't believe his ears.

"They really mean it?" he asked in wonder.

"Listen to them, Charlie!" Zadie exclaimed.

*"Ride, Charlie! Ride!"*

The spirit of resistance broke loose in the audience. Silas Black had struck the chord of rebellion in the nation's souls. He gave their voices an outlet for the song of protest in their hearts. They'd been pushed down, forced aside, pressured, and threatened. The people cheered Charlie on with the long-forgotten triumph of the small against the mighty. It was their David's roar to the monster of Goliath. The band kicked back to a trumpet riff to give the audience time to hoot and holler in wild enthusiasm -

Then the radio went dead.

"That was the government, giving you their regards along with the people," Tucker snorted.

"Too late," Zadie cheered. "Ten million listeners too late."

She was right, the tune stuck in people's heads. They were humming it at the grocery stores. The gospel churches down south sang it like a spiritual. Charlie's relatives muttered the lyrics under their breaths. Lupe's kids sang it in the school playground. Aubrey whistled it on his balcony as the sun rose over the city skyscrapers. The nation shouted it out like a prayer for their freedom.

*"All you want to do is ride around, Charlie . . .*
*Ride, Charlie! Ride!"*

# CHAPTER EIGHTEEN

. . . . .

*Dandelion Politics*


Lupe Hernandez-Booker popped onto the computer screen with her youngest son in her arms and a fire in her soul. The security of the Alternet allowed her rebellious spirit to come out of hiding and courage had blossomed in her heart. The calculating look of her mother glinted in her eyes. The passionate determination of her sister shone in her face. Federal agents had been harassing her for weeks trying to find *the Man From the North* and Lupe's patience had finally worn out. Her older boy, Marcos, had been questioned as he walked home from a friend's house. Todd had been placed on probation at work for suspicion of anti-American activities. Two weeks ago, her unsuspecting daughter had carried the final straw home from school in her pink backpack, and triggered a chain of unexpected events. Finally, Lupe contacted Charlie through the Alternet.

"Eva came home with anti-terrorism literature that justifies why the government is destroying our democracy!" Lupe exclaimed in outrage. "I drew the line. I pulled out the Constitution and the Bill of Rights and gave my kids a lecture on civics. My kids don't know the first thing about democracy, not even Marcos! He's ten and he didn't even know what voting was!"

"Civics hasn't been part of the school curriculum for decades," Charlie pointed out. "It was cut from the budget when I was a kid. The government doesn't really want an informed citizenry. They want soldiers and consumers. The model American follows directions, obeys orders, works hard for little reward, and doesn't question authority."

Lupe sniffed.

"Well, they aren't going to get that from my kids. *¡Ya basta!* Enough is enough. I'm not going to let the government ruin my children! Not this government. Not my children! You know what I'm doing?"

Lupe's eyes turned bright with rebellion.

"I'm teaching people how to fight back."

Charlie closed his eyes against the sudden image of Lupe as a gun-toting revolutionary with a baby in her arms. She laughed as she read his expression.

"Don't worry, *querido,* it's not what you think. You wrote about undermining the pillars of this corporate dictatorship, and I've decided to attack them in the only place that counts . . . their profits! It's time for boycotts. I'm putting the Suburban Renaissance to work! They're ready. We've been talking about doing this for weeks. I've been putting trilingual versions of your articles in the Suburban Renaissance newsletters," Lupe told him, the corners of her eyes crinkling with laughter, "in the recipe section under dandelion salad, soup, and tonics. This group read them and contacted me. They said they wanted to teach about real democracy. All they needed was a living room and people, so I said, no problem. Inez had already started doing this in the city. She has been taking her people - especially the ones who have been kept from voting by unfair laws - and getting them involved in community self-governance based on participatory democracy. Inez starts by teaching people how to respectfully disagree! Nothing is more important to functional democracy than citizens being able to discuss their viewpoints, she says." Lupe took a deep breath and barreled onward. "Then, after I organized some democracy classes, people wanted to know how to join the insurrection, so I got ahold of some people who teach methods of nonviolent struggle and asked them to train us. Inez and I talked it over, and it's all arranged, every Suburban Renaissance group and the urban neighborhoods in most of the cities are all lined up and - "

"Wait! Wait!" he interrupted as something like hope exploded in his chest. "Are you telling me that you have thousands of communities across the United States training in nonviolent resistance?!"

"Well . . . *sí*. More or less. Some places, only one or two people," she said modestly.

"Lupe! Do you understand what this means?" he cried.

"Of course," she answered simply. "The people are getting ready for change."

This short, motherly woman who was transforming the American landscape one household at a time shook her head at Charlie's excited words of praise.

"*De nada*," she shrugged, *it's nothing.*

She picked up her baby and fed him.

After she hung up, Charlie bent his head over his writing paper like a penitent worshipping in church. The magnitude of Lupe's commitment stunned him. In a few short weeks, she had shifted from almost throwing him out of her house for fear of the police to truly becoming, as the anarchists claimed, *the largest subversion of the dominant paradigm in American history.* Charlie wrestled with words to describe the beauty that had unfolded in Lupe Hernandez-Booker. She had blossomed with conviction and courage. In his mind, he could hear Lupe's voice thick with emotion. He could see her round face both illuminated with passion and shadowed by worry. He sighed. How could he condense Lupe Hernandez-Booker onto the page? What was it about people that defied the written word?

He tapped the pencil to his lips, scratched the eraser through his shaggy hair, gnawed the yellow paint, and -

"HOT DIGGITY!"

- nearly poked his eye out as Tucker erupted like a stuntman from the cannon's mouth of the basement.

"We got it!" Tucker shouted, leaping into the air.

"Got what?" Charlie asked.

"Proof of last fall's stolen elections!" Tucker exclaimed.

"What?!" Charlie gasped.

"Yes!" Tucker assured him. "The Alternet team has been working on it for months."

"Who? How many are implicated?"

"Most of the elected positions last fall were manipulated in some way."

"But," Charlie gasped, "that means - "

Tucker nodded, waggling his eyebrows expressively.

"The President, the Vice President, conservatives and liberals alike. At least a third of the politicians blatantly cheated their way to power . . . and that's just the statistics from this last election. Undoubtedly, this isn't the first time."

"But that's like impeaching an entire Congress," Charlie said in shock.

"Exactly," Tucker answered, "and the governors, the mayors, the county supervisors; everybody! We don't even have a legal process for that."

"We've got to tell people - " Charlie started to say.

Tucker cut him off.

"It's a delicate thing," he warned. The thin man began pacing the kitchen, running his hands through his wild spikes of hair. "If the people aren't ready, this information is worthless. If the people are too angry, they'll erupt into violence. If the Dandelion Insurrection isn't primed for strong action, the governmental suppression of this will destroy everything. But then, even if all the factors are right and we actually can sweep the political scene clean . . . what kind of angels or monsters are waiting in the wings?"

Tucker had been carefully sniffing and snooping around the minority parties as best he could. He knew there were militant extremists and religious leaders just itching to gain a foothold. There were also incredible people boxed into political corners and true revolutionaries of the heart just waiting for an opportunity. Tucker perched on the precipice of sweeping change, knowing an ounce of caution would prevent a ton of chaos later.

Zadie burst through the backdoor.

"Your apple tree is blossoming - " she broke off when she saw their expressions. "What's going on?"

They told her. Zadie split into a wide-eyed grin.

"That election information is the whistle-blowing start of incredible change," she told the other two, nodding with fierce certainty. "Tucker's right, though. We've got to get ready. Government by the people, for the people won't just fall from the sky," Zadie told them. "We have to reach for it and pull it into reality."

She trembled with passion. Her face flushed with enthusiasm. Her heart pounded like she had waited her whole life for this moment.

"Charlie, you should start writing about the necessity of a multi-party system," she urged him, "and put in something about the need for transparency, open dialog with citizens, a real commitment to being a public *servant*, and the importance of kicking corporate money out of political campaigns! Write about the power of compassion in governing bodies and the readiness of the people for revolutionary change." She grinned to the two men. "We're going to spread the seeds of dandelion politics and grow a strong new government from the roots up!"

"Dandelion politics?" Charlie frowned. "What does that mean, exactly?"

"Participatory democracy led by the people. We're not weeds to be rounded up. We are human beings, each unique and fully capable of governing wisely, especially if we bring life, liberty, and love to the center of our politics."

"They're going to nominate you for President," Charlie teased her.

Zadie laughed at the notion.

"I'm too young, and you need a high school degree for that."

"No, you don't," he replied, "any ignorant citizen born in America and over thirty-five qualifies."

"They're going to have to wait ten years then."

"Maybe they can get the age requirement waived. In ten years, the ice caps will have melted and Washington will be underwater," Charlie pointed out.

"I'll be clinging to the spire of the flooded Capitol building, shouting *for life, liberty, and love!*" Zadie joked, striking a pose in her blue jean jacket and cut off shorts.

Charlie smiled, picturing the scene perfectly.

# CHAPTER NINETEEN

· · · · ·

*Mother, In Progress*


Ellen Byrd shook out her brushes and stood back to admire her handiwork. This was her largest painting yet, covering the entire side of the barn. The mural blazed in vibrant colors, still glistening wet. Every person traveling along the main road would see the phrase, *pour la vie, la liberté, et l'amour!* For life, liberty and love! Old Valier Beaulier had cleverly passed it off as a traditional French Acadian drinking toast. Behind the backs of the investigating agents, the valley's inhabitants raised a glass to Charlie and the Dandelion Insurrection.

"Ellen!" her husband hollered from the farmhouse door. "Phone call!"

"Who is it?" she yelled back.

"It's about your favorite painting!"

*Zadie!* Ellen raced up the driveway to talk with her daughter. Bill banged out of the house shouting something about having to fix a tractor and tell Zadie he loved her and would talk next time. Ellen smiled at the sight of her daughter's round eyes. Twenty-five years of memories of those eyes flooded through her; the first time they opened in a wrinkled red face, the way they popped awake in the morning, their quick darting flight over books, bees, skyscrapers, the world. Ellen remembered the first night she had taken her grumpy adolescent stargazing when they moved to the valley. Dark wonder had tilted Zadie's head back as the stream of stars poured from the sky right into her open mouth. *You are stardust, my girl,* Ellen had told her. *Not from the distant past, but right now, as it enters and becomes you.* She remembered the terrible vanishing act Zadie had pulled on them at sixteen, and the way Bill's eyes lost the fiery temper that Zadie used to spark in them. She recalled, with a sudden plummeting of her gut, Zadie's first phone call from the road, when the lies flared like sparklers from her mouth, fizzing and popping with brilliancy, but not fooling her mother in the least. They had come on a long, long journey together.

"So," she asked, "what's going on?"

Zadie cringed. Moms can make a child's secrets wriggle like night crawlers on hot cement, but that election information was a ticking time bomb, and it was best if no one knew about it just yet.

"Oh," Zadie said, "I've just been thinking."

"Mmm-hmm," Ellen answered, instantly suspicious. "About what?"

Zadie saw the hackles of intuition rising in her mother, so she responded carefully.

"I've been having this feeling that this country is about to get a once-in-a-millennium chance to radically shift," she said, thinking about the election fraud and the upheaval it would create. She shivered with excitement. A rush of words poured out of her. "I can see it, Mom, a whole different way of doing things. We can do so much better in governing ourselves, listening to each other, and taking the time to do things right, not just expediently. We've never even experienced real democracy in this country. The constitution that the founding fathers wrote was just one more step on the long road to equality, and even after suffrage and civil rights, we've still got a lot to improve on. The environment needs to be cared for, and so do the people. Money drives politics right now, because it drives the mentality of our people, but when the heart erupts

with love, and compassion becomes the driving force of politics
. . . imagine the world we could create!"

Ellen saw the passion shining in Zadie's eyes and was
suddenly faced with the greatest challenge of courage she had
ever encountered as a mother. This glimpse of Zadie's potential
chilled her soul as fast as it thrilled it. She calmed her breath,
once, twice, thrice. She forced her mind to look not at the
dangers her daughter might face, but at the possibility
incubating in the womb of the universe. It hung there
impatiently, a bold spark of life just waiting to be born, an
infant set of ideas formed from the lifeblood of Zadie's mind,
nurtured by the passion of her heart, and now bulging against
the amniotic sac of the subconscious, laboring to cross the gate
of reality.

"Zadie?" she asked finally. "You invented an insurrection.
Are you willing to start a revolution to finish it?"

*     *     *

Late that night, as Tucker and Charlie worked in the
basement, Zadie hung on the backdoor of Tucker's house,
staring out into the blanket of darkness, shaken by the
afternoon's conversation. Ellen had rocked her parameters of
possibility. *You could be the mother of a nation,* Ellen had said.
*Mother of a nation?* It was enormous. It was a crazy suggestion.
*Her?* Zadie's thoughts mocked her, scoffed at her, derided the
arrogance of the notion, and yet . . . there are moments when
fate looms large and present in our lives, holding out the
ultimatum of our destiny. Zadie knew such a moment had
come.

Dry laughter parched Zadie's throat. Fate's humor is blacker
than the night. Irony is a bitter companion. Twice, her womb

had pulsed with life. Twice, she had rejected it. For ten years, that decision had snuck into her dreams and stared at her with sullen eyes. She had thrown away a lineage of lifetimes in a terrified moment long ago, her father's line, her mother's line, and all her unborn children, too. She had erased an entire twisting strand of the human family tree.

This afternoon, Zadie's mother had delivered an ultimatum to her girl.

"You won't ever be a mother of a child of your own blood," Ellen had said, "but there is a whole new way of life just waiting to be born. It is standing on the threshold of reality, begging for a mother."

It hung out there in the night sky as visible as the stars. Ellen had seen it. As soon as her words curled around the notion, the nebulous shape took form.

"This country is ready to be reborn. Something fresh and new is fomenting in the fertile crumbling of the old. Compassion, connection, collaboration, and clean environments churn impatiently in the ethers. Bring them in, Zadie. I know you can."

Mothers stand on the bedrock certainty of births. Ellen had carried Zadie as a part of her own life's blood for nine months and delivered her into the world kicking and screaming. Ellen read her daughter like a book; corners turned down and favorite passages underlined with the pencil marks of memory. She knew, beyond a doubt, that Zadie could bring a world of change to this country, powerfully, swiftly, and without hesitation . . . if she chose to do so.

Zadie leaned on the doorframe of Tucker's back porch watching the moths and mayflies dart in dizzy circles around the lamp. She snapped the switch off, releasing the poor insects from their frantic lust for light. The night's depth climbed the porch steps and curled up against the curtained windows. As her eyes adjusted, stars emerged across the black expanse. She sat down on the porch steps and let the worn wood press against her, cool and firmly reassuring. Her uncertain heart thudded frantically in her chest. The child of an idea waited breathlessly for her answer.

*Show me*, Zadie thought, *show me what you are.*

*Truly?* the looming concept replied.

*Yes*, she answered firmly.

*All of me?*

*Yes.*

It hesitated. Zadie sensed that whatever hung out there hoping for her acceptance drew back in concern that its truth would not set her free; it would send her running away in terror. Zadie felt a fire rise within her. Women who stood up to become mothers of nations often died in the process. History attested to that. Zadie wanted stark clarity about this creature asking to be born. There could be no holding back. No flirtatious games of hide and seek. No presentations of little cherubs or perfect angels. She demanded to know the mysteries that other mothers can only guess.

*Show me who you are!* she commanded fiercely.

It gathered like the breath of a tsunami. A flicker of fear touched her gut. Enormity amassed. Without warning, reality cracked open and split the night down the middle. Light so bright it defied the eyes blasted through Zadie's body. She was blinded and deafened as Love roared from the depths of the universe. This was not the love of pink valentines and pecks on cheeks. This was a blazingly fierce and painful force that raked its talons through the soul and sliced all nonsense into shreds. This Love tore open the body of reality, splitting the pumping heart of blood and aortas and vascular chambers like an obstacle to truth. Death came and went, passed by as inconsequential. Thoughts of religion withered before its blaze. Notions of race and class hid themselves in shame, crying, *we are nothing, we are nothing, we are nothing to the greatness of this Love.* Zadie screamed in silent agony or ecstasy, there was no telling which. Words formed within the soundless roar of Love.

*I was here before the Universe. I will remain when all is gone. I am coming to walk the Earth again . . . inside every human form.*

Zadie died. She resurrected. She died again. She returned. Some tiny strand of sanity shuddered. Truth began to tear apart her being. She could not hold on much longer.

The last message shot out from the infinite.

*Love is coming back to Earth . . . get ready.*

And then it was gone.

Zadie sat shaking on the steps of Tucker's porch. The black fabric of the night hung still and silent. One woman cannot be the mother of *that,* she thought in awe. Never in a thousand years. We are not designed to be the vessels for that power. Zadie wrapped her arms around her torso, feeling the frailty of ribs and skin. She breathed deeply, shivering. She could not carry all of that. It would take all of us, Zadie thought; every single person must be the mother of this vision. Suddenly, she froze. Each gleaming star in the sky sharpened into crystalline clarity.

She was not meant to be the mother of this nation . . . she was being asked to be the midwife to its Love.

# CHAPTER TWENTY

. . . . .

## *The Coming Storm*

"Are you ready, Zadie?" Charlie called out the back door to where she stood watching the storm clouds sweep across the cornfield. *Click*, Charlie thought, taking a mental photo of her leaning against the pillar that held up the porch roof, one hand sliding up above her black curls, the other resting on her hip. She turned and Charlie caught a strange expression on her face. A fleeting sense of finality went through him, as if today were the last day of . . . what? Confused, he shook the feeling off.

"There's a big storm coming," Zadie told him.

"Tucker says it'll pass by sunset," Charlie answered, opening the screen door for her.

They twined their fingers together as they climbed down the basement stairs. Tucker looked up as Zadie drew close. The young woman reverberated with the tension of a tornado that hadn't quite touched ground. It was as if she was gathering unspeakable power up into her whirlwind, swirling with intensity, just waiting for the storm to break.

The computer beeped as the group connected. Charlie had set up a video conference with a handful of journalists, underground radio broadcasters, and filmmakers. The security of the Alternet presented the Dandelion Insurrection with an unprecedented opportunity to sway the hearts and minds of the people, and Charlie intended to use it to its fullest capacity. The team began to appear on the screen. Zipper gave them a merry little wave as his face popped up. He began to say something, but another journalist came online, intense and serious, and

211

barged right into the conversation.

"I'd like to thank whoever got this Alternet thingy up and running, because without it, we'd be screwed. The mainstream propaganda machine represents an enormous arsenal of control. They've been shutting down the Internet in certain areas and blaming it on domestic terrorists . . . which we all know is an abject lie."

"We've been able to trace them doing it," Tucker offered. The blustery journalist raised his eyebrows. Tucker shrugged. "We're a little skeptical of being able to prosecute them with their own justice system."

The journalist shook his head.

"You should go for it. The judicial branch is in mayhem. On one hand, they're pocketing bribes like there's no tomorrow. On the other, they're panicking because *there is no tomorrow.*"

Charlie frowned.

"What do you mean?"

"When the Constitution is flapping like a shredded flag in the breeze, there isn't much need of a judicial system to interpret it, now is there?" the journalist pointed out. "The black robes are splitting right down the middle. Half of them are swinging toward lawless bribery. The other half are digging in their heels and protecting the Constitution. The ACLU is playing the scene like a bunch of Wild West heroes, going in ready to fight to the death, slinging fast and furious. If you've got goods on not-so-legal government activities, you should contact Tansy Beaulisle. She's a real firecracker of a lawyer, always ready for a showdown."

"Speaking of showdowns," a somber woman put in, "I think we're headed for a media shootout on the Dandelion Insurrection. It's growing too fast and powerfully for the propaganda machine to ignore. They're already bashing Charlie

Rider like he murdered the nation's firstborn sons."

"I say," the first journalist interjected, "that we strike first. Get our own propaganda out before they start beating our image. Shoot them with a smear campaign or a series of muckraking exposés."

The blustery journalist's gruff suggestion resonated with the others. They began shooting out ideas.

"We've got to expose the brutality - "

"Images of injustice!"

"People rising up in outrage - "

"Police tear gassing them - "

"The beatings - "

"No," Charlie and Zadie said in one breath.

They had seen thousands of these images. The scenes of brutality woke them up in the night. The images of the awful capacities of the power elite crept into their daytime minds, lacing them with fear.

"We can't play the government's fear-mongering game," Charlie blurted out. "You know what they do . . . they report on violent protests, riots, tear gassings, and even beatings, not to *inform* people, but to scare them into submission."

The journalist cut in.

"Well, that's the news. We have to report the facts of what's going on - "

"Forget the facts," Zadie suddenly spoke up. "Go deeper than the facts. Tell the truth." Her vision burned inside her chest. The blaze of Love slammed up against her. In her mind, Zadie rolled up her sleeves and got to work. The time of midwifing had finally arrived.

"Do you want to be on the defensive or the offensive?" Zadie challenged them. "I'm not big on war terminology, but let me put it to you bluntly; we're not going to win this using defense."

Charlie blinked at the determination in Zadie's face. The male journalist scowled at her. Tucker sat back with a knowing look as her tornado swung close to touching down. *Not yet,* Tucker thought, *but it's still close enough to pull the roofs off of those journalists' minds.*

"History is won by the most convincing story," Zadie told them, "and I say that the story people need to hear is that life and love are triumphing over all efforts to defeat them. Always have, always will. Every day, children are born, plants grow, lovers are reunited, flowers blossom."

"Yeah, but we have to expose what's going on; the arrests, the death threats, the interrogations," the journalist insisted.

"If you want," Zadie shrugged, "but I wouldn't waste my breath. This whole government is a grand flaring sunset . . . it looks fiery, but it's actually on its way out."

She paused, almost distracted by the blazing sensation inside her. Her hands were tingling. She could see compassion straining to break loose in the others. The woman's sorrow held it back. The man's cynicism nipped it in the bud. It shone in Zipper's face. The other woman, too, showed some faint traces of understanding. She tried again.

"Every morning, the sun rises on a whole new world," she told them. "Look at what is coming on the horizon. Tell *that* story. Track it down. Listen to the whispers in people's hearts."

"All you can hear is their hearts hammering," the gruff journalist argued. "Everyone is scared stiff."

"Nonsense," Zadie said curtly. "I'm not scared, Charlie's not scared, and if you run into someone who is, your job is to look for what is hidden under the fear."

"My job is to report the truth," he shot back, "and the truth is, people are angry and scared."

214

"Truth is a mighty deep river," Zadie retorted. "Don't get stuck on the surface. Beneath that anger and fear is a swift flowing current of longing. People are aching for a better life, a future for their kids, some hope, some safety. You're not a fish caught on the end of a hook. You can be visionary. In our reporting, we have to inspire the people to action through love, not fear. We have to give them hope, answers, and ideas. Those three things are no harder to track down than sealed FBI files and government corruption."

The media team chuckled at that. They knew the laborious and dangerous journey of tracking down a story. They had all risked life, limb, and career to get the goods on an important report.

Charlie weighed in to support the concept.

"Zadie's right. The most powerful story we can tell is the proactive one," he said, holding up a hand to stop the journalist's protests. "There's no reason we can't use the stories of the government's terrible abuse as a contrast to the vibrancy of the people, but let's tell our story. Let's tell the people why we have every right and reason not just to resist the death sentence of the government, but to rally for a whole new way of life. I'm not going to keep scrambling to put out their fires. I want the government chasing us because we're leading the revolution."

Zadie saw the lights turn on inside the group. The one journalist's bitterness kept his love winking in and out, but Zadie guessed he would open the shutters of his heart eventually.

"Give your writing every last drop of your faith in humanity," Zadie urged them. "Don't hold back one iota. Pour your hearts and souls into this moment of human history. It will either be the beginning of a new world . . . or our last days on earth."

Above the house, Zadie heard the first crack of thunder and the pattering of rain. Sorrow climbed inside her heart as she looked at Charlie. The quiet lull in their lives was over. She left them abruptly, pulling her fingers free from Charlie's, and climbed up the stairs with his questioning eyes on her back.

"So," one woman questioned, "is that your girlfriend?"

"Why?" scoffed the gruff journalist. "Are you going to write a love story?"

Charlie laughed.

"The whole Dandelion Insurrection is a love story. It's the greatest love story ever told . . . and Zadie is right; it is the story that people need to hear. They're starving for love. We have the bread . . . let's feed them."

Charlie hunkered down into the subject.

"We must remind people that *they* are the Dandelion Insurrection, ordinary and extraordinary, all at the same time," he told the journalists. "Let's get images of children laughing, parents sneaking kisses above the soapy dishes, fiddleheads unfurling in the forest. Let's release a stream of hope like a fire hydrant uncorked in the inner city on a scorching day. We've got to wash the tired minds of the public in reminders of why life is worth living. Let's bathe them in the inspiration of their fellow human beings. No ounce of beauty is too small to share; clotheslines flapping in the breeze as the sun streaks through them, a woman bringing a glass of water to a tired policeman on the street corner, the tears of relief that ran down the people's cheeks when martial law was ended . . . that sort of thing."

They strategized ways to counter the government's glossy, heart-pounding advertisements about Charlie Rider, the terrorist bent on destroying the foundations of the United States. Some people believed them, but others scoffed. They knew Charlie Rider wasn't a terrorist. The advertisements had only caused their distrust of the government's manipulations to deepen.

"Let's expose as much of the people's suspicions as we can," Charlie said. "Once citizens recognize that their fellow Americans are also questioning what's going on, the strength of our movement multiplies, and we can begin to undermine the current government's authority."

Tucker and Charlie worked through lunch. Zadie made them sandwiches, then sat and watched the falling rain. The drops splattered fat and heavy on the porch roof, rolling off in rivulets and trickles that churned up frothy puddles on the ground. The damp air snuck inside Zadie's clothes and licked her bones. She let it. Rain brings solace to the mourning. All things shall pass; this moment would, too. Zadie quietly watched the ebb and flow of the storm, accepting the changes that were coming. Twice, salty tears slid down, releasing the perfect days with Charlie, leaving her open to the time that was coming.

*     *     *

That night, Charlie and Zadie walked the long farm road that shot out straight behind Tucker's house. The rain clouds had swept past, leaving behind a moist tenderness that softened the ground. The damp grass glistened. The round moon gleamed like the bone-white eye of a whale. The corn trembled around them like silver-black seaweed in the night ocean. The spring breeze licked them with the edge of its lapping tongue. They walked a mile in silence, content with the stretch of sinew and swing of legs. They strolled together in no rush to arrive or return, no destination, just a slow padding of strides down an open road. The flat flapping slaps of the corn leaves grew quieter and more distant. Charlie squinted into the silvered fields.

"We must be on the conservation land that Tucker said was out here," he said.

They stepped off the road into the soft prairie. The raindrops that clung to the grasses soaked their shoes. They kept walking until the touch of human roads felt distant and the tracks of other species wove through the grasses. Their footsteps halted. They stood shoulder-to-shoulder, facing the fullness of the moon.

"Zadie," Charlie asked softly, "why do I feel like I'm about to lose you?"

She swallowed hard. He had felt the churning force of change. The expression on his profile waited anxiously for her answer, afraid to turn and look for it. Zadie bit her lower lip, wishing she could erase his unease, but knowing she could only deepen it. He turned and his face dipped into shadow.

"Are you leaving?"

It was all right there, cracking through his voice, the unending departures and heart-pounding arrivals, her disappearing acts, the longing and the losing. In the silence, he began to prepare his heart for loneliness.

"No, Charlie, it's not like that - " she started to say. He pulled his fingers from her grip. She darted to catch them again, holding them firmly even when he twitched to get away.

"What is it then?" he asked, agony shredding his words.

She pulled him to her, pressing her whole body into his, trying to communicate *I'm not leaving you. Even when I go, I won't leave you!* She laid her forehead on his. They stood at almost equal heights, she just a fraction taller than he. His breath trailed across her lips.

"I love you, Charlie," she told him.

His eyelashes fanned against hers.

"Then why are you leaving?" he asked.

She sighed and pulled back, pushing his sandy hair out of his face before she turned to look up at the moon. Charlie traced a line down her arm, reminding her of his question.

"We won't win this insurrection without a revolution, Charlie," she answered. "There are three hundred million people in this country and someone has to pull their love from the womb of their hearts and spur them into action."

He froze in the moonlight, looking younger than the night. She stilled beside him, seeming more ancient than the stars. Their feet sank into the fertile soil of the heartland. The country spread out around them in a compass rose. North, south, east, and west, change pulsed against the surface of reality. A new world was waiting to be born. Charlie saw it reflected in Zadie's determined eyes. She peered into the void and saw kindness and compassion, connection and caring. Her long fingers slid across each other, ready to reach into the womb and pull out the future.

"I'm going to midwife this coming world," she told him, certain.

He said nothing at first. Shivers ran up and down his spine, tingling across his scalp. He licked his lips. They split. He tasted blood.

"How?" he asked her.

"I have to find the mothers of the nation," she said. "They're out there. I have to pull their love from inside them and send it howling out into life. Then I have to find the fathers and hand them this newborn compassion. I have to lay it in their arms, tender and fragile, and let them love it like a child. Then I have to find the teachers, the aunties, the grandparents, the cousins . . ."

As she spoke, the vision gleamed in her eyes. Charlie caught himself glancing out into the night, hoping to see what she saw, but finding only the stark silver lines of the fields, the black river of road, and the whispering grasses that swept up to his feet.

"Do you have to go?" he asked. "Can't you just track them down online - "

"You can't deliver a baby online," she said, laughing at the notion. "What if it's coming out the wrong way? What if the mother is too narrow or scared? Or all alone in the middle of nowhere, frightened? You've got to be there with them, Charlie."

Charlie heard the conviction in her voice. She looked so ancient, this young midwife of the world, peering into mysteries that no one else could see. It was a Zadie he had never seen before, and yet had been there all along.

"I want to come with you," he admitted quietly.

"Oh, Charlie," she sighed. She reached for him. They clung tight for a moment. The rational reasons for him to stay whipped through their minds, undeniable. They both knew he couldn't come; he was safer here in Kansas and his presence would bring the authorities cracking down on them both. She laid her head on his shoulder and tried to tell his heart all the myriad emotions that suddenly flooded through her: love, sorrow, longing, loss, excitement. She felt the aching pulse of his heart.

"It's not forever, Charlie," she murmured.

Charlie shook his head.

"Don't make promises, Zadie."

Uncertainty had become a way of life. Charlie would rather live by that truth than believe in a lie. Anything could happen to

Zadie, to him, to the world. It was better to accept the unknown.

"Just love me now," Charlie told her. "If there is meant to be a later, it will come."

"Everything *Insha'Allah,*" she replied. "It means *if God wills.* The Muslims use it to take the sting of arrogance out of making plans, such as, I will see you tomorrow, *Insha'Allah.*"

"I'll stand here all night with you, *Insha'Allah,* if God wills?"

"Exactly. That's how it is with everything; you, me, the Dandelion Insurrection. Everything *Insha'Allah.*"

Charlie stroked the bright curve of moonlight on her cheekbone then kissed her, hard, heartbreakingly, longing to capture the taste of her before she was gone. She matched his hunger, devouring the sensations of the touch of his hands, the press of his mouth, his scent, the way his body fit against hers, tucking the memories away to savor during the separation that lay ahead.

*Please God, if you will, let this night last forever*, Charlie prayed.

"Remember when you asked me how to write about the Dandelion Insurrection?" Zadie whispered.

His lips parted against hers, smiling as he remembered. A cool strand of air slid between their bodies. There's only one way to write about it, she had said. Write like you're on fire. *I am*, his body had answered. Write like the love of your life is on the horizon and every word hurtles you toward her. *I'm coming*, his thoughts had cried out. Find your passion, Charlie, Zadie had urged him. *I'm looking at it*, he had silently replied. Build a fire of it, she had told him. *I'm incinerating in it*, he thought. Write from there, she had said.

He had written a million words since that day. He had hurtled across the horizon toward her and, still, words could not help them now. In his mind, he tore up every page he had ever written. He tore up his past. He ripped apart the future. He set his memories on fire, his triumphs and failures, his pinpricks of heartaches, losses, and joys. This moment was burning like there was no tomorrow. Everything *Insha'Allah*. His lips were inches from hers. The scalp of his hair was rippling with fire. Their bodies blazed like a pair of human torches against the dark coolness of night. He leaned. Their torsos brushed.

"Zadie?" he croaked.

"Yes."

He froze. It was not a question. It was a command. He shut up, crossed the last half-inch of separation, and ignited the bonfires within them.

# CHAPTER TWENTY-ONE

· · · · ·

## *Change of Heart*

Zadie shot eastward in a burst of speed as a buried ultimatum resurrected in her chest. Five years ago, a pair of dark, piercing eyes had pinned her and asked the soul-shattering question, *do you have the courage for this?*

She hadn't, not that day, but the offer never faded from the eyes of her friend. It stood between them over the years, brazen and sharp. Zadie flew between the skyscrapers of the city, darted low between the buildings, and dove through the old neighborhoods until she found the other woman standing in a patch of earth opened in the concrete. The small woman's black hair was pulled back tightly at the nape of her neck. Her calloused fingers curled around the spade handle. Her head was tilted heavenward. The sunlight slipped through the buildings' shoulders. Her dark eyes stared back fearlessly.

"Inez," Zadie said, "I'm ready."

There is an alchemy to leaders; a light that blazes and gathers everyone around. Inez had long seen it smoldering in Zadie's eyes; similar embers burned within her own. Inez riveted the listener. Zadie gathered the crowds. Two kinds of strengths, two kinds of grace, two kinds of flames to set the world on fire. Long ago, she had asked Zadie to help her ignite the courage of the poor.

"We have our bodies and our hearts and nothing else, but all across the world, that is what has pushed for change."

She had asked five years too soon. For Inez, walking in the trenches of the city's suffering, it was agony to wait while gunshots rang out, and families faced evictions, and drugs sucked living souls away. Inez had known Zadie was too young then, but her heart had been splitting like a drought-cracked landscape, desperate for a rain of change. The passage of time had tempered the steel of her convictions as Inez strengthened herself and her community, pushing back against the suffocating despair that sank into the neighborhoods like polluted harbor fog. Five years had changed the landscape, the buildings, the people, and especially Inez. Everything collided at once; the time had come, the people were ready, and Zadie Byrd Gray had come of age.

The two women whipped into action, gathering people in churches and homes, nineteen at a time, skirting just under the need for a permit. Zipper filmed their speeches and the Alternet multiplied their viewers into thousands.

"How long will you suffer without taking action?" Inez demanded of them. "We have nothing. Our children are hungry. Debt enslaves us merely for survival. We all know the joke about the man who sold his organs on the black market to pay for the medical care to get them fixed!"

They laughed, but the bitter irony hit close to truth.

"How long will you live and die by thousands without rising up for change?" Inez asked them. "When will the day come when you say, *enough!* We have nothing left to lose, and everything to gain."

Seeds sprouted that had been planted weeks ago. During the time of the evacuations, people had learned more about the statistics that accounted for their lives. Fifty percent of the population lived at the poverty line. The richest one percent owned more than all of them put together. People knew it was not through hard work that the upper class became so wealthy. Aubrey Renault had often heard the wealthy gloat, *the reason we are so rich is because everyone else is so poor.* The quote ripped through the Alternet, fanning the flames of resentment. Inez and Zadie decried the tax code that was written by the wealthy, for the wealthy. They outlined in stark clarity the way that corporate influence on politics effectively disenfranchised all but the extremely wealthy. Only millionaires could run for Congress; the poor were taxed without any hope of representation.

"This is wrong!" Zadie said. "If the poorest in this country are fifty percent of the vote, then *we* are the majority party! How can millionaires represent us if they have never felt the stab of hunger and their children have never suffered?"

"*Aii Díos,*" Inez added with a breath of prayer, "may all children be free from the suffering ours have seen . . . but until our children are part of the Congress that makes the laws, no one will ever see the end of this!"

They spoke to people without the credentials of suits, ties, or résumés. They related to people from the truth of who they were. Zadie wore her ubiquitous boots, short skirt, and jean jacket. Inez pinned a cluster of dandelions in her hair and tucked her mother's embroidered blouse into her blue jeans. The women held their purses upside down. They turned their pockets inside out, showing that they had no riches, no trust funds, no money. They had nothing but their words and even then they could make no promises.

"Only God can make promises that can be kept," Inez said passionately, "the rest of us can only do our best . . . but I swear to you, with every breath that enters my chest, I will speak and act to help you. You know these are not the empty words of politicians. I have said this vow every day of my life. Have you ever seen me break it?"

They hadn't. Inez Hernandez served the soup when she was

hungry and handed out bread when her own shelf was bare. They had seen her body block policemen's punches from the beaten and abused. God sleeps more than Inez Hernandez, the joke went. Some people gossiped that she slept in church, but since her waking life was an act of prayer, Inez reasoned that God's church could cradle her when she rested.

"All my life I have served the poor, but the abuse of power creates a roaring ocean of hunger that I cannot silence. You must take your roar," she told them, "take that hungry ocean in you and turn it into waves of change."

Inez called for a nationwide resistance to the poverty draft.

"Do not enlist in the war machine! The wealthy warmongers will send you to your death. Come to me! I will put you to work feeding our families. We have Victory Gardens for people all over the country. We will triumph over oppression by planting the seeds of health, peace, and equality."

The young people came to Inez. The recruitment offices sat empty. Reenlistment rates plummeted. The Victory Gardens flourished. Songs that had lain dormant in the heart of America blossomed on lips in the cities. *Gonna lay down my sword and shield* shot out from one garden plot, and *down by the riverside* echoed back from another.

On Sundays, at the behest of Inez Hernandez and Father Ramon, preachers called upon their congregations to withdraw their support of war, bring their brothers and sisters in the military home without judgment or blame, and to become true followers of the Prince of Peace. The preachers concluded their sermons with the immortal lines of Isaiah.

*". . . and they shall beat their swords into plowshares, and their spears into pruning hooks: nation shall not lift up sword against nation, neither shall they learn war any more."*

The power elite lifted its head from its perpetual feast. Eyes narrowed. Fury heaved in chests. The sanctity of war must continue unquestioned. The unholy crusaders of death rallied their spies and agents.

"Zadie-cherie," Aubrey warned her, "be careful. Be very careful."

Caution slowed her visible actions; but the dormant seed of powerful soulfulness Inez had seen in Zadie roared from the depths of her being. She was potent, hot, burning with energy. Zadie and Inez had to flirt with the knife's edge of visibility as they grew the movement. Everything had to be cloaked in secrecy and hidden underground. The Alternet was a great tool, but it was not foolproof. The corporate agents were twice as crafty as the government's and the local police hauled people down to the station for questioning like tunnel spiders catching their prey.

Education was pivotal to the success of the struggle, so Zadie and Inez built on the trainings Lupe had instigated, arranging evening sessions in civics, political philosophy, history, current events, and contemporary law. They discussed the statistics that accounted for their lives. They broke through notions of passivity, disempowerment, and despair with education about successful nonviolent revolutions and struggles for social change.

"Civil rights, women's equality, labor reforms - these things didn't just fall from the sky," Inez told people. "They took years of education, struggle, hardship, and sacrifice. This is the reality of fighting for change."

Inez didn't just make lemonade out of lemons or sugarcoat hardship into pies. Inez planted an orchard of lemon trees and made the sour knowledge of truth an emblem of pride.

"The laws of this nation enslave us," she said. "The protections put in place for the upper class perpetuate our suffering. For us, the police symbolize cruelty and injustice. Politicians represent tyranny and corruption. Democracy is a hollow word; it means nothing to people who have been stripped of their ability to vote by criminal convictions, discriminatory laws, and simply because they don't have billions of dollars to get their candidates into office!"

Inez shared this bitter truth like a hard-to-swallow medicine. Democracy was not dead; it was twisted beyond recognition. She pruned the whole corrupt system down to its root. In Inez's eyes, everyone was created equal, and everyone had a vote, rich or poor, criminal or not, young or old, educated or ignorant. She instituted community governance boards and invited everyone to attend, teaching participatory democracy as they grappled with the issues that plagued their communities. It was arduous work, full of frustration and argument, but Inez tried to have faith in it, nonetheless.

The urban poor brought strength, perseverance, and courage to the table. They were survivors of hard times, as pragmatic as Pilar Maria, savvy, calculating, sharp, and observant. For Zadie, raised by pacifist, activist parents, nonviolence was a philosophic imperative, but in Inez's communities, it had to be explained as a tactical move. They weren't going to get involved if they weren't going to win. Inez persistently repeated the exact process through which tyrants crumbled, showing them the pillars of support that propped up the ruling elite, discussing how they could erode those like water and stone, until their eyes began to glow with Gandhi's soul-force, and Inez knew they would ultimately be unstoppable. Day after day, Inez saw people come alive with purpose and conviction.

"This is our real work," Inez said to Zadie one night. "On the surface, we are planting gardens and growing food; at the roots, we are growing people. We strengthen health through good food, bodies through honest work, minds through education, and hearts and souls through action."

Pilar Maria's coffee flowed like a black river. Hair-curling bitterness became the taste of those times. Zadie swigged it down with a grimace, accepting its harsh energy as penance for starting this insurrection with her lies.

"You didn't lie, Zadie," Charlie told her finally. "You saw the stories of the Dandelion Insurrection spread like stars in the sky and dared to point out the constellation that they formed."

Zadie drank his sweet words with a smile. They softened the challenges of the struggle and made the coffee less bitter. One morning, she realized she had grown fond of the brew's painful honesty. It kicked you into action. It seared lies from your throat. It jolted clarity into your mind. It left no room for idealism, only absolute truth. Pilar served it black . . . as stark as the reality they lived in. She made no apologies. She offered no milk. Cream and sugar had to arise from the soul.

One night, Zadie and Inez sat in the echoing chamber of the church, discussing the next move of this struggle. Their soft voices barely dented the silence. The ever-present votive candles lined the altar before them. Zadie leaned back in the pew, staring at the dark void of the ceiling.

"Inez," she said quietly. "How deep into this revolution do you want to go?"

Inez frowned at her.

"Do you want to prune the problem down a little," Zadie asked, "or pull it out by the roots?"

"The roots, of course," Inez answered immediately.

"Then we've got to tackle greed," Zadie said. "If we don't address it as a spiritual and moral failing, no amount of revolution will bring lasting change. The greed of our society must be uprooted, or we will grow into that which we despise."

*Consumption* had once described a deadly disease. Now, as a practice, it wasted the soul. It devoured one's life. It crippled societies. Consumption had become the symbol of American society, and it stamped its demise in clear ink. Greed was a disease that would kill them all. No one was immune to it. Inez recognized the signs of infection in the poor. Lupe diagnosed it in the suburbs. Charlie knew his rural relatives suffered from it as well. Zadie spoke up for the remedy.

"We have been taught greed," Zadie told people. "We were sold consumption as a measure of our worth, but look around you! You are a human being with measures of love and kindness to offer. When you have nothing, you are still worth more than the millions of dollars locked up in a bank! Money is a pale substitute for the riches of our hearts. Hidden within our greed is our longing for something greater; something money cannot buy and products cannot deliver. We want to love and be loved. We want to share a meal together. We want shelter from the storm. We want peace. We want joy."

Inez and Zadie urged people to stop all forms of excessive consumption. If they wanted equality, they had to embody it themselves. Inez told them to give of their time and their love. Zadie asked people to turn their eyes from advertisements and listen to each other. The women went a step further and urged the people to emancipate themselves from the greed that enslaved them all. Zadie urged people to stare with cold eyes at consumerism. She told people to spit on the sidewalks when fancy cars drove past, to spit when they saw billboards for gold watches, spit when the radio told them they couldn't live without the newest gadget on the market!

"Spit out your enslavement to a culture of greed," Zadie said. "Feel that addiction leaving your body. Then raise your head high and walk onwards. You are one step closer to freedom!"

The women told people to withdraw not only their worship of wealth, but also their approval of the wealthy.

"When children go to bed hungry," Zadie said, hot with passion, "the diamonds of the rich become the emblems of their shame! Turn your backs on them. Withdraw all approval from people who have amassed fortunes from the suffering of others!"

Ostentatious status symbols began to vanish as the Dandelion Insurrection pointed out the parasitic connection between the rich and poor. The situation dripped with irony. The wealthy vilified the lower class as suckers on the system while the rich sucked the entire nation to death, person-by-person, drop-by-drop. The fattest ticks were the ones at the top, the nastiest worms stole the food from the babies, and, as the new slogan went, *one man's treasure is another man's hunger.*

Inez could feel the rising tide of tension. She could smell the scent of the city turning ripe with readiness for action. Eyes no longer dripped with envy as they trailed after fancy cars. They burned with injustice. The ache of knowledge seethed. The elite began to double their security forces when traveling in public. The city police reinforced the blockades around Greenback Street.

Uptown, Aubrey Renault anxiously watched the efforts of his friends. He writhed in painful emotions as he served the people who opposed his little bird. He clenched his jaw while *the Butcher* complimented his cooking, he nodded politely when *the Banker* came in the door, but he knew how easily they would hurt his beloved Zadie, this girl who had shown up on his doorstep years ago. He tossed sleeplessly at night. The strain of guilt plagued him. He had grown rich catering to the wealthy. He gave generously, but the bottomless pit of suffering

231

swallowed every penny without ceasing. There was no amount of money he could give away in penance for participating in this injustice. The cry of his soul was no longer solaced by his Robin Hood games. His Lady Liberty gleamed at him from the harbor. The unfulfilled promise of her creed echoed accusingly in his thoughts.

*Give me your tired, your poor,*
*Your huddled masses yearning to breathe free . . .*

One night, he paused over the flames as he grilled filet mignon. He scorched one side, then the other, inhaling the stench of charred meat like a bitter perfume. The time had come. He shut off the flame, handed the kitchen over to the *sous-chef de cuisine*, and walked out into the night still wearing his apron. He contacted his little bird and sent his private car to bring her in secret to his apartment. Zadie and Aubrey spoke long into the evening, sitting side-by-side on his balcony overlooking the city. Finally, Zadie nodded. They shook hands. She left. He prayed to the saint of liberty. At dawn, he went to get ready.

The anniversary celebration of the world's most successful and exclusive restaurant was touted as the event of the year. Café Renault's illustrious clientele vied to be present. *The Butcher, the Banker, the Candlestick Maker,* the Mayor, the President, the Chief of Special Operations; every last one of the richest, most powerful members of the elite accepted the invitation of the world famous Aubrey Renault. When the night arrived, Aubrey welcomed his guests. His obsidian eyes glinted. He knew that on this anniversary, he would offer them an unforgettable feast, a repast that would change the face of politics. This lavish meal contained only one ingredient . . . dandelions.

"In twenty minutes," he informed his astonished guests,

"the hungry are coming to join the party. Give them a place at your table . . . or get out of my restaurant."

A mad shock and scramble erupted as the private security guards evacuated the elite from the restaurant. At first, *the Banker* scoffed, calling it a hoax. However, he, too, fled when the rumors were confirmed.

The poor were marching to Greenback Street.

\*       \*       \*

Far up north, Ellen Byrd and Bill Gray watched with bated breath as the mainstream media claimed riots had broken out on Greenback Street. On the coffee table, Bill's laptop streamed actual footage via the Alternet.

"Look at that," Bill snorted. "There aren't any riots. The television is using old footage. I don't think those images are even from the United States."

"Shhh!" Ellen shushed him. "There's Zadie!"

She stood in the doorway of Café Renault, explaining the events that had transpired. At six o'clock, a small group of ten democratically elected representatives from the neighborhoods had attempted to cross through the curfew barricade around Greenback Street holding an invitation to Aubrey's anniversary celebration. They had come to enjoy the graciousness of Aubrey's offer and, for the first time in their lives, to sit at the table with the powerful people who controlled so much of their daily experiences. When the police refused to allow them through, Zadie placed a phone call and in fifteen minutes a thousand readied citizens had assembled. They had been preparing for this anniversary dinner as meticulously as Aubrey Renault. Swiftly and calmly, before they could be stopped, Zadie walked the people through the police barricades and entered Greenback Street. By seven o'clock, the elite had hastily vacated.

Zadie stood on the fountain outside Café Renault, surrounded by people who had never once set foot on the street, but now stood determined to show that Greenback Street belonged to the people, *all* people. They were not here to destroy it, but to bring the wealth of the nation back to the people upon whose backs it was earned.

"Police officers," she called out, "you may go home. Not one storefront on this street will be harmed. Not one flower in the landscape will be destroyed. We came to sit at the same table with the elite. I am very sorry to hear that they have refused to meet with us like civilized people."

The sergeant replied over a bullhorn.

"We have orders," he said, "to clear this area of your kind of people."

"Not my kind of people," Zadie answered, stepping off the fountain and walking halfway to meet him. "*Our* kind of people. This gentleman, here, is you when your pension runs out. This woman is your wife when her heart fails and you can't afford the surgery. This young mother is your daughter when her mortgage turns upside down. This venerable old lady is your mother when Congress cuts her social security money." Zadie clasped hands with each person as she pointed them out. "You have a choice," she told the police officers, "to protect and serve the people or to become the paid mercenaries of the upper class."

Far up in northern Maine, Ellen's chest split with emotion. *Get away from those cops, Zadie,* she urged silently. That body she had birthed, the limbs she had nourished, the wild crop of curls that defied constraint, and the thin armor of Zadie's skin all stood just a few feet from certain harm. Ellen, with the heightened senses of a mother hen on alert, saw goose bumps on Zadie's arms from the coolness of the air and felt a ludicrous urge to tell her daughter to put on a coat. *Never mind,* she groaned silently to herself. That girl should have on full body armor if she was going to walk toward armed officers.

"If you do not clear this street immediately," the sergeant announced, "the National Guard will be called in to assist us."

"Who here has a family member in the military, serving because of the poverty draft?" Zadie called out.

Eerily, in utter silence, every hand in the group was raised. The silence was frightening. The stark and absolute sense of conviction and clarity ran shivers up Ellen Byrd's arms. Her daughter had built a Peace Army. These people were *organized.* They had moved beyond anger or fear, transforming those emotions into fuel for their determination. They had tempered the heat of fury into the strength of perseverance, and hardened fear into courage.

Ellen and Bill read Charlie's breaking news report anxiously, worried about the inevitable eviction or arrests.

*Thus far,* he wrote, *the police are just waiting. The strategy seems to be, ignore them long enough and they will go home. This might be the most intelligent tactical move in the history of the United States,* he mentioned with irony.

"It is only a matter of time," Aubrey warned Zadie as they sat side by side on the edge of the fountain. "The wealthy will not meet with you, and the police won't allow this to continue. They cannot."

"We knew that," Zadie reminded him. "This was a symbolic gesture from the start." She looked up and down the street. The storefront owners were the worst agitators, demanding the immediate eviction of the riffraff. Every minute that passed sank a hole in their profits. The poor smudged Greenback

235

Street with their presence, tarnishing the allure of the street. Zadie wished the demonstrators could remain long enough to crumble the sickening elitism of the wealthy class' cultural oasis . . . but it was only a matter of time.

Aubrey shifted on the fountain beside her.

"Soon, they will begin to use tear gas," he warned her.

"Then we will change the game first," Zadie answered. She squinted out at the city's apartments where citizens were flicking their lights on and off in solidarity with the demonstrators. She stared at the incredible patterns that formed and dissolved. Her eyes tracked the motions. Everything around her vanished for a moment as her focus telescoped onto a particularly beautiful sequence of flashing lights. *That's life,* she thought, *a flash of brightness, here and then gone, an ever-changing permutation of presence and nothing.*

"Let's start the murmurations," she decided. She gathered the demonstrators. "If the police don't want us in one place, fine. We'll go everywhere like flocks of birds. We don't want just Greenback Street. We want our whole country! Let's get this insurrection moving!"

The word relayed out through the Alternet. The people left Greenback Street, but even as *the Three Men in the Tub* toasted their success, an unexpected form of resistance blossomed in cities across the country. Zadie and the Dandelion Insurrection initiated a series of spontaneous movement demonstrations nicknamed *the murmurations.* Flash mobs crossed with marches as groups of people joined together, split apart, reformed, and wove through the city streets without destination or predetermined routes. They walked. They ran. They sat on the sidewalk for a while and then moved again. They marched in circles in the intersections and then continued on their way. The cops couldn't figure out what was going on. The people, however, knew the simple rules of the game; *fly forward, the leader changes at every shift in direction, keep equidistant, and don't leave your wing-mate out on a limb.*

Just as Greenback Street began to resume its normal atmosphere of high-end shopping and dining, a murmuration of well-dressed 'shoppers' suddenly swooped through and startled the wealthy during their luncheons. By the time security was alerted, the murmuration had vanished. These demonstrations formed nearly hourly for several days. Finally, private security cordoned off the street completely. It was too late, however. The mystique of the cultural oasis crumbled. The upper echelon whispered that it was no longer safe to go into the area.

The murmurations were the nonviolent guerrilla strategy of the Dandelion Insurrection, appearing and disappearing, growing in strength and volume. Zadie's principles of multi-nodal movements - *create, copy, improve, and share* - offered ordinary people simple instructions for protest and change. One person walking down a city street would pull out a pot and a spoon, and a thousand person cacerolazo would erupt. A few people would stop in the crosswalk and, in two minutes, traffic slammed to a halt as dozens slowly and silently raised up their hands, answering the unspoken question; who has sacrificed family to the poverty draft? In a park, a lone voice would holler out, *what do we want?* And inevitably the cry would be returned, *Life!* The second shout would be heard, *what do we want?* A score of voices would reply, *Liberty!* And by the third cry of *what do we want?* every voice within earshot would join in, *Love!* The murmurations were maddening to the authorities. Nothing could be done to stop them.

"It is a dance," Zadie told people via the Alternet. "A dance of human beings working together to show that *we* are our own authorities. Sooner or later, the officials will realize that they must listen to us, because we have now learned to listen to each other."

After the high visibility leadership role at Greenback Street, Zadie was forced to do her work from hiding. The Chief of Police, with the full support of the wealthy class, had sworn a personal vendetta against Aubrey, and hounded the man mercilessly until he was finally arrested and thrown in jail without bond. The wealthy then turned their wrath on Zadie. The propaganda machine reared its despicable head and labeled her *the Most Hated Woman in America*. Tucker hacked into the mainstream media networks and changed the slogan to *the Most Hated-LOVED Woman in America*. Charlie released an article explaining exactly why Zadie Byrd Gray was rising in popularity even as the government hunted her.

*Zadie exemplifies the indomitable spirit and passion of the Dandelion Insurrection. She strives ceaselessly for life, liberty, and love, refusing to be mowed down or rounded up. The corporate-political powers hate her precisely because she is so worthy of our love!*

Hidden in the basement of an apartment building, Zadie ached to see Charlie, not through a screen, but with her flesh-and-blood eyes. The strain of their efforts affected Inez, too. The small woman longed to sink her fingers into soil and tend her garden peacefully. They clamped down on their complaints, however. Their sacrifices seemed minor compared to Lupe's, who had sent her children into hiding for fear they would be kidnapped or used against everyone in the movement. Pilar Maria, who endured challenges like the Rock of Gibraltar, broke down in tears over the plight of her family.

Even as Zadie's heart ached, she redoubled her efforts to build popular resistance. The release of Tucker's election fraud information relied on getting the citizens used to demonstrating under the authoritarian thumb of the government. Surveillance drones swept the streets while Zadie and Inez kept their eyes out for the infiltration of government and corporate agents. A raid on the anarchist bike co-op caught Hawlings and Spark Plug. Charlie warned Zadie to be careful. His suspicions about ole Sparky still plagued him.

Zadie reluctantly mentioned to Charlie that she shouldn't keep contacting him. The tension and stress of the week lined her face.

"They're getting closer. I can feel them getting ready to pounce. If they find you through me, it could be a disaster."

Charlie nodded in agreement.

"Come back," he suggested. "I'm holding down a one man occupation of Tucker's spare bedroom. I could use some solidarity here."

She smiled and reached out to touch the screen.

"I love you."

"Love you right back and a million times over," Charlie replied.

That love propelled her through the arduous days. Death threats for Zadie and Inez were stapled to Pilar Maria's door. Inez gritted her teeth and wrapped martyrdom around them like a thin veil of protection, warning the world that their deaths would cause revolution. She planted the notion in people's minds, watered it with prayers, and watched as it grew into an eerie possibility that made Zadie shiver. Revolution would come whether they were assassinated or not . . . and frankly, she preferred to stay living.

One evening, Zadie leaned against a wall, wearily waiting for a discussion to start. The six core organizers in New York had arranged for a secret meeting. Zadie had been nervous about attending, but Inez thought it was important to help strategize the next move. Zadie sighed. It had not been an easy time for the young midwife of Love. She had been up to her elbows in the bloody laboring of humanity; sweat, tears, straining, shoving, gritted teeth, screaming. Zadie looked around at the half-dozen faces in the room, where stress and anxiety were inscribed right along with passion and determination. Her heart ached for them. They were parents in the difficult process of birthing change. Memories swelled up in Zadie and haunted her. She bit her lip, wondering what she could tell these parents when it seemed that change was bringing more heartache than beauty to their lives. She had been in their shoes. Twice, she had aborted her children, repeating her excuses like mantras, *too young, too immature, not ready, wrong time.*

A sudden rush of tears pricked her eyes. If only there was more support, she thought. If I had known that my children would have been fed and clothed . . . if I had known my children would not be sent off to war, beaten, or jailed unjustly . . . if the fathers had been full of love, like Charlie - Zadie stopped. The endless maze of *what ifs* led nowhere. She was here, now, with her choices made and the future opening according to them. She pushed off the wall and walked to the center of the room.

"Tonight," she said, "let's talk about Love."

There had been much discussion about putting forth political candidates as they set up self-governing communities, and it was a golden moment to plant the seeds of dandelion politics.

"I've been in abusive relationships before," she told them honestly, "and I've got a zero tolerance rule now. I'm not going to stick around with politicians who are bent on abusing, stealing, starving, or poisoning me. If someone hurts me, we're done. No excuses. I'm not voting for that person again. The American people deserve political partners who will treat them with respect. I'll vote for anyone who can honestly say, *I love you* . . . and then act like it."

The small group nodded in agreement. Zadie went on.

"I fell in love with this great guy and he has shown me that if you want to be in a relationship with somebody, you've got to listen to them. That's the relationship public servants must build with citizens . . . a truly caring, sincere partnership."

"Who is this guy? Maybe I can call him up for advice," a wisecracker joked.

Zadie's heart made a split-second decision. If she had to work from hiding, she'd just as soon be in hiding with Charlie. Inez froze as she read Zadie's thoughts. *Don't Zadie,* she begged silently, but her young friend said it anyway.

"Charlie Rider, sweetest man on earth."

That juicy tidbit of gossip raced out into the streets like a fire truck blaring down the block. The thrill of knowing that Zadie Byrd Gray and the infamous Charlie Rider were a couple ran through all the stop signs of secrecy. The news barreled through the neighborhood, reaching the ears of Spark Plug like a screaming siren.

"I met them once," he said casually to the woman who told him the news. He pointed to his battered face. "When I got arrested, the Feds tried to beat their whereabouts out of me."

"I think," the gossip whispered, "they must be somewhere around here."

Spark Plug looked up sharply.

"Why's that?"

"Well, Zadie was just seen at this meeting . . . and if he loves her, he would be close, don't you think?" the gossip's eyes gleamed with excitement.

Spark Plug's eyes glowed, too, but for other reasons. He limped off, called the agent who was tracking his every move, and negotiated a deal for his continued release from prison.

# CHAPTER TWENTY-TWO

. . . . .

## *NOT A TERRORIST*

"What?!" Charlie gasped when Tucker ran out of the basement and told him.

"They locked down the city! A massive mobilization is conducting door-to-door searches. Zadie vanished - no one knows where - Pilar is getting Inez out of the city, Zipper's claiming that some guy named Spark Plug turned into an informant - "

Charlie swore and cursed that yellow-bellied punk to an eternity in hell.

"The whole Alternet is being probed like a colonoscopy," Tucker groaned, "and these posters are everywhere!" He handed a printout to Charlie.

TERRORIST was stamped across a photo of Zadie Byrd Gray. The caption underneath read *closely associated with Charlie Rider.*

*The Hunt for the Zadie-bird* obsessed the mainstream media. The evening news featured footage of gun-toting police kicking down doors and shouting, *freeze!* The lockdown of New York City to capture *the Most Hated Woman In America* occupied the front page of every major newspaper. The radio interrupted its programming every five minutes to give folks an update on the terrorist madwoman at large in New York City. Tanks motored up and down the streets. Police forces arrested people left and right.

The attack on Zadie infuriated everyone who knew her. It was an assault on themselves, their families, and everything they had hoped and dreamed. They watched the persecution of a woman who had brought them nothing but love, and felt a gut-twisting sense of outrage at the government. Charlie's writing seethed.

*These corporate-political thugs must be condemned for their immoral persecution of Zadie Byrd Gray. The indiscriminate use of the terrorist label is a clear violation of human rights and a flagrant affront to justice. The corporate-political elite abuse the label of terrorist to control politics, social movements, and, most importantly, to hurt the people we love.*

That, of course, was putting it mildly. His words burned across the page, countering the allegations of the government and sharing the outraged responses of everyone who knew Zadie. Ellen Byrd and Natalie Beaulier-Rider went together to the local post office with sharpies in hand. The postmistress looked the other way as the two mothers scribbled *NOT A* on the TERRORIST posters of their children. Soon images of Charlie and Zadie across the country bore the slogan *NOT A* TERRORIST.

Bill Gray got so mad at the hyped-up portrayal of Zadie as a terrorist that he hauled his television down to Main Street and publicly smashed it. Charlie whipped out an article about the despair Zadie's father felt at seeing his only child slandered by propaganda and hunted by the government. Television smashings broke out across the country. Alternet usage surged. Charlie watched videos of the demonstrations with bitter pleasure, knowing that with every broken television, *the Three Men in the Tub* were losing control of the populace. Predictably, the government banned the smashing of televisions. People dumped the propaganda machines on their sidewalks, labeled with signs; *FREE LIES*. The government responded with television and online ads featuring a boot crushing a dandelion

244

and the phrase *Stamp Out Terrorism.*

Signs appeared in the front yards: *Dandelions are not terrorists.*

Bumper stickers graced the nation's fenders: *A world without dandelions is no fun at all.*

Posters handmade by the children were posted in the windows of schools, homes, churches, and local markets: *Dandelions grow here.*

The government banned the words *dandelion* and *insurrection.*

The golden symbol sprouted everywhere. Posters of dandelions sprung up faster than the flowers themselves. Banners were strung on clotheslines in inner cities.

The government banned the 'image of terrorists'.

Ellen Byrd rattled her artistic sabers and rallied an army of artists. Abstract painters threw yellow dots and green lines on canvas. Spray paint taggers left stenciled dandelions everywhere. A fashion line came out with dandelion bras that sported little fuzzy yellow blossom pasties. Feminist activists formed flash mobs, converged, tore open their shirts, hollered, *the Dandelion Insurrection is here!* and vanished.

Tucker hacked into mainstream television and interrupted primetime news with Zipper's new film. Breathtaking clips flashed by showing Lupe's children and Zadie in a backyard surrounded by yellow dandelions. Seeds blew from puffed up cheeks and small chins glowed yellow with pollen as Zadie patiently wove chains for the children. The film concluded with Eva solemnly crowning Zadie with dandelions. Underneath, a single caption read: *We are not terrorists. We are people. With love, the Dandelion Insurrection.*

Charlie allowed himself a small smile. By that evening, however, another assault of bad news punched them.

"They raided Bill and Ellen's farm," Tucker informed Charlie. "The Feds used the anti-assembly laws to break up a meeting with your extended family. Around a hundred people were arrested, including Bill, Mack, and your cousin, Matt. Ellen came home from your mother's and the place was turned upside down. Your grandfather, Valier, locked himself in Bill's outhouse so they couldn't arrest him."

Charlie's stomach dropped. His breath caught in his chest. His mind reeled. Mass arrests were sweeping the country. Pre-existing jails had no room for the new wave of arrests. The evacuation centers were used as prisons. The courts claimed an unmanageable backlog, and citizens were being held without bail until trials could be scheduled.

"In other words, indefinite detention in the camps," Charlie groaned.

He scoured his mind for a response as people vanished off the streets.

*We cannot allow ourselves to forget them,* he wrote. *Put out a place for them at the dinner table. Leave an empty chair at the office for them. Let their absence become visible. We cannot be complacent in the face of injustice.*

People put up small signs with quotes from his articles.

*A vanished person is a sign of your vanishing freedom.*

*You have no freedom until all are free.*

The government placed a total media ban on the prison camps, but Mack managed to get word out from the inside.

*Bill, Matt, and the rest are all fine,* he wrote. *We're trying to put a bad situation to good use with trainings.*

The next note relayed bad news.

*A crackdown killed the trainings. We're working as forced labor now, but trying to keep sane.*

The third message sent chills down Charlie's spine.

*We're not allowed to talk anymore.*

A week passed before the next note arrived.

*Whispering is forbidden.*

And then no more messages came.

Charlie prayed for Mack, Bill, young Matt, all the other Acadians that had been arrested in the raid, and for Aubrey Renault, who was still being held in New York City. The table grew into an altar, decorated with candles, offerings, and small scribbled prayers.

One night, Charlie set Zadie's photo on it.

"We haven't heard from her," Charlie said quietly.

Tucker said nothing, staring at the despair in the young man's face.

The phone rang. They flinched. Tucker answered, suspicious at first, then increasingly more solemn and quiet. Without a word, Tucker hit the speakerphone button and Charlie looked up from the table.

" . . . my friend's friend said to call this number and tell this story, even if it was just on a machine. I gotta be anonymous, so I can't tell you what camp I used to work at . . . but I can't keep silent no more. This is America! Christ, I know these people ain't done nothing."

Charlie grabbed a sheet of paper and started taking notes.

"We were told to keep them silent. No talking. No whispering. But I started to see these signs, you know, secret communications. I didn't say nothing about it, but this fellow caught me watching. I dunno, maybe he could tell somehow that I was just as scared as he was. He told me, a smile meant, *be kind;* a touch on the hand meant, *be connected;* and a look in the eyes meant, *be unafraid.*"

The man's voice cracked. Charlie's breath clenched in his chest. Tucker's eyes grew bleak and round. The slogan of the insurrectionists brought tears to their eyes and chills to their hearts. Charlie wrote down every word the man said. At dawn, he sent the story across the country like the ray of the sun, scorching with painful illumination.

*       *       *

Charlie pushed his writing to its limits as arrests continued and fear laced the hearts of the insurrectionists. The leaderless movement reached a breaking point. People wanted answers and direction, but it seemed there were none to give. At a time when all eyes were looking for leaders, Charlie could offer only one message.

*Look within. Leaders reflect the courage or the fear that already lies inside us. Cast out fear, grasp courage, and move forward.*

He tried to take his own advice to heart as sleeplessness and anxiety took their toll. Charlie wrote night and day, frantic with worry for Zadie as the Dandelion Insurrection heaved with action. Images rolled through the Alternet from the front lines of the extraction resistance. People joined hands across the railroad tracks as the freight trains moved coal toward the ports. They stood firmly as the mass of steel thundered toward them. The train slowly decelerated, screeching to stillness in the last few feet of track. The sweating engineer laid his face in his shaking hands. His orders had come from an office far away: *run them over if they don't get off the track.* His soul rebelled. In other places, the engineers shut their eyes, closed their hearts, and barreled onward. The activists scattered. So far, no one had been killed . . . but it was close.

A haunting video from the oil pipeline resistance came through the Alternet of police beating a protestor viciously. The man took blows to his face, his chest, and his groin. His lip split and bled down his chin.

"If you beat my body," the man said laboriously, "you beat the earth . . . in the end . . . you beat yourself."

Charlie's draft was damp with his own grief as he wrote a response. He urged the people to talk to their police officers and reach for the human underneath the uniform.

*Reveal yourself as a person, not a statistic,* he wrote. *Ask the police if they would beat your children if ordered . . . would they beat their own? We must remind them of their humanity. It is our only hope to stop the violence.*

Just as Charlie felt they were making some headway with the police, a new kind of force began to wreak havoc in the cities.

"We don't know who - or what - these guys are!" one activist cried. "I've never seen this kind of uniform. They're brutal - awful - no hesitation, no way to connect to them. We tried."

Tucker put the Alternet team on it. The word came back, *hired guns.* These were not public servants. These were the private security forces that *the Butcher* had been building for years. *Greenbacks,* the people began to call them, bought and paid for by *the Three Men in the Tub.* The people's cries of illegality seemed to fall on deaf ears, but one of Charlie's journalists urged them not to give up.

"The justice branch is having apoplexy over this issue. Two Supreme Court Justices devolved into a shouting match over it yesterday. A fissure is opening up. I'll give you the names. Get people contacting the lawyers and judges who want to keep some semblance of democracy around. The situation's smoldering, Charlie, keep the heat up."

It wasn't easy. The hired forces cracked down in dozens of cities. Charlie was wracking his brain for a solution when

Zipper contacted him with an astonishing story. In multiple cities across the country, the uniforms of every known brutalizer had been swashed with a green stripe of paint.

"Greenback stripes," he told Charlie with a grin. "Rumor has it that the marks are courtesy of the nation's dry cleaners."

The story cheered his heart, but bad news kept relaying through the Alternet.

"Did you write this?" Tucker asked one day, handing Charlie a printout. Charlie quickly scanned it, frowning at the article written in his name that advocated the use of violence to bring down the government.

"Of course not!" he exclaimed.

"We're being co-opted," Tucker grimaced. "It was bound to happen."

That night, the six o'clock news ran a story on the article.

"Insurrection leader Charlie Rider is calling for violent attacks as the dandelion movement fails," the newscaster announced.

"Dandelions are never violent," Charlie said to Tucker, "and we ought to point out that they violated their own ban on the word dandelion."

Charlie wrote a fast exposé of the article, warning people to use discernment. *The Dandelion Insurrection has advocated peaceful resistance with every breath. The heart of love never promotes violence. Honesty is a sharp enough tool for us.*

He wrote furiously, fueled by the suspicion that the phony article was just a foreshadowing of events to come. He worked long into the night, plastering words over his worry for Zadie, but Tucker, passing bleary-eyed by his door, was not fooled.

*It's always darkest before dawn*, Charlie wrote. Then he scratched it out. Dark was dark. His sun had set the day Zadie disappeared and dawn was a promise that might never come.

Each day passed with a solid ache in his chest. Insomnia began to grip him. He spent long nights looking out the window as his pencil scraped absently at the page. A word here, a phrase there. When he looked at the scribbles the next morning, poetry sat on the page.

*Every form of cruelty boils down to this:*
*me, here*
*you, there*
*separated*
*by this foolishness.*

In the darkness, Charlie's heart flew across the country seeking Zadie, and along the way, he heard the unspoken thoughts of sleeping souls. He wrote them down in scrawling lines, placed them at the beginning of his articles, and slipped them out to people. They hit a tiny bell of truth that reverberated throughout the nation. *The Man From the North* crept deeper into the people's hearts. He was real. He was human. He lived and breathed like them. He longed for love and life. The poems were mounted on refrigerators, pinned to bulletin boards, and scrawled on the backs of notebooks. One night, Charlie turned his gaze slowly upward to the stars. His pen moved sadly across the page.

*Stars . . .*
*you are not so distant*
*as the one I love.*

\*       \*       \*

One evening, the rising drumroll of intensity struck its inevitable crescendo. Charlie and Tucker had made themselves a weary set of sandwiches and turned on the television to check for news of Zadie. No one had heard from her within the insurrection, so Charlie had taken to watching primetime news to see if the government would announce her arrest . . . or death. Tucker flipped the channel to the main station and his mouth fell open in disbelief.

"Tragedy struck today as Lt. Gibbs was killed when two violent insurrectionists launched an attack on police officers," the newscaster announced. Images flashed by of a man lobbing a canister at the police as a second activist tried to stop him. An explosion burst. A rain of gunfire shot out. Silence. An image of bodies on the street. A photo of Lt. Gibbs in dress uniform.

"Not a word about how the police gunned down the two men!" Tucker shouted in fury. "Not a word about how one activist tried to stop the other man!"

He threw his sandwich at the television as the mainstream news replayed the footage of the attack.

"Ten bucks that guy was an agent provocateur hired by the government to incite violence," Charlie said, his voice laced with disgust. "Watch, we might see something as they replay the scene."

They squinted at the screen. There was the first activist, turning and shouting something. There was the second man, his face covered with a bandana. And, yes, sure enough, there it was; as the announcer brazenly claimed the violent insurrectionist had stolen a canister of tear gas, there were the police, clearly handing it to the man. The footage rolled on. The peaceful activist tried to restrain the man as he lobbed the canister. Gunfire broke out. The two men spun as they fell. Charlie leaned forward as the bandana fell off the man's face.

"Spark Plug," Charlie gasped. "That was Spark Plug!"

A wrench of emotions twisted inside him. He stared at the falling bodies, appalled and infuriated. Betrayal stung him. He remembered the man pushing him up against the wall of the tool co-op. *You can't make me hate you,* Charlie remembered saying, *you can't make me feel anything but love for you.* He scoffed at his earlier idealism as he shook with anger. Then images of Spark Plug's falling body replayed. His emotions drained away to a dull weariness. It didn't matter. Spark Plug was dead.

Tears ran down Tucker's cheeks.

"I knew him," he said.

"Who?" Charlie asked. "Spark Plug?"

"No, Lee Walker, the one who tried to stop the violence." Tucker stood up wearily and pulled out a photo of a young man offering the peace sign to the camera. Tucker put the photo of his longtime friend on the altar. He shook his head and turned the image face down. Lee was not missing. He was never coming back. Tucker's body shook. The table reverberated. The photos of missing friends trembled. Grief was an earthquake that rocked them all. Tucker let his tears fall like rain over the landscape of the altar. When he looked up, his face was stony and ashen.

"There's too many, Charlie. This table can't hold them all."

Charlie turned on his heel without a word. He closed the door to the bedroom . . . and wrote.

On doorsteps and roadsides, they appeared. Altars, memorials, and shrines sprang up across the country. Prayer came out of its private residence in people's hearts and spilled its sorrow openly onto the streets. Larger memorials formed in alleys and in the corners of parking lots. Grief became visible, uniting the people through sorrow and vulnerability. It was shocking to see the numbers and staggering to gaze at the photos of the faces. People walked by the shrines and their hearts turned cold toward a government that would do this to its citizens. The authorities forbade the altars in public parks, so people offered up their lawns. Churches mounted shrines on

253

their front steps. In the cities, people hung the altars on wrought-iron railings. The names of the dead, the incarcerated, the beaten, and the missing were written on the sidewalks. The authorities came to wash the chalk away. The people wrote the lists again the next day.

"I have written my daughter's name Every day," one woman said, "and Every day, they try to wash her away." Her lips began to tremble. "*Nothing* will ever do that. Nothing."

One set of images repeated at every shrine, propagated by the Dandelion Insurrection. Photos of three faces, the most recent on the list of casualties, were linked together with names and titles underneath:

| Lt. Gibbs | Spark Plug | Lee Walker |
|-----------|------------|------------|
| Officer | Agent provocateur | Activist |

The media called Lt. Gibbs' death: *the tragedy of insurrection.* Everyone else called all three deaths: *the tragedy of oppression.*

*     *     *

A shift occurred. The tide changed direction. An eddy in the current broke free and the course of history's river altered. Charlie could hardly believe it. The shrines galvanized people into action more strongly than anything else the Dandelion Insurrection had ever done. The names and faces of the fathers, sons, daughters, sisters, and mothers who had been harmed by tyranny renewed the determination of the people to resist. From the north, south, east, and west, the reports began to roll in hopeful. Lupe's boycotts drove a dent into corporate profits. Rolling blackouts swept the nation as citizens shut off their own electricity to send *the Candlestick Maker* the message: we don't want your dirty energy! *The Banker* watched in alarm as people withdrew their money. Institutions started to divest from the highly controlled chains. The stock market took a nosedive. In a multitude of ways, the people hunkered down and put up a fight against business as usual.

"They've stalled the pipeline paperwork," Tucker informed Charlie one afternoon.

"Who?" he asked, looking up from editing.

"Who knows? It has been lost in bureaucracy for a week. Now the clerk who is supposed to sign something is 'sick' for the fifth time this month."

"Well," Charlie smiled faintly, "illnesses can be recurring."

"Mmm-hmm," Tucker agreed, "and contagious."

Police deployment orders began to fall through the cracks. Dispatchers sent cops to the wrong addresses. Pepper spray canisters arrived defective.

"It's the people," Charlie said incredulously. "The people are standing up for themselves, even if it means sabotaging their own professions."

Work on natural gas extraction froze in Pennsylvania. The filling stations for fifty miles in each direction of Rudy's town were out of order. The restaurants were all closed for renovations. The motels were all booked up. Local bank tellers refused to serve the corporations. Folded placards were placed on the counter that informed the corporations that *the buck stops here.*

*Sorry,* a sign in one window read, *we're not servicing our extinction.*

Everywhere, a resistance pushed back against the tide of destruction. Like grains of sand wearing down the cogs of machinery, the system began to falter. Belligerent oils refused to slide things along smoothly. Fuses wouldn't ignite. Tires went flat. Memos disappeared. Uniforms weren't cleaned. Deliveries failed to show up.

"Total incompetence," the authorities grumbled.

*Dandelion Insurrection,* the people whispered.

# CHAPTER TWENTY-THREE

. . . . .

## *A Cream and Sugar Woman*

A low bank of clouds pressed down overhead as Charlie wearily went through the motions of beginning another day.

"We're out of cream," Tucker warned him as Charlie fumbled with the coffeemaker, "but there's a carton of Zadie's soymilk in the cupboard."

Zadie. Charlie closed his eyes and exhaled slowly. She was always there, teasing at the corners of his mind. Lately, he found himself staring at the front door expecting Zadie to walk right through. All his life, she'd been disappearing and reappearing . . . maybe this time would be no different. He leaned his forehead on the cupboard. Tucker put a hand on his shoulder.

"Sit down. I'll put the coffee on before I go downstairs."

Charlie sank into a wooden chair, rubbing his palms across his stubbly chin. His whole body ached with too many late nights, worries, and longing. As the hot water hit the coffee and a frothy trickle spouted into the pot, Charlie laid his red eyes on his hands. For the first time since hearing the phrase *the Dandelion Insurrection*, a feeling of *I don't want to do this anymore* hit his heart. Words of revolution choked as dry as dust in his aching throat. His palms pressed into his eye sockets. He became aware of every inch of his vulnerable flesh-and-blood body as he sat hunched over and exhausted. The sharp aroma of coffee stirred up memories inside him. His eyes scrunched back a wave of emotion as he allowed his mind to escape the heartache of the present for a memory from the past. As the

257

coffee dripped, Charlie's mind slipped back to an afternoon in high school, when he'd been waiting for Zadie in Pierrette's little cafe. He remembered inhaling the steaming coffee, romancing the enticing brew, wishing he could screw up his courage to tell Zadie how he felt.

"So? Woman trouble?" Valier had called out knowingly.

"None of your business," he had answered.

"There are one hundred and seventy-two girls between the ages of fifteen and forty in this town," Valier had informed him, "and we are related to them all, by marriage, blood, or gossip." The old man sat down in a chair, one hand on his knee, the other palm slapping the table as he scoffed at his grandson. "You're too young to know anything about women."

"Well, you're no expert," Charlie retorted. "You were married to the same woman for fifty years."

"Eh, see?" Valier exclaimed proudly. "I know about women."

Charlie snorted.

"You're Catholic. Divorce is practically illegal."

"Exactly," Valier leaned in whispering, "you see? I was married to Bette for fifty years . . . and I am still alive! I know about women, no?"

The two convulsed in laughter. The old man's face lit up like a delighted schoolboy. Then Valier wiped the mischief off his expression.

"Charlie, I must tell you some things because you have no papa to tell you - "

"Well, don't feel obliged to volunteer," Charlie warned him.

Valier took an enormous swig from his own mug that promptly scalded his tongue. He coughed as the liquid seared through his body. Charlie blew across his coffee and sipped it with a sigh. Valier scowled.

"You have to learn to drink bitter coffee, Charlie," his grand-père admonished him. "I know you. You like cream and sugar, but what is going to happen when times get tough, eh? No cream. No sugar."

"I'll just stop drinking coffee," Charlie answered, shrugging. "Or maybe I'll get a cow and sweeten the coffee with some honest-to-god maple syrup."

Valier scowled ferociously.

"Holy God, Charlie, don't take the Lord's name in vain! Cream and sugar will not get you through tough times, no, no."

"Yeah," Charlie argued, "but what's a life full of nothing but bitter old coffee?"

Valier shrugged.

"It's not so bad. You get used to it."

Charlie snorted. *Get used to it* . . . maybe getting used to things was a substitute for love, but it sure wasn't the same thing. Carob wasn't chocolate; chicory wasn't coffee; and Aunt Jemima's wasn't maple syrup. Charlie didn't want pancakes if he couldn't have the real deal. The bell above the door tinkled, interrupting his thoughts. Valier looked up, squinting.

"*Qui est cette femme?* Who is that?"

"*That*," Charlie replied as Zadie burst in laughing, "is a cream and sugar woman!"

Zadie. A thousand miles away and a decade later, Charlie shook his head. He stood up in the Kansas kitchen, dizzy from the vertigo of memory. He poured a cup of coffee and suddenly saw his grandfather's own wrinkled hand serving a beautifully rich brew, proclaiming in his gravely Acadian voice that coffee had to begin strong, or else the cream and sugar would have nothing to caress, eh?

Charlie wondered if his grandfather had known, even then, that Zadie Byrd Gray wasn't just the cream and sugar supplement to his life; she was the eye opening, invigorating force that propelled him. He sipped the hot sting of the black liquid and blinked furiously, reeling from deep emotions. His eyes darted up to where his personal shrine of missing and departed friends encircled the whole kitchen. Photos and mementos hung on the walls. Names had been scrawled onto scraps of paper and pinned to wooden doorframes with bright thumbtacks. Over the splashboard, the wax of vigil candles trailed down into the kitchen sink.

*Don't they realize what they're doing?* Charlie thought. The government and the corporations were destroying all this life - all this history - all these incredible, beautiful people living and breathing and loving, one generation to the next . . . how could they throw it all away for a moment of profit?

Outside, the cornfield rippled in a sudden gust of wind. *Who is They?* the breeze whispered. *The Butcher, the Banker, the Candlestick Maker, the President?* Well, Charlie admitted, those four men hadn't done it alone. Soldiers fired guns and dropped bombs. Someone's daughter stamped the final papers of foreclosure. Another person's father ignored the early warnings of oil leaks. Lawmakers voted on bills. Officials denied or approved permits. Accountants worked the numbers. Judges ruled on cases. The deeper Charlie looked, the more *They* became a pronoun with a billion faces, one of which might be his own.

*We,* Charlie realized. *It is always we who are ultimately culpable.* He thought about the subtle shift that was occurring. Thousands of people had recognized their complicity in destruction, and were now taking a stand for life. *Ah,* Charlie thought, *when we stop blaming Them and take responsibility for our actions . . . when we consciously withdraw our cooperation from injustice . . . that is when real change begins to occur.* Not from the top, and not just from the bottom, but from all sides at once as every person wakes up and makes a conscious choice to preserve the goodness of life on this earth.

The aroma of coffee lapped his face as Charlie bowed over his mug in prayer. *Please,* he cried to whatever spirits, God, or holy hosts listened. *Please give humanity another chance. Give us a chance to live and love. Please.* The coffee gurgled. The corn rustled. A small brown bird alighted in the apple tree outside. A knock rapped on the front door. Charlie looked up. Tucker went to open it.

Zadie stood on the doorstep, a bouquet of dandelions in her hand.

# CHAPTER TWENTY-FOUR

. . . . .

## *In Absentia*

Their first embrace crashed with a gasping shock akin to plunging into cold Maine waters. Their limbs flailed frantically. The breath was punched out of their chests. When air rushed back in, a torrent of words poured out of both of them: *Bill? I heard. Inez? She's fine. Where were you? Hiding. Oh my god, you're back! You're back! You're back!* Finally, the surreal became real in a painful jolt of realignment. His hands pressed too hard as he held her. Her fingers left marks on the back of his neck. Their chests heaved together.

"I didn't think I would cry," Zadie complained, wiping her eyes with the back of her hand.

"You should have warned me that you were on your way," Charlie stammered. "I'd have shaved and cleaned. My room looks like an infamous Kansas tornado strike," he groaned, thinking of the disaster of papers, books, articles, dirty clothes, grimy cups, and forgotten sandwiches that would have to be shoveled aside.

"I warned you," Tucker reminded him. "I told you she was going to show up one day and you would regret that disgusting madness."

"Tucker," Zadie answered as she kissed Charlie, "you are a very wise man."

For the rest of the morning and long into the afternoon, they lay together in stunned contentment under the apple tree in the backyard. The grass pressed against Charlie's back as he breathed in gulps of the cool damp air. Zadie's head rested on

263

his chest, tickling his chin with her curls. Bruised black and blue clouds chugged ominously across the sky. A gust shook the branches of the apple tree and a little bird flew off, calling, *Don't wait! Don't wait!* Zadie's eyes darkened, mirroring the slate-grey sky above. Life is short. Time is fleeting. Love now. Don't wait.

"I shouldn't have waited so long to come back," she whispered.

Charlie could feel the long weeks in her body as if each day had stolen a sliver of Zadie. She'd thinned. Dark circles had formed under her eyes. The rose in her cheeks had slid off somewhere. He felt the crick in her neck that comes from constantly looking over your shoulder. Her heartbeat had notched up from her flight. His pulse hammered slowly in counter-rhythm as she told him about her days hiding and running, traveling alone, not daring to come home. She lifted her head, looking at Tucker's backyard. Home? Where was that? She had nests in trees across the country, a flight pattern comprised of perches and roosts, but home? Wearily, she laid her head back down.

*Here. Right here.* Charlie's heart tried to tell her. He traced the tired lines on her face. Zadie kept talking, telling him how she had met with people in secret, one by one, persuading the cloud of fear away and tearing open the fabric of reality so love could come shining through like a new day rising.

"And?" he asked, hardly breathing, not daring to hope for the answer.

"It's coming," she said firmly. "Brighter than any star in the night sky, bigger than any constellation. It's a sunrise building in the darkness before dawn. I can feel it, Charlie."

Thunder shook the clouds. The sky drooped black toward the ground. Rain curtained the distant horizon. Hard green apples bounced like marbles as the wind shook the tree. One fell. Zadie looked at it curiously.

"Do you remember that time when Dad launched into a sermon on the Fall from the Garden of Eden?" she asked Charlie.

"I remember," he answered.

Bill had spent an hour lecturing on the Biblical story, telling them that the Garden of Eden was a place within their hearts beyond good and evil, a sanctuary from the storm of judgments where we dwelled in our own innocence. Charlie grew solemn, thinking of Zadie's father in prison. He sensed sorrow creeping into her bones like the chill of a storm in the air.

"Zadie," he said, "if I was standing in the Garden of Eden, looking at the fruit of knowledge, you know what I'd do?"

She shook her head, bewildered.

"I'd eat the whole damn apple. Then I'd take the seeds and march off like Johnny Appleseed to plant a whole world of knowledge. I'd bake pies if I had to, or make it into cider, but I'd get awareness into every person that I could. We can't keep living in ignorant bliss. It doesn't work."

Charlie moved the green apple toward his mouth, ready to bite. Zadie stopped him.

"Don't Charlie."

She took it from his fingers and threw it away. His eyes tracked it up until the sky swallowed it.

"Don't you wonder, though?" he asked.

She shook her head. The sour nub hardly seemed a fair exchange for paradise. When the apples dripped with sweetness, then she would wonder. Later, when the cold crisped the last touch of summer into perfect ripeness, she would run her tongue across her lips and reach for the tantalizing unknown. But today, when the storm clouds rumbled overhead and the apples bobbed green and mocking, she wanted no part of it. The Garden of Eden is within, she thought, and she intended to stay in paradise for one tiny moment. The night stretched out ahead of them and she wanted to taste only the sweetness of his mouth.

The first drops of rain tumbled out of the sky as she pulled him to his feet.

"Come on," she said, "let's go make something tastier for dinner."

They raced inside as the drops stung their skin and hurled into the kitchen with the wind on their heels. Tucker protested the commotion as he stirred the pot of soup that simmered on the stove.

"Smells like poetry!" Charlie told him.

"That reminds me, Charlie!" Zadie exclaimed. "Your poetry is everywhere! Train stations, park benches, bus stops; I went into a public restroom and someone had written one of your poems in sharpie across the stall door!"

"Which one?" Charlie asked.

She quoted it.

*Greyhound Station loneliness*
*halfway destinations*
*homeward bound*
*and wondering*
*where my home*
*- my heart -*
*is?"*

"That one meant a lot to me," she said quietly.

"Just you wait," Charlie boasted. "They'll be inscribing tonight's poetry onto statues!"

"Hah!" she retorted. "If it isn't raunchy enough for the bathroom stall, Charlie Rider . . . "

"You can send me back to rewrite it," he promised. "I'll keep trying all night."

She whacked him with the dishtowel and he leapt for her, chasing her around the kitchen, buzzing as lustily as a spring-crazed bumblebee.

"Look at this bee . . . me!" he incanted, inventing poetry as he grabbed Zadie. "Nuzzling head first . . . this woozy pollen." He sighed and swooned dramatically. "Rolling in it, delirious with you!"

"You deserve every ridiculous story the foreign paparazzi is writing about you," Tucker said. He laughed and put on his raincoat to run down to the store to get fresh bread. He winked as he went out the door.

"What did that mean?" Zadie asked.

Charlie grinned.

"We're an internationally famous couple, Zadie Byrd Gray."

"No!"

"Mmm-hmm. We're more popular than Silas Black's latest fling and more infamous than Bonnie and Clyde. We're practically national heroes in France!"

He tossed a tabloid from the stack by the phone. Zadie caught it. Her mouth dropped open, flabbergasted. Their pictures were on the front cover with the headline, *Revolutionary Romance.* She flipped it open.

"*Charlie Rider, civil liberties activist* -that's nice," she commented. "They're not calling you a terrorist overseas."

"No," he laughed, "it's exclusively an American sort-of-a-thing."

" *- is being called 'the American Scarlet Pimpernel' as he continues to give U.S. authorities the slip,*" she read. "*Is he in heaven? Is he in hell? That damned elusive Pimpernel!*"

"No," Charlie joked, "I'm in Kansas, which, depending on

your perspective, could be either." He rolled his eyes as a whip of rain slapped the side of the house.

"*Meanwhile,*" Zadie read, "*Rider's paramour Zadie Byrd Gray continues to serve the people like a nonviolent Zorro, devoted to liberty and love.*" She snorted with laughter and flung the tabloid onto the table.

"I've got a whole collection of them," Charlie informed her. "Some of them are quite steamy. I'll read them to you later."

"Do I faint in your arms?" she asked, raising an eyebrow.

"Several times. I nearly die twice, bust you out of prison, and evade a legion of FBI agents," Charlie said proudly.

"I'd be appalled," Zadie sighed, "if it wasn't so close to the truth."

"The good news is that half a dozen international groups have been calling on their governments to offer us amnesty," Charlie pointed out optimistically.

"Great," Zadie rolled her eyes. "I've always wanted to live in an embassy."

"It's better than solitary confinement," he replied.

He dodged the whack of the dishtowel and stole a kiss.

"Zadie - "

The door banged. They flinched and spun, but it was only Tucker.

"Where's the bread?" Zadie asked as he hurtled into the kitchen empty handed.

"Forget the bread. We've got bigger problems," he said. "Look at this."

He threw the thick weight of a newspaper down on the table.

INSURRECTION LEADERS TO BE TRIED
FOR TREASON.

"*What?!*" Charlie exploded. "How can they try us for treason when they haven't even managed to arrest us?"

Tucker pointed to the first line and read it aloud.

"The United States Government has accused Charlie Rider and Zadie Byrd Gray of intellectual terrorism and intends to try them *in absentia* if the duo is not apprehended by the beginning of the trial," Tucker quoted.

"*Intellectual terrorism?* What the hell is intellectual terrorism?" Charlie demanded to know.

"Must be the new buzzword for freedom of thought and expression," Tucker answered.

Charlie pulled the newspaper over and read it.

"*In absentia?* Is that legal?" Charlie frowned.

"No," Tucker answered, "but it's the new legal. The article says you'll be tried in a new form of court specifically for domestic and intellectual terrorists."

Zadie's mouth fell open as she read over Charlie's shoulder. They were accused of treason against the United States, and of engaging in intellectual terrorism aimed at destroying the values, morality, and spirit of the American people.

"Are they joking? *We* should be charging them for those crimes!" Charlie spat out. He began to pace the kitchen, furious. "They don't have a single accusation that could actually hold up in a court of law!"

Tucker shook his head.

"I suspected they were working on something like this. I thought they just couldn't make up their minds whether to shoot you on sight or capture you. From their perspective," he said, pointing to the article, "this is brilliant."

They stared at him in disbelief. He shrugged.

"This is their chance to completely gut the old justice system, rout out the people who won't be bribed, and destroy the remnants of constitutional justice. Starting right here, with *in absentia.* It's utterly unconstitutional, but it doesn't matter. If you refuse to show up, they'll rack up so many legal charges against you that it will take years to dig your way out of them." He ticked the list off on his fingers. "Avoiding arrest, refusing to sign paperwork, failure to respond to deposition, not showing up for your own trial, flaunting justice - "

"This isn't justice!" Charlie growled through gritted teeth.

"No," Tucker agreed, "but by not showing up, you're endorsing lawlessness. I can see the headline now: Charlie Rider Ignores Justice, Continues Terrorism."

"Damned if I go, damned if I don't, is that it?" Charlie muttered.

Tucker looked down at the article. His lean face clouded with thought.

"Maybe you should go," he suggested hesitantly.

Charlie reared back.

"Are you nuts? This trial is a death warrant." He snatched the paper from the table and shook it at Tucker. "If we even made it through the trial alive - which I doubt - they could drag it out for decades while we rot in solitary confinement." Charlie shuddered. He shook his head and flung the paper back at Tucker. "I say that if they can try me *in absentia*, they can incarcerate me *in absentia*, too."

"But if we won," Zadie said, holding up a hand to stop Charlie's retort. "I know, we stand as much chance of surviving as a peanut in an elephant farm, but, *if* we won, it would be a tremendous thing for the justice system, for the nation . . . and for us." She grabbed Charlie's arm as he turned away. "Think about it, Charlie," she begged him. "We've spent months hiding and looking over our shoulders because of these insane charges. This is our chance to get rid of them!"

"This is our chance to end up dead," he responded cynically.

"Maybe. But maybe the FBI will raid us tomorrow," Zadie said pragmatically, "and maybe we'll be shot dead in the street. If we go to the trial, at least we have a chance to keep the label of terrorism from being used to destroy democracy. We might even get back those civil liberties that we know the Dandelion Insurrection needs."

Her eyes shone with the possibilities, but Charlie stared back, unconvinced. He had been running from the government for months, housebound here in Kansas for most of that time. His world had shrunk to four walls, a backyard, and the creepy sensation that, any day now, the FBI would catch up to him. The past weeks had ripped a hole of anxiety through his stomach. He wasn't sure he had much hope left inside him. Until Zadie had reappeared, he had just been doggedly getting up each day, writing to keep despair from killing him.

"Go without me," he said coldly.

Zadie reeled back like he had hit her. Hot tears leapt to her eyes. Without a word, she turned on her heel, stalked into the bedroom, and slammed the door so hard the framed photos on the walls shuddered. Charlie followed her with his gaze. Tucker shifted uncomfortably.

"Charlie," he began.

"Shove it, Tucker."

Tucker flung himself away from the table in frustration. He brushed past Charlie, crashing out the screen door into the backyard. Tucker's dim shape bent over in the twilight, looking for something under the overhang of the porch. The wiry little man straightened up and banged back into the kitchen.

"You make me so dead mad I could spit," Tucker snapped. "Here you've got the most courageous woman on earth ready to stand up for the most worthy cause, stick by your side, fight you clear of this madness, and you say, *go without me*." His tone mocked Charlie's words. Tucker held up his fist. In it, a silver-seeded dandelion, dry from the shelter of the roof, quivered.

"Do you know why the dandelion is invincible?" Tucker asked. "Even when it's about to topple over, it doesn't give up. It offers a promise to every man, woman, and child; *make a wish, the dandelion says,*" Tucker said, quoting one of Charlie's articles, *"and this lowly weed will do its best to carry your seed-borne hope to fertile ground."*

He closed his eyes for a moment, puffed out his cheeks, and blew. Charlie flinched as Tucker's breath hit his face. The seeds clung to his cheek. Tucker opened his eyes. One silver seed stuck to the tired gray head of the dandelion. Tucker's mouth twisted sadly.

"Guess it won't come true."

Charlie stared at him.

"What did you wish?" he asked.

"I wished to be you."

Tucker's eyes burned with passion. He had given up his peace, his quiet, his solitude, and his home to help Charlie and the Dandelion Insurrection. His work didn't bring him the notoriety of Charlie's writing. No one saw the tremendous efforts he put into making the Alternet viable and secure. He worked unimaginably long hours, but he still felt like he wasn't doing enough to help.

"I wished I was on trial," Tucker said. "I wished I had the chance to risk all, to gain all. This is so much bigger than you, or me, or any hopes and dreams we've ever had for ourselves. Are you afraid they're going to kill you? I'm not. The way things are going it's just sooner rather than later. I wished I could take your place at that trial, because at least I wouldn't live out my days, regretting - " he broke off.

"Regretting what?" Charlie challenged him, daring him to

say it to his face.

"Regretting that after telling other people to stand up . . . I didn't have the courage when my time came."

Charlie's gut clenched. His head dropped. The bands of muscles along his back tensed. Tucker waited. Standing up to an enemy pales to speaking hard truth to a friend. Charlie raised his head and took the scraggly dandelion from Tucker's fist. He closed his eyes, made his wish, and blew the last seed back into Tucker's surprised expression.

"What did you wish?" the man asked him.

"Can't tell you until it comes true," Charlie answered, "but I hope there are more of these outside. We're going to need a whole field of dandelions to get us through this one."

He held out his hand. Tucker shook it.

# CHAPTER TWENTY-FIVE

. . . . .

*Southpaw Curveball Pitcher*


Tansy Beaulisle knocked on the door like a tornado come calling. Tucker let the lawyer in and was promptly whiplashed by her non-stop stream of conversation. She was a short woman, dressed tonelessly in a gray suit and pumps with a halo of dense curls that shot out in all directions in a bleach-blonde fuzz that contrasted with her darker skin.

"Well, how-do, Mr. Jones?" she said. "Where'd you hide the terrorists?"

"They're on a phone call downstairs, Ms. Beaulisle," Tucker replied mildly, feeling like a quiet leaf swept up in the storm of this woman.

"Aw, you can call me Tansy, so long as I get to call you Tucker."

"Agreed. Would you care for a cup of tea?"

"Not unless it's cold sweet tea, 'cause, Lord, I am hotter than an egg frying on the blacktop!" She fanned herself dramatically with the folder she was pulling from her briefcase. Tucker motioned for her to follow him into the kitchen. She pulled off her suit coat and sat down, looking around in a lively fashion.

"Well, glory be," she exclaimed. "Look at your walls!"

Tucker glanced up.

"Oh yes, our shrine. We had it on the table, you know, but it got too big."

She inspected the images of the friends and fellow activists who had disappeared, died, or been incarcerated. She touched

275

the photos of Gandhi, Martin Luther King, Jr., Rosa Parks, and other heroes of the nonviolent lineage. Then she rummaged in her briefcase and pulled out a photo of Jesus.

"Y'all can put him up there, too. The Quakers read the Bible the way Jesus intended, shared it with Tolstoy, who inspired Gandhi, who set the stage for Dr. King. We got a tradition and we all gotta learn it, study it, and walk in it all our days." Her eyes filled up with passion. "I've got my own altar, too, for my friends who are in trouble right now. We're up to bat on those indefinite detentions in a few weeks, so keep your fingers crossed."

"Excuse me?" Tucker asked.

"ACLU's got a case up with the Supreme Court, trying to prove that those indefinite detentions are utterly unconstitutional, for one, and a violation of human rights, for another. Y'all should be praying, 'cause it's gonna affect Charlie 'n' Zadie's trial, too. But then, I don't reckon y'all ever let up praying 'round here. I don't mean just to Jesus!" she clarified as Tucker stammered. "I seen y'all's Buddhas and Kwan Yinnys. That's fine by me. To each his own." She pointed to the statues with a long red fingernail.

"Tansy?" Tucker asked, eyeing the gold band around her ring finger. "May I ask you something?"

"Spit it out, whipper."

"How does your husband keep up with you?"

"He don't. That's why I left him 'n' the first one behind. Why? You offering to be my lucky number three?" She battered her eyelashes outrageously at Tucker.

"No! I mean, no offense, but - "

"You swinging for the other team?" she asked pryingly.

Tucker suddenly caught a glimpse of what a ferocious hawk this woman could become in the courtroom.

"Tansy," he sighed, "I'm the umpire, coach, and water boy all rolled into one, just trying to get the whole world to play nicely, praying for world peace, and trying to contribute through a secure communications network."

She grunted approvingly.

"Tucker Jones, I don't care if you worship frozen pizza so long as you're working for peace, equality, and love. I ain't keen on discriminating 'tween religions when there ain't enough angels to go around already."

She stuck out her hand boldly. Tucker smiled and shook it. Her grip was firm and her gaze clear. Honesty blazed out along with her ballsy words.

"I'm glad you're not a stone statue in a gray suit," Tucker admitted. She laughed a bray that bounced off the walls.

"No way in hell! I try to simmer it down for appearance's sake, but I always burst out around the edges. The ACLU sent me down here because I wouldn't let them send anybody else. I'm the Dandelion Insurrection in a legal nutshell, and I'm gonna wreak havoc in that contemptible excuse for a justice system that we got going on. Then again," she leaned in conspiratorially, "nobody else was too keen on taking the case."

"And why's that, Ms. Tansy?"

"Well, they're all taking bets on how quick my life insurance rate is gonna go sky-high!" She grinned wickedly, absolutely unconcerned. "Bunch of weenies," she snorted. "Lawyers come in three categories; weenies, balls, and bitches."

"I presume you're the latter," Tucker replied weakly.

"Naw, I'm none of the above. I'm trouble on two legs. This trial may be a circus, but, by golly, I intend to steal the show!"

Zadie's laughter broke over them as she swung up the stairs.

"Please say that you're my lawyer . . . because I can tell we're going to get along just fine!"

Tansy spun round and sized up the long-legged, mini-skirted, wild-haired Zadie. Charlie squeezed in behind her and Tansy's scrutiny swallowed him whole. *Good God Above*, she thought in alarm, *they really are just a couple of kids, aren't they?* She had twenty years on them, minimum. She had weathered storms and hard times, fought like hell, triumphed and failed, all before they were out of diapers. *What is this world coming to?* she sighed to herself.

"Nice to meet you, Ms. Beaulisle," Charlie said, reaching out a hand. She shook it with enthusiasm.

"Mmm-hmm, and it's nice to meet a young man who can pronounce my name properly, *bo-leel*."

"Must be our French heritage," he hinted. "My ma's a Beaulier, from the Acadians up north."

"My pa was Louisiana Cajun, my mamma a Creole, and I've got French, English, Spanish, African, Choctaw, and a few things they forgot to name jumbled up in my family tree," Tansy said enthusiastically. "I could be related to you!" She waggled her thin-plucked eyebrows.

Tucker caught the boiling teakettle and began making some tea.

"You ain't gonna drink that hot, are you?" Tansy challenged him.

"Hot water will cool you quicker on a warm day," Tucker replied evenly.

"I've been swimming in hot water since the day I was born. Pour a cup for me and stick it in the freezer for a minute or two. Now, kids, let me tell you something straight off. You're gonna hear all sorts of rude comments about me along this ride. *Tansy the Pansy*, I've heard them call me. They lob their hardballs at me fast as they can, but I'm a southpaw curveball pitcher, and when my team takes the field, they just can't handle me at all."

She held their gaze steady, looking from one young face to the next. Tansy could tell from Zadie's expression that she was born on the fly and lived on the go. Charlie, though, he was more of a calculator; sharp, observant, and inclined to keep his distance.

"Alright," she launched in, "this is what we got going on. They say you violated several clauses of the Freedom of Defense Act, which is one of the foulest pieces of unconstitutional garbage I ever ran 'cross in my life! If I had my druthers, we'd be suing the paint off the White House walls over it. I'm a damn fool twice over for not getting to you two sooner and pushing this case through as prosecution, not defense! The only good thing 'bout being on the defense is that the burden of proving your guilt lies on them."

"So, the Freedom of Defense Act can't be overturned by this trial?" Charlie asked.

"No, not exactly, but here's where it gets real sticky. You haven't done any acts of terrorism as defined by any law prior to this unconstitutional baloney that they passed. And since the Freedom of Defense Act is labeling speech and assembly acts of terror, the government is basically arguing that our Constitution allows acts of terror!"

Tansy's eyes gleamed with fire, incensed by the outrageous convolutions of law.

"Let me tell you something: dissent is democratic. Discussion is democratic. Dictatorship is not. We're in a showdown, folks, and the justice system is the Wild West. I never saw anything like this trial before. It's a new-fangled thing they've cooked up, 'bout halfway between a military tribunal court and a lynch mob, if you ask me. 'Course, out in the frontiers of justice, anything can happen and we might just win."

Tansy gave a wry grin and hunkered down into the particulars. The kids had thrown the prosecution for a spin when they announced they were coming to the trial. Tansy reckoned the powers-that-be were already regretting putting a jury on this case. Of course, the judge had the final say by confirming or denying the verdict. That's where it got real slippery.

"The prosecution's pushing this trial through faster than anything in the history of U.S. law, and, meanwhile, the judges are dropping this case like a bunch of drunk jugglers and nobody can figure out who is presiding!" Tansy threw her hands up in utter confusion.

By supper, Charlie couldn't remember the last time he had laughed so hard. Tansy was a wisecracking lunatic . . . but he liked her. He told Tansy that they had been contacting their friends throughout the Dandelion Insurrection, asking their opinions about the *in absentia* trial.

"And?" Tansy asked in her bold, direct way. "What're they saying?"

"Tell Tansy exactly what Inez said," Charlie encouraged Zadie.

"¡*Madre de Díos!*" Zadie mimicked her. "*If the justice system doesn't stand up for itself, I'll start my own court of law and try them for being idiots!*"

"It's not so farfetched," Charlie pointed out. "Mahatma Gandhi told the Indian lawyers to give up their licenses in the British system and form their own arbitration courts."

"I'm 'bout ready to do the same if my colleagues can't get their act together!" Tansy declared. "We've got a right to a fair trial and we've got to stand up for it."

Charlie snorted.

"Of course we do. We've got a right to speak out. We've got

a right to assemble. We've got a right to govern ourselves. We've got a right to resist tyranny within our own government. We've got a right to protect our children from poison."

Tansy reared back in her chair and startled them with a sudden eruption of song that rattled the photos on the walls. The old spiritual leapt from her throat, powerful and reverberating.

*"You've got a right! You've got a right!*
*You've got a right to the Tree of Life!"*

"Did you know," she commented as they blinked at her potent voice, "that there were two trees in the Garden of Eden?"

Charlie and Zadie exchanged looks. In their discussion of the Tree of the Knowledge of Good and Evil, they had forgotten about the Tree of Life.

"Everybody's got a right to the Tree of Life," Tansy said emphatically. "I don't care what the preachers say on the subject. They think the Tree of Life is about immortality. Well, maybe the one in the Bible is, but that song I sang? It goes back to slavery times, when the white colonists were putting together the Constitution and Jefferson was saying folks had a right to life, liberty, and the pursuit of happiness. Black folks said they had the same rights, but weren't nobody listening to them, so they started singing that message so their children wouldn't forget that they had a right to live."

She shook her head in disgust.

"I look at what this corporate-controlled government is doing, and you know what I think? God ain't gonna forgive them for doing Satan's work. This whole world is humanity's cradle and God's children are dying in it. I sing that song to remind folks, we got a right!"

The melody burst out of her again as if the long lineage of

people who had stood up for freedom hummed in the back of her throat, demanding to be released through song.

*"Got a right, you got a right,*
*You got a right to the Tree of Life.*
*The voice is heavy but you got a right,*
*You got a right to the Tree of Life.*
*Some ups and downs but you got a right,*
*You got a right to the Tree of Life."*

Tansy hummed the melody thoughtfully. Then she shrugged off the ghosts of her complex past and settled down to dealing with the present.

"Now, I've got to ask you something hard," she warned them.

"What's that?" Zadie asked.

"Do y'all got faith?"

They blinked at the unexpected question. Tansy's mouth pursed into a tight line for a moment and raised an eyebrow at Zadie.

"You ain't Christian," she observed. "Otherwise, I wouldn't be askin'. God bless my religion," she said, rolling her eyes, "but it requires more faith than any other spirituality on earth. You've got to *believe* because nothing about Christianity makes much sense and there ain't no way in hell that rational thought is gonna get you to heaven. What we got here," she tapped the legal documents, "is a question of miracles and faith. One, we've got to have faith in justice." She raised her hands at the immediate snort that shot out of Charlie. "I know, I know, it's a long haul for the rational mind. Lord, I've been a lawyer for most of my life, and it's only my unwavering faith in an often deaf, dumb, and blind thing called justice that has kept me devoted to this field. But I got *faith* that justice is gonna come someday, so I keep on workin' toward it. Now, miracles? Well, we ain't gonna win without one, so get praying now." She laughed at them and shrugged. "But, y'all got this far, so that leads me to think," she paused and regarded them with somber admiration, "God must love you two something special."

"How's that?" Charlie sighed.

"Well, He put me on your case, didn't He?"

Charlie looked at this southpaw curveball lawyer with her bleach-blonde halo of curls, red fingernails, and hellfire in her eyes . . . and started praying.

# CHAPTER TWENTY-SIX

. . . . .

## *Conundrum*

A storm rumbled its thundery belly overhead and Tansy's temper snapped like lightning bolts. Zadie had already retreated to the basement with Tucker, leaving Charlie to diffuse the lawyer's frustration.

"Our biggest problem," Tansy declared, "is how to get you two to the trial alive."

Tansy made no bones about her distrust of the FBI. She had seen too many dead witnesses and twenty-year indefinite detentions to advise her clients to cooperate with the authorities. In the past few years, that strategy just hadn't led to health or longevity. Charlie and Zadie's mothers had both received death threats. Valier was warned several times that his grandson *had it coming.* Tansy considered assassination to be a real likely option.

"Before y'all got internationally famous, it would have been a simple murder, but now that you've inspired half the country to start standing up for the Bill of Rights, the world is watching, and knocking you out counts as assassination."

The breakdown of justice in the United States of America was no joke. With the military budget equivalent to the rest of the world's nations combined, the tenuous state of the Constitution had international officials nervous. The efforts of the Dandelion Insurrection had not gone unnoticed by the global community.

"Once I get you to Washington, we've got help," Tansy told Charlie. "The legal team is riling up the international powers-that-be and we're aiming for house arrest at the French Embassy. We can't have y'all dying of mysterious causes in jail. We've even got the formal arrest lined up in paperwork, so they can't drag you down to the station for a once-over. But mind you, this isn't a joy lark. You'll be guarded by the French security forces at all times. Y'all won't be able to talk to the press, meet with anybody except me, and you can forget any ideas of escape. I had to trade your right to seek asylum for your right to a fair trial. The President has threatened to drop the atomic bomb on France if they whisk you out of the country." Tansy rolled her eyes. "I tell you, it's taking a good dozen of us workin' our balls off to manage you two."

"Thank you," Charlie answered.

"Shucks, I ain't done nothin' yet. Still got to figure out how to get y'all *into* Washington. I've got to go select a jury that ain't half crazy, but if you come with me, y'all will be sitting ducks for trouble." Tansy fumed and steamed, wracking her brain to find an option. Finally, she shrugged. "What you workin' on in those scribbles?" she asked, flicking her eyes down toward his notebook.

"Oh," he said sheepishly, "nothing special. Just some poetry."

"Love poetry for that Zadie-girl?" she groaned. "I tell you, y'all are the living end. You got FBI agents on your back and you're writing love poetry? Write something with fire and torch people's lazy butts off the couch. There's an insurrection going on, you know!"

"Love is as great a motivator as fear," Charlie retorted.

"Well, then write a love poem that'll get the nation roaring!"

# CHAPTER TWENTY-SEVEN

· · · · ·

*Revolutions*


In the fields of northern Maine, Ellen Byrd fumed to herself as she turned the old tractor around in a slow grumbling circle. Revolutions don't happen because we wake up bored in the morning. Ellen lined the front wheels of the tractor up with the row. Revolutions happen because your husband is locked in jail and the harvest might rot in the ground. She plunged the throttle forward. Revolutions happen because your daughter is forced into hiding. She rumbled down the long row, beating down the potato tops to toughen the spuds for picking. Revolutions happen because a young man can't get to his trial alive. Her eyes looked toward the heaving country that lay beyond the pine forest. Revolutions happen because people get tired of abuse and injustice. She scanned the horizon of heartache that spread in all directions. Revolutions happen because a woman aches to hold her family once again. The reverberations of the engine throbbed in her bones. Revolutions happen because your heart throws down the gauntlet of its love.

Halfway out, where the farmland crested in a rocky rise, Ellen killed the engine. The rumble of the machine faded into the lonesome silence of the farm. She climbed down from the tractor and marched through the rows of potatoes. Her rubber boots whapped the sides of her calves. Her willowy frame bent against the wind. Her long, lone figure left the farmland behind.

Revolutions happen because one woman says, *enough.*

# CHAPTER TWENTY-EIGHT

. . . . .

## *The March*

The scent of showdown laced the air. The trial began in one week. Rumors marched in great strides over the hills and farmlands. Legend stepped over suburbs and city rooftops. The love poem of *the Man From the North* murmured in people's minds. The King of Rock 'n' Rebel's folksong rendition echoed in their ears.

*"In the heart of darkness,*
*dead of night,*
*heat of danger,*
*burning bright,*
*I'll meet you, love*
*at the break of day.*
*Say where, my love,*
*say when,*
*say now,*
*I'm already on my way."*

They said he was coming from the north. They whispered that she was coming from the south. It was thought that an army of insurrectionists marched with them.

"What's going on?!" Charlie gasped when Tucker told him the news.

"Zadie's mother started it, then your mother joined in, then the rest of the valley, and now it has all collided into the craziest-damn notion that the Dandelion Insurrection has ever had - "

Charlie's jaw dropped as he realized what was happening.

"They're marching to Washington?" he exclaimed.

"Everyone," Tucker confirmed. "The entire Dandelion Insurrection is marching to Washington to demand justice for you and Zadie."

From the north, south, and west, a great migration of people assembled. No one knew where, but rumors claimed that Charlie and Zadie were walking to their trial, protected by the bodies of the people. Every woman bragged that she had marched alongside Charlie Rider and every man swore Zadie Byrd Gray had smiled at him.

Ellen Byrd's words flew from person to person, swelling the ranks of the march with each repetition; *we must show them that the greatest force on earth is not the government, not the corporations, and not the military . . . the greatest force on earth is the love of the people for each other!* She walked hand-in-hand with Natalie Beaulier-Rider as they led the tide that swept down from the north to defend the rights of their children.

A thousand miles away, Charlie's marrow quaked at the danger the people were marching toward.

"They'll be massacred," he whispered. "A thousand, ten thousand, even one hundred thousand people . . . the President will call in the soldiers, everyone will be shot dead in the streets! We've got to stop them."

"No," Zadie answered. "We've got to help them."

"How?" he asked her.

"By growing that march until it is unstoppable."

"That would take millions," Charlie argued.

Zadie nodded in agreement, her eyes burning with fire. She leaned on the table with both hands, shaking from the power of Love that coursed through her veins. Her mother was risking death and imprisonment for her. Charlie's mother was vowing to protect her son's body with her own. Hundreds of Dandelion

Insurrectionists were standing up for justice and love. Zadie took a deep breath as every gritty, heart-pounding step of this midwifing journey, every threat of arrest, every assassination attempt, every victory, every loss; everything slammed together in this moment of decision. A crucial junction had arrived, triggered by the ferocious love of her mother. Zadie looked at Charlie, then at Tucker. For months, they had sat on a secret, strengthening the people for change. Zadie closed her eyes and checked the pulse of the nation. She ran her mind over the vital signs of the corporate government. She took note of the strength of the people. In the quiet Kansas kitchen, she nodded. They were ready. The time had come.

"Tucker," Zadie said, "release the election fraud information."

\*      \*      \*

The news rocked the nation. Nothing had ever whipped so fast through the Alternet. It was the proverbial straw on the camel's back. The size of the march doubled overnight. Emails and phone calls poured into the Capitol demanding resignations. The White House and Congress immediately began to throw the legal book around, stalling for time. They told the people that the impeachment process took months, the data must be verified, don't come marching to Washington, everything was under control, due process would happen. Nobody believed a word of it. They wanted action, *now!*

Warnings were issued to the marching insurrectionists to cease at once. The marchers refused. Reasons for marching grew by the mile, multiplying with every person who joined. Escorting Charlie and Zadie to their trial shrank into a single steppingstone on a whole path of actions. The Dandelion

Insurrection planned to throw their list of demands down on the table: the immediate resignation of all public officials implicated in the elections' fraud, the restoration of civil liberties, the repeal of the Freedom of Defense Act, revision of the tax code, reformation of debt law, cessation of corporate financing of politics, renewed protection of the environment, and an end to export and extraction.

"We're not going home until major change occurs!" Inez Hernandez promised. The tiny woman threaded through the northern marchers, strategizing a plan for when they arrived in the Capitol. Pilar trailed her daughter like a shadow, her sharp eyes scanning snipers and police. Surveillance drones trailed them constantly, and once or twice, people thought they saw the black shapes of predator drones in the distance. Such machines were armed to kill. Even the sound of their ominous low reverberations sent shivers down people's spines. A leaked order containing plans for Charlie and Zadie's assassinations had circulated through the Alternet. *Shoot Gray and Rider on sight*, the order read.

"If we don't stand up for Charlie and Zadie's rights," Ellen Byrd declared, "the rights of every human being on this planet will vanish. Your last name may be Jones or Smith, but we are all Gray Riders now."

The name stuck. The March of the Gray Riders swelled in volume. The Suburban Renaissance opened their doors and laid out blankets on the floor. Along the routes, children placed bouquets on front stoops and hung chain-linked wreathes on their doorknobs, sending the message, *dandelions grow here, sanctuary within*. As the march swept past their homes, many followed the example of Lupe Hernandez-Booker and joined in.

Tansy Beaulisle appeared in Washington D.C. without

either of her clients and fired through the jury selection faster than Annie Oakley at her finest.

"There's gonna be upwards of a million people coming to watch this horse-and-pony show!" she declared. "We had better be ready when they get here!"

That same week, the Supreme Court ruled indefinite detention to be unconstitutional and ordered the immediate release of all citizens. Ellen Byrd sat down on a street corner and cried in relief. Just west of Rudy's town in Pennsylvania, Bill Gray stepped out of prison and immediately started marching toward Washington. Young Matt Beaulier and the rest of Charlie's relatives joined him. Yellow-bearded Mack, thinner than he had ever been in his life, flagged down an off-duty school bus driver, explained where they were headed, and asked for a lift. The man cranked up the radio in response; Silas Black was singing Charlie's love poem. He gave the group a ride to the western flank of marchers, parked the bus, and walked along with them.

At night, when the march rested, Inez, Ellen, and Natalie held meetings about the road ahead of them. Ellen spoke eloquently about the philosophies and strategies of nonviolent struggle. Inez drilled people in practical skills and tactics. The majority of the marchers had attended some of the earlier trainings instigated by Lupe and Inez. Ellen breathed a deep sigh of relief as the commitment of the people became clearer. The southern branch of the march had reported that people were showing up with rifles and shotguns. The western and northern branches urged them to demand a commitment to nonviolence from every single person and to insist that all weapons were left behind.

"If we meet violence with violence, a civil war will erupt," Ellen told her marchers. "We must commit to nonviolence, passionately, and with great faith."

One night, they camped out in a farmer's hayfield. Sentries were posted in case of attacks from the military or the police, or even from the citizens who believed the mainstream media's portrayal of the March of the Gray Riders as an insurrection of terrorists.

"Let me be utterly honest," Ellen said. "We will be met with violence, possibly even extreme violence. People may die. Certainly, we will be subject to beatings, abuse, pain, and suffering. Before we take one more step on this journey, you must be clear about the monumental commitment you are making. Some of us," she said with eerie conviction, "will not make it home."

She looked at the field of faces glowing with nervous excitement, creased with grim determination, and shadowed with inner worries. Her heart swelled for the frailty of humans and for the courage that could course through such a tender structure of capillaries and skin. Their eyes would weep on this journey. Their mouths would cry out in pain. Their hands would reach for each other in fear and assistance.

"We are going into the battlefield," Ellen told them, "armed with nothing but justice, courage, and committed love. Are we lunatics? Perhaps, but fools like us have shaped history more than once. It has been shown, time and again, that change wrought through nonviolent means endures far longer than the havoc of war and violence. We approach our nation's capitol not as armed insurrectionists, but as citizens dedicated to the foundational rights of our democracy."

She paused, for the commitment to nonviolent struggle was no small vow. It could not be just a lofty ideal. It had to become an inner conviction; a willingness to forgive in the heat of suffering; a deep fortitude to hold back the strike of retaliation.

She asked them to bear the great cross of Jesus; not the wooden one or the crown of thorns, but the powerful, invisible cross that had been shouldered by a man who hung crucified and still found room in his heart to forgive. When the police callously shot people dead; when pepper spray was pumped into their eyes, when soldiers pointed bayonets at the innocent; when bodies fell in the streets; when women were bloodied and men crippled; at these times, Ellen demanded that the marchers step beyond the limits of human patience and walk in the realms of the saints.

Not all would achieve it. Not every hand would be restrained from fighting. Not every heart would bear outrage without yearning for revenge. Some would find their resolve crumbling in the face of terror. Others would feel righteous anger whip through them unchecked. Ellen knew, though, that if enough marchers could achieve such strength, they could carry many others along with them. Such self-governance and sincere leadership, together, would be the foundation that resurrected the nation.

The next morning, good news cheered the marchers onward. Tucker's election fraud data had been analyzed, and though the mainstream media continued to insist that the data was fraudulent, the official reports verified its authenticity. Tucker and the Alternet team ensured this news reached not just the people, but the public officials, sheriffs, and the entire chain of military command.

Dissension fractured the military. The Oath Guardians openly refused to obey the orders of the illegitimate president. High-ranking generals held hasty conferences. Lower levels of command watched the shifting winds, uncertain which side to defend. Police departments nationwide splintered. Citizens contacted the local and state police, asking them to look favorably on the march. In the north, state troopers began to trail the Gray Riders. People eyed the vehicles nervously until Natalie Beaulier-Rider lost her patience and boldly rapped on a window.

"Look, if you're here to give us a speeding ticket, hurry it up, eh?"

"I'm not here to harass you," the officer protested. "I'm here to help."

"*Voyons!* You're joking?"

"No ma'am. You're peaceful citizens standing up for your rights. I won't cross the state line, but until you hit D.C., I intend to make sure you get no trouble on my highways."

Natalie counted her blessings and thanked God. The northern marchers experienced no problems. The western Gray Riders reported minor incidents, but had not been halted yet. The real trouble struck in the south. In Virginia, the police cracked down with such violence that the north and west paused to tremble. Then the message came from the south: *We're smaller in number, but we're not stopping now.* Hasty strategy sessions convened. An idea shot through the three flanks like a bird in flight: *Disperse, but move forward.*

The people vanished.

All that remained was a rumble, an unease, a sense of a tidal wave approaching. Officials grew nervous, uncertain about the rumors that persisted. Something was coming. The invisible march of people gathered strength like water tumbling from the hillsides into creeks. Rivers flowed toward the ocean. The suburbs swelled, doubled, tripled, and the people kept coming. As they reached the city limits, their numbers grew so large that they could no longer remain out of sight. At twilight, a teeming mass appeared on all sides of the city. The army was sent out to barricade the streets. The march halted. The trial began tomorrow. In the morning, the people were determined to pass through.

The sun slowly rose in the gray sky. The people climbed to their feet, stiff from sitting overnight, but resolute. On the south side, riot police awaited the marchers. Hearts thudded in chests, but their feet stepped forward. A voice lifted in an old spiritual, then sputtered and died in the throat-choking tension. They walked toward the barricade, praying for a miracle. A voice barked out an order. The eyes of the riot police snapped toward the speaker . . . and a miracle arrived on the scene. A cheer erupted from the people as Oath Guardians forced the riot police to stand aside and allowed the people to move forward in peace.

"Watch out for Greenbacks," the uniformed men warned them. "They're waiting for you. Godspeed and good luck! Defend our democracy."

Insurrectionists shook hands with soldiers. The march moved quietly and quickly onward.

In the western quarter, Greenbacks confronted the marchers donned in full riot gear and wielding tear gas and rubber bullets. The western contingent of marchers was the smallest and weakest of the three. The Greenbacks had orders to disperse, not kill. Crowds of protestors were already forming inside the city; unnecessary brutality at this stage could pitch the building frenzy over the edge. The orders were to wait for the insurrectionists to strike first, badger them with beatings and tear gas; and send them packing.

The western marchers slowed as the Greenback forces came into sight. A solid wall of shields blocked them. A second and third line formed beyond the first. The marchers split up and wove through the maze of streets, looking for a way past. For miles, it seemed a cordon of mercenaries prevented the peaceful demonstrators from entering. Word spread that the southern flank had broken through. The Gray Riders turned toward the rumored entry, but the Greenbacks moved to block them. Bill Gray saw the reinforcement lines split formation and turned to young Matt Beaulier.

"This is our chance," he said grimly. The stint in prison had left him hardened and fearless. Only one line of Greenbacks protected the street they were on.

"Let's charge," Matt suggested.

The two men shook hands and shot forward. Others joined the rush and, together, they fractured a hairline crack in the dam of the blockade. Panting, Bill Gray and Matt Beaulier sprinted down the streets as the Greenbacks chased them. Rubber bullets fired. Tear gas filled the air. Chaos broke out . . . but they were still headed toward the courthouse!

In the north, the Gray Riders halted. News of the clashes in the west had reached both the marchers and the authorities. Soldiers had been ordered to reinforce the riot police in the north. Armed infantry awaited the people. The red laser sights of assault weapons gleamed amidst the shells of black helmets and shields. The Gray Riders stood in place as Inez Hernandez walked slowly forward and spoke to the soldiers.

"We are not your enemy. We are your people. These are our streets. Your streets. Our children's streets. Let us pass by."

The soldiers stood unmoving. They had orders. The troops raised their guns.

"Look into their eyes!" Inez cried. "Look into their eyes and see love."

No one knew whether she spoke to soldiers or citizens. The two front lines tensed. Activists and soldiers each had their trainings, as different as night and day. One lanky fellow stood in the front line of the Gray Riders, hearing the echoes of

Charlie's voice saying, *someday, the soldiers will lay down their guns, tired of killing people who love them.* Zipper swallowed hard and prayed for that someday to arrive.

"Someday," he murmured, "they will lay down their guns, tired of killing people who love them."

A tall, willowy woman joined her hands and voice with his.

"Someday, they will lay down their guns, tired of killing people who love them."

A third voice joined.

A chorus grew.

"Someday," the marchers chanted, "they will lay down their guns, tired of killing people who love them."

Eyes locked with eyes. Shoulders tensed. A finger tightened on a trigger. Zipper reflexively shut his eyes, waiting for the bullet in his chest.

"Someday," he prayed.

He opened his eyes and looked straight into the soldier's gaze.

*Someday,* he prayed.

The barrel wavered . . .

. . . and that someday came.

One soldier in the front line lowered his gun. His commander barked out an order. The soldier shook his head.

"No."

One word. A miracle rested on that one word. The soldier slowly backed away from his ranks as the commander threatened to court-martial him. He moved to the side of the Gray Riders, refusing to kill civilians who had a right to protest what was going on. A second soldier lowered his weapon with a cry of frustration. A third soldier straightened into a standing position.

Inez Hernandez spoke.

"If you allow us to move forward peacefully, we will walk quietly to the courthouse, that is all. We are not here to destroy anything. Please, do not turn this into a massacre. Allow us to walk through peacefully."

The Gray Riders, still looking down the barrels of guns, watched breathlessly as the commander's face contorted through a series of expressions. No one moved as the situation hung tenuously close to erupting. Inez continued her efforts to persuade him. An agonizing ten minutes passed.

A flurry caught their eyes as a soldier ran up to the commander. A hushed conversation whipped between the two men. The commander's expression leapt from surprise to confusion to irritation. Inez tuned her ears to the low murmurs.

" . . . southern marchers through, western headed toward courthouse . . . the Colonel says to let them through. Sir, yes sir, he knows the President's orders, sir. It's just - " the soldier broke off.

"Just what?" the commander barked loud enough to be heard by everyone.

"The Colonel's orders came from the General, sir."

Inez's eyes widened at the subtle insinuation of internal scuffles between the President and the high-ranking General. *Division in the command*, she thought, *there's a General who doesn't acknowledge the President's legitimacy.* She tucked the knowledge away for later.

The commander's eyes flicked to the marchers, swept over his troops, lowered to the ground in a brief moment of calculation, then finally lifted into a decisive nod.

"Let them through."

Cries of relief broke out. The three insubordinate soldiers released heavy breaths. The march moved forward.

"Thank you," Zipper said as he passed the first soldier who

had stepped down against orders. The young man gave a tight nod. Sweat ran down his face.

"Thank you," Ellen Byrd repeated, though nothing could express the overwhelming sensation in her chest.

"Thank you," Natalie Beaulier-Rider told the soldier, her voice cracking with emotion, trying to squeeze the importance of what had just occurred into two tiny syllables.

Within the hour, the March of the Gray Riders reached the steps of justice. The northern flank poured into the broad courtyard where the southern flank awaited. The western flank ran in coughing on teargas, bruised from rubber bullets, carrying injured companions, but still managing a ragged cheer upon arriving. Bill Gray scanned the crowd for the tall figure of his wife, caught sight of her curly silver-black mop of hair, and dove through the crowd with twice as much determination as he had shown the Greenbacks. Young Matt Beaulier, battered, bruised, and out of breath, mounted the courthouse steps and raised his arms high in a gesture of victory. The crowd cheered with him briefly before the guards chased him off the steps. A ring of Oath Guardians stood around the assembly, watching for the inevitable appearance of Greenbacks. Inez quickly appointed people to go urge the Oath Guardians not to use violence.

The air crackled with volatility. The people waited expectantly for Charlie and Zadie to appear. They stood on tiptoe, craned through each other's heads, tapped their neighbors' shoulders, and asked *do you see them?* Now and then, a person was caught looking skyward as if expecting them to come winging down like birds. The crowd shifted impatiently. On the top step of the courthouse, the officials smirked. After all this, wouldn't it be ironic if Charlie Rider and Zadie Byrd Gray didn't show up for the trial? The officials got ready to announce this to the people.

"Excuse me," said a soft voice, weaving through the crowd.

"Pardon me," another voice said as he slipped between a pair of shoulders.

"Move out of the way!" someone bellowed. "They're here!"

Heads turned. Shoulders slid sideways. People parted.

Zadie and Charlie emerged from the crowd. They walked slowly up opposite sides of the courthouse steps, hearts pounding, expecting catastrophe at any minute. They met in the middle under the implacable gaze of the guards.

"Charlie Rider," Zadie said quietly.

"Zadie Byrd Gray," he sighed with a smile.

"Never a dull moment, hmm?"

"Or private," he replied, waving to the crowd. She grabbed his jacket and pulled him into a kiss. The madness of the world faded to nothing . . .

. . . and roared back to life a moment later as cheers pummeled the white walls of the courthouse.

"Well, that's a first," Zadie murmured.

"What is?" Charlie asked.

"A crowd of thousands cheering on a simple kiss."

Charlie smiled.

"I'd say it was a sign of great progress in this country," he replied.

And he kissed her again, just to hear the people roar for love.

# CHAPTER TWENTY-NINE

. . . . .

## *The Trial*

Just outside the courthouse doors, the police attempted to arrest Charlie and Zadie. Tansy Beaulisle blasted them apart with a bevy of lawyers, guards from the French embassy, and a written order from the judge to leave the defendants in the custody of the French officials. A team of burly security guards hustled Charlie and Zadie inside while Tansy squawked ferociously at the police. *Out of the frying pan and into the fire,* Charlie thought, *that's the story of my life.* In a few moments, Tansy burst in behind them and bowled them over with a whirlwind of words.

"Look at the size of that crowd! The ACLU is working hard and furious to get 'em a special permit or court order or something to keep them all from being massacred in the next twenty minutes! I tell you, it has been a helluva week. The prosecution has been pitching hardballs at me so fast I started praying to Jackie Robinson instead of Jesus. The opposing team is now being led by my dear ole pal, Ron Warner," she grimaced. "They switched him in just to rile my buttons, I'm sure. He has been the all-star player of every nefarious, low-down shameless trial I've ever worked on, and he has beaten me 'n' justice into a pulp on numerous occasions. I keep hoping he'll give himself a legal hernia one of these days," she grumbled. "On the bright side, Judge Samuel J. Bowker is presiding."

"Is he a friendly judge?" Charlie asked her.

"Hell no. Ain't no such thing as a friendly judge. Bowker's

the real deal. I can't wrap my head around what he's doing on this horse-and-pony show. Musta been bought out or bribed 'cause he used to be an old legal stickler. Now don't get me wrong, he's so conservative he makes me wake up in a cold sweat praying for my vagina rights! But he's a bull in a china shop when he gets ornery, and if there's two things he don't like, it's power-grabbin' militants and politicians messing with the Constitution. So, there you have it."

"Have what?" Charlie asked, reeling.

"The faintest chance of a miracle," she declared. "Back when Congress got nasty over gun control, they took away Bowker's hunting rifle, and, Lord, he's still stewing over it. He don't care too much about free speech, but his hunting rifle? He might just defend the Bill of Rights on account of that."

"Why didn't he pull strings to get a special permit?" Charlie asked.

"Honey, it's the principle of the thing. A full-grown man shouldn't have to bribe somebody to go duck hunting in his own damn pond."

"Well," Charlie shrugged, "that's how I feel about protests. A citizen shouldn't have to ask the government's permission to make a ruckus in their own darn streets."

Tansy beamed.

"See, Chuck? Y'all are best friends in the making."

Inside the courtroom, Charlie eyed the judge with his hangdog jowls and had some doubts about Tansy and her crazy ideas. He had thrown her a curveball early on in this case, and she hurled it on up to the judge thinking Bowker would appreciate Charlie's unique legal perspective. As the minutes ticked by, however, Charlie grew increasingly uneasy about Tansy's ballsy strategy. The presence of the insurrectionists, cops, and soldiers outside the courthouse made everyone's neck hairs stand on end. Judge Bowker was not amused by the flagrant disregard of law occurring outside. He didn't like the smart-aleck look on that young terrorist's face, nor the fact that the defendants' parents had made a stink until they were allowed into the courtroom. He certainly didn't appreciate that they hadn't even gotten through the preliminaries before Charlie Rider was challenging due process.

"Mr. Rider," Judge Bowker growled, "it's a matter of procedure. Do you plead guilty or not guilty?"

"Neither, sir."

"Neither is not an option."

"Rather short-sighted of the justice system, don't you think?"

Judge Bowker accused him of mocking the court.

"Your Honor," Charlie protested, "with all due respect, the fact that Zadie and I are on trial at all is a mockery of this court. The Freedom of Defense Act is a mockery of this court. Every law passed by Congress this year has been a mockery of - "

The judge cut him off with a wave of his hand.

"I will ask you again. To the charges of violating the Freedom of Defense Act, Sections 326B and 327A, do you plead guilty or not guilty?"

"I exercised my constitutionally given rights of speech and assembly."

"So, you plead not guilty?"

"I plead that I am beyond guilt in this case, sir, and refuse to term my actions in any such language. I believe Congress is guilty of violating my constitutional rights."

"Mr. Rider, the United States Congress is not on trial today. You are."

"Your Honor, regardless of what the court docket says, the Constitution, the Congress, the President, and the people of

305

the United States are all on trial today."

"It is your lawyer's role to make speeches, Mr. Rider," Bowker said reprovingly.

Charlie shrugged.

"So, sue me."

A twitch flicked across the judge's expression. Charlie had a fleeting sense that Bowker had smiled. Then a ferocious scowl curled down through the man's jowls and dissuaded him of that idea.

"For the purpose of court proceedings," Bowker snapped out to the court recorder, "take note that the defendant pleads not guilty to the charges, though this is not technically accurate according to his philosophic perspective. You may step down, Mr. Rider."

"Call me Charlie," he said. He reached out his hand across the bench. The courtroom froze. Judge Bowker pursed his lips, glaring severely over his glasses. Charlie didn't back down.

"You're a man; I'm a man," he said quietly. "We're going to get to know each other real well. I'm just introducing myself as one man to another."

Judge Bowker coldly ordered him back to his seat.

\*       \*       \*

Prosecutor Ron Warner was a snake in a silk suit, and that was an insult to snakes. Charlie watched the man slink back and forth, and a shudder ran up his spine. In the first row of court benches, Bill Gray and Ellen Byrd sat next to his mother. Natalie's sharp retorts and stubborn persistence had gotten Bill, Ellen, and herself in the door. He could see the flush of indignation still burning in her cheeks. Natalie sniffed critically as she scrutinized the jury. She pursed her lips as her glance raked across the prosecutor. Commotion could be heard outside the courthouse as Charlie was called up to begin the questioning. His eyes flicked to the doors, but the frosted glass prevented him from knowing if the crowd was being attacked. Warner wheeled on Charlie and struck with his first question.

"Charlie Rider, are you the instigator of the Dandelion Insurrection?"

Charlie flinched from the man's venomous ferocity, and quickly counterattacked.

"Your Honor," he said, turning to the bench, "would you please have Mr. Warner arrested?"

Consternation and confusion shot through the courtroom. Judge Bowker demanded that he explain himself.

"There's a nationwide ban on those two words," Charlie said. "I request that the law be equally applied in this court."

Judge Bowker stared at him sourly before swinging his gaze to the prosecutor.

"Mr. Warner, is it possible to refrain from using those words?"

"I would suggest a temporary lifting of the ban within the confines of this court," Warner said smoothly.

Charlie snorted.

"I would suggest a permanent repeal of such an obvious violation of the first amendment. If the journalists reporting on this trial don't censor the words, will the people be arrested for reading them?"

"Mr. Warner, perhaps you can use a set of replacement words, such as *Dog Inaction*?" Judge Bowker requested.

Tansy stood up, objecting.

"That would leave an inaccurate court record for history, possibly leading to errors in judgment in future cases."

"Your Honor," Warner interjected in his oily tones, "we

could refer to this as *the terrorist group.*"

"That has not been proven!" Tansy protested.

Bowker's eyebrows lifted to his hairline.

"I'll make a court exemption for the duration of the trial. The journalists can take their chances. The people should respect the law."

Charlie exploded.

"The people should refuse to acknowledge the unjust laws of an illegitimate government! It's ridiculous to be in court fighting for my freedom of speech and kowtowing to a ban on the name of our own movement. If this court will not stand up for the first amendment, then the people must!"

Charlie's words whipped out of the courthouse. In the streets, Charlie's defense of the first amendment reached the ears of young Matt Beaulier and Inez as they organized the people to hold their ground against the Greenbacks. The two exchanged a quick look and the words *dandelion insurrection* began their struggle for liberation. Inside the courtroom, the muffled chant of voices climbed in volume until they were clearly heard.

*"Insurrection Dent-de-lion! Insurrection Dent-de-lion!"*

*"Insurrección diente de león! Insurrección diente de león!"*

No one had ever thought to ban the words in French or Spanish.

Tansy chuckled softly and sang under her breath.

*"We've got a right! We've got a right!*
*We've got a right to free our speech!"*

Bowker banged the gavel. Tansy shut up. The cut-and-dry proceedings continued. Warner seethed beneath his slicked hair. Charlie decided that he appreciated the prosecutor about as much as a root canal.

"Mr. Rider, is it true that you founded the Dandelion

Insurrection?"

"No."

Warner paused and frowned at him. Charlie explained.

"The Dandelion Insurrection is a leaderless movement. It wasn't founded. It erupted in the hearts of the people in response to the increased levels of governmental corruption and control."

"Did you incite this insurrection against the government?"

"That phrasing is incorrect," Charlie answered.

"Answer the question," Warner insisted. "Did you instruct the people to resist the government?"

"I instructed the people to resist unjust, destructive, and unconstitutional laws."

"In other words, to revolt against the government."

"No," Charlie said firmly, "there are no other words. We have never fought government itself, merely the corruption of democracy in the United States. Should the current political leaders restore civil liberties to their constitutionally granted status, I could simply encourage citizens to use them in the context of functional democracy."

"That is wonderfully idealistic, Mr. Rider," Warner scoffed, "but it is beyond the scope of the actual question. Please answer, yes or no, did you urge the populace to break the law?"

"I cannot answer that question with a yes or a no," Charlie responded.

Warner spun to the bench.

"Your Honor, the defendant is obstructing justice."

"On the contrary," Charlie retorted immediately, "I am insisting on justice. You asked if I urged the populace to break the law. I can only answer that I urged the populace to *uphold* the laws outlined in the Bill of Rights."

"Which necessitated the violation of the Freedom of

Defense Act, Sections 326B and 327A."

Charlie shrugged.

"It is the opinion of the court, and not myself, that the unconstitutional laws of Congress are not on trial today."

It was grueling. Zadie watched Warner badger, beat, and provoke Charlie with every word. Her body tensed in empathy. Sweat beaded up in her palms. Warner worked ruthlessly. He was vicious and unrelenting. Tansy watched him like a hawk and took copious notes.

"Use this as study," she warned Zadie. "You'll be next."

Zadie willed herself to silence the whisper of fear that arose. She fixed her eyes on Warner and tried to see the person beneath the soldier in a business suit. She saw his red nose, the signs of drinking, the bitter heart, the wary tension he carried in his shoulders, and his deep-rooted anger.

Charlie blew out a hot sigh of frustration that caught Zadie's attention. He rubbed a hand across his eyes, a sign that his patience was about to break. Zadie coughed. He looked at her. She smiled, *be kind.* He lifted his fingers. She touched them from a distance, *be connected.* She met his eyes, *be unafraid.* Charlie turned back calmly to the prosecutor.

"I'm sorry," he said politely, "could you repeat the question?"

*     *     *

The next day, dandelion symbols plastered the streets between the embassy and the courthouse. The crowd outside throbbed with flags, banners, and posters. The Dandelion Insurrectionists had been ordered to disband. They refused. A crackdown was anticipated at any moment. Inez managed to warn Tansy that they were going to form murmurations to delay direct confrontations with the Greenbacks. Teams of insurrectionists intended to deliver their demands to Congress today. The victory of the march's arrival was fading quickly under the mounting pressures.

"You're up, Zadie," Charlie murmured as they entered the courtroom.

From the start, Charlie could sense trouble brewing. A satisfied smirk oozed out of Warner's expression. He took his time beginning his questioning, looking at Zadie with a gaze that could curdle milk. The court waited while he shook his head and raised his eyebrows. Zadie fidgeted. The jurors shifted in their seats. Judge Bowker looked on impassively.

Tansy rose.

"Objection, Your Honor."

Warner wheeled to face her.

"How can you object when I haven't said anything?"

"That is my objection," Tansy stated, startling Charlie as she lassoed her usual slang into sharp legal speech. "Your dramatic attempts to intimidate my client are an utter waste of this court's time."

Charlie hid a smile. Good ole Tansy. She never missed a beat. Judge Bowker scratched his nose. It was impossible to tell if amusement or annoyance - or both - was hidden behind his wide hand.

"Mr. Warner, would you begin, please? We are not here to spend all day looking at the defendant."

"Ah, yes," Warner said, "the lovely Zadie-bird is - "

"Objection," Tansy said. "My client's name is Zadie Byrd Gray and the prosecution should use either her full name or the honorific of Ms. Gray when speaking to or about her."

"Is this relevant, Tansy?" Judge Bowker frowned, pulling off his glasses. His expression revealed a long history of court cases with this fireball lawyer.

"Yes, Your Honor. I would never address you as Sammy-Bo or the prosecutor as Ronnie-Wonnie. Any attempts to demean my client through the contraction of her name must be addressed as an issue of court prejudice against women. And, for the record Your Honor, I prefer to be called Ms. Beaulisle."

"Not Tansy the Pansy?" muttered Warner.

Without looking at him, Tansy addressed the judge.

"I suggest Your Honor hold Mr. Warner in contempt of court," she snapped.

Judge Bowker sighed. It was going to be a long day.

"Mr. Warner, I would urge you to use the proper honorifics and appellations for all persons in the court or we will never get through the trial. Continue."

Tansy sat down satisfied.

"Operation Diffuse Dramatics was successful," she whispered to Charlie.

Warner stalked to the witness stand.

"Ms. Gray, you're a lovely young lady - "

"Objection," Tansy said. "My client's physical appearance has been repeatedly referred to by Mr. Warner - "

"I was merely complimenting Ms. Gray," Warner interjected.

"This isn't a nightclub, Mr. Warner," Tansy shot back, "and she's taken."

The jury laughed.

Warner spun ferociously to Zadie. "Why did the government put you on the terrorist watch list?"

"I believe my ability to unite the people in defending their democracy made the corporate power elite a little nervous," Zadie answered.

"Is this the only reason?"

312

"So far as I know," Zadie sighed. "Perhaps you could ask the Head of Homeland Security."

"People are placed on that list because of suspicion of engagement in terrorist or other illegal activities," Warner informed her. "Have you ever engaged in illegal activities, Ms. Gray?"

Charlie heard a small gasp of sound from Zadie's mother. He spun around just in time to see Ellen's startled look vanish behind a steely expression. Tansy leapt to her feet.

"Your Honor, my client's juvenile history was sealed seven years ago and is not legally permissible in this court," Tansy said.

"Mr. Warner?" Judge Bowker motioned him to the bench. They had a quick, hushed conversation. Bowker frowned, harrumphed, and finally cleared his throat.

"Objection has been overruled," Bowker said sternly. "Juvenile records may be opened under the Freedom of Defense Act, Section 117A, if considered relevant to a charge of terrorism. Proceed, Mr. Warner."

"Gosh darn it," Tansy swore softly as she sat down. "Hang in there, girl, we'll get you through this."

"What's up?" Charlie asked.

Tansy just shook her head and motioned him to silence.

Warner spun fiercely and pointed at Zadie.

"Ms. Gray's criminal past shows a track record of immoral and illegal behaviors, including, but not limited to underage prostitution, use and distribution of intoxicants, possession of illegal substances - "

"Objection!" Tansy called out. "The records show those 'illegal substances' to be nothing more than the possession and serving of alcohol as a minor. Mr. Warner is misleading the jury."

313

"Mr. Warner," Bowker warned him, "please accurately portray the facts."

"Very well," Warner shrugged, "I was going to discreetly cover the shameful history of this woman, but if you insist . . . " He launched in before anyone could object. "Zadie Byrd Gray is a prostitute who has had repeated illegal abortions, forged identification, and lied about her age, occupation, and activities."

"Objection!" Tansy called out. "I repeat that the prosecution is both misrepresenting the facts and conveying information that is not relevant!"

"Oh, but it is," Warner snarled back. "Forgery of identification is a hallmark of terrorism. The sex industry is well-linked with other criminal activities and despite this woman's frequent profusions of *life and love* to the unwitting American public . . . tell me," his voice rose in dramatic outrage, "what kind of reverence for life is it to have two abortions? Not one, but two!"

Zadie sat like stone beneath the staring eyes of the jury. Her lips twitched once, but Charlie couldn't tell if it was anger or hurt that raged behind her expressionless face. She flinched as Warner spun back toward her.

"What do you have to say to this?"

"That was close to ten years ago," Zadie answered, emotionless.

"Oh?" Warner said in a tone that twisted Charlie's gut into knots. "What about during the last week of March? Were you or were you not, *stripping* at Tits Galore, the Dive-in Bar, and Mel's Hotties, all located in the Blue Ridge Mountains?"

"Stripping is not against the law - "

Warner cut her off.

"It calls into question your morality, Ms. Gray. You profess to be a worthy leader of the American people. Yet, how can this jury view your behavior as anything more than the self-serving actions of a woman who has engaged in depravity to suit her own purposes?"

Warner proceeded to badger Zadie with questions so ferociously that the color drained out of her cheeks. He grilled her on her history of radical activism, insinuating a trend toward extremism. He questioned her motives behind the events around Greenback Street, claiming that the murmurations were riots. He referred to her underground educational campaigns as brainwashing and anti-American propaganda. Charlie clenched his hands into fists and jammed them between his knees. Warner raked through the coals of Zadie's past, dragging it all into the present, quoting and mocking her. Charlie could hardly stand to look at the disapproval that pinched the jurors' faces. When Warner finally sneered *no further questions,* Charlie and Zadie sighed in tandem relief.

Tansy rose with the wrath of God in her.

"One moment, please," she asked the court, visibly trying to collect her outrage. "I am appalled at the tremendous breach of legal ethics displayed by the prosecution, shocked and horrified to see smear tactics applied in the case of a young woman who was unable to access conventional systems of money due to unlawful persecution by government agents - "

"Objection," Warner said, smirking.

"Overruled," Bowker barked out, startling the man.

Tansy quickly hid her own surprise with a polite nod.

"Thank you, Your Honor. You restore my faith in justice." She regarded Zadie for a moment then turned to the jury.

"The relatively common criminal infractions of a juvenile aren't indications of a person's proclivity toward crime, and furthermore, the economic injustices of the male dominated market that drive women to use their bodies for income are not on trial today . . . though I surely hope to prosecute this issue until it lies buried in the dust of human progress."

"Objection," Warner called out, "feminist dogma is not relevant to this case."

"Sustained," the judge answered. "Ms. Beaulisle, please stay relevant to the subject."

Tansy nodded politely, but a tiny smile flitted across her face. She now had the riveted attention of the female jurors. Tansy turned to Zadie, who seemed to be breathing easier now.

"Ms. Gray, did you exercise your freedom of speech and right to assemble, and encourage others to do so as well?"

"I did."

"And you did this knowing it would violate the Freedom of Defense Act?"

"I did it knowing it was necessary to defend the foundational principles of our democracy."

"Do you believe our Bill of Rights is an essential part of our democracy?"

"I do," Zadie answered fervently.

"Have you ever considered violent actions against the state?"

"No, never. I have always advocated and engaged in methods of peaceful resistance."

"Ms. Gray, exactly what does the Dandelion Insurrection resist?"

"Well, some say we resist tyranny in the government, economic injustice, and environmental destruction, but I maintain that such views are a flawed conception of reality. In truth, we resist nothing."

Tansy asked for clarification.

"The Dandelion Insurrection stands *for* life, love, civil liberties, participatory democracy, economic equality, and environmental sanity," Zadie answered. "When this movement is framed as oppositional, the proactive, life-supporting aspects of the Dandelion Insurrection are ignored. In truth, it is a handful of greedy, corporate elitists who are resisting the rest of humanity. They're doing a heck of a job, but they're not going to win. Life wants to live," she pointed out, "a fact that those destructive few should be very grateful for since our will to live is keeping them alive, too. I'm not expecting a Congressional Medal of Honor, but if anyone can get them to stop attacking me, I'd be most grateful."

The jurors laughed and by the time Zadie left the stand, they were openly applauding. At the end of the day, the security forces from the French Embassy escorted Charlie and Zadie out. Tansy paced alongside them, planning to ride over to the embassy with them for a strategy session. Charlie looked at the vacated courtyard and wondered with painful poignancy about the fate of the insurrectionists that day. A forlorn cardboard sign left on the pavement caught his eye. *Be kind. Be connected. Be unafraid.* Tansy followed his gaze.

"Don't worry," she exclaimed. "Got a message a while back that they're all over at the White House, and only a couple hundred have been arrested so far. Apparently, the police are refusing to obey orders. Rumor says there's a task force of Greenbacks in police uniforms being assembled to break the crowd," Tansy frowned, "which would be tantamount to treason, hiring mercenaries to butcher citizens. It could be true, though, if the police won't obey orders. Even the military seems to be splitting down the middle; some insisting on protecting that phony baloney president, others standing alongside the Oath Guardians in supporting the people."

Charlie bit his lip anxiously as Tansy continued on.

"Inez Hernandez managed to get the list of demands into

317

Congress today," Tansy told them. "A couple politicians walked it onto the floor all legit and everything."

"I guess not all politicians are crooks," Charlie commented.

Zadie snorted.

"I bet Pilar Maria bribed them."

Charlie choked.

"Inez wouldn't let her do that!" he exclaimed.

"You know," Tansy declared, "that four foot firecracker has got my vote. Inez for Prez! Why, if she was running the show as Commander-in-Chief, the wars would be over before they got started!"

Zadie smiled to herself. *Exactly,* she thought.

Tansy's stream of conversation continued nonstop as the guards nudged them toward the armored car. As they rolled toward the embassy, Tansy turned her attention to the trial.

"What on earth was Bowker doing today?" she complained.

"Uh . . . presiding?" Charlie guessed.

Tansy gave him a look.

"What?" Charlie protested. "I thought he was great, standing up for Zadie and all."

"Chuck," Tansy explained in exasperation, "Bowker's not supposed to be helping y'all out! He outta be bending every rule *against* you two, otherwise they wouldn't have let him near this trial with a forty-foot pole. That's why I want to know what he's doing on this case. The government's got plenty of other hanging judges they coulda strung you up with." Tansy let out a hot sigh of confusion. "I swear, something is cookin' behind the scenes and it sure ain't fried chicken."

Zadie chuckled.

"Maybe the Dandelion Insurrection is happening in his heart, too."

Tansy shot her a startled look. *Bowker?* She thought of her

318

long history with the judge, the deepening of his wrinkles and hangdog jowls over the years, the sharp bite of his irascible temper. When he signed onto this trial, she had been sure as death and taxes that he was getting a hefty bribe. Most of the judges wouldn't get within half a continent of this case. It was a career wrecker. Find them innocent and the power elite would blacklist you forever. Rule against the kids and the whole country will hate you - not to mention you could kiss the Constitution goodbye. Bowker should have been hunkered down, hanging on until retirement, but here he was in the heat of new territory, a regular John Wayne of the Wild West. Tansy looked up at Zadie again.

"The Dandelion Insurrection . . . in old Bowker?"

"Crazier things have happened," Zadie said hopefully. "He's got this penchant for the Constitution, remember. He could be playing the powers-that-be to defend what he knows is right."

"I wouldn't place my bets on it," Tansy said cynically, "but if it turns out to be true, I swear to the Man Above, I'll scale the bench and smack that old dog a kiss!"

# CHAPTER THIRTY

· · · · ·

## *Le Grand Ménage*

The next day, surprises awaited them at the courthouse. The insurrectionists had returned and appeared to be sweeping the wide area in front of the building. The guards from the French embassy frowned and took firmer grips on Charlie and Zadie, moving them swiftly up the steps. An old man turned in the crowd and let out a loud exclamation. He hobbled rapidly in their direction, one hand waving in the air, the other gripping his cane. The guards froze, anticipating an attack. Charlie squinted.

"*Pour la vie, la liberté, et l'amour!*" the gravely voice called out.

"Grand-pere!" Charlie cried.

Valier staggered up the steps, spilling his breath into a stream of French. He impertinently batted the guards away as they moved to restrain him from reaching for Charlie.

"I'm not a terrorist, you fools! I'm the boy's grandfather! *Mon Dieu!* Let me have a look at him before I die, eh?"

Valier cajoled them in his deep Acadian accent until they nodded curtly to one another and allowed him to approach. Valier wrapped his quivering limbs around Charlie, drawing him close, and laying his gnarled hand on the back of the young man's head.

"*Ah voyons,*" he cried emotionally before whispering in Charlie's ear, "*la mémères* sent you a message."

Charlie froze. His *grand-mère*, Bette, had been dead for eleven years, and besides, the old man clearly said *mémères*. He

321

frowned. What could the blue-haired old ladies of *La Vallée Saint-Jean* possibly want to tell him?

"They said to tell you, *it's time for Le Grand Ménage.*"

"The Spring Cleaning?" Charlie hissed back. "What are they talking about?" *Le Grand Ménage* was an old Acadian tradition. Every spring, the people of the valley cleaned their houses from top to bottom. They washed down walls, scrubbed inside the cupboards, laundered every piece of clothing they owned, aired the sheets, turned the beds, repainted the shutters, shook out the curtains; everything submitted to the compulsive cleaning regime.

"Eh, I don't know," Valier shrugged innocently as the guards looked in their direction. He waited a moment and then hugged Charlie to him again. "The *mémères* say it may be summer already, but better late than never! First, we clean our souls, then we clean our homes, then we clean it all!" Valier waggled his eyebrows. "Not just down here, Charlie, all over the country. The *mémères* say, *no work, no play, no school, no shopping. Nothing but Le Grand Ménage until everything is swept clean!*" His eyes darted toward the security officer standing nearby. He couldn't say more.

The guards insisted on ending the conversation. They had bent the official agreement with the U.S. government far enough. The couple was supposed to have no communication with anyone but their lawyer while they were in custody. Valier hastily hobbled after Charlie and Zadie as they were escorted toward the courtroom, commenting in a steady stream of French that he had been determined to come to Washington, even if his obstinate daughter had ordered him to stay home.

"Natalie said I was too old to dodge rubber bullets, so I decided to lead the grand finale of the march," he said with a twinkle in his eye.

"You may still get your chance at dodging rubber," Charlie warned Valier.

"Eh? Not me! I've got to keep my eye on you! I'm coming to the trial."

Charlie sighed in relief. The chaos on the streets was no place for the old man. Out of the corner of his eye, he saw his mother catch sight of Valier. Charlie bit back a smile as a volley of French erupted between them.

"Remember, Charlie!" Valier called out. *"Le Grand Ménage!"*

\*     \*     \*

Ssshhh. Shhhhht. Shhhck. Way up north on the edge of the nation, a little old *mémère* paused in her sweeping. She leaned on her broom as a border guard walked by. She twisted her lips in annoyance. The cry for impeachment, resignations, and re-elections beat in the pulse of her blood. The demand for justice swept through the bones of her body. She rapped the bristles of the broom sharply against the sidewalk and brushed the dust briskly into the street. Those corrupt officials would resign, she swore, or they would all be impeached!

Shhweet-shhwitt. Shhweet-shhwitt. Todd Booker scrubbed the hood of his car as his kids soaked him with the hose. Lupe had sent him a three-word message: *Strike. Boycott. Kids.* Todd Booker led a walkout at his work, shot an email to the Suburban Renaissance to halt all purchases, shopping, and consumption, and wept in relief as he drove to where his kids were in hiding. The economy ground to a complete halt as a total consumer boycott erupted. The Dandelion Insurrection also urged a general strike until the demands of the people were met. They were determined to pull the plug on *the Three Men in the Tub* and sink them in the ocean of their greed! Home from work

323

midweek, the suburban families joined in with *Le Grand Ménage*. Voices hollered up and down the blocks of the suburban neighborhoods as they shared a hose and conversation, swapping stories of the attempts to disperse the rapidly growing crowd of protestors in D.C. Some hair-raising reports indicated that the Greenbacks had cracked down brutally. Others claimed that the police were standing up for the people. Todd suspected both rumors were true and prayed for Lupe's safety in Washington.

"Just a few more days until she scrubs their hides right out of there," he told his kids proudly.

Fssst-fffffpht, Tucker absentmindedly swept the feather duster around his basement. His eyes were locked on the computer screen watching the ones and zeros. He froze. He dropped the duster. He slid into his seat. *Here we go*, he thought, *it's happening*. In an effort to stop the insurrection, the President ordered the entire Internet to be shut down. Tucker Jones shook his head at the President's folly. The shut down triggered a hidden function in the Alternet to flare into action. The programming rose up from dormancy in computers across the nation, invaded the server stations, and in one tyranny-induced swoop, the Alternet devoured the Internet.

"When the Internet falls, the Alternet rises!" Tucker said.

Tucker's programming strained under the massive weight of its expansion. Secretly, Tucker crossed his fingers and hoped the system would hold up. He watched it like God setting the Earth into orbit. Utter fascination glowed in his eyes. The Alternet hummed with vitality . . . it heaved with the strain . . . and it held!

"People of the United States," Tucker said proudly, "the Alternet is at your service."

Officials panicked. Authorities claimed it was the largest

single-handed cyber-terrorist attack in the history of computers. Tucker ignored their histrionics. Terrorism was in the eyes of the beholder. By next year, they would be giving him the Nobel Prize.

Shwuoolp-shwoomp-shwlup. Mops across the Capitol swiped furiously. Zipper filmed the people as they washed down the worn steps in front of the courthouse in appreciation for the show of solidarity that was literally sweeping the country. He had been denied media access to the trial, but he covered the swelling crowds that grew by the hour. He kept in contact with other reporters covering the White House, the Mall, and several side streets. Masses of people were pouring into the Capitol, millions, all told. Zipper glanced at the multitude in front of the courthouse. *Five hundred thousand,* he estimated at midday. *One million,* he amended by dusk.

Shhhhurerp. Inez's wiry arms reached up. The squeegee screeched down the windows, then plunged into soapy water. Inez scoured her soul, purifying her heart for the struggle ahead of them. Her lips murmured prayers, requesting the compassion of the Virgin, the strength of St. Michael, and the forgiveness of Jesus, himself. Absorbed in the divine, she didn't see the Greenbacks whipping around the corner. A bullet shattered the window she was washing. She whirled. The red light of a pistol placed its stigmata on her forehead.

"*Aii Dios, no!*" she cried . . .

. . . and a man tackled the Greenback.

"Run!" young Matt shouted at Inez. He jumped up and pushed her out of her shock. Together, they hurtled down the street, into an alleyway, and hid out of sight behind a dumpster.

"Are you alright?" he asked as their chests heaved.

She nodded.

"Matt Beaulier," he introduced himself.

"Inez Hernandez," she gasped back.

"I know," he said. His eyes - and his heart - had been trailing her for days.

Down the block, Pilar Maria confronted a Greenback, cursing Inez for the restraint of nonviolence. If she could just sock him in the eyes, knee him in the balls, gouge her fingernails into his cheek . . . Pilar settled for hurling her bucket of dirty water at him, then scuttled away like a beetle.

"*El Señor*," Pilar prayed to God, "help us survive one more day!"

Tension mounted by the minute. Riot police harassed the Dandelion Insurrectionists at every turn. Arrests were made for threatening officials with spray bottles and soapy water. Buckets of cleaning solutions were said to be bombs. Up and down the city streets, yellow gloves flashed along with the lights on top of the riot police vans. Greenbacks attacked without warning. Nostrils flared on the smell of ammonia and tear gas.

The scchhhhrk, ssshhhwwpp, sscccrrrpp's of bristles and scrub brushes haunted the Capitol. Politicians placed frantic phone calls. Corporate powers cursed. Things were getting out of hand. Down the hall from the Oval Office, the late night custodian turned on the vacuum machine. The Commander-in-Chief of the world's most powerful military flinched. Lower level officeholders started jumping ship like fleas off a drowning dog. The highest-ranking officials gritted their teeth and prepared their legal battleships. The wealthiest in the country readied their private jets. Letters, emails, and phone calls flooded into offices. The people were clear: *anyone who was not implicated in the elections' fraud had best pick up a broom or get out of the way.*

By midweek, the nation shined. The city buildings gleamed. Suburban neighborhoods squeaked. Rural farmsteads glistened.

The people scoured their souls along with their homes. They cleaned out their hearts, scrubbed out their minds, washed the grit of corruption away from their lives. Mouths drew into thin determined lines. *Tomorrow at noon*, the people agreed. *We will give the politicians until tomorrow at noon to resign or be impeached.*

That night, the prayers of a thousand faiths wafted from millions of lips. From coast-to-coast, the nation's heartbeat hammered in sleepless anticipation of the morrow. Millions stood vigil in the streets of the capitol. Thousands more would rise up in the morning. Hundreds of cities and small towns quaked in readiness. In New York City, the Chief of Police resigned and Aubrey Renault was released from prison. He walked home and stood on his balcony, listening. In the thick of night, the French devotee of liberty could hear the whispered prayers of the nation's souls. It wasn't singing . . . but it was something close.

# CHAPTER THIRTY-ONE

· · · · ·

## *In the History of the Universe*

The night before their trial ended, Charlie and Zadie could not sleep. The scent of tear gas flooded the streets. The Greenbacks had killed two insurrectionists that afternoon. Thousands were being arrested. The streets heaved with chaos and attacks. Outside the embassy, Charlie and Zadie could hear the cries of the people in the streets below. The coming verdict on the trial loomed impossibly large and uncertain. They lay side-by-side on the bed, fingers laced together, staring at the ceiling.

"What do you think will happen tomorrow?" Zadie asked Charlie.

He paused before answering.

"Does it matter, Zadie?"

"It does to me," she admitted. Charlie's silence stretched for a long time, ticking by as slowly as the clock. She drew in a breath to ask him - for suddenly she had to know - did he believe that freedom awaited them tomorrow . . . or was this their last night together?

"Charlie, do you think we'll win?" she asked.

"No."

She froze. Throughout the trial, she had sensed this thought creeping up like choking vines, strangling all hope. The last days of the trial had swept by in a steady grind. The lawyers had wrung out every angle, squeezed the last drops of juice from the testimonies, and shaken the witnesses dry as bone. Charlie and Zadie had been examined and cross-examined so many times that they were run ragged into threadbare sheets of human souls, torn and frayed around the corners. Finally, the wringer exhausted its machinations, leaving Charlie and Zadie flapping in the breeze of surrender, hung on the clothesline of the jury, awaiting their fate.

"With the big thrust of *Le Grand Ménage* looming tomorrow, there's no way they're going to let us walk free," Charlie said. "Judge Bowker is probably accepting his bribe from the President right now."

Zadie felt his answer hit her in the gut. Justice was a long shot in the dark night of the nation and the odds had been stacked against them from the start.

"You were right, Charlie," she admitted, biting her lip. "We shouldn't have come."

He rolled over suddenly, looking down at her.

"We didn't have much choice, Zadie. Our only other option was the bullet-in-the-back style of justice. We've been damned if we do, damned if we don't, from the day you mentioned the Dandelion Insurrection."

"I should never have done that," she moaned.

Charlie held a finger to her lips. Once, he would have agreed. Months ago, he had hollered at her on a dusty Kansas sidewalk, furious that she had gotten him into this predicament . . . but now, imprisonment hardly seemed to make a difference. Without life, liberty, and love, the whole world would turn into a prison. Humans were all inmates on death row, hoping for parole. If any pardons or releases came, it would be because Zadie Byrd Gray dared to pull apart the veil of delusion and shake people like him awake. He touched her brimming eyes.

"Don't cry, Zadie," he begged.

"But Charlie," she whispered, "what if the Dandelion

Insurrection doesn't succeed? What if I never get to see you again?"

He swallowed.

"Never is an awfully long time," he responded.

"Life imprisonment is long enough," Zadie protested.

"Well, Tucker got me thinking about reincarnation," Charlie replied, shooting for some hope. "Let's come back and raise hell."

She laughed sadly.

"No, let's come back and raise vegetables . . . or kids."

"Got to raise dandelions, too, Zadie. Kids and vegetables won't be the same without them."

The thought silenced them for a moment. Life hung by the most fragile of threads. The next generation of children would slip from the wombs of their mothers onto the streets of upheaval. *But so what?* Charlie thought. We are not born to die; we are born to live. Our first breaths are an insurrection against destruction. Charlie shook his head. When the road of humanity led off a cliff, those who turned toward life had to battle the traffic, face policemen and tickets, beatings and arrest, simply for wanting to *live*.

"Charlie," Zadie said, "if the *Grand Ménage* fails . . . will that be the end of the Dandelion Insurrection?"

He looked out through the bars on the windows as if trying to read the future history of the country that lay hidden in the darkness. There were no stars above Washington D.C., no pinpricks of possibility shining through the black blanket of the sky, no signs of any world other than the glaring lights of the entrenched systems of the nation.

"It's not the end," he answered. "I know that much." The Dandelion Insurrection could never end, for it never began. It was old as time, older than human beings. It was a spark leaping from the dawn of creation, ever-present through the evolution of the world. "Anywhere that life reaches out with compassion," he told her, "the Dandelion Insurrection will endure."

"Do you really believe that?" she asked, aching to have hope.

"Yes," he said passionately. He remembered Tansy Beaulisle bursting into song in Tucker Jones' kitchen. The lawyer's deep brown eyes held generations of freedom seekers in them. The spirits were alive in her: Jesus, Sojourner Truth, Gandhi, King, Chavez, and countless more whose names were lost to memory. Even if the court case failed, even if he and Zadie never saw each other again, he understood from that woman's song that not one effort toward love is ever lost in the records of the Universe. It goes on, imprinting into the hearts of total strangers, carried like a spark into generations untold. Love leaps past the boundaries of genes, education, and class to erupt in the hearts of humans. On the long road toward freedom, Charlie suddenly saw that he and Zadie had reached the immortal Tree of Life. As long as life pulsed on the planet, as long as two hearts entwined, as long as a tendril of compassion continued, their legacy in this world was assured.

He kissed Zadie and a smile blossomed across her face.

"See?" he murmured. "It doesn't matter if we win or lose tomorrow . . . "

Her fingers leapt up to silence his lips.

"In this moment," she finished, "we've already won."

# CHAPTER THIRTY-TWO

. . . . .

*Judgment Day*


Day dawned in a roar of light. A little bird perched on the glowing telephone line. She ruffled her feathers and tilted her head at the great mass of people. She was the remainder of a once mighty species, a flock that had blackened the skies when they flew. She had flown north against the bitter winds, warbling *don't wait!* Now, she puffed up with a breath of hope and sent a new message into the sky. *Today! Today! The chance for life is now upon us! Today! Today! Today!*

The cry struck Charlie like an alarm. His nerves were shot with adrenaline and worry. All across the country, political juggling balls were being hurled up into the air. Corrupt politicians were wrapping their money around them like suits of armor and fleeing the country in a great flock of private jets, leaving paperwork to convict them. Fear of military coups and factional takeovers soared. The people planned to march on Capitol Hill at noon. Uncertainty surrounded everything.

"Y'all look like you been chasing billy goats instead of counting sheep," Tansy commented when she came to collect them to go over to the courthouse. She rubbed her weary eyes with a sigh. The lawyer had been lobbying hard to get their case thrown out of court, but Judge Bowker refused to budge.

"He told me something about innocence and guilt needing to be proven in a court of law," Tansy snorted, "and I told him to go to hell."

Zadie groaned.

"You shouldn't have pissed him off. He's bound to convict

333

us now."

"Tansy," Charlie asked urgently, "what if we didn't go to the trial?"

The lawyer dropped her briefcase.

"That was a joke, right?"

"No," Charlie answered, dead serious. "Look at that crowd outside! Revolution is on the doorstep and we should be out in the streets with the people, not pandering to a corrupt justice system."

"If you don't show up, Bowker'll convict y'all *in absentia*," Tansy warned him.

"Just tell him to add storming Capitol Hill to the list of charges," Charlie shrugged.

"I'm gonna pretend you didn't say that," Tansy answered in alarm. "The French Embassy promised to keep you in custody 'til this trial is done. This is not the time to be flaunting international law or the processes of justice! The country is in chaos. The chain of law and order is being split in dozens of places. You can't go scampering out into the streets! We're at a crux. The verdict of this trial could sway the whole nation, Chuck. If we win, the people will rise up in victory!"

"And if we lose?" Charlie challenged her.

Tansy clapped him on the back with a determined expression. This was her final ultimatum for the legal system. If justice abandoned its post, Tansy Beaulisle swore to tear off the badge of her license, turn her back on the courts, and fight for justice as an outlaw.

"If we lose," she promised with a grim look, "I will personally rally the people and come bust you out of prison!"

*     *     *

On the way to the courthouse, people packed the streets so

tightly that the car could only narrowly slip through. In an hour, the streets would be impassable. They could hear the muffled chants of the crowd, crying, *the Dandelion Insurrection is here!* The reply echoed from every direction; *Here! Here! Here!*

Tansy looked out the window of the armored car with a thoughtful expression on her face. She grimaced as if regretting her fiery promise to Charlie.

"Tansy," Charlie asked her bluntly, "do you think Bowker will let us off?"

"Not on your life," Tansy replied, certain.

Charlie sighed in exasperation.

"What?" Tansy protested.

"Maybe you should lie to us," he said shortly.

"It's not a good practice for folks who are waiting on miracles," she sniffed. Tansy had her fingers crossed and her prayer card in her pocket. She'd been pestering God so bad it was a wonder he hadn't struck her dead with a lightning bolt. Tansy knew, though, that this circus wasn't over 'til the fat lady sang, and Jesus specialized in miracles not justice. Warner had crucified their case with the strict nails of law, but Tansy sat on a secret that could save them all, her lips sewn shut by legalities. There was justice to be won that could only be found in the hearts of the jury. It was a long shot, but then again, the southpaw curveball pitcher was known for striking out the opposing team on the last pitch of the ninth inning.

"Come on, y'all. If you wanna win something, you gotta set your sights on it. Can't look at the pitcher. You gotta look at the ball to knock out a home run!" Tansy nudged Charlie in the ribs. "Keep your eyes on the prize, kid, or you'll get stuck in the muck."

"What's your prize, Tansy?" Zadie asked.

"Liberty and justice for all," she said without hesitation. If she was going to knock out a home run, she intended to shoot it straight into the sky like a star. The angels in heaven were rooting her on, God was her umpire, and when her three strikes were up, she'd be running all the way home to His plate.

*     *     *

Judge Bowker looked particularly sour as he growled out instructions to the jury. Palpable tension laced the courtroom. The air tingled with nervous energy. The rallying cries of the crowd outside made the blood pulse faster in everyone's veins. The defendants' parents, relatives, and a throng of reporters sat in the benches. Hands twisted. Feet jiggled. Bowker glared at the jurors.

"Your charge is to decide whether Charlie Rider and Zadie Byrd Gray are guilty or not guilty of violating the Freedom of Defense Act, Sections 326B and 327A. In a court of law, jurors must turn a blind eye to extraneous events and stand firm in the pursuit of justice," Bowker told them in his slow and grumbly voice. His scowl left no doubt that he expected each juror to do his or her duty regardless of the upheaval going on. He looked over the top of his glasses, meeting the eyes of each juror, impressing upon them the grave responsibility of this moment.

"Rarely do jurors, in which the true power of the land is vested, find themselves presented with such a weighty decision. You have heard from the prosecution, Mr. Warner, representing the United States government, who urged you to keep the integrity of lawfulness in place. You have also heard from the defense, represented by Ms. Beaulisle, who asks you not to go quietly into this dark night of democracy, but to take a stand for the principles of this country and find the defendants not guilty."

Judge Bowker glared at them through the iron mask of his face.

"Back when the term conservative had some meaning and morality behind it, a man named Barry Goldwater, a Republican Senator and presidential candidate some fifty years ago, said something powerful. I am going to conclude my remarks with a quote of his for you to contemplate along with your verdict."

Tansy frowned. Warner smirked. Judge Bowker cleared his throat.

*"Extremism in defense of liberty is no vice. Moderation in the pursuit of justice is no virtue."*

With that, he banged the gavel and there was nothing to do but wait. After a hasty conference with the courthouse security, Charlie and Zadie were taken to a small anteroom. The crowds outside had blocked the roads, making a return to the embassy impossible. *This is it,* Charlie thought. There was no escaping this one. They sat quietly together, pressed side-to-side, taking in each other's closeness with painful poignancy. Tansy warned them that a quick deliberation boded ill news for them, and if the jury returned swiftly, they would most likely be found guilty. Zadie pushed all that from her mind. She sat next to the man she loved and let the madness of the world fall away.

People restlessly paced the courthouse halls, not wanting to miss the verdict, suspecting it would come soon, but hoping it wouldn't. They ran to the restroom, checked watches, texted girlfriends, whispered anxiously, and prayed silent prayers to any deity that would listen. The tension of the day hung like thick humidity. Everyone fidgeted, anxious and uncomfortable, until just before noon the jury sent word through the bailiff that they had come to a verdict. Zadie and Charlie were escorted back to the courtroom. The benches filled. Bowker took his seat. The jury filed back in, frowning.

Charlie licked his lips.

"Doesn't look good, Zadie," he murmured.

She tore her gaze from him and scanned the somber expressions. She nodded in agreement. There was no spark of happiness in those faces, no joy, no hope. Her eyes prickled with tears. The room blurred.

Then something caught her eye. She choked. The lips of one juror twitched. She snorted. A second juror pressed her lips together. Laughter shot out of Zadie like fireworks of the soul. The judge frowned at her. Zadie stuffed it all back inside her throat where it sizzled and tickled and kicked to be let out.

"Have you made your verdict?" Judge Bowker asked the jury.

"Yes, Your Honor," the spokesperson replied.

"Charlie," Zadie hissed, "look at the lapels."

Charlie squinted at the jury. His eyes flew open.

There, in the lapels of the jury members, were twelve quietly understated, but undeniable - unbelievable - indomitable . . .

. . . dandelions!

Cheerful, yellow, outrageous in their context, hinting . . .

"Your Honor," the spokesperson of the jury said, "we find the defendants to be not guilty!"

An explosion of sound shot through the court. Zadie and Charlie slammed back in their chairs, wild with amazement. The jury burst out in face-splitting grins. Bill's cheer roared. Ellen lost her voice. Natalie Beaulier-Rider shrieked. Tears rolled down the wrinkles in Valier's face. Tansy whooped a holler worthy of a yodeler and squeezed the living daylights out of Charlie and Zadie.

"Jury nullification! Jury nullification! I couldn't say a word, y'all, but I've been praying nonstop for this!" she cried.

Hands reached across the bar and pummeled Charlie and Zadie. Tears ran down cheeks like faucets. Someone slammed out the courtroom door and hollered the news from the front steps.

"NOT GUILTY!!!!"

The crowd exploded. Cheers roared back. A wave of sheer joy, utter relief, and unbelievable hope reverberated the walls. Judge Bowker hammered to no avail. Pandemonium rocked the courthouse. The parents of the defendants climbed over the bar to embrace their children. The security officers struggled to keep the crowd outside from flooding into the court. Cynical as he was, the old judge bit his lip to hide his smile. Never in all his years on the bench had he allowed such nonsense in his court. *Jury acquittal.* His lips twitched. He looked in the direction of the Capitol, where the people were about to sweep out Congress. Underneath the raucous celebration, Judge Bowker leaned over to the court recorder.

"Take note that the jury, utilizing their undisputed power to acquit as it appeals to their logic or passion, has found the defendants not guilty. This court upholds their verdict. And, for the record . . . "

He paused. A smile formed in the corners of his eyes.

" . . . the Dandelion Insurrection is here!"

*Rivera Sun*

# CHAPTER THIRTY-THREE

. . . . .

*Immortal Song*


Charlie and Zadie linked hands as they stepped out of the courthouse into a cascade of cheers. Bright symbols of dandelions were lifted high on banners and flags, woven into crowns, and painted on cardboard signs. Charlie took a breath, feeling in his chest the breaths that had been taken by countless courageous people on the long road to freedom. He sensed the long lineage of teachers and leaders looking over the court and the people gathered outside it. Zadie felt a surge ripple through her body and saw spirit run through the crowd like a tidal wave. The life force of the planet rose up in that moment and pulsed in their hearts. They lifted their hands up in victory and a triumphant roar broke loose. It swept down the streets and burst into maddening excitement. A howl of readiness leapt from the throats of the people. Eyes turned toward Capitol Hill.

Zadie pulled him close and whispered in his ear.

"No rest for the weary, hmm?"

He shook his head. A revolution was a wheel turning inexorably toward change. One moment could bring triumph, the next might bring disaster, but strength lay in never giving up. Beyond this moment stretched another. After this push came many more. Charlie could see the struggles lining up on the horizon. He squinted into the future, trying to discern what lay ahead: challenges, possibilities, wild excitement, utter despair. He smiled slightly and returned his attention to the present. He drew a breath to speak –

- and choked as his eyes fixed on something in the distance. "What is it?" Zadie asked.

He shook his head, mute, pointing skyward. She narrowed her eyes. It seemed to be a flock of birds, but no, birds did not fly like that. Zadie gasped. The sound hit their ears. A pounding thump-thump, deep as a monster, and the buzz that reverberated the bones - the sound of predator drones. The people swiveled in the streets, crying out as they realized that these weren't the ever-present surveillance machines; these were loaded to kill.

Charlie's mind slammed into shock. *Are we nothing to this government? Mothers, fathers, old women, children!* He scrambled for sanity as the bottom dropped out of his stomach. Every step of the way, he had tried to prevent unnecessary violence, bending over backwards to sway the police, the soldiers, even the people themselves away from brutality, and now, this falsely elected president, boxed into a corner, facing imminent impeachment, was sending drones out to murder the people.

Zadie roared into action with a force that astonished them all. Every shred of trepidation fell away from Zadie in the blazing fire of crisis. Her face was an open book of honesty and passion. Her blue-gray eyes shone fearlessly. Beside her, Charlie glowed in the flame of her determination. The two young people had traveled so far into the heart of the nation's darkness that they gleamed like a pair of stars in the night sky.

Zadie held her hands up for silence. The crowd froze as the murderous hum of the drones throbbed above them. Zadie knew beyond a shred of doubt that they could not back down from this threat. Now was the time to stand firm. This moment would never come again, not with millions in the streets and a revolutionary turn of government at hand. They had to stand firm and show the forces of destruction that the will of the people could not be dominated by fear.

"This is terrorism," Zadie said, pointing to the black shapes. "They have called Charlie and me terrorists for standing up for democracy, but *this* is true terrorism! This illegitimate president and his corporate allies have taken over our cities and towns, our land and water, our health, our economy, our laws, and now they dare to wage war upon the people!"

*Join hands,* she told them.

"We have no time for fear or panic. There is nowhere to run. There is nowhere to hide. We must join hands with each other and face this together."

*Join hands,* she repeated, *and vow.*

"Vow that you will give tyranny no compromise. Vow that if one drop of blood is shed you will hound these criminals at every turn, sabotage their efforts, refuse cooperation, and resist until they are stripped of power!"

*Join hands,* she urged the people in the streets.

"Feel the strength of the people coursing through your palms. Feel the force of love alive in your body. Join hands and remain firm. We will not run. We will not hide. We will remain . . . and we will win!"

In the streets, one hand reached out to another. A finger tapped a shoulder. A palm opened to a stranger. The hands linked, two-by-two, then by the dozen, then the score. A drumroll of connection rippled through the crowd, a magnetic surge joined the group, electric hands leapt together, and a mass of strangers became a force called *the people.*

A lightning strike of Love cracked through Zadie's body. The young midwife trembled as it rose up and towered like a giant. *I am here!* the infinite roared and Love returned to earth, walking through the bodies of the people.

Beside her, Charlie shook as he saw the crowd glow electric

with connection. The wisdom of his grandfather echoed in his heart: nations vanish, cities tumble, politics come and go, but the people will inevitably endure. They will rise like a song through crisis and upheaval. They will outlast drone strikes and dictators, alike. Charlie's gaze swept across the people and up into the sky. *You are dust,* he said silently to the machines. *You may win for a moment, and that moment may last lifetimes, but in the end you will crumble and we will rise.*

Time began to freeze under the shadow of the drones.

A quarter-hour passed by in agony.

Ten minutes ticked like eternity.

Five minutes crept past slower than shifting plate tectonics.

The world's heartbeat stopped in suspense as political insanity unfolded. Greenbacks seized the drones; the military arrested the Greenbacks, a General tried for a coup, the Oath Guardians revolted. The fate of millions hung by a thread and the drones hovered on standby while politics convulsed.

"Be kind," Charlie murmured.

"Be connected," Zadie said.

"Be unafraid," the people called back from the streets.

Tansy stepped forward as if pulled by the spirit. Her eyes locked on unseen figures and long gone ghosts. Zadie shivered as she witnessed history and destiny colliding. Tansy bowed her head before her God. She stood silent for a moment. Then she lifted her throat and the song of freedom-seekers lofted.

*"We shall overcome . . . "*

Tansy fixed her eyes on something mightier than the drones and more powerful than death. She lifted her voice and the vehicles of destruction shrank into flies. Her song scaled the heights like a bird in stormy weather. Drones could not daunt this woman's faith. When the dogs attacked at Selma, when the fire hoses hit the children, when the bullets felled the students at Kent State, the song had vowed to rise again, to return throughout the ages, to fight injustice until its promise had been met.

*"We shall overcome someday . . ."*

Tansy turned her gaze to the people and gave the song to them. The melody of laborers and suffragettes erupted from their chests and the song of freedom seekers was lifted like a shield against oppression. It was the song of America, of our legends and unsung heroes, the song of humanity through the ages. It encompassed all that had come before, and all that still awaited; it resounded in the uncertainty of the present.

Charlie looked at all the people, the millions of faces in this ocean . . . the tide of history ebbed and flowed through their bodies. He watched them sing, saw them cry, caught one smile to another, and his heart broke into infinite shards of compassion. Breath swelled in their chests. Love rippled, surged, and crested. A thought crashed through Charlie like a wave . . .

We are one people, indivisible, not by allegiance or by force, but entwined through the love in our hearts. Through our pulse, and our breath, and our frail human skins, the body of *the people* stands immortal. We rise and we fall; we sweep by in waves of faces; we roll in the rushing tide of life. We are foolish, we are proud, we are loving, we are tired; we weep for beauty, laugh in sorrow, cry out lonely in the night; we hurt and cause harm; we are lovers and beloveds; we shall live, we shall die, we shall pass, and still remain; for the body of *the people* lives forever.

Charlie wept unashamed. He raised his tears toward the drones. Laughter burst from the depths of his soul. *You are nothing,* he cried. *You are dust in the wind!* Death's shadow cannot darken the light of love. They would overcome, not through force, but through their indomitable will to live.

345

Charlie knew this deep within his heart. He turned his back on the drones, took Zadie's hand, and started walking toward the Capitol with the people.

The promised *someday* of the song would come through them.

## Author's Note and Acknowledgements

Many readers contact me with the straightforward question, "How do we make *The Dandelion Insurrection* real?" My answer is simple: it already is. Every day, I meet more and more warm-hearted people like us standing up for life, liberty, and love. Real life stories abound and since publishing this novel, I have shifted my writer's focus to sharing some of the incredible people, organizations, and events that inspired this book. I invite you to read these essays on my blog and to contact me with your own stories, too. (My information is listed under my author's bio in the back of this book.) Please note, however, that bringing *The Dandelion Insurrection* to life requires that you do something radical:

**Be kind. Be connected. Be unafraid.**

**Be kind.** If you do nothing else, bring kindness to the forefront of your daily life. Our lack of respect for one another holds us back not only from working together for change, but also from creating a civil society that embraces complexity and diversity. A considerate and empathic approach to one another should be the root of how we work for change. Our lack of compassion allows cruelty, injustice, casual violence, and abuse to succeed in becoming systemic. Simple acts of kindness and consideration create a platform for showing a way out of the abusive and self-centered culture in which we live. Remembering the humanity of our 'opponents' or 'enemies' shows them that we demand that they live up to the highest standards of their human nature. I will not allow anyone the excuse of being 'evil', 'demonic', or a 'monster'. They are human beings and must answer for their actions as such. Kindness is not just a noble sentiment; it is a powerful platform demonstrating change.

**Be connected.** Through your kindness, reach out and support one another. Build friendships. Bring people together. Create community. Oppressive forces succeed through the atomization or isolation of individuals. Consumer society, in particular, thrives on isolating us from each other. However, by our very biological nature, we are interconnected beings, inseparable from the whole of this earth. Connection between us is an act of resistance. Reaching out to support one another is essential for social change. Because of this, I encourage every inspired reader to cast aside shyness and contact me. I'm quite friendly. I am also a good switchboard operator to connect you to incredible thinkers, information, reliable news sources, discussion groups, films, etc. . . . and I love to hear from you!

**Be unafraid.** Build up your courage for these wild times. In French, there are two words for dandelions. One is *dent-de-lion,* tooth of the lion, a brave and tenacious term that, sadly, has fallen out of use. The more modern phrase, *pissenlit,* piss-in-the-bed, now describes the scraggly-leafed dandelion. My friends, by the time this novel is translated into French, I should hope there is no question as to which term applies to the current crop of human beings on this planet. We live in a pivotal juncture in time - a time when it is essential that we grow out of our adolescent, egotistical, and destructive ways, and blossom into the kind of people we have always yearned to be.

*The Dandelion Insurrection* is a prophetic mirror, both foretelling and reflecting the story of our times. Between the first pencil-scratched draft and the publishing of this edition, many details of the novel have shifted from this author's wild imagining into a stark and sobering reality. As a result, the story resides in a foggy realm between fact and fiction. To address this, I have posted a page on my blog entitled, "Fact & Fiction

350

in *The Dandelion Insurrection*". There you can find references to laws such as the National Defense Authorization Act - our real life version of the fictional Freedom of Defense Act that allows the U.S. government to indefinitely detain citizens without access to a lawyer or to a fair and speedy trial. It also will direct you to inspiring real life groups like Food Not Lawns, the Urban Renaissance, and other organizations that offer us hope through forms of practical rebellion. My blog also tracks some of the strangely prophetic aspects of this book - the extensiveness of the government spying and surveillance being only one of many eerie moments in which I realized I could not invent fiction stranger than our reality!

That said; this novel is fiction. It is not a blueprint or a roadmap or even a strategic study on how we could create the change that we seek in real life. At best, the novel works to inspire you to struggle for what you believe in and to know that it is possible to achieve these goals nonviolently. If you are sincerely interested in working toward change, I strongly suggest looking up the Albert Einstein Institution and the works of Gene Sharp. (www.aeinstein.org)

In preparation for writing this book, I studied this scholar's seminal works on historical and contemporary nonviolent struggles. Gene Sharp's writings have been used around the globe to topple dictatorships and liberate people from oppressive and tyrannical control. I have reprinted with permission a list of 198 methods of nonviolent struggle to give you a taste of the depth of his research. Reading this list and launching into action is akin to opening a toolbox and starting to build a skyscraper . . . tools require knowledge to be used effectively. Become knowledgeable. Read Gene Sharp's work. Many shrug this off as unnecessary, thinking they are the foot soldiers of change, not the tacticians or the generals. My perspective is that when the general falls, the foot soldier leads the charge. Even the tactician relies on intelligent individuals to react strategically when the situation shifts unexpectedly. A single leader cannot be everywhere at once, but a leader-full movement can. For that to be feasible, we must all become knowledgeable of the strategies of nonviolent struggle.

**"Be a light unto yourself." -the Buddha**

I believe in you, in us, and in the human yearning for peaceful, respectful societies. In the madness of this world, it is your courage and kindness that show the way out of darkness.

This author's note could not be complete without my humble acknowledgement of the great many people who made this book possible: Gene Sharp and the incredible lineage of teachers of nonviolent struggle who have walked this earth; the wonderful supporters of our Community Publishing Campaign; my friends and family who offered feedback and inspiration, Dariel Garner, Delores Cook, Skylar Cook, Tangerine Bolen, Keith McHenry, Cindy Reinhardt, Ethan Au Genauer, Velcrow Ripper; Marirose Nightsong for her detailed editing; the Acadians of the St. John Valley, especially Michelle Dubé-Morneault, Andrea Chasse, Valier and Florence Dumais; my improvisational dance teacher, Susan Sgorbati, who taught me about general systems theory and murmurations; David Wright, who introduced me to the phrase "Everything Insha'Allah"; the editors and journalists of Dandelion Salad, Revolution Truth, Schwartz Reports, and many more; to whistleblowers like Daniel Ellsberg, Jesselyn Radack, Thomas Drake, Private Manning, and Edward Snowden who sacrificed deeply to expose corruption and tyranny; and to activists who stand up to injustice and destruction throughout the globe. To these and to my readers, I offer a deep bow of thanks.

Yours in love and revolution, Rivera Sun

# 198 METHODS OF NONVIOLENT ACTION

Far too often, people struggling for democratic rights and justice are not aware of the full range of methods of nonviolent action. Wise strategy, attention to the dynamics of nonviolent struggle, and careful selection of methods can increase a group's chances of success. Gene Sharp researched and catalogued these 198 methods and provided a rich selection of historical examples in his seminal work, *The Politics of Nonviolent Action* (3 Vols.) Boston: Porter Sargent, 1973.

# THE METHODS OF NONVIOLENT PROTEST AND PERSUASION
## Formal Statements
1.  Public Speeches
2.  Letters of opposition or support
3.  Declarations by organizations and institutions
4.  Signed public statements
5.  Declarations of indictment and intention
6.  Group or mass petitions

## Communications with a Wider Audience
7.  Slogans, caricatures, and symbols
8.  Banners, posters, displayed communications
9.  Leaflets, pamphlets, and books
10. Newspapers and journals
11. Records, radio, and television
12. Skywriting and earthwriting

## Group Representations
13. Deputations
14. Mock awards
15. Group lobbying
16. Picketing
17. Mock elections

## Symbolic Public Acts
18. Displays of flags and symbolic colors

19. Wearing of symbols
20. Prayer and worship
21. Delivering symbolic objects
22. Protest disrobings
23. Destruction of own property
24. Symbolic lights
25. Displays of portraits
26. Paint as protest
27. New signs and names
28. Symbolic sounds
29. Symbolic reclamations
30. Rude gestures

**Pressures on Individuals**
31. "Haunting" officials
32. Taunting officials
33. Fraternization
34. Vigils

**Drama and Music**
35. Humorous skits and pranks
36. Performances of plays and music
37. Singing

**Processions**
38. Marches
39. Parades
40. Religious processions
41. Pilgrimages
42. Motorcades

**Honoring the Dead**
43. Political mourning
44. Mock funerals
45. Demonstrative funerals
46. Homage at burial places

**Public Assemblies**
47. Assemblies of protest or support

355

## THE METHODS OF ECONOMIC NONCOOPERATION: THE STRIKE
Symbolic Strikes

# THE METHODS OF POLITICAL NONCOOPERATION

121. Refusal of public support

122. Literature and speeches advocating resistance

## Citizens' Noncooperation with Government

123. Boycott of legislative bodies

124. Boycott of elections

125. Boycott of government employment and positions

126. Boycott of government depts., agencies, and other bodies

127. Withdrawal from government educational institutions

128. Boycott of government-supported organizations

129. Refusal of assistance to enforcement agents

130. Removal of own signs and placemarks

131. Refusal to accept appointed officials

132. Refusal to dissolve existing institutions

## Citizens' Alternatives to Obedience

133. Reluctant and slow compliance

134. Nonobedience in absence of direct supervision

135. Popular nonobedience

136. Disguised disobedience

137. Refusal of an assemblage or meeting to disperse

138. Sitdown

139. Noncooperation with conscription and deportation

140. Hiding, escape, and false identities

141. Civil disobedience of "illegitimate" laws

## Action by Government Personnel

142. Selective refusal of assistance by government aides

143. Blocking of lines of command and information

144. Stalling and obstruction

145. General administrative noncooperation

146. Judicial noncooperation

147. Deliberate inefficiency and selective noncooperation by enforcement agents

148. Mutiny

## Domestic Governmental Action

## THE METHODS OF NONVIOLENT INTERVENTION

## Social Intervention

174. Establishing new social patterns
175. Overloading of facilities
176. Stall-in
177. Speak-in
178. Guerrilla theater
179. Alternative social institutions
180. Alternative communication system

## Economic Intervention

181. Reverse strike
182. Stay-in strike
183. Nonviolent land seizure
184. Defiance of blockades
185. Politically motivated counterfeiting
186. Preclusive purchasing
187. Seizure of assets
188. Dumping
189. Selective patronage
190. Alternative markets
191. Alternative transportation systems
192. Alternative economic institutions

## Political Intervention

193. Overloading of administrative systems
194. Disclosing identities of secret agents
195. Seeking imprisonment
196. Civil disobedience of "neutral" laws
197. Work-on without collaboration
198. Dual sovereignty and parallel government

For further inquiry, please contact
The Albert Einstein Institution
PO Box 455, East Boston, MA 02128 USA
tel: 617.247.4882   fax: 617.247.4035
email: einstein@igc.org   web: www.aeinstein.org

# About the Author

**Rivera Sun** is the author of *Billionaire Buddha*, *The Dandelion Insurrection* and *The Way Between*, as well as nine plays, a study guide to nonviolent action, a book of poetry, and numerous articles. She has red hair, a twin sister, and a fondness for esoteric mystics. She went to Bennington College to study writing as a Harcourt Scholar and graduated with a degree in dance. She lives in an earthship house in New Mexico, where she writes essays and novels. She is the cohost of a weekly radio program, a nonviolence trainer, and an activist. She writes several essays each week for peace and justice journals. Rivera has been an aerial dancer, a bike messenger, and a gung-fu style tea server. Everything else about her - except her writing - is perfectly ordinary.

Rivera Sun also loves hearing from her readers.
Email: info@riversun.com
Facebook: Rivera Sun
Twitter: @RiveraSunAuthor
Website: www.riverasun.com

## Also Available!
## The Dandelion Insurrection Study Guide
## to Making Change Through Nonviolent Action

You'll love this lively, engaging journey into the heart of *The*
 *Dandelion Insurrection*'s story of nonviolent
action! Taking lessons off the page and into
our lives, author Rivera Sun guides us through
the skills and strategies that created the
thrilling adventure of *The Dandelion
Insurrection.* Using your favorite scenes from
the book and also drawing on historical
examples of nonviolent struggles, this study guide brings the
story to life in an exciting way.

Find Group Discounts, Bulk Orders, and Book Club Specials
on Novels and Study Guides at:
www.riverasun.com

# New! The Way Between
## by Rivera Sun

Between flight and fight lies a mysterious third path called *The Way Between*, and young shepherdess and orphan Ari Ara must  master it . . . before war destroys everything she loves! She begins training as the apprentice of the great warrior Shulen, and enters a world of warriors and secrets, swords and magic, friendship and mystery. She uncovers forbidden prophecies, searches for the lost heir to two thrones, and chases the elusive forest-dwelling Fanten to unravel their hidden knowledge. Full of twists and turns and surprises, *The Way Between* is bound to carve out a niche on your bookshelves and a place in your heart!

"This novel should be read aloud to everyone, by everyone, from childhood onward. Rivera Sun writes in a style as magical as Tolkien and as authentic as Twain."
*– Tom Hastings, Director of PeaceVoice*

"Rivera Sun has, once again, used her passion for nonviolence and her talent for putting thoughts into powerful words."
*–Robin Wildman, Fifth Grade Teacher, Nonviolent Schools Movement, and Nonviolence Trainer*

"A wonderful book! It is so rare to find exciting fiction for young people and adults that shows creative solutions to conflict, and challenges violence with active nonviolence and peace. Ari Ara is a delightful character and this story is a gem."
*– Heart Phoenix, River Phoenix Center for Peacebuilding*

# Reader Praise for Rivera Sun's
## Steam Drills, Treadmills, and Shooting Stars

*Steam Drills, Treadmills, and Shooting Stars* is a story about people just like you, filled with the audacity of hope and fueled by the passion of unstoppable love. The ghost of folk hero John Henry haunts Jack Dalton, a corporate lawyer for Standard Coal as Henrietta Owens, activist and mother, wakes up the nation with some tough-loving truth about the environment, the economy, justice, and hope. Pressures mount as John Henry challenges Jack to stand up to the steam drills of contemporary America . . . before it's too late.

"Rivera Sun paints the truth of our environmental crises, but also the hope and the challenge for all of us." - *Nancy Audette*

"I highly recommend this inspiring book for the magic it creates and the change it inspires!" - *Dawn Hayes*

"It took me on a literary ride that tickled my own activist soul. This book is a powerful, exciting, and just plain fun story that will keep you reading to the end, and then be sorry that it's over." - *Barbara Wilder*

"Rivera Sun offers up a soul-drenched world full of nuance, faith, secular truths, and a love of nature. This is a beautiful work by a very gifted young writer." - *Christopher Palermo*

"I was swept into the story from the first page and could hardly put the book down." - *Sharon Riegie Maynard, Women Weaving the World."*

## Praise for Rivera Sun's *Billionaire Buddha*

From fabulous wealth to unlimited blessings, the price of enlightenment may bankrupt billionaire Dave Grant. Emotionally destitute in the prime of his career, he searches for love and collides with Joan Hathaway. The encounter rattles his soul and unravels his world. Capitalism, property, wealth, mansions: his notions of success crumble into dust. From toasting champagne on top of the world to swigging whiskey with bums in the gutter, Dave Grant's journey is an unforgettable ride that leaves you cheering!

". . . inspirational and transformational! An enjoyable read for one's heart and soul."
*-Chuck Collins, senior scholar, Institute for Policy Studies; co-author with Bill Gates Sr. of 'Wealth and Our Commonwealth'*

". . . inspiring a skeptic is no easy task and Rivera Sun manages to do so, gracefully, convincingly, and admirably."
*- Casey Dorman, Editor-in-Chief, Lost Coast Review*

"People, if you haven't gotten your copy of *Billionaire Buddha* yet, you are letting a rare opportunity slip through your fingers. It's that good."
*- Burt Kempner, screenwriter, producer and author of children's books*

"This is the kind of book that hits you in the gut and makes you stop and think about what you just read."
*- Rob Garvey, reader*

"A clear and conscious look at our times and the dire need for a real change to heart based living."
*- Carol Ranellone, reader*

If you enjoyed *The Dandelion Insurrection* . . .

Spread the word about the book.
Tell your friends.
Post about it on social media.
Review the book on your favorite online bookstore.
Recommend it to your book group.
Suggest it to teachers and students.

**Thank you!**

Made in the USA
Middletown, DE
23 February 2020